Jake's Redemption

The Angel Eyes Series Prequel

Jamie Schulz

Jake's Redemption

ISBN: 978-0-9980257-1-1

For information contact: www.jamieschulzauthor.com

Book Cover design & illustrations by Jamie Schulz and Natina Norton
For more information contact:
www.jamieschulzauthor.com or www.natinanorton.com

This book is dedicated to my Mom, Dad, and N & M – 143!

To all my friends who helped with the story, plot, editing, ideas, brainstorming, dinner, or who just listened to me rant: Thank you!

And, of course...with all my love and gratitude to my "Mr. Wonderful"!

Jake's Redemption

1

JAKE NICHOLS KNELT in defeat on the cold ground of the mountain meadow, directly beside his best friend, Bret Masters. Defenseless, with their fingers laced together behind their heads, their eyes scanned the surroundings for any escape from the Raiders who had attacked their camp in the early morning hours.

Both men scowled up at their captor, a woman Bret had foolishly—and against Jake's repeated warnings—loved to distraction. Jake risked a quick glance at his friend, knowing the pain Bret must be suffering in the wake of her betrayal. He felt the bite of it too, only for a different reason. Bret was family, and what hurt him, hurt Jake. His protective nature made him long to shield Bret from the misery this woman inflicted.

"I don't care for you," Amy had said only moments ago, indifferent to the devastation Jake saw in every line of Bret's granite-hard face. What made her confession even worse was the bit she added about only wanting to use his body.

"You do have such a pretty face, but no brains in your head," she went on, and then laughed at Bret's seething look. His expression made Jake ache for his friend, and he silently hoped she had nothing more to torment him with. But Amy wasn't done with Bret yet.

"How could you think any self-respecting woman would want you for anything more than your gorgeous face and hard body?" she asked, not waiting for a reply. "A decent woman would never accept you as an equal. Any woman who would is worse than the slave you will shortly become."

A deep growl rumbled up from Bret's chest, and to Jake's surprise, Bret lunged to his feet and attacked her. Seeing an opportunity, Jake and all the other prisoners immediately joined him in a last, desperate attempt to gain their freedom. Their female adversaries, however, had a new genetic advantage. It may have taken a few seconds for the hysterical-strength to kick in, but once it did, the fight, strength-wise, was no longer in the men's favor.

The skirmish didn't last long, but in a brief moment before it ended, Jake turned to see Amy about to drive a long-bladed knife into his best friend's back. Jake didn't think, he moved, tackling Amy as her weapon plunged downward from its high arch. Amy tried to wiggle away from him, but he held on, desperate to keep her from harming Bret.

"Run!" He heard Bret's frantic shout. "Run!" The sound of pounding feet and continued battle assaulted Jake's ears. He tried to roll away from Amy, but now she held on to him. On his hands and knees, he jerked his arm to shake her loose and follow his friend into the forest, but she wouldn't let go.

Pain bloomed sharp and bright in his ribs as a booted foot slammed into him—once, twice—and he fell. The boot kept coming. He curled up, protecting his vulnerable areas, but his assailant still landed several blows to his head and back.

"Enough!" Amy's voice rang out, and the assault ended. Jake spit blood from his mouth and struggled to catch his breath. The dizziness in his head and the stabbing ache in his side told him getting to his feet might be harder than it was a few minutes ago.

Definitely broke a rib or two, he thought, tonguing his split lip and rapidly cataloging the pain in the rest of his body.

"How many do we still have?" Amy shouted to someone nearby.

"Ten got away," a woman said. "With this one," Jake assumed she was pointing at him, "we still have twenty-seven men, along with some traitorous women and children too."

"Is there a tall man, black hair, green eyes, very good-looking, among those we recaptured?" Amy asked, describing Bret to a tee.

"No."

"That sappy, pretty-boy son of a bitch," Amy swore, undoubtedly meaning Bret. "I should've known he'd try something like that." She cursed again.

"You know their hiding places now," the other woman said. "We'll catch them and their friends too."

Jake and Bret had come across Amy by accident—or so they had thought at the time—almost seven months before as they traveled the mountains, hunting for food. She'd been hungry and in need of aid. Unsurprisingly, she took an immediate interest in Bret. Although he had a mistrusting nature, she spared little time wrapping his love-starved heart around her finger. Jake had never liked her and the two friends argued about her more than once, but despite his misgivings about Amy, Jake refused to alienate his boyhood friend. Yet as a result of her relationship with Bret, she now knew the location of most of their woodland hiding places.

"That's true," Amy replied to the other woman's comment. She tapped her chin with her index finger as if considering, and then she glanced down at Jake.

He had lain very still during their interaction, hoping against hope they might forget about him.

No such luck.

"And you," she said coming toward him. "You—"

He didn't give her a chance to finish; he had a fairly good idea of what came next. Instead, he ignored his dizziness and the pain in his chest as he surged to his feet, pushed her aside, and ran for the trees. He'd made it six feet when he heard a crack behind him. Then something hard and thin snapped around his neck and yanked him backward. He saw stars as his head and back slammed to the ground, sending a new wave of misery through his abused body. He groaned, trying to place what just happened, and then Amy was leaning over him.

She jammed her knee into his chest, and pain shot through his damaged ribs. He lifted his arms to shove her away, but the leathery rope wrapped around his neck yanked at him again, choking off his air. Desperate, needing to get her off him, needing to breathe, he tugged at the cord strangling him. His eyes widened as Amy grabbed him by the hair and tilted his head back to expose his throat. He reached for her again, but the minute the edge of her knife grazed his flesh, his arms collapsed to the ground and he froze.

The binding around his neck loosened and fell away as Amy glared into his face. Blessed air came freely, but the simple act of breathing caused his ribs to twinge more.

With the suffocating rope gone, his hands automatically lifted off the ground to defend himself. Amy's knife cut a tiny fraction deeper. Blood tickled his neck as the warm liquid trickled over his cool skin, and he froze once more, afraid to even breathe.

"Uh-uh," Amy warned as she increased the pressure slightly, widening the gash a bit more and digging the point of her blade into his Adam's apple.

His mouth went dry. *Is she going to slit my throat?*

"Looks like Bret didn't value your friendship as much as you thought, huh, Jake?" Amy said with a nasty smile, her dark brown eyes glittering down at him.

Jake cringed inwardly. He knew that wasn't the case. In the chaos, Bret probably hadn't even realized Jake had been captured, and wouldn't until he failed to show at their rendezvous point. But her implication twisted at his guts nonetheless.

A second woman stepped up behind Amy, coiling the long black length of a bullwhip in her hand.

So, that's *what was strangling me...I should've known.*

"You fucked up my plans, Jake, just as much as your damned friend," Amy hissed at him when he didn't respond to her earlier comment. "If it weren't for you, he'd be mine and you'd both make me rich. Now, I have to settle for you and those other losers we caught today."

"What're—you going—to do with me?" He stifled a groan for his halting speech and glared daggers at the woman hovering over him.

"Oh, I think you know what we do with captured men," Amy chuckled. She tilted her head, and a strand of her amber-blonde hair fell into her face as her eyes raked over him.

"You know, Jake," she said reflectively, "you're a good-looking guy. If Bret hadn't been around, you would've been my target. It's only next to a man like him that you'd seem second best. But then, you were always suspicious of me, weren't you? Maybe once you've been trained, I'll pay you another visit."

He clamped his jaws tight and didn't respond, but his mind was in overdrive. He wanted to fight, but moving meant death. He didn't want to know what it was like to bleed to death from a severed artery. Instead, he scowled all the more. If he wanted to live, it was all he could do.

The woman beside Amy crouched down, but he couldn't see what she was doing. The next thing he knew, he jumped as a needle jammed into his hip and something injected into his body.

Ah, shit... He knew what *that* was; he'd heard dozens of stories about it but luckily had never had to deal with the drug, until now.

It started working almost instantaneously, driving up his anxiety level, making him shake and cringe. A few seconds passed, while Amy's gaze bore into his, and the effect of the chemical doubled.

Oh, God, this is worse than I thought it would be. He had never felt so weak and vulnerable in his life.

"Now," Amy said as she removed the blade from his throat and stood. She tucked the knife in her boot and then plopped her rear down on his chest, knowing he would be too terrified, thanks to the drug, to do anything to save himself. "What shall I do with you?" She ran a finger down the side of his face.

He flinched away.

You could let me go, he thought and tried to force out the sarcastic remark, but the substance surging through him wouldn't allow it.

"I think you deserve a particularly horrible punishment for always interfering in my plans with Bret," she said, answering her own question while tapping his bearded chin with one finger. The slight contact amped up his anxiety, and he shivered. "He may have listened to you complain about me, but he *loved* me." Her derisive tone told him what she thought about that. "He would've never turned me out the way you kept telling him to do. And now, you've ruined my chance to have him how I always wanted him: in chains. So, how shall I make you pay for all of it?"

Jake's body shook with fear, both real and chemically induced. Amy was far more lethal than he had once thought.

"I know just the place you should go," she continued with a bright smile, as if she'd come up with a brilliant idea. "I have an acquaintance near here, a woman who's exceptionally adept at training men to be perfect little slaves. I'll bet she'd *jump* at the chance to make you a willing breeder. You'll make her a lot of money. Once she pays me a high price for you that is."

"P-Please..." Jake pleaded involuntarily, the drug wreaking havoc with his willpower. No matter how much he wanted to resist begging, he couldn't stop now that he had started. "P-Please..." he muttered again, his voice shaking while fighting the drug—and losing. "Let me go..."

Amy laughed.

"Darla's going to tear you to pieces, Jake," she told him, her sinister smile sending waves of dread prickling up and down his spine. "A little bit at a time, she'll peel away your pride—"

A loud thud from down the hall jolted Jake's mind back to the present. Darkness surrounded his sweating, trembling body as terror from his nightmarish recollection lingered in his mind. As much as he hated the bleak confines of his concrete cell, he was thankful to be alone. No one expecting anything. No one demanding he perform acts that made him want to retch. No one hurting him. He waited for the sound in the hallway to repeat, but when it didn't, he exhaled in a grateful rush and ran an unsteady hand over his face.

Why can't I stop obsessing about what happened that day?

He slumped against the cold stone walls of his tiny prison cell, staring into the midnight-black nothingness. Scurrying sounds of small creatures sounded nearby, and in the distance he heard the soft sobs of another slave. A burning wetness welled in Jake's eyes, and a thick ache formed in the back of his throat for the other man's suffering. Or maybe it was for his own. He shook his head, wiped at his face again, and tried to block out the other man's weeping.

The concrete chamber in which he sat was smaller than the walk-in closet in the tiny two-bedroom apartment he'd rented years ago. That room had seemed huge back then; this one felt claustrophobic. He had enough room to lie down and turn over, but that was about it.

His first frantic attempt to find a way out yielded nothing. Several times since, his hands had methodically slid over the wet, rough stones of his cell. His fingers dug into the concrete joints, every nook and cranny, until they hurt; still, he found no way out. Even if he had, he couldn't have gone anywhere. The chains connected to the heavy shackles around his neck, wrists, and ankles anchored him to the wall, but he kept trying. So many times, sweat had trickled down his face and chest as he gritted his teeth, his fingers gripping the chains with a desperate strength. He strained every muscle in his body, but after hours of repeated yanking, he released them with a despondent cry and sprawled on the damp floor in exhausted defeat.

The lump in his throat returned. Would he ever see the sun again? Ever see his friends? But then, only one of those remained. Bret Masters.

He sighed and rubbed his forehead, attempting to ease the ache caused by thinking about Bret. He dropped his hand and sighed again. The long story of their friendship had led Jake to this fate. A part of him blamed Bret for everything that had happened to him in this place, which was unfair, but rationalizing didn't stop him from being angry.

His fingers unconsciously moved to his chest. They kneaded rhythmically, trying to release the knot of despair tangled around his heart. In constant battle, resentment warred with the brotherly regard he still harbored for Bret, and the victor was, as yet, undecided.

Jake rubbed at his temples and shivered. *This damn room is freezing.*

Even in the spring, the room was damp and cool. Of course, being naked all the time didn't help, but his Mistress, Darla Cain, couldn't be bothered with clothing her slaves. Only when required to work in the cold and wet or the sweltering heat were they given the minimal basics to cover their nudity. The rest of the time, they were all bare and vulnerable to whatever their Mistress wanted from them. Or what she wanted to do to them. After witnessing much of her cruelty personally, Jake suspected she hated men—she took too much enjoyment from their agony not to. Adept at causing pain, she tormented her captives, changed them, ruling them utterly. When she tired of them, they were tossed aside and left to molder as Jake was doing now.

Jake had to admit, Amy's choice of punishment had been well made. The things his Mistress did to him were terrible—demoralizing and humiliating—and he didn't want to remember, but he had nothing else to do here in the lonely, oppressive darkness.

As the memories came, his mind flinched from the incident that had landed him in this cell.

Piercing agony burned across his back, and he screamed. Over and over he screamed, but he refused to give them what they demanded, would not provide them their sick pleasure.

A moan escaped him. He shivered at the memory of his short-lived rebellion, hating himself more for his eventual submittal, for being weak, and for the loss that eventually came of it.

The act that followed his failing though—when his Mistress tried to force him into another vile game for her entertainment—that one he relished.

"You sick bitch!" he had roared at his Mistress as he surged against the three guards who blocked his way. Fear trembled in the back of his mind, but reckless rage kept it there. "I'm going to fucking kill you!"

When alarm crossed his Mistress' face, his lips twitched upward as satisfaction flooded his system. *Good, she's scared,* he thought bitterly. *She should be!* Then his muscles tightened and he redoubled his efforts.

He lunged with all his strength, his gaze locked on his target, determined to reach the red-headed bitch and end her for good. His bigger, heavier body drove the guards back several steps before more joined in. He swung at them, but the chains on his wrists hindered his movement. Again, he gathered his diminishing strength and strove to reach the cause of all his pain and fury. He surged against the human barrier, but too many bodies now stood between them. He hadn't moved fast enough. Hysterical-strength kicked in, and the women guarding his Mistress grew stronger.

A sharp yank on the chain attached to the collar around his neck wrenched him off his feet. He landed on his back, knocking the breath from his lungs and cracking his head on the hard floor. Dazed, he blinked, and then saw the next blow coming. The end of his own lead chain slammed across his heaving chest with a loud thud. Ribs vibrating with pain, he grunted and rolled into a ball as the next strike fell, knowing he had lost the fight. Knowing his Mistress' treatment of him would now grow much, much worse.

And it did.

Instead of preventing his Mistress from ever forcing something so terrible on him or anyone else again, the guards had stopped him, beat him severely, and dragged him down here. For hours, he'd lain almost lifeless where they dropped him, licking his wounds and berating himself. He didn't know how long ago that was now. Days, weeks, months—they all blended into one. Regret for his inability to end his Mistress' reign of terror left him feeling hollow and weighted down by the enormity of his failure. Though, if he'd succeeded, they would've killed him, disappointment still pierced his heart like a flaming arrow.

But that first act, the unthinkable thing his Mistress forced him to do—the one that led to his futile assault and lonely imprisonment—that event *haunted* him.

"Leave it alone," he growled into the abyss of his cell, his heart heavy in his chest. "You can't change anything now."

But he couldn't leave the memory alone.

Her soft brown eyes filled with terror and tears.

Her trembling body, cringing against him.

Quiet whimpers wrenching at his heart.

Her misplaced trust in *him*.

Jake's hands curled into fists and he shook his head, the recollection tearing at his insides, killing him slowly.

I was supposed to protect her.

A sob bubbled into his throat, but he swallowed it down and rushed to his feet as self-loathing roared in his ears. His chains rattled along the rock as he paced, five steps one way, five steps back. *A path should've worn through the stone by now from all my pacing*, he thought.

He stopped at the door imprisoning him. His hands clenched tightly at his sides, and in his helpless anguish, he hammered on the steel with his fists.

"Let me out!" he bellowed in a cracked voice, welcoming the pain in his knuckles, his hands, his wrists. "God damn you. Let me out!"

His cries and the dull pounding of his fists ricocheted through the long corridor outside, the echoes mocking him with their freedom. The cries of the other slave stilled as inarticulate roars of fury ripped through Jake's aching throat, every muscle in his body quivering as he released the rage inside him.

You're being stupid! a voice in his head shouted. *Stop it!*

His throbbing fists ceased pummeling the immovable metal, and his hands splayed out over its cold surface.

His forehead fell against steel with a muffled thud.

Waves of shudders crashed through him.

Despair, like a living thing, coiled tightly around his heart, and a sob finally escaped him.

Squeezing his eyes closed, he concentrated on breathing.

I will not give them any more.

No more blood. No more sweat. No more tears.

Pushing away from the cell door, he wiped his hand over his face, brushed at his damp lashes, and sat back down.

Maybe Bret had it right all these years, he thought. *No more trust either.*

He shook in the aftermath of emotion. Or perhaps he should blame the drug. He was more than a day overdue for his booster of the nasty stuff, so the fear and submission it caused were minimal now. In nearly two years, he'd never gone so long without an injection. He wondered if they figured his obedience didn't matter because he was chained, locked up, and half-starved.

His fingers rubbed at his chest again. Still sore from the beating they had given him after his ill-fated, rage-induced attack, he felt weak and tired, and he didn't care anymore.

Again, resentment burned in his chest.

"Run!" Bret had screamed that day, and—after all they'd been through together and all Jake had done for him over the years—Bret had left him behind to be captured and enslaved.

You know that's not fair, a part of Jake murmured, the familiar war waging inside him. Despite their agreement not to attempt to rescue each other, the fact that Bret didn't even try made Jake unreasonably angry.

"He couldn't have saved you from this," Jake mumbled into the gloom, "and you would hate yourself worse if he had gotten captured or killed by trying. Let it go."

"Jake?"

The sound of the soft voice filtering through the steel door made him jump. Only a few minutes had passed since he howled his rage at the world. She must've heard him screaming because she sounded uneasy. Not nervous or afraid, just uncertain of what she would find when she opened the door.

The voice belonged to one of the handful of halfway-decent guards working for his Mistress. The guard's name was Hailey Tate, and there weren't enough like her. She talked about leaving this place one day to move into her own home with her own slaves. Though he didn't know her well, he would miss the kindness she had shown him and the other slaves. When she eventually did leave, there would be one fewer of the kindly guards working here, just one more face forgotten.

He didn't answer her call. They would come in whether he wanted them to or not, and though she had been kind to him in the past, he would no longer cooperate. They could fill him up with the fear drug, beat him unconscious, but he wouldn't do one more thing for them. Or so he kept telling himself. Trying to stay alive for the hope of escape was like slow, agonizing torture, and he would not do that to himself, not anymore—unless they dosed him with the drug again. Then its effects would leave him no choice but to submit.

A key fit into the lock. The mechanism clicked, and the heavy door slowly swung open on squeaky hinges.

"Jake?" Hailey called again, but he refused to respond.

He closed his eyes and turned away from the intolerable brightness coming from the lantern she carried. After sitting in the dark for so long, even the dim illumination burned.

"Jake? Are you all right?"

He chuckled, an unpleasant sound bouncing off the walls of his small stone prison. "Well," he croaked, "if you count being beaten, starved, and chained to a wall as *all right*, then I'm just dandy."

"I know it's been a while. I tried to get some food to you yesterday," she said as she crouched down beside him, "but there was a problem."

He glared at her but didn't speak. Even through his hurt and anger, he appreciated her aid, especially since she didn't have to offer it.

"Someone's here to see you," she said, changing the subject.

"There's no one out there I want to see."

"It's one of the council members."

Jake laughed, still bitter. He looked down at his filthy, naked body and reached up to scratch his bearded cheek. "I'm not in any condition to perform sexual favors. Send her away."

Hailey frowned and glanced over her shoulder at the open doorway.

"Keep your voice down, Jake," she hissed, leaning closer to him, her tone hardening as she spoke. "And mind what you say. I might not agree with all the rules here, but I will enforce them if I must."

He cringed inwardly as his last comment replayed in his head. He didn't intend for it to, but it did come out like a command. A shiver of dread slid up his spine. Hailey might not punish him for that, but he didn't know about his visitor if she had overheard. Quickly, he changed the focus of their murmured discussion.

"I'm going to die down here, Hailey." He couldn't help the forlorn note in his voice.

"Don't use my name, Jake."

"Sorry. Ms. Tate. My Mistress doesn't care if I live or die, and I will die down here, just like all the others."

"I don't think so," she corrected, and he aimed another sharp glance in her direction.

"No?"

"No. That's what your visitor's here about."

His brows twitched together in confusion. "What?"

"She has an offer for you," Hailey told him. "If you give me your word you won't try to harm her, I won't restrain you as *she* ordered me to do."

Ordered. He knew who ordered that: his Mistress. A slave attacking a fellow council member in Darla's house would make her look bad, but even if he failed, the effort might also set him free from his unbearable existence. *Is it worth it?*

Jake sighed. "She won't take it well if she finds out you disregarded her orders."

"Do you plan to try to harm your visitor?"

He stared at Hailey and then shook his head. "I don't want to hurt anyone, even though you all will hurt me."

That sounded sufficiently noble, he mocked himself. *What happened to not giving them any more?*

"Just do it," he said when she didn't move or respond, not caring how his words could be construed.

It didn't matter anyway.

She didn't argue, and soon his wrists were locked together above his head, connected to a steel ring embedded in the wall. She glanced down at him, still seated on the cold stones.

"Take the offer, Jake," she whispered as she bent over him, and his eyes snapped up to hers in surprise. He opened his mouth, but she straightened and stepped out of the room before he could speak.

An older woman entered. She was impressive; her gray-streaked black hair, pulled into a bun at the nape of her neck, exposed a pretty face, now lined with wisdom. She wore jeans and a lightweight white work shirt. She appeared stern, but a kindness resided in her amber eyes that calmed his initial fear. When she smiled, her whole face changed, and he relaxed even more, before reminding himself to stay on guard.

"Good afternoon, Mr. Nichols," she said in a clear voice.

Jake only nodded and stared at the floor.

It's what they expected of slaves.

Whatever she wants, I will not give it.

"My name is Jewel Stewart. I'm a member of the section's governing council, and I have a few questions for you."

He flicked a withering glare at her and looked away again, but still refused to answer.

She paused, and he could feel her eyes assessing him like ants crawling over his skin. He wanted to squirm under her perusal, but he forced himself to remain still.

At length, she spoke again. "Do you like living here?"

Astonished by the idiotic question, he met her gaze and barked out a rude answer before he could stop himself. "That's a stupid question."

"Does that mean yes or no?"

Is she dense?

"No."

"I didn't think so," she said and smiled again as she joined him on the floor, sitting directly across from him. Her actions, disarming as they were clearly meant to be, shocked him too. The floor was filthy, and the room stank from his unwashed body and his waste—which hadn't been emptied from the overflowing bucket in the corner since before they last fed him three days ago.

What's she up to?

"Tell me about yourself, Mr. Nichols."

"What do you want to know?" Curious now, he told himself that talking required nothing from him. Besides, he had been alone too long. Seeing and speaking with another human being was...nice.

"How did you come to be here?"

He scowled at her. "The same way every other man came to be enslaved."

"A raiding party took you?"

"We fought a war and lost."

"I meant something a little more recently."

Jake hesitated. This was his most civil conversation with a woman since before the war, which sent people running for their lives while its destruction leveled cities and towns across the globe. Again, a pang of regret twisted inside him. So many had died in the war that destroyed their world and altered its social conventions completely. Women, no longer considered the weaker sex, controlled everything now. Men were their slaves, thanks to losing a second civil war they foolishly started themselves.

Raiding parties, like the one that had captured Jake, traveled into the mountains searching for runaways, uncaptured men, and the women who helped them, to sell at auction. In Jake's case, the Raiders had help in acquiring him.

Another reason for his resentment of Bret Masters.

"A woman fooled my friend and betrayed us," he finally responded to her question. "The Raiders showed up, I was taken, and sold at the Auction Hall to Dar...uh...Miss Cain. When she got tired of abusing me, she locked me up down here and left me to rot." He sounded angry and bitter, but he didn't care.

"Tell me what you did before the wars. What kind of work did you do?"

He glared at her, wondering again what her game was, but he saw no reason not to tell her. Giving her the answers was far preferable to another beating.

"I worked in construction for a number of years," he said, "and did some ranching for several more after that."

"So, you're trained in building houses and caring for livestock?"

"Yeah..." he said warily.

Jewel asked for more details about the work he did and he told her, but his suspicions amped up his anxiety level once more. He sat taller, his whole body and consciousness on alert. *What the hell does my work history have to do with anything?* No one had asked him any of this before. No one cared.

"That's quite a resume," she said, smiling again.

Jake grunted in reply and averted his gaze.

"Would you like a chance to leave here for a few months?"

His eyes snapped up to her face. He frowned as his heart rate sped up and he waited for the punchline. Was she screwing with his head like

Darla? Dangling a carrot in front of him, getting his hopes up, only to snatch it away again?

"It's not a trick," she told him, apparently reading his thoughts. "There's a job in need of your particular skills if you're interested."

"What kind of job?" he asked, still cautious. This seemed too good to be true. "And where?"

"A friend of one of the other council members is building a new home," Jewel told him. "Her ranch foreman, who also happened to be responsible for the construction, had an accident and died. She has a number of decent workers, but no one with enough experience to oversee the work now. She asked the council if we knew of anyone who could fill in, and your name came up."

He croaked out a rusty laugh. No way did his Mistress tell anyone about him. She wanted him to suffer. Jewel smiled when he said as much.

"I didn't say it was Darla."

He scowled at her again. *Is this for real?*

"The job would last about six months or so," she said as if he'd asked. "Do you want it?"

He stared mutely at the floor. Could he trust her or believe her story? *What if this was just another one of Darla's mind games?*

He was silent so long she must've assumed he wasn't interested, because she stood up and dusted herself off. "I'm sorry we couldn't come to an agreement," she murmured and stepped toward the door.

"Wait!" The chains connected to his wrist shackles rattled against the wall as he abruptly sat forward.

She turned back to him and looked down into his upturned face, her expression impatient now. "You have something to say?"

He took a deep breath, wavered, and then dived in. "What's the woman like? The one who needs the house built?"

Jewel smiled again, the annoyance melting away.

"She's nothing like Darla if that's what you're worried about. She won't beat you or starve you. You'll be working in the sun, have three meals a day, and a bed to sleep in at night."

He dropped his eyes to the floor. His mind blazed through the assorted possibilities, while his chest tightened with uncertainty.

Sobs from the slave down the hall had started up again. The other man's torment spurred Jake's decision.

Jewel shifted her feet, and Jake tilted his head to meet her amber gaze.

"Are you interested, Mr. Nichols?"

He hesitated. Wary prickles crept over his skin and his heart stuttered, but there really wasn't any other choice.

"Yes," he said, and a shudder of hope passed through him. The reemergence of the once-lost emotion sent another wave of terrified tingles racing up and down his spine.

"Very good," she replied with a smile. "Let's get you out of here. Your temporary Mistress is anxious for you to start right away." She turned to the guard outside. "Hailey, would you unchain him, please?"

As Hailey released his shackles from the wall and helped him to his feet, Jake's stomach fluttered with the shock of escaping this hellhole, where he had expected to die. Heart racing, he reeled and stumbled into the wall, but Hailey steadied him. His head spun and his stomach churned from lack of food, but he fought down the nausea and clenched his jaw, determined to keep going. He would not stay in this place one second longer than it took to get on a horse, or in a cart, or whatever transportation waited to take him away from here.

One foot in front of the other, he thought, his whole body feeling somehow lighter with every step. *Just keep going.*

"Lead the way, ma'am," he told Jewel when he stood beside her in the hallway, swaying slightly, but resolutely staying on his feet.

She smiled and started down the hall.

Jake Nichols, with a rapidly lightening heart, followed in her wake.

2

DARLA DIDN'T BOTHER clothing him for the trip to his temporary home, so gooseflesh prickled his whole body before they even left her front yard. They also filled him so full of the damned drug he shivered with fear and flinched at every sound. And they chained him again, but this time, he didn't have to wear them long.

Once he reached his destination, Darla's guards dragged him from the back of the cart and threw him to the ground. He landed on his knees and stayed there, knowing they expected him to be submissive. And, since they dosed him with the drug again, he didn't have much choice.

"Be careful with him," a woman's voice warned, but he didn't dare look up to see who defended him.

No one else spoke as Darla's women climbed back in the cart, jangled the reins, and drove away. As soon as they were on their way, someone was at Jake's side to help him to his feet, but he jumped and grunted, shying from their touch.

"It's okay," a man told him as he gripped Jake's arm. Jake peeked over and met the other man's dancing brown eyes. "I'm the foreman, Shawn Brohm," the man said with a crooked grin, "and she runs the place." He nodded to the woman opposite him as they helped Jake to his feet.

"Hello. I'm Monica Avery," the blonde woman said as she released his arm and moved to face him.

Upon laying eyes on her lovely curves, bright smile, and twinkling hazel gaze, Jake blinked in surprise before he recalled his circumstances and dropped his gaze. Something in her direct stare, in the kindness of her expression, unnerved him as much as the woman did herself.

"Welcome to our home," she said in a friendly voice.

He flicked another glance in her direction, but only nodded in reply. He was so wound up with dread and anxiety from the drug, he could barely communicate; yet he was not so unnerved or disorientated that he didn't notice her breathtaking beauty.

He couldn't work any moisture into his mouth. His throat was too tight and his shaking so bad, he knew he would stutter unintelligibly if he tried to utter a single word.

"Are you cold?" the woman asked.

He shook his head, still unable to speak.

"What's your name?"

He looked up again and then back at the ground. He opened his mouth, but nothing came out. Coughing, he tried again.

"J-Jake...Ni-Nichols."

"Jake. I like that."

Something in her tone, or maybe it was just his fear of being close to another woman with power over him, sent an icy shiver of dread down Jake's spine.

"So, you're not cold," the woman said, "but you're trembling like it's twenty below. Did they give you the drug before you left?"

He nodded again.

She rested a hand on his arm and looked up into his face. He wanted to pull away, but something in her eyes held him immobile.

"You won't have to suffer that again for as long as you're here," she told him. "I don't use the drug and never will. You'll be treated like a person here, not a possession, and you'll be expected to treat others the same. Do you understand?"

He nodded once more.

The tightness in his gullet spread to his chest, and his breathing hitched uncomfortably with her standing so close.

"No chains either," she said as she fit a key into the lock of his wrist shackles. "I hate to see these on you."

He glanced at her face as she removed his restraints, and he met her eyes again when she reached for the one around his neck. He pulled back, a little alarmed, and she smiled at him.

"I won't hurt you," she said in a soft voice. "You'll learn that in time." She pulled the restraint from his neck and grimaced upon seeing the angry, red rawness beneath the metal, but she didn't comment on it. "Are you hungry?"

He moved his head in the affirmative, and she turned to Shawn.

"Shawn, would you show Jake where he can get cleaned up, then find him some clothes and get him something to eat?"

"Sure," Shawn agreed, his crooked grin once again adorning his suntanned face.

"You'll probably want to rest after eating," Monica told Jake. "The room Shawn will take you to is all yours. No one will bother you there. However long it takes, feel free to lie down and recover. Shawn or Rosa"—Monica tilted her head to indicate an older Latina woman standing a few feet away, scrutinizing them closely—"will check in on you to make sure you get anything you need."

Jake nodded once more, understanding her words but not entirely believing them.

Shawn took him to a long, finished two-story building set to one side of the main house's construction site. The building contained several one-room apartments with shared bathrooms and showers on both floors. Shawn showed him to a shower with hot running water, and Jake was in heaven. He hadn't set foot in a hot shower in years.

Once he had cleaned up—he wished he could shave and trim his beard, but he was still shaking too much—he dressed in the hand-me-down clothes they had found for him and followed the foreman to the dining room for something to eat.

Afterward, he returned to his own private room with a double bed, small side table, and a window. Jake hadn't slept in a bed in years either. Well, other than when required to service a woman who wanted to use his body, that is. He wondered, staring at the blue-quilted bed, if sexual services were a requirement here as well, whether Miss Avery or one of her guards would arrive one night to press him for favors. He'd seen the appraising looks women in the surrounding crowd gave him upon his arrival. One brown-haired young woman, in particular, had ogled him more closely than he would've liked. Not that there was anything he could do about it. He was a slave. The guards and other women could do what they liked with him; at least, that was the life he'd become accustomed to. Things seemed different here, but he wondered how different they could actually be.

On the afternoon of his first day on the ranch, a male doctor came to give Jake a checkup. Dr. Beck lived at Miss Avery's friend's place. Nearly seventy years old, stocky, and somewhat sickly himself, the doctor didn't allow his ill health to stop him from helping others. He chatted amiably as he examined Jake's numerous injuries.

"Well," the old man said as he pushed his stethoscope back in his small leather satchel, "I can diagnose your shivering as too much of the fear drug, which should dissipate in a day or two, but your other injuries will take a little longer. I'm prescribing you bed rest until the shaking ceases and to give your body a break."

"But I'm supposed t-to be wor-working," Jake argued while struggling to sit up on the bed, worry written all over his face.

"Don't worry, son." The older man gave him a reassuring smile as he pressed Jake back down to the mattress. "Monica Avery is nothing like Darla Cain." He patted Jake's shoulder consolingly and grabbed his bag. "Get some sleep, Jake. You should be feeling better in a few days."

With that, he left the room.

Not feeling so cared for since before Bret's mother passed away years ago, Jake curled up beneath the warm blankets in the softest bed he could remember and fell into fitful dreams.

He lay in bed for two days, quaking from the effects of the drug. The head guard, Rosa Santos, checked on him two or three times a day, often bringing his meals and monitoring his recovery. She came across as busy and distracted, but he didn't mind. She made him almost as nervous as Monica. During Rosa's first visit, the evening he arrived on the ranch, she stayed for a little while to chat him up, but her first off-hand comment caught him off guard.

"You've already caused quite a stir among the young women on this ranch, Mr. Nichols," she stated in a playful tone as she set his dinner tray in his lap, but her comment struck Jake completely opposite from her intent.

His whole body froze, and his eyes went wide as he gaped at her in fear. "I-I didn't d-do anything," he stammered anxiously from beneath the covers. "I don't wa-want to cause tr-trouble."

Rosa frowned in confusion, staring as if he had suddenly grown horns. His unreasonable distress over her lighthearted comment was an overreaction, but he couldn't help it. The fear drug, still strong and flowing through his system, had surged to life the minute she walked into the room. But the implication that he had inadvertently attracted women living at Monica's sent panic rushing through him that had nothing to do with the drug.

"You haven't done anything wrong, Mr. Nichols," Rosa said, backing away from the bed to give him some room.

Jake breathed a little easier, but her previous statement still bothered him. His experiences with women over the last twenty months were mostly unpleasant, to say the least. The last thing he'd meant to do was to invite attention he didn't want and wasn't prepared to handle.

"I...don't m-mean to s-sound ungrateful," he stuttered. "I appreciate b-being sprung from m-my prison, but I d-don't want—" He stopped abruptly, realizing he was about to make a demand. Doing such a thing at Darla's would bring on a painful lesson in etiquette, and despite Miss Avery's claims earlier that afternoon, he was unsure what the practices here actually were.

"You don't want what?" Rosa probed lightly.

Jake dropped his eyes to the food in his lap without speaking. A shudder passed through him, causing the silverware on the tray to rattle against the dish.

"You can speak your mind, Mr. Nichols," Rosa told him gently, her tone reminding him of Bret's when he worked with a terrified horse. "Nothing bad will happen to you."

He glanced at her, saw the empathy in her eyes, and shook his head. He didn't want her pity either.

"We can discuss this more later, if you like," Rosa said with a gentle smile as she headed for the door.

"Wait!" Jake called; he suddenly needed her to know what he had intended to say. He needed to test what he'd been told too. He sucked in a deep breath and braced himself to speak the words burning inside him.

"I don't want...a...woman," he said quietly, staring at his blankets. "I can't... I don't... I...I just want to do my job and stay out of trouble." His last words were said in a rush.

"I understand," Rosa murmured, and Jake's head lifted. "Don't look so surprised. I'm well aware of what life is like where you came from. What you need to understand is it's different here. If you don't want a woman's attention while you're staying here, you're under no obligation to accept it. We want you to be happy here, Mr. Nichols."

He stared at her, still shuddering slightly, amazed by her short speech.

"You—" His voice cracked. He had to ask the question, even though he might not believe her answer. He swallowed and began again. "You mean that?"

"Absolutely," Rosa smiled. "You'll see the difference soon enough." She went to the exit. "Either Shawn or I will pick up the tray later," she said as she opened the door. "Just leave it on the floor when you're done. Get some rest, Mr. Nichols." With that, she left the room.

* * *

Shawn Brohm checked on him after dinner that night. Both in their early thirties, he and Jake had a lot in common, though they'd grown up differently. Like most of the others here, Shawn was a city boy and had never lived outside of a metropolis until the wars forced him into hiding. As a result, he possessed little ranching knowledge, and once he discovered Jake's prior experience, Shawn consulted with him about everything.

"How hard is it going to be to work with cows?" Shawn had queried that first night.

Despite his wariness and poor physical condition, Jake laughed.

"Well, first of all," he said, "they're not all cows. Some are bulls and others are steers. Then you have heifers, calves, mavericks, and a whole lot of other names I've forgotten."

"So, what do I call them then?" Shawn asked straight-faced, making Jake chuckle again. "Is there one word to cover all of them, other than cows?"

"Cows are females, bulls are uncut males, and steers are castrated males," Jake told him, thinking he liked Shawn Brohm a lot, "but you can call a group of them cattle, or the herd. You're going to have to learn the differences though."

"So what's the difference between all the other ones you mentioned?"

Laughing again, Jake shook his head before explaining the terms he remembered. He didn't mind; he liked ranch work too. He enjoyed being outside, sweating under the sun, doing something he loved. And in a day or two, he would be.

3

JAKE SAT IN BED, propped against several pillows, finishing the fried chicken, mashed potatoes, and generously buttered corn Rosa had brought him for dinner. It was his second night on Monica Avery's ranch, and he was feeling better after sleeping through most of the morning and afternoon. He still shivered once in a while and felt twinges of fear when unknown voices sounded from the hallway or children screamed as they played in the dooryard outside, but his anxiety was lessening. Yet sadness twisted his heart whenever the everyday sounds reminded him of his previous life and the freedom he'd lost.

He had dreamed about his teen years with Bret as he slept that morning. About all the trials they battled together once they finally got past their initial animosity. About how Jake's father had accepted Bret as part of their small family and how Bret's mom had comforted Jake when he missed his own dearly departed mother. When images of his capture and Bret running away without him finally entered his slumbering visions, Jake had jolted awake, covered in sweat. He'd lain there, staring at the ceiling and brooding about his friend, until Rosa appeared with his lunch tray.

"How are you feeling today, Mr. Nichols?" Rosa had asked, smiling as she set the tray down in his lap and stepped back.

"Better," Jake had said, and returned her smile when he realized her nearness didn't elicit any nervous trembling in him.

"You look a little better," she said and tilted her head. "Are the shakes and headache gone?"

"Not completely," he said after swallowing a ravenous bite of the sandwich he had taken from the tray.

"Looks like your appetite's returning." She grinned again.

Jake smiled now, remembering the earlier visit as he washed down the fried chicken with a swig of the chocolate milk he couldn't believe they had here. He hadn't freaked out once during his short conversation with Rosa at lunch. He only hoped he continued to improve.

He had just finished the last of his dinner and set the tray on the floor when someone rapped on his door. He jumped at the sound but chided himself for his reaction. *You were doing so well.*

"You decent in there?" Shawn called from the hallway.

The corners of Jake's mouth twitched in the beginnings of a smile, but a frown replaced it. Shawn seemed to be overly carefree for a slave. It made Jake curious and a little cautious.

"Come in, Shawn."

"I come bearing treats and entertainment," Shawn said cheerily as he stepped into the room. He carried two glasses of chocolate milk and a thin, ratty cardboard box under his arm. "I heard you were fond of chocolate milk." His eyes danced with mirth.

"Yes, I am," Jake said, grinning again at the surprise. "I can't believe you can still get it. I haven't had chocolate since before the wars."

"We get a little here and there," Shawn said, pressing one of the glasses into Jake's waiting hand. "It gets shipped up from somewhere down south a few times a year. Don't know the specifics, but I'm glad to have it when we do."

"Me too." Jake took a drink and then nodded toward the package under Shawn's arm. "What's in the box?"

"Mmm," Shawn said, gulping a quick bit of milk and hurriedly setting the glass aside. He held the battered, patched-up cover toward Jake and arched his brows. "Do you play chess?"

Jake tilted his head and shook it slightly. "Not well, and I'm not sure I remember all the rules."

"Not a problem," Shawn said, his eyes still dancing. He set the box on the bed beside Jake and then seemed to bounce as he went back to the door. "I'll teach you...that is..." He paused at the open door as if suddenly unsure of himself and glanced back at Jake over his shoulder. "You feel up for a game?"

Jake glanced at the age-worn box, gauging whether he was up for company and a game of mental acuity. "I don't know how long I can stay alert, but I think I could play a game or two."

"Good." Shawn grinned and reached for something in the hallway. He returned with a ladder-backed chair, which he set next to the bed after closing the door.

Shawn quickly explained the rules. Jake nodded as memories of playing with his old friend returned. They played one quick game to test his recollection and Jake lost in a rout, but he was enjoying the company and the challenge.

They were in the middle of their third, tiebreaking game when Jake finally got up the nerve to ask the first of many questions buzzing in his brain.

"Do you like living here?" He bit the inside of his cheek and looked up from the board.

Shawn sat back in his chair, cocked an eyebrow in Jake's direction, and then grinned. "Hell, yeah. Some piece of paper may say she owns me, but Monica never treats any of us like slaves."

"She doesn't..." Jake's voice trailed off as he stared at the other man, unsure how to finish his inquiry.

"What?" Shawn leaned forward again and rested his elbows on his thighs. He seemed truly interested in whatever Jake had to say.

"She doesn't...u-use her breeders?"

A long pause followed Jake's question, and he shifted uncomfortably under the weight of Shawn's steady gaze. Jake was about to tell him to forget it when Shawn threw his head back and burst out laughing. Jake glared at his new friend darkly, making Shawn laugh harder. He wasn't sure if Shawn's amusement came from the question itself or if it embarrassed him as much as it did Jake.

"No," Shawn said, sitting back in his chair and wiping at his eyes.

Jake, somewhat offended by Shawn's reaction, assumed the man had finally gotten ahold of himself.

"The men here aren't forced," Shawn continued. "She doesn't allow it or practice it herself."

"So, she's never...?"

Shawn shook his head.

Jake ran his fingers over his scraggly beard. "Not with anyone here or...anywhere else?"

"No, I told you, she doesn't force anyone or allow any other woman to do so here. If anyone wants to get together, including her, both parties must consent freely. As far as anywhere else, no way would she use the sexual services of slaves offered up for a fee by other owners."

Jake only nodded, slightly stunned that Shawn knew about breeders being sold by the hour, but something on Jake's face must have hinted at his thoughts, as Shawn wasn't done.

"Don't get the idea Monica doesn't like men," he said hurriedly, while giving Jake a suggestive look he didn't like but didn't have a chance to refute. "She's had boyfriends over the years, but nothing serious and no one for a long time now."

"So, you've never...?"

Shawn straightened, his chin dropped, and his head recoiled slightly.

"Me? And Monica?" Shaking his head, Shawn chuckled. "No."

"Why not? She's—" Jake clamped his jaw shut to stop himself from saying more. He didn't want to give anyone the wrong idea.

"What? Beautiful? Sweet?" Shawn's crooked grin returned, and his eyes twinkled with amusement. "Yeah, she's definitely both of those things. Which is why I convinced her to try kissing once, a long time ago, but she's too much like a sister to me." His lip curled and he shivered dramatically, groaning with disgust. "It was weird and awkward and we never thought of it again. She broke up with the last man she was seeing shortly before moving here."

"And where was he?" Jake wanted the question back the second it left his lips, but Shawn didn't seem to think anything of his curiosity.

"We all lived at her friend Angel's place for a couple years." Shawn's gaiety dimmed a bit and Jake wondered why, but the next instant his smile returned and he continued. "The man, Theo, was a ranch hand there. Like us, men aren't treated like slaves on Angel's ranch either."

"But Miss Avery still left him there," Jake said. For some reason, the idea that Monica left a man she once cared for as a slave in another woman's home unsettled Jake's stomach and made his whole body feel tight and heavy.

"Not exactly. They mutually agreed to stop seeing each other before we left. And from what I've seen since, Theo's happily involved with another woman now."

"I see," Jake replied, though still a bit lost in all the new information. He tilted his head as another question occurred to him. "Why were you living there?"

"At Angel's?"

Jake nodded.

Shawn sighed and glanced at the floor, but only for an instant. Then he shrugged and met Jake's eye again. "Monica didn't have enough to start this place on her own, so we helped Angel get hers up and running and she gave Monica the funds to buy this land and get the ranch started."

Jake frowned. "Where did Angel get the money?"

"I've no idea." Shawn's open expression said he spoke the truth. "She and Monica took off on their own for a few days and came back with a bag full of gold. Neither of them ever explained where it came from."

Jake snorted. "And why was this Angel woman so generous?"

Shawn chuckled again. "They've been friends for a while, been through a lot together. When they decided to move here, they made a pact. Monica took care of her ranch, and Angel joined the governing council. She spent a lot of time helping to rebuild the town and the electrical grid. That was touch and go for a while, but from what I understand, the town has access to a stable supply of power from parts of the old wind farms nearby and the hydroelectric dam on the Columbia about fifteen miles east of town. The outlying areas like Angel's ranch and ours," he shrugged and slouched back in the chair, "not so much. We rely a lot on solar to supplement certain necessities like refrigeration and the water pumps when the regular power fails for whatever reason. The rest of the time, we mostly use old-fashioned frontier ways."

Jake stared. He'd wondered how they got the power running again. "How did they manage that? The repairs to the grid, I mean."

"Angel and a few other women on the council began interviewing slaves. They asked about their skills and found several with enough knowledge to train others and get the job done."

That sounded familiar, but it left a bad taste in Jake's mouth. "Insightful of her," he said, his scorn ringing clear. "Just one more thing to use us for."

"It's not like that," Shawn said, a little too sharply, as he straightened up in the chair. Jake wondered at the strength of his retort. "Angel's a lot like Monica. Neither of them like the way things have turned out, and they do their best to counter the effects of women like Darla Cain and her friends. But Darla has been here a long time; she'd built herself a little kingdom before any of us arrived. The power she wields over the council is vast, and after a year, Angel is only starting to make a dent in it, though it's been hard." He lifted a shoulder and sighed, then continued in a calmer voice. "Soon Monica will be a member too, and together they'll have more influence over the others. They're not all cruel, they're just afraid of Darla."

Jake nodded. He could relate to that fear.

"How long have you known them? Monica and her friend, I mean. You make it sound like you've known them for years," Jake blurted, without thinking.

"I have, but the details will have to wait for another time," Shawn said as he got to his feet. "You're tired, Jake. We'll talk again tomorrow. We still have to finish our tiebreaker game." He set the chess board on the chest of drawers in the corner and went to the door.

Suddenly reminded of the late hour and his own weariness, Jake yawned and nodded.

"Get some sleep," Shawn said with a friendly grin.

"Yeah, good night," Jake muttered as Shawn left him to consider everything they'd discussed.

Jake lowered his head to his pillow and pulled the blankets over his shoulders, while his mind turned to the beautiful woman who temporarily owned him. Usually, now, he only felt dread when a woman touched him, uncertain about what kind of torment she would put him through for her entertainment. Yet everything about this situation seemed different from what he'd grown accustomed to in Darla Cain's care. He would've been punished a half-dozen times already for his words and actions the last two days if he were still in Darla's domain. If Shawn were to be believed, life on this ranch would be as close to normal as any of them had experienced since before the wars. He wasn't sure he could believe that.

Jake yawned again, and his eyelids dropped as if weighted down. He turned over on the bed, shifting under the blankets, and sighed. He was too tired to think of all the possible ways this could be an elaborate lie. Darla liked to play games, but this didn't feel the same.

And Monica...

Yeah, he thought, *she's beautiful, but she still owns slaves. Life might be good here, but don't get your hopes up. You can't stay anyway.* If this all proved to be real, God only knows how much he would want to remain here. Then, perhaps, he could heal and learn to be whole again, not the confused, terrified, fragmented man—no, slave—he had become.

4

THREE DAYS AFTER his arrival, Jake felt well enough for Shawn to give him a tour of the homestead.

"What do you think?" Shawn asked, waving his arm to indicate the work already completed on the house.

As he considered his reply, Jake eyed a group of three young women who had been studying him from afar. They stared right back at him, shared whispers, and giggled. Jake frowned and turned away. Shawn's voice receded as Jake's chin dropped, his eyes closed, and his hands balled into fists. He shivered and took a deep breath, battling almost two years of indoctrinated fear.

Shawn's hand on his shoulder made him jump.

"Ignore them, Jake," he said in a quiet aside, while tilting his head toward the women. "They'll get tired of your newness soon enough."

Jake nodded and tried to do as Shawn suggested, but the young women made it difficult. Despite his unease, he still answered Shawn's question with a hint of excitement.

"I think it'll be an easy job," Jake said, visually inspecting the framework already in place. "I'm surprised so many of the ranch buildings are already up though."

"Yeah," Shawn replied.

"Why didn't she build her house first?"

"Monica wanted to be sure to have beds for the single men, the guards, and the families with the dozen or so kids living here. Altogether, there's about sixty of us. So, the bunkhouse apartments were first. Then, as you can see," he waved a hand around the dooryard, "the barn, outbuildings, and most of the fencing came next."

"And she saved her house for last?" Jake asked with raised brows, an air of incredulity infusing his tone.

Shawn nodded. "Yep. It's so typical of her to think of her own comfort after everyone else's."

"You've worked for her for a while then?" Jake couldn't help the question, though just like his inquiries the night before, he didn't know why he asked. He kept reminding himself he was not interested in Miss Avery, but his curiosity about the woman, who for the next few months held his life in her hands, got the better of him.

"I've known her for years," Shawn said with a smile. "Since before the wars. Her whole family were good people. Monica is too."

He's never known life as a real slave then. Jake's ribs squeezed, and an envious knot tugged at his gut. *Lucky bastard.*

He didn't reply to Shawn's comment as he glanced at the three women still staring at him: two blondes bracketing a brunette with long straight hair. The one in the middle winked at him, and he stifled a groan as dread trickled down his backbone like ice along his flesh. He averted his gaze and replayed Shawn's last comment.

Good people, he thought as Shawn led him toward the back of the construction site and away from the ogling women. Dr. Beck had told him something very similar about Miss Avery a few days ago. He wasn't sure he believed Shawn any more than he did the doctor.

MONICA AVERY STOOD in the shadows near the half-open window of the small building she currently used as her office, watching her foreman touring around the dooryard with the new man.

Jake Nichols... His name floated through her mind, and her chest tightened a little. She hadn't intended to spend this morning standing idly by, secretly gawking at the man, but there was something about him that held her attention.

As the men walked through the yard, a group of younger children ran up to them. The little ones were always full of questions for anyone new on the ranch. She smiled as she watched Jake interact with them. He seemed a little unsure of himself at first, but he was soon chatting with them easily. One of the younger boys appeared to acquire Jake's full attention. Jake casually tipped his hat back on his head with one finger while he crouched down to the boy's level, a small smile curling his lips.

Ah, his lips... She sighed. She certainly found him attractive. At one time she would've considered approaching him, but she didn't need or want to jump into another fling. Still, despite her misgivings, Jake Nichols piqued her curiosity. Shawn told her he was a smart man, but hurting and leery of women. Well, she hadn't needed Shawn to tell her that. Considering where he came from, she expected his skittishness. She just didn't know how to help him through his apprehensions so he could enjoy his time with them. Monica had seen the fear in Jake's eyes the first time he met her gaze. He seemed broken in ways she could only imagine. She could understand that feeling. She'd been lost and afraid before, but then she had Rosa and Shawn to help her. Jake didn't seem to have anyone. Watching him smile at the boy in her dooryard and shake his hand, as if they'd struck some kind of bargain, warmed her heart but also made her feel oddly sad. Still, the touching scene gave her hope that Jake wasn't so damaged he couldn't heal. But then, he'd have to permanently get away from the danger of Darla Cain for that to truly happen. She shied from that, refusing to think about the horrors Jake Nichols may have faced all alone and would again in the fall.

Outside, Jake adjusted his hat and stood up, still smiling at the kids as Shawn shooed them on their way. Jake glanced toward her office, and she receded farther into the shadows of the unlit room. Curious as to what he was looking at, she also wondered what he thought about her and his temporary home.

"He will be mine," said a voice Monica recognized, floating in through the partially open window.

Jake kept glancing in the direction of three women—all guards on the ranch, now standing a few feet from Monica's office window—his hands balled into fists. Shawn put his hand on Jake's shoulder, turned him around, and led him behind the building site. Monica noted how much taller Jake was than Shawn, how broad his shoulders were, and how he walked with a masculine grace that sang to her.

"I can't wait to get him alone," the same voice said decisively to her friends.

"Do you really think you'll get him into bed, Kristine?" one of the women asked. "Rumor is he came from Darla Cain's. He didn't look too able or accommodating when he arrived."

Monica's stomach lurched. The fact that they were talking about Jake was bad enough, but the conversation got worse the longer she listened.

"Darla's slaves are well-trained," Kristine replied, with too much conviction for Monica's taste. "He'll be anxious to please me."

"Well, I must admit," the third guard said from Kristine's other side, "I'll be jealous if you do get to have sex with him. Just look at him."

"Oh, I am," Kristine said. The greedy lust in her tone irritated Monica on several levels. "And don't get any ideas about trying to beat me to him."

"We wouldn't think of it," the second guard said, brushing back her blonde hair and winking at her friend.

"I mean it," Kristine said in a commanding tone. The other two sobered immediately. At twenty, Kristine was young, but in Monica's estimation, she knew her worth. Not only did men find her attractive, but more often than not, she got her way. The others seemed a little afraid of her, and that, too, set off warning bells in Monica's head.

"We wouldn't interfere," the third guard said, tilting her dark-blonde head and fixing Kristine with an intense stare as she lowered her voice. "But you should be careful. Monica doesn't allow us to force them. You'll lose your job and get kicked out of your home if you do."

Well, Monica thought, *at least* one *of them listened to me.*

"I won't need to force him," Kristine said. "Men are easy to manipulate. A look, a touch, a kiss, and he'll come running. Besides, even if he's not willing now, he'll be going back. If he doesn't comply, he'll be sorry he turned me down later. Darla will punish him for his rudeness, and I'll have him anyway."

Her friends giggled, though their laughter sounded more uncomfortable than amused.

Monica fought the urge to storm outside and shout that Kristine would do no such thing. She only just succeeded.

As a girl and young adult, Kristine had known no other world except one where men were slaves. *She needs guidance, not punishment,* Monica thought. Unfortunately, most of the women Monica had hired on as guards or ranch hands—who received room and board and a little pay, once the ranch started to earn a profit—had come from other homes or from town, where that kind of behavior was the norm. Monica refused to hold that against them. She had high hopes for all of them and wanted to give them every chance to change their ways.

As she stood debating whether or not to confront them now, the three women wandered off toward the barn, murmuring complaints about work they needed to do, and the opportunity to immediately deal with their attitude went with them.

It's not as if I don't know where to find them, Monica thought as she went to her desk. Postponing the task for later, she made a quick note in her log to speak with Rosa about their guards and the overheard conversation. If she had any chance to alter their perceptions, while giving the men here a safe home, she would need help. She couldn't be everywhere at once, and Rosa would have some motherly insight on how to deal with the young women.

She might also know what Monica should do about the unexpected and troublesome attraction she felt for Jake Nichols.

5

THE RIVER WATER cooled Jake's overheated skin as he knelt on the bank and held his head beneath the fast-moving, gurgling surface. He sat up and sucked in a lungful of air, allowing the cold flood of water to run down his neck and into his shirt. His close-cropped, sandy-brown hair held little back, and rivulets dripped from the dark-golden goatee adorning his chin and upper lip. He pushed back and sat on the heels of his cowboy boots, his eyes closed as he turned his face to the warmth of the low-riding sun.

It was the end of May, and Jake's fortune had changed drastically. In the last four weeks, he had gained back the weight he'd lost in Darla's dungeon and recovered from most of the abuse he had suffered at her hands. The memories were still there, and he still harbored suspicion for any woman who approached him. But things were looking up.

On his fourth day after starting work for Monica, she had passed him as he ate dinner in the temporary dining room, and she stopped to ask how he was fairing. He had interacted with her on a couple of occasions before, when she helped with work on the house's construction, and her straightforwardness always threw him. That night, still adapting to the free environment of her home, he had endured her very direct gaze and told her he was doing fine.

"Anything you need?" she had asked, her hand resting on his shoulder. "I mean for the house or yourself?"

He inhaled sharply at her touch. His muscles tightened, but he refrained from pulling away from her.

"Ah...no, not right now," he fumbled, far too aware of her hand on him, not because of the drug, but because she was beautiful and a stranger to him. He didn't know what to expect, and despite her kind behavior and all the positive accounts he'd received about her, anticipation of the unknown kept him on edge.

"Good." She smiled at him, and his heart stuttered. "If you do, please let Rosa know right away."

Right. Rosa, he thought, disappointment swirling in his chest, though the emotion confused him.

Looking up at Monica, he nodded in response. Her gaze dropped to the table. Uncertainty flashed in her eyes, but disappeared just as quickly. She smiled at him again and then patted his shoulder amicably.

"Enjoy your dinner," she said before walking away.

He released the breath he'd been holding and turned back to the table. His fork, held tines-up in his white-knuckled fist, caught his eye. He groaned and then glanced at the others sitting around him, but no one paid him any mind. He loosened his death grip on the utensil and went back to his meal.

Whenever he thought back on that incident—and other similar ones since—his clumsy communication made him feel awkward and idiotic. There was no reason for it, but he couldn't make it stop. Luckily, he didn't have to interact with Monica much. His dealings were mostly with Rosa, which was fine with him since he didn't seem to have trouble speaking to her. A few times, he noticed Miss Avery watching their work and wondered if she would call him out on the modifications he'd made to her home's building plan. But aside from a wave or smiling hello, she hadn't approached him again in the three weeks since their last short conversation, and Rosa had made no comment about the revisions either.

He took their lack of criticism as a good sign.

Now, sitting on his heels by the river, he ran his hands over his face and sluiced the remaining water from his head. Kneeling on the thin, sandy bank within sight of Monica's new house, he dropped his hands into his lap, and sighed.

Another, slightly more exaggerated version of Jake's sigh rang out a few feet away, and Jake glanced toward the sound. He found a little boy of about nine, his normally wavy brown hair slicked to his head and his shirt soaking wet, mimicking Jake's every movement. He chuckled softly. The kid had been following him around for almost two weeks now, watching him closely, curious to learn more about ranch life, and asking questions about everything they did. At first, Jake was worried the kid would get hurt, but surprisingly, he did as he was told, stayed out of the way, and was a good helper.

The boy's name was Trevor, and he had decided Jake was his new best friend. That wouldn't have been so bad, except that Trevor also had a younger sister who wanted to do everything her brother did. She didn't always listen, and she asked twice as many questions.

Another sigh followed Trevor's, and Jake leaned back over his heels to see the boy's sister, Kara, kneeling beside her brother. Her long ash-blonde curls hung in a messy mop around her face and dripped river water onto her oversized, dirty blue T-shirt. She'd clearly been mimicking Jake's movements as well.

"You two get a lot of work done today?" Jake asked with a smile.

"Yep," Trevor replied. "Shawn told us we could help the guys dig the new duck system for the cows."

Jake chuckled again at the boy's description of the aqueduct system. He had spoken to Shawn about building the channel to take advantage of the nearby waterway. Once the watercourse was finished, they wouldn't have to rely on the well as much to water the livestock.

"I dug, too," Kara volunteered, and Jake stifled another laugh. They were good kids, and despite his apprehensions about getting attached, he liked having them around.

A couple of days after they started tagging after him, Jake had paused, his hammer halfway to the nail in the subflooring they were securing, when Trevor announced their parents were dead. He'd gazed over at the boy, afraid to ask any more about them, unsure of what the kid and his sister had already endured.

"So, who do you live with then?" he had asked instead.

"Sally's mom takes care of us." Trevor pointed out a brown-haired girl about his sister's age running with the other kids in the yard. Apparently, children were still a priority to the women of this new world. This was not the first time he'd heard of orphans or unwanted kids being taken in by other families. When he and Bret had been hiding in the mountains, many of the people there had banded together out of necessity. That others had done the same here surprised him at first, but now it only seemed natural that good people did what needed to be done.

"Do you like living with them?"

"Yeah." Trevor grinned. "She makes us cookies—" Distracted by shouts from the other children playing, Trevor ran off, ending the conversation, for which Jake was grateful. The thought of what those kids must have gone through in their short years disturbed him, and he hoped they were as content as the boy said.

"Well," Jake said to the children now, as they knelt on the sandy riverbank, gazing at him expectantly with big smiles of accomplishment on their little faces, "you must have worked up a mighty big hunger then."

"Yep!" the children replied in unison.

"You want to head back for dinner?" He grabbed his straw cowboy hat off the ground and stood, before placing it on his head.

"Yeah."

"Yeah."

The siblings jumped to their feet and rushed toward him. Kara held her arms up, her denim-colored eyes earnest, and Jake had to swallow the lump in his throat. She'd only started asking him to carry her a few days before, and the familiarity of the act, the open trust in her face, affected him as much now as it had the first time she did it.

"Carry me," she demanded when he didn't immediately move to pick her up. Understanding he wouldn't be living there long, he knew that encouraging their growing friendship wasn't a good idea, but he couldn't help wanting to find the same connection the children seemed to have found in him. He was fond of them too.

"You want a ride to the house?"

"Yes!"

"All right, come here then," he said and gathered the little girl in his arms. He looked down at Trevor and saw the boy's mood had darkened. Guessing the cause, he shifted Kara to his hip and offered his hand to her brother.

"Hey, Trev, would you lead me back? I'm a little tired, and carrying your sister is hard work. I might need a little help. I don't want to lose my way."

Trevor looked at him with the same denim-blue eyes as his sister and frowned, as if Jake had lost his mind.

Again, Jake had to hold back a smile. *Damn kid's too smart for his own good.*

"Okay," Trevor said, as if Jake's request was an arduous task, but Jake caught the hint of a grin curling the boy's lips as he began leading him to the house.

Jake dropped the kids off with their new mom, promising he'd be back to go in to dinner with them, and then made his way to his bedroom to clean up. When he went back to meet them, he was a little surprised to find Shawn waiting too, but he made no comment about it. Kara wanted another ride, and Trevor didn't need an offer to take Jake's hand; he simply grabbed hold and they started walking. Sally's mother smiled at Jake as they turned toward the dining room. He gave her a brief nod but no indication he wanted any other interaction with her, as Trevor tugged at his hand to go. Thankfully, she appeared more interested in Shawn than him.

They joined the other ranch workers for the meal, and the lighthearted banter at their table made Jake feel more at home than he had in too many years. It also reminded him of his long lost friend.

He could almost see Bret's green eyes light up in his too-handsome, suntanned face as a broad grin pulled at the corners of his mouth.

"I'll make a cowboy out of you yet, Jake." He heard Bret's voice plainly in his head as he recalled the hours of training his friend had given him.

Jake took a lot of ribbing from the other cowboys the first few months after he joined Bret on the ranch he ran, before the war drove them into the mountains. He'd been trying for days to learn how to rope a steer but was wretchedly inept at the chore. Bret stuck with him until Jake could finally loop the lariat over the stationary practice head consistently. Bret's regular praise, patience, and enthusiasm never waned, even when they graduated to working with moving targets and it seemed to Jake that he had to start all over again.

"You're doing fine, Jake," Bret encouraged more than once. "Just keep at it. You'll get it."

Bret was a good friend and Jake knew how much the man cared about him, but Bret didn't trust easily. His personal demons often caused him to push people away, even Jake, and his need to be loved had left them open to attack.

"Amy's brainwashed you, Bret." The memory of his own voice sounded loud and coarse in Jake's mind. "You're just too blinded by her beauty and your need to prove your uncle wrong to realize it."

His uncle's harsh treatment was a sore subject with Bret. The hurt and anger Jake read in Bret's silver-green eyes when he said those words still haunted him. Perhaps if he'd found a better way of convincing his friend to rid himself of the conniving woman, Jake would've never been captured.

Leave it alone, he told himself. *What's done is done. There's no changing it now.*

Despite everything though, he missed his friend, missed his witty banter while working a job, his loyal friendship, even his occasional dark moods. But Bret was long gone by now. Or a prisoner himself somewhere, though Jake hoped not. Being enslaved and owned by a woman like Darla Cain would kill Bret as surely as a bullet or a well-aimed arrow to the heart. Jake's stomach churned at the thought, but he had no way of knowing, so he chose to picture Bret still living in the mountains as a free man.

"Jake?" Shawn's teasing tone brought him back to the present. "Earth to Jake." The man was always joking around.

"Sorry. What?"

"Where were you?" Shawn scolded with a grin. "We were speculating on how long we have before we start working on the roof."

"Two or three weeks," Jake answered shortly, still distracted by his previous musings.

"Can I work on the roof too?" Trevor piped up from the end of the table. Jake glanced at the woman caring for the boy and his sister, saw the sudden unease on her face, and shook his head.

"I'm sure we'll have plenty of work for you on the ground, buddy," he said and caught Trevor's new mom's grateful look.

"Me too!" Kara chimed in, and Jake grinned.

"Yes, you too, squirt."

After a generous meal and enjoyable conversation, a quick good night to everyone, and a swift once-over of the construction site, Jake was ready for bed. Rosa had lent him an old crime novel after learning he liked to read, and he was looking forward to burning an hour of lamplight reading and relaxing in bed.

Upon entering, he flicked the switch beside his bedroom door, but the room remained dark.

Power's still out, he thought as he stepped inside and closed the door.

He didn't bother to immediately light the lantern on his bedside table; enough illumination crept in from the curtained window for him to undress without a lamp. His shirt untucked and unbuttoned, he was sitting on the bed, pulling off his last boot, when he caught movement out of the corner of his eye. Startled, he clumsily jumped to his feet, boot in hand. Unthinking, he tossed his footwear aside, and it hit the wall with a loud bang. Jake didn't hear it. All of his attention wholly focused on the person moving toward him from the darkest corner of the room.

This was *his room*, yet an uninvited someone moved silently toward him. Unsure how to react, Jake prepared to meet an attacker.

"You're not supposed to be in here," he growled at the shadow still slowly strolling toward him, as his fingers curled into fists at his sides.

A feminine giggle skittered over his strung-out nerves like the unpleasant screech of a violin in untutored hands. *A woman*, he thought, but the realization didn't lessen his anxiety.

"What do you want?" he demanded, sweat breaking out along his hairline. His breath came in short gasps, and his fists clenched tighter. He had been waiting for this, knowing eventually someone here would demand things from him he didn't want to give.

"Don't be afraid," she said, so close now he could grab her. "I'm not here to harm you." A small hand stroked his furred chest through his open shirt, and it was all he could do to hold back the shout that leaped into his throat.

"What do you want?" he repeated, stepping back and away from her roaming fingers. His back bumped up against the wall, and he froze.

She moved closer again as he suppressed the urge to shove her away.

"I wanted to spend some time with you," the woman said, and Jake almost groaned. He knew what she wanted.

"I'm not interested." His heart rate kicked up, and he swallowed the lump of terror in his throat. His jittery stomach instantly threatened to hurl up his dinner.

"You're not?" the woman sounded sulky.

"No." He wished he could see her face more clearly, so he would know who to avoid.

"And why is that?" she asked, her hand once again caressing his chest, her fingers combing through the crisp mat of hair. "A big, handsome man like you, not interested in sex with a beautiful woman? Seems strange to me. I think you're playing hard to get."

"I'm not playing anything," he snarled and grabbed her wrist, being careful not to injure her. "I'm not interested." He pushed her away and released her.

"You will be," she promised and lunged at him. Her arms snaked around his neck to pull his head down to hers, and she kissed him.

His whole body stiffened when her small form collided with his, and he stood immobile while she plied his lips with hers. He couldn't say her soft curves pressed against him and her eager mouth teasing his were bad sensations, but the memories crashed in too. He didn't want to remember. He didn't want to feel. But his mind gave him less of a choice than the woman did.

He started to shake, and anger bubbled to the surface. In a fit of self-preservation, he clutched her shoulders in a tight grip and shoved her away from him.

"I said, 'No!'" he shouted and kept shouting. "Stay away from me. Don't touch me. Don't *touch* me!"

Someone knocked on the door. They kept calling his name, but Jake couldn't reply. He grabbed the first thing his hand touched and threw it at his attacker while sensations of pain and fear assailed him.

Glass shattered against the far wall.

"Get out!" he cried, stepping toward the woman this time. He didn't think about his actions; he only wanted to escape her and the torment in his mind.

"What's wrong with you?" the stranger asked, but Jake was beyond answering.

"Out!" he screamed, panting and short of breath. "Get away from me."

The stink of kerosene assaulted him.

Did he smash the bedside lantern?

Voices and footsteps bustled in the hallway.

Glass crunched under the strange woman's shoes as she backed away.

"You're crazy," she said, alarm straining her voice. "I would've treated you well."

"I don't want you. Get—out!"

The door opened, and lantern light filled the dark room. The woman who'd propositioned him was not quite within reach. Seeing her clearly for the first time, he glared furiously and yelled at her again to leave.

She stared at him with big brown eyes, looking shocked and afraid of his overreaction to her advances. Jake remembered her. She was one of several women who'd been staring at him for weeks. She was attractive, and if he wasn't so screwed up, he might've taken her up on her offer—that is, if she hadn't treated him the way all the others had. She expected him to comply whether he wanted to or not, and when he didn't, she intended to take what she wanted without his consent. If she had taken it slower, he might've given in, eventually, but just like all the other times he had found himself in similar situations, she didn't care what he wanted.

Approaching him in the dark like that was a bad idea. It creeped him out and left far too much to his imagination, which took him right back to the hell he had lived in. This time, however, he could fight. He wasn't chained, and he wasn't so full of the fear drug he couldn't move. This time, he could defend himself.

He took another menacing step toward her, fury gleaming in his cold, hazel-green eyes, and she stumbled backward.

Suddenly, another woman stood in front of him, but his gaze stayed locked on the brunette who'd assaulted him.

"Jake," the woman blocking his path called softly, being careful not to touch him, but standing her ground. When he leveled the power of his angry glare at her, she blinked but she didn't move. "Jake?" She whispered his name this time, and the note of concern in her voice reached inside him and coiled around his heart.

His breath hitched and then rushed out in a whoosh as the rage seemed to flow from his head, through his body, down his legs, and out through his stocking feet. A puddle of fury and fear pooled around his socks. The image made him want to giggle.

What the hell is wrong with me?

"Jake? Are you all right?"

Panicked and peering around the room, he tried to remember what just happened. It only came in bits and pieces, but as they fit together, terror flooded him and his rapidly beating heart felt about to explode. The melodious voice calling his name drew his attention, and his eyes scanned the face of the lovely blonde woman who stood before him. As recognition finally dawned, a completely different type of dread banded his chest.

"Jake?"

"I-I didn't m-mean to hu-hurt her," he stammered.

"You didn't hurt anyone," Monica assured him before she shifted her attention to the others in the hall. "Please go back to your rooms now," she told them, and then focused on the young brunette who had caused the whole ruckus. "Kristine, I will talk to you in the morning. For now, go back to your room and stay there."

Monica turned to her head guard. "Rosa? Would you have someone bring me some towels, water, and a broom to clean up this mess?"

"Right away," Rosa answered in her soft, Spanish accent, and giving Monica a knowing look Jake didn't understand at all, she turned to the others. "Okay, everyone, you heard Monica. Back to bed. Tomorrow's going to be a long day."

Monica closed the door, leaving the rest of her people in Rosa's capable hands. When she turned back to Jake, he was standing where she'd left him, staring at the floor and trembling.

From the corner of his eye, he marked her unhurried approached, how she carefully kept her distance. *Good, maybe she heard my shouts not to touch me.* He also noticed her sympathetic expression and didn't know what to make of it. *Does she think I'm crazy, too?*

"Why don't you sit down, Jake?"

He nodded and went to the bed. He perched on the edge, staring at nothing.

"I'm sorry," Monica said, adjusting her dark-red robe. "Did she harm you?"

He shook his head and lifted his gaze to hers.

"How will you punish me now?"

"Oh, Jake." Monica sighed. She took a step toward him, her arm outstretched.

Jake stiffened and straightened up, squaring his shoulders to face an enemy.

Monica stopped. She dropped her arm and waited until he met her gaze again.

"I'm not going to punish you. I told you we don't do that here. Besides, you didn't do anything wrong. At least, I don't think you did."

He frowned at her, but looked away again. *Does she really think that?*

"Will you tell me what happened?" Monica was closer to him now, trying to meet his eyes.

He shook his head and scooted a little farther away.

Deliberately, Monica tucked her hands behind her and leaned against the wall opposite Jake. She seemed willing to wait indefinitely for him to speak.

A part of him didn't want to discuss it. The brunette had only kissed him, but he'd flashed back to other abuses and situations in which he'd be unable to protect himself. He'd suffered through far worse than a kiss during those.

Still, he thought, *what could it hurt to tell Monica? She said she wouldn't punish me for denying the other woman what she wanted.* At least Monica didn't ask him to reveal the full extent of what caused him to act like a crazy person so often; she was only asking about what happened tonight.

He sighed before he spoke. "She was in here when I got back from dinner."

"Did she threaten you?"

He shook his head again. "She... She kissed me and I..." He squeezed his eyes closed, and his hands clenched around the edge of the mattress.

"Go on," she said, her voice raspy. "Nothing bad will happen to you."

He glanced at her, nodded, then focused on the floor. "I told her no but she didn't listen. I guess I...freaked out a little." He closed his eyes again, shocked and embarrassed by how he had reacted to the situation.

Monica knelt on the floor at his feet, and he allowed her to take his hand gently in both of hers. She stared up into his face and spoke kindly but firmly. "It's okay, Jake. If you told her no, she shouldn't have pursued you. She should've listened. I'm glad you stood up for yourself." She paused for a breath, clearly trying to think of the right words to console him. "I know life at Darla's is far different than here, so I want to make sure you understand you did nothing wrong."

His cool fingers still trembled slightly as he met her gaze, but he didn't pull away. On the contrary, an abrupt desire for more contact flooded his senses; so much so, he almost got lost in the fiery deluge. Strange, considering his reaction to the other woman he just nearly attacked for wanting to touch him. He doused the arousal inside him, then swallowed and coughed to clear the lump in his throat.

"Thank you," he murmured hoarsely. "That means a lot to me."

"It won't happen again. I'll make sure of that."

"I don't want to make more trouble," he replied, anxiety edging his voice, and his hand tightened around hers.

"You didn't make any trouble. I don't let my guards harass the men here. She *knows* better, and tomorrow morning I will remind her of that."

She released him and got back to her feet; her hands trembled slightly, and he frowned at the sight.

"Will you be all right? Do you think you can sleep?"

He nodded.

A soft knock sounded at the door.

Monica opened it and found Rosa, who had brought the cleaning supplies herself. She set down the bucket of water and handed the remaining items to Monica, then went to open the window.

"It reeks in here," Rosa declared, throwing open the sash. "Did you break a lantern or something?"

"Or something," Jake said quietly.

"We'll clean this up and let you get some sleep," Monica told him.

A little flustered, Jake rushed to his feet, insisting he should clean up his own mess, but Monica told him to relax and urged him to sit on the bed.

"We got this," she said as she stepped on the towel she had dropped over the kerosene puddled on the hardwood floor. "All you need to worry about tonight is getting some rest."

At length, she convinced him to sit down, but only after it became clear nothing was left for him to do. She and Rosa had swept up the last of the glass, gathered up the wet towels, and tossed everything into the hallway when he finally complied.

"Go to sleep, Jake," Monica said and patted his arm consolingly. "If you need anything, anything at all, please wake Rosa or me. I mean that."

Rosa nodded at him from the doorway.

He looked at Monica and saw the concern in her gaze. Insight filled her eyes as if she knew exactly what had happened and why, and her perception disturbed him. Her warm hand resting on his shoulder was more comforting than he wanted to admit, and that disturbed him too.

He suddenly wanted to be alone.

He nodded.

Monica smiled at him and patted his arm once more.

"Good night, Jake," she said as she stepped through the doorway.

"Night."

She smiled again and closed the door with a soft click.

Jake stared at the doorway for several seconds after she left, trying to rein in his galloping heart.

What the hell is wrong with me now?

He wanted to pretend he didn't know. But he did.

He was attracted to Miss Avery.

He didn't want to be, he just was.

Her kindness, more than her beauty, drew him. But her behavior also intrigued him, and he wondered if she was really the tenderhearted woman she appeared to be. She seemed to sense what he needed, and he felt the resonance of her deep within him. It's what calmed the rage inside him earlier, before he lost complete control and did something stupid.

The unexpected impulse to take comfort in her gentle reassurances had been strong, and if he kept responding to her with the increasing intensity he felt tonight, he wouldn't be able to resist the urge for long. Worse than that, her manner indicated she felt sorry for him and nothing more.

He shook his head. *Damn it, you know better. You're here to do a job, stay out of trouble, and maybe find a way to escape. Not be distracted by a pretty face.*

But he already knew the admonishment came a little too late.

6

JAKE AND SHAWN WERE BUSY supervising Trevor, Kara, and a few other kids working on the framing and stairs for the front deck on a bright summer morning. Shawn had given them the standard lecture about safety—reminding the helpers and the crew that someone with experience had died from an accident not too long ago—before allowing the children to participate. Despite the gloomy safety lecture, everyone except Jake seemed to be in a cheery mood. Shawn in particular was especially jovial and had been joking around with the kids and Jake all morning.

"Hey, John," Shawn had called to one of the teens earlier. "Hand me the left-handed wrench, would you?"

Jake had grinned to himself. He'd been the brunt of that old joke years ago and been witness to it many other times since.

The young man dug through the tools and looked up confused.

"What's wrong?" Shawn asked with a straight face.

"They all look the same," John replied. "Which one is it?"

Shawn burst out laughing along with several other workers. The teen blushed, unsure what all the hilarity was about.

Taking pity on the young man, Jake explained. "There's no such thing as a left- or right-handed wrench."

Shawn had played a similar trick on Jake a few days before by nailing a wooden toolbox to the subflooring and asking him to retrieve it.

"Damn it, Shawn," he'd said, immediately knowing why he couldn't budge the box from the floor. "You need to get that off the floor before someone hurts themselves."

Shawn just laughed.

A short time later, Shawn had forgotten all about his joke and tripped over the same box. Aside from a bruise on his knee and some slivers in his hand from the subflooring, Shawn was unhurt, and the rest of them got to have a good laugh at the prankster for a change.

This morning though, Jake was feeling the weight of the tool belt he wore, and his mood had turned grumpy.

"Damn this belt," he complained while adjusting the heavy leather around his hips. He heard snickering behind him, and when he glanced over his shoulder, he was surprised to see Trevor laughing with Shawn, when the boy usually avoided the man.

Jake's suspicion tingling—and feeling idiotic for not checking sooner—he dug through the pockets of his belt.

"What the hell?" he mumbled as he pulled handfuls of pebbles from two rear pockets half-full of the small stones secretly piled into them.

Shawn, the kids, and several other workers laughed uproariously when Jake discovered their shenanigans.

"Not cool," Jake said. The glare he leveled on a clearly unrepentant Shawn conveyed his unhappiness, but he couldn't entirely blame his friend.

I should've guessed what he was up to hours ago.

The siblings seemed a little unnerved by his reaction. He glanced at Kara, her face frozen in an uncertain smile somewhere between laughing and fear of his anger. He gave her a playful wink that made her and her brother giggle again. Then he tossed aside his obvious irritation and laughed at his own expense.

He considered Shawn a friend, and despite his clowning, the easy camaraderie they shared gave Jake a sense of belonging he hadn't experienced since he lost Bret. The conflicting mix of emotions Jake still harbored for his old friend thundered inside him whenever he thought of Bret, but, as always, he could not deny how much he still missed the man he called his brother.

As Jake's comfort level on the ranch grew, he became more sociable at meals, during which the others often inundated him with questions.

"How do you get the cows to breed?" one younger man had asked curiously a few nights before as they gathered around him in the dining hall.

A few chuckles rounded the table, and Jake smiled.

"There used to be a whole process that didn't involve the two animals being anywhere near each other," he explained and provided a brief description of artificial insemination. At first, he was a little unnerved by all their attention being so focused on him, but as he got into the conversation, he forgot all about his unease.

"Things are more natural now," he continued. "The way it was before everything got so scientific and complicated. Of course, this life can be more frustrating too, backbreaking at times, but it's still worth the effort."

"What do you know about chickens?" a guard inquired as she joined them at the table.

"They're good fried with a side of mashed potatoes," one of the other cowboys joked, and a half-smile tugged at Jake's lips as another twitter of laughter sounded around the table.

"Not a whole lot," Jake admitted somewhat warily once the chuckling died down, and the young woman—who had thrown a glare at the male speaker—turned back to him with an expectant but friendly look on her face. Though Jake's anxiety bloomed to life with her direct gaze, he refused to let it show. "But ask away and I'll tell you what I know."

Each day, they queried him on something new, everything from raising crops to caring for cattle, and Jake did his best to give them the information they sought.

Most of the people living there were unfamiliar with ranching life. Like Shawn, many came from cities or suburbs and had to learn how to survive in the wild during the wars. Thousands headed into the hills to escape the bombs and destruction. Some returned to the ruins of their homes once the hostilities dwindled and some semblance of civilizations started anew, only to discover things had changed.

During the war, women discovered a new ability that science and the media labeled "hysterical-strength." This change was created in secret by a global genetics project that gave women bursts of unnatural strength during times of stress, particularly fear. The strength it awarded them only lasted until the need to protect themselves abated. The upside was they could individually contend with a male opponent in physical skirmishes for short bursts and longer if they worked in groups. The downside was that it could take up to thirty seconds or more to take effect, leaving them vulnerable for those few seconds.

By the time the global conflict ended, the male population had dwindled to precarious levels. When the less-depleted female populace took control, they treated the men no better than slaves.

The men fought back.

They lost.

That second war—known as the Sex War—turned men into nothing more than chattel to be bought and sold and used. Some ran back to the mountains to endure the harsh life of backwoods living once again. Until Raiders hunted them down and dragged them back to the Auction Hall.

That's what happened to Jake, sold at auction like an animal to Darla Cain, who took pleasure in ensuring he—and all her other slaves—never forgot his place or who owned his body, if not his soul. He tried not to dwell on his story. He tried not to remember what living under Darla's thumb was like and would be like again when—or if—he returned.

In the few weeks that he had been living on Monica's ranch, he'd begun to feel like a man again, a man regaining control of his life. He felt stronger, more sure of himself, the way he once had, before all the fear and running and deprivation. Being here reminded him of his job in construction when he was younger, and later, when he worked the ranch with Bret before the wars finally reached the Pacific Northwest. When the bombs came, he and Bret escaped into the mountains and lived rather well, considering, due to Bret's wilderness survival skills. That didn't mean they thrived; they just survived a little better than so many others.

Now, about seventy-five miles east of the Cascade Mountains, he enjoyed a life he'd almost forgotten how to live. His subjugation under Darla Cain had been total and brutal, but Monica's home was a paradise in comparison, and without the multiple daily injections of the drug, much of his self-confidence had returned. That was the best part about coming to live here. He could be himself again, do things he enjoyed, like creating beautiful things that would last and caring for the animals. Feeling like a man again—a respected and liked human being—was more heartening than he could ever convey. Despite his leeriness and temporary position, he couldn't deny he felt safe here with these people. They accepted him, and though he understood this reprieve would end in the fall, he couldn't help but enjoy the new friendships he was building with the other members of the ranch. His wariness around the women remained, but lessened significantly with the kind treatment he received from almost everyone.

Two days after Shawn's last prank on him, Jake stood in Monica's dooryard, supervising the installation of a new, enormous picture window. Jake felt comfortable and confident, more like himself than he had in a long time.

"Why don't you get up here and help us," Shawn joked without looking Jake's way, as he and three others maneuvered the frame into place.

"Then who would direct you?" Jake asked with a smirk and glanced at the drafted drawings in his hands. "You really want to do the installation by brail?" He didn't mind the ribbing, and he understood Shawn wasn't serious; neither was he. As soon as they had the heavy glass pane lined up in the opening, Jake would be up on the partially completed deck, working alongside them again.

"Hello, Jake," a female voice said from somewhere behind him, and he froze. The paper in his hands crinkled as he inadvertently crushed it in his fist.

His whole body tensed.

Sweat started along his tingling spine.

He tried to breathe, but his throat seemed to have closed after his first shocked inhalation.

He knew that voice; it haunted his nightmares. *What's* she *doing here?*

"Looks like they didn't exaggerate your skills," Darla Cain said as she drew nearer.

An almost overpowering desire to run, to hide, to get away struck Jake, but his feet remained rooted in place.

"Don't you have anything to say?" Darla questioned from directly behind him, a very real threat ringing in her voice.

"Thank you, Mistress," he muttered, still unable to move and falling into the submissiveness she had beaten into him long ago.

He couldn't see her, but he felt the superior smile that pulled at her lips. An unwanted picture of her filled his mind: long red hair, cruel gray eyes, pale skin, a pretty face with more than a hint of age lines around her eyes and mouth, and an evil smirk intent on making him squirm.

"Are you doing your best work for Miss Avery?" she asked, and a new threat laced her tone.

"Yes, Mistress," he replied without thought, ashamed that even without the fear drug he still wanted to cower in her presence. Her feigned interest in the job didn't fool him; she had no interest in his work. She was there to terrorize him and make sure he remembered his life belonged to her.

"Is that *all* you're doing for her?" she probed sweetly, but the question was anything but sweet. Darla was a jealous woman, and though she sold her breeders' services to others, she always made sure her slaves understood that she held their chains.

Jake's muscles tensed further.

"Yes, Mistress," he murmured.

"Good," she said, and he nearly sagged with relief.

Several seconds passed as her eyes carved into his back, and then she spoke again.

"Turn around, Jake," she ordered.

Grudgingly, he let the drawings fall and did as she said.

Head down, eyes on the ground, he strove to remain meek and humble, but terror and fury rocked through him all the same.

Does she know what happened that night in my room?

Is she here to make sure they punish me?

Is she here to do it herself?

Questions raced through his mind as he stood submissively before her. He could sense the malice of her regard like sandpaper against his skin as her gaze raked over him.

He flinched when she plucked his straw cowboy hat from his head. She let it drop to the ground behind her, where it landed with a quiet thud and a rustle of grass. Her fingers trailed across his cheek, his jaw, and down his neck.

"You've filled out nicely," she said, flicking the collar of his white work shirt. The tenor of her voice sounded pleased and...hungry.

"Thank you, Mistress," was his automatic reply, though his mind seethed. His weak and shabby physical condition had been all her doing. The heat of anger for all he'd suffered at her hands flushed outward from his chest and raced over his skin. He immediately bottled it up; fighting would only make things worse.

"Remove your shirt," she commanded, and he flinched again.

They stood in the middle of the dooryard. His entire crew of workers, gone silent at her arrival, was arrayed around the house behind him, watching. Darla wanted to humiliate him in front of her captive audience.

Thank God all the kids went to the river, he thought, but he still hesitated.

"Did you hear me?" she asked, her voice dangerously low.

He had no choice.

"Yes, Mistress," he said as his fingers slowly unbuttoned his shirt and pulled it from his jeans.

"The T-shirt too," she instructed, once his first garment landed on the ground.

Is she going to make me strip naked? Here? Now?

It didn't matter. If he didn't find a way to escape her, which seemed an insurmountable feat at the moment, a little embarrassment today would save him a lot of agony later, though there would be pain, nevertheless.

He tugged his undershirt from his jeans and was about to pull it over his head when another voice called out from the barn.

"What's going on here?" Rosa exclaimed as she hurriedly crossed the short distance to them. "Darla? What are you doing here?"

Darla flashed a dismissive glance at the head guard, and then her hard eyes locked on Jake. She crossed her arms and tilted her head. "I've come to check on my property," she said with a meaningful smirk.

Jake saw Rosa's shadow come up beside him and he glanced at her briefly as she turned toward Darla. Rosa nodded her head and he heard someone he couldn't see hustle away from the scene, but he didn't dare investigate who or why. He focused all his attention on Darla, careful not to look her in the eyes, but still keeping her face in his peripheral vision.

Striving to appear compliant was the best way to avoid her unpredictable wrath. Monitoring her facial expressions, he'd learned, prepared him for her inevitable cruelty.

"Have you talked to Monica?" Rosa queried, as if the redhead had not spoken.

"Not yet," Darla said with a calculating grin that made Jake cringe. "I wanted to look my slave over first."

"You've no right to do anything here without discussing it with Monica first."

"He's mine." Darla bristled, and her arms dropped to her sides, hands balled into fists. "I can do anything I want with him."

Rosa's gaze darted between Darla and Jake.

Jake could hear the laughter coming from the river, and he hoped none of the kids wandered back to witness this mortifying fiasco.

He shivered under Darla's icy glare. Sweat sheathed him, and even though he was standing in the warm summer sun, the slight breeze caressed his skin like an arctic blast.

"Take off your shirt, slave," Darla said again, and Jake's eyes flicked to Rosa.

"No, Jake," Rosa said. "Do not move."

"You've no authority in this, Miss Santos. He's mine."

"Not right now he's not."

Darla ignored her and turned to Jake. "Did you hear me, slave?"

"Yes, Mistress."

"No," Rosa repeated when Jake moved to comply. The steely power in her voice caused him to drop his arms again. He didn't know whom to obey. He wanted to follow Rosa's directives, but refusing Darla would bring him an unavoidable beating upon his return, or even now.

Darla's hand flashed toward his groin, and Jake knew he'd hesitated too long. He squeezed his eyes tight and inhaled sharply, his whole body cringing in anticipation of the pain to come.

But nothing happened.

"You will not touch him," Rosa said in a tone he'd never heard from her before. She sounded dangerous, like a mama bear protecting her young.

Jake's lids lifted, and he was stunned to see Rosa's work-hardened hand tightly gripping Darla's pale wrist and forcing her back, keeping the hated woman from hurting him the way she had so many times before. He sagged in a moment of utter relief, before dread and shame washed it way.

He'd just frozen in place, waiting for Darla to lash out at him. And now, he just stood there letting Rosa defend him.

You're worthless as a man, he thought bitterly. No longer inhibited by the drug, righteous anger roared through him, along with the desire to do something about it. Nothing was stopping him now, except fear of reprisal, but his fury burned that away too. Although it would be a stupid move, he desperately wanted to confront Darla himself.

Man up and look at her! his long-lost pride demanded, resurrected by weeks of normalcy, revived self-esteem, and the courage Rosa's support instilled in him now.

He turned his gaze to glare at the flame-haired woman who had caused him so much grief. He opened his mouth to speak, but before he could, Darla lunged forward, attempting to reach him, to punish him for daring to challenge her, if only with his eyes.

Rosa stepped between them and pushed the other woman back once again.

"I may not be able to keep you from speaking," she said, returning to Jake's side, "but you will not touch him without Monica's permission."

Darla stepped toward Jake and he tensed to meet her attack on his own this time, but Rosa moved into Darla's path. She glared at the head guard, then her eyes shifted over Rosa's shoulder to Jake.

"You're *mine*, slave," she hissed, leaning forward, her eyes boring into his. "Don't let Miss Avery's soft-hearted practices go to your head. You'll do as I say or you *will* pay for your disobedience."

His shoulders slumped as his rage and unexpected courage deserted him.

She was right. Defying her would gain him nothing. She'd make sure the Section Guard patrols doubled, tripled around Monica's home and he'd never escape. He might salvage his pride for a few months, but she'd only rip it away from him again in the end. He dropped his head and lowered his eyes. He couldn't win.

His hands trembled slightly as his fingers reached for the hem of his white T-shirt.

7

MONICA RAN ACROSS THE DOORYARD, horrified by what she saw happening on her land. Jake's handsome face was set in a mask of despair as he slowly lifted his shirt from his body.

"Stop!" she shouted, and wanted to sob when Jake jumped. Fear and anger ripped through her as she came to a stop beside the cruel woman who had no business being there. Sickened and infuriated that Darla would dare defy the rules of her home, Monica struggled with losing her temper, not wanting to cause problems she couldn't afford. The all-too-plausible tales of Darla's revenge against other women who tried to stand up to her replayed in Monica's mind as she swiftly weighed the pros and cons of dragging this hateful woman off her property. Barely refraining from yanking Darla away from Jake, Monica clenched her fists and barked out an order instead.

"Get away from him," she demanded, but Darla didn't comply.

"He's *my* slave, Monica. I have a right to inspect him and reprimand him as I see fit. Your guard doesn't seem to know her place."

"Not on my land, you don't," Monica railed. "And Rosa did exactly what she should."

Darla's spine straightened as if outraged by Monica's assertions, and then she slowly spun around.

Monica inhaled and tensed, preparing for the worst.

Darla's expression appeared placid, almost bored, but her eyes were filled with disdain and mockery.

"You're an idiot, Avery," she said. "One day, you and your friend Aldridge will regret your lenient practices with your slaves. I only hope I'm there to savor it."

"You have no business here," Monica said, ignoring the other woman's comments and striving for a calm she didn't feel. "You were not invited, nor did you ask permission to enter my property to do anything. The law still states you must confer with me prior to performing any dealing on my land, does it not?"

"This slave," Darla pointed at Jake, "*is—my—property*. I have a right to check on his welfare."

Monica held back a laugh, but could not keep from rolling her eyes.

"Not right now you don't," she answered. "Our contract says he belongs to me until his work is complete. His ownership will revert back to you in a little over four months and not before. Until then, you have a right to updated reports or to request a visit, but you do not have a right to torment him while he's in my care."

Darla looked away and crossed her arms over her chest, clearly vexed. Monica could tell she wanted to argue further, but she had no grounds.

"As you can see," Monica waved a hand at Jake who—head down, jaw clenched, and eyes squeezed shut—still stood in the same spot, "he's in good health and his work is impeccable, as my last report indicated. No need for you to concern yourself further today."

Darla huffed but said no word in reply.

"Rosa?" Monica turned to her friend.

"Yes, ma'am?" Rosa's overly formal address made Monica blink. Their relationship was normally that of equals, but one glance at her head guard revealed naked dislike for Darla on Rosa's face, and Monica understood. Rosa was purposely showing her employer the respect due her position, her expression broadcasting the act as an intentional slight to Darla. One that Darla didn't miss. She glared at the olive-skinned woman as Monica spoke again.

"Please take care of this." Monica nodded toward Jake and the other workers. "I'll check back with you later. I need a word with Miss Cain."

"Yes, ma'am, right away." Rosa tossed a loaded glare at Darla before she turned to Jake.

Darla opened her mouth to retaliate, but Monica cut her off by taking her arm and leading her back toward her horse and the two guards who had accompanied her.

She looked to Shawn, who had summoned her from the river to break up the drama in her dooryard, and tilted her head toward Rosa and Jake. He nodded his understanding and went after them.

Take care of him, Monica thought, and turned her concentration to getting Darla off her land.

"Not that I don't appreciate your facilitation in lending him to me, but I must insist, if you plan to pay another visit in the future," Monica said as she led the other woman away from her people, "that you send word at least twenty-four hours in advance of your arrival."

"It's been almost two months," Darla stated. "I only wanted to make sure his work was satisfactory."

Right, Monica thought and fought to keep from rolling her eyes once more. *You wanted to remind him* and me *of the power you hold over him.*

"Then I don't expect your company again until October," she said aloud in a pleasant tone.

"Yes, of course," Darla retorted peevishly as she mounted her horse. "Until then, keep a close eye on my property," she warned in parting. "He's unpredictable and dangerous, and quite likely to attempt escape. I'd hate to learn he harmed you before running for the hills."

Sure you would. Monica seethed as her uninvited guests headed back to town.

"I will, and thank you for your concern," she replied, then clamped her jaw tight to keep from saying anything she might regret.

In silent speculation, Monica watched them ride away. She loathed alienating Darla Cain further, because the woman wielded a great deal of influence. She already disliked Monica for her allegiance to Angel Aldridge and for their less-abusive practices with the men in their care. Still, Monica longed to put the woman in her place, though she currently lacked the financial stability to confront Darla outright. Despite that, however, she would not allow the woman to torture or humiliate Jake. Besides, she had a powerful friend of her own, and Angel would back her up no matter what.

Monica turned to her house and saw everyone working once again. One or two peered toward the bunkhouse, where she just glimpsed Rosa and Shawn accompanying Jake inside.

Jake, she thought and sighed. What was it about the man that kept tugging at her thoughts? He was attractive, sure, but it wasn't just that. She liked men, had spent time with more than a few, but none affected her the way this quiet man did. She didn't even know anything about him, except that she liked his slow smile—though he had yet to bestow one on her—and the gentle way he dealt with the children and everyone else on the ranch.

His clever mind and growing confidence also intrigued her.

Because she hadn't known precisely what to expect, Jake's skill and obvious intelligence were a surprise, though they shouldn't have been. The reports she'd received said he'd been educated and knew construction. Still, Monica was more than a little impressed.

When he had mustered the courage to voice at least some of what happened with Kristine several nights ago, he'd stunned Monica again. For some reason, he'd trusted her that night, showing an inner strength she admired, which not only piqued her fascination but also warmed her heart.

There was more to him than the trembling, half-starved, pitiable man who'd first arrived, and definitely more than just his handsome face. All of it made her wonder what else lay beneath his wary, kind, and sometimes curious eyes.

Maybe it's time I got to know him better, she thought. *Maybe it's time he got to know me too.*

8

JAKE SAT ON THE EDGE of his bed, trembling. Heat burned inside his rib cage, radiating outward in waves, boiling his blood. Every muscle felt tense to the point of breaking as he stared at the floor. All he wanted to do was put his fist through the wall. Not that it would do any good.

She couldn't just fucking leave me alone!

Head down, heart racing, he clenched his hands in his lap and squeezed his eyes shut, silently willing the other two people in his room to leave. It was bad enough they had witnessed his humiliation outside; now he didn't want anyone to see him fall apart or break something.

At least the kids didn't see anything...

But Monica did.

He groaned at the thought.

Rosa mumbled something to Shawn about staying with Jake and then left the room. A few seconds passed before Jake lifted his eyes and met his friend's worried gaze.

"You don't need to stay," Jake rasped, barely in control of the storm inside him. "I'd rather be alone."

"Hiding won't make it better," Shawn said sagely, and Jake laughed without humor.

"You saw what she's like. You know I'll be going back to that. There's nowhere I can hide."

"I understand you're angry—"

"Angry?" he slammed his fist on the bedside table, and his voice shook as he shouted. "Shawn, she *humiliated* me! The only reason she showed up was to make sure I remembered she's waiting to throw me in chains and fucking torture me again."

"No one blames you for being afraid."

Jake glared at his new friend, but Shawn had struck the nail right on the head.

Jake looked away.

He was outraged by how Darla had treated him—how she always treated him and the rest of her slaves—but he was totally embarrassed by his utter fear of her too. He'd always been ashamed of the terror she roused in him, but back then he had the excuse of the drug to placate his wounded pride. That pretext was no longer valid. He couldn't blame his lack of courage on the chemical to justify his reactions to Darla Cain. No, now, he must face the truth of his cowardice.

"You're not a coward, Jake."

"How can you say that after what just happened?" Jake didn't question how Shawn knew what he was thinking. He was positive the truth was like a neon sign flashing "Coward" in bright crimson across his forehead.

"Because I've heard the stories of what she's like, and I've gotten to know you over the last couple months. I was also there when you first arrived. You're a different man now than you were then."

Jake huffed derisively, uncertain how true the last part of Shawn's statement was and doubting his ability to ever truly get over his fear.

"But I'll be going back. Facing women here is very different than what

I'll be returning to. There's no end to the torment there. Coming here only reminded me of how much I lost when they enslaved me. How can I survive going back now?"

"I don't know," Shawn said sadly, and they both fell silent.

Elbows on his knees, Jake dropped his head in his hands as if its weight was too much to hold up any longer. Slowly, the rage receded, leaving only his worry and fear for the future.

"You don't have to be afraid here, Jake," Shawn said in a tone very unlike his usual lighthearted self.

Jake lifted his head and stared at him, clearly disbelieving.

"Why don't you try to enjoy the time you have with us?"

"And how do you suggest I do that?"

"There are several pretty women living here. Chat one up and enjoy yourself a little."

"I'm not interested in that."

Shawn gave him a stunned look, clearly confused, and even before he spoke, Jake knew the man had jumped to the wrong conclusion.

"So...you...don't like women?"

Jake shook his head and sighed. "It's not that. I like...women. I'm just not... I can't..." he stuttered through the words, unable to finish a single thought. "Where I came from... The things they did... The things they *made* me do... I just..."

"I get it," Shawn interjected between Jake's uncomfortable pauses. "I do. But you're still a man, and I've seen the way you look at Monica."

Jake's eyes widened and he started to speak, but Shawn lifted a hand to halt his objection.

"It's not an accusation and I'm not making any claims. I told you, she's like my sister and I love her. She's a wonderful person and she deserves someone who'll treat her well."

"What are you talking about?" Jake demanded incredulously, stunned by the apparent implication in Shawn's words. "I'm a coward and a slave. I can't offer anything to anyone. Besides, we barely know each other.

There's no reason to assume anything simply because I noticed she's pretty."

"Maybe you should ask her what she thinks." Rosa's voice sounded from the doorway, making both men jump with the suddenness of her appearance. She stepped into the small room and extended a glass filled with water to Jake. "Here."

He took it gratefully and swallowed a long drink before setting it aside.

"May I ask you a personal question, Mr. Nichols?" Rosa said softly, her kind ebony eyes intent on his face as she stood at the end of the bed.

Jake took a deep breath, let it out slowly, and then nodded.

"Why are you spending so much time with the children?"

Jake looked away. "Why do you want to know?" he inquired, partly because he wanted to know and partly to give himself time.

"I've seen you with Trevor and his sister. You're good with them, and I wonder, now, why—if you're so worried about having nothing to offer—why do you encourage the children? Is it because...you're missing your own?"

Jake snorted. She didn't know half of what went on at Darla's.

"I'm not trying to hurt them," he said about the kids. "They wouldn't quit following me, and I didn't want to scare them away. Maybe it's wrong, but I like them being around. That doesn't mean I have any of my own."

He saw Rosa's assessing look and elaborated.

"The woman who sold me to Darla wanted me to suffer for ruining her plans for my friend," he said quietly, unable to meet their eyes, but his tone hardened as he continued. "She made my punishment part of the deal when Darla bought me. Because of that, I never received a reprieve from abuse. Many of the women who come to Darla's... They... They usually...aren't there for...conception. Some are...interested in it, but..." His voice cracked and he swallowed, but he didn't stop. "Most of those who...used me...weren't. They come there to relieve their own stress by taking out their frustrations on men who can't fight back. I'm sure some men have a few kids as a result of their...encounters, but not me."

"And why do you believe that?"

He slanted her a quick glance, expecting condemnation in her expression, but all he saw was compassion. His eyes dropped to the ground once again. He released a long, shuddering sigh before he said in a rough voice, "Because I...know."

Rosa nodded and, apparently recognizing his discomfort, didn't press him further.

"I'm sorry to pry, Mr. Nichols, but I've been worried about those kids. They are quite fond of you. I don't want them to get hurt."

"Me neither," Shawn said, but there was no malice in the comment. Jake had already figured out that Shawn wanted something more with the woman who had taken Trevor and Kara in; he just didn't know how deeply his friend's desires went.

"I don't want that either," Jake said and met Shawn's eyes. "I'm not trying to invade your territory—"

"We're not at war, Jake," Shawn interrupted, though he seemed pleased by Jake's words. "It's okay if the kids like you, as long as you're careful with them."

"They know I'm not staying, if that's what you mean. I told them weeks ago." He lowered his gaze and shook his head. "I'm not sure how much they understand, but they know." He huffed out a breath and shrugged as he looked up at Shawn again. "They keep asking me, 'How much longer will you stay?'"

Eyes down again, Jake sighed, and they were all quiet for a long minute before Rosa spoke again.

"Well, I should get back to work." She looked at Jake. "You don't have to go out again today if you don't want, Mr. Nichols, but it might be better if you do go back to work. Many of those people have started looking up to you. This would be a good time to show them and yourself how strong you really are." With that and a nod to Shawn, she left the room.

Jake stared at the floor, unsure what to think about her comment but knowing she was right. Still, going out again meant facing the stares of silent question and pity.

That would be hard.

"You don't know how lucky you are to have ended up in a place like this, with a woman like Monica," Jake said, still sitting on the bed, staring at the ground. "You're damn lucky, Shawn."

"Yeah, I'm beginning to see that more clearly," Shawn murmured.

They both fell quiet, lost in thought.

"I'm not trying to push you into something you're not ready for," Shawn finally spoke up, breaking into Jake's morbid thoughts, "but being alone indefinitely doesn't seem like a great option either."

"It's...not," Jake said without taking his eyes from the floor.

"Then maybe you need to face your fears more directly."

Jake's brows drew down and he lifted his head. "What?"

"Spend some time with a woman who won't hurt you. There are still many who won't treat you like a slave."

When Jake's expression darkened, Shawn raised his hands in a placating gesture. "I'm not saying you should run out and have a physical relationship with someone...unless...you want to. I'm just saying, let yourself relax a little. You were starting to do just that before..." His voice faded and he shrugged, but Jake knew what he didn't say: before Darla Cain showed up.

Jake's eyes fixed on his hands clasped between his knees. *Maybe Shawn has a point.* Perhaps he could work on healing and relishing life a little while he was here. He'd gained most of his strength back, and he'd already considered the lack of restrictions in this place. If he took advantage of the low security here and ran for the mountains, he could regain his lost freedom before Darla came back for him. Why not enjoy himself a little before then if he could?

When Shawn spoke again, his careful tone turned light and teasing. "If you let yourself loosen up a little, it might—just might, mind you—put a smile back on that ugly mug of yours." Shawn couldn't stay serious for too long.

Jake snorted, frustrated and annoyed by Shawn's ignorance, but, understanding his friend's desire to help, he refused to be offended. He also didn't want to talk about it anymore. Summoning up a brighter tone, he replied to Shawn's lighthearted comment. "You might be right about that. About the smile part, not the ugly part."

Shawn laughed outright. "Yeah, enjoy yourself a little while you're here. Make some good memories for a change."

"Yeah," Jake said softly, sobering once again, "but then I'll have to go back."

"There's no harm in letting yourself have a little fun until then."

A long silence followed while Jake considered Shawn's comment.

"Maybe," he finally answered, "but I'm afraid what it'll do to me when they take me back."

9

THE NEXT DAY, Monica couldn't keep herself from seeking Jake out as he and the other hands labored around the building site. She hadn't been available to help with the work for several days, and she still had other duties to attend to today, but she wanted to check up on him.

He seemed at ease as he gathered four long wooden planks over his shoulder to tote them back to the partially completed deck. She couldn't help noticing the way the corded muscles in his arms and back flexed in this unpretentious display of strength. As she watched his long-legged, cowboy-like stroll to the deck, her body clench deep inside. Shaking her head, she pressed a hand to her fluttering belly and inhaled sharply. His physical attractiveness was obvious, but despite her body's reaction to him, her interest lay in the flashes of intelligence and kindness he often displayed, and the deep well of courage he'd shown yesterday.

She was happy to see him outside again after the disaster with Darla. Rosa and Shawn had both told her how the woman's sudden appearance and treatment of Jake had shamed him. Seeing him return to work, when he knew there would be curiosity and sympathy, made her proud of him in a way she didn't expect. Once again, she admired his strength to continue as if nothing had happened, as well as the way he quietly accepted his co-worker's empathy and the reactions of those who were not so kind, particularly Kristine Collins.

"He disobeyed," she had argued a little too loudly with one of the other guards sitting at her dinner table the night before. "He got what he deserved. Should've gotten more."

"You know men are treated differently here," the other woman had replied.

"He still belongs to her," Kristine said. "If you ask me, she has every right to make sure all his training isn't undone here."

"No one asked you, Kristine," Rosa said from the table next to her. Kristine glanced in the head guard's direction, another argument on her lips, but she clamped her teeth shut when she saw Monica approach.

"You've been told to leave Mr. Nichols alone," Monica reminded her quietly as she hovered over Kristine's chair. "Leave this alone too."

The gentle but grim admonishment shut Kristine up.

Today, some of the kids helped with the easier construction tasks, while others screamed and laughed as they chased each other around the yard. As Monica stood by the barn, watching the men work, a group of the younger children ran up the back porch steps through the house, dashing around and jumping over obstacles in their way, before they exited out the front, giggling madly. Shawn shouted something at their backs about staying out of the work area and tanning their backsides if they do it again. She saw how the delighted terror of irritating the ranch foreman brightened their little faces, and she chuckled to herself. The instigators knew Shawn was a big softy. She shook her head at their antics, and before she knew what she was doing, she was standing on the partially finished front porch where Jake was on his knees, hammering in finishing planks. She tapped him on the shoulder, and he jumped before glancing back at her.

"Hi," she said, grinning.

"Hi." He slowly tucked his hammer in his tool belt and straightened, glancing around nervously.

When he met her gaze, she had to resist the sudden urge to touch him, to reach out and smooth the worry from his brow.

"I wonder if you'd give me a tour?" she asked, feeling ridiculous for being so coy. "I'd like to see it all up close if you have the time."

He shrugged. "Sure. It's your house. What do you want to see?"

"Everything."

"Okay," he chuckled lightly. "Follow me."

He walked her through the first floor, explaining how it would all look once the interior was complete. The details barely registered with Monica; she was too wrapped up in listening to his voice. His deep timbre resonated through her, making her shiver as the warm, comforting, longing sensation he caused settled into her bones. The feeling was a little surprising.

"You want to check out the upstairs?" he inquired, his eyes dancing and the corners of his mouth turning up slightly. "It's obviously not finished, but you can see where everything is at least."

A smile bloomed on her lips. "I'd love to."

Something tightened in the center of her chest when he grinned in return.

"This way then," he said, and they turned toward the stairs. Monica's heart skipped a beat when his hand angled toward her back, as if to guide her. She didn't think he realized what he was doing at first. It was simply a polite, masculine gesture, but at the last second, his arm fell back to his side.

Still, for a long heartbeat, Monica could almost feel his palm against the small of her back, its heat seeping through her shirt, waking her body. Her stomach tightened and tingles raced over her skin in anticipation, raising the hair on her arms and the back of her neck. When nothing more happened and his hand dropped without making contact, her shoulders slumped, and she bit her lip to keep silent, wondering at her visceral reaction.

Upstairs, his hand reached toward her once more, and her breath caught. Yet again, he stopped inches short of touching her, but just his proximity seemed to be enough to heighten her awareness of him. Her pulse raced. Her skin flushed with warmth. Her knees wobbled unsteadily. So wrapped up in her body's sudden responses to him, she had to remind herself to breathe.

He led her to Rosa's room, then to the guest room, and then on to where her own room would be. Following him, Monica was again struck by the easy way he moved. Head up, back straight, long legs eating up the short distances. He walked with a quiet confidence that his insecurities couldn't conceal, she noticed, and a rush of thankfulness gladdened her heart.

Monica had designed her house similar to her friend Angel's home, though on a smaller scale, so she knew the layout well. But she liked listening to Jake speak, the way his self-assured tone soothed her hyperaware senses. She liked being near him, catching a whiff of his masculine scent—a mixture of pine and musky man—and she liked the tingling excitement in her belly whenever he was close. She could chat with him for hours about the house project, or anything else he wanted, for that matter.

"And here," Jake said, stepping toward the back wall and breaking her from her thoughts, "is where the French doors will open onto the deck."

She smiled at the obvious pride shining on his face.

"It's beautiful," she said, admiring the panoramic view of the meadow-like lawn, the tree-covered hills in the distance, a cloudless blue sky, and the far-off mountains. From the corner of her eye, she saw his gaze flick between her and the gorgeous scenery before them.

"Yes, it is," he agreed, and she turned to him with a soft smile. Looking at him, a light, cheerful feeling bubbled up in her chest, like champagne in a glass. His breathing matched the rapid pace of hers, and she wondered if his heart was thumping as hard in his chest as hers was. Her lips parted.

Her skin prickled. Heat flooded her insides, and she felt his presence with every cell in her body.

My God, she thought at this new sudden rush of sensation.

His feet shifted, he swallowed, and a muscle in his clenched jaw twitched. Appearing suddenly rattled, he shoved his hands in his pockets and quickly turned toward the stairs.

"You've done a wonderful job," she said as she followed him downstairs, feeling a little rattled herself. And a little disappointed too.

"I'm glad you like it," he replied, his tone reserved and noncommittal.

They exited out the back door, and she noted, unhappily, that he kept his hands in his pockets as they strolled through the short grass and open dirt patches behind the house.

"We're on track to meet the scheduled completion date," he said somewhat woodenly.

She nodded her understanding as they passed several other workers. They came to a tall ladder propped against the wall, and Monica followed the rungs upward to see a woman near the top.

"Hey, Kim!" she shouted up at her.

The woman lowered her head and tucked a strand of chestnut-colored hair behind her ear as a bright smile filled her face. "Hi, Monica! What do you think?" She gestured to indicate the progress on the house.

"It looks great."

Kim smiled and waved before going back to work.

Monica glanced at Jake, standing silently beside her. "You do know everyone, right?"

"The men, yeah," he answered, glancing up at the woman on the ladder. "Not all of the guards though. Her," he lifted his chin upward, "I only knew as 'Sally's mom.'"

Monica chuckled, pausing her steps and stopping him with a hand on his arm. The hard strength beneath his warm skin amped up her awareness of him and how close they stood. "That's right," she said after only a slight hesitation, "Trevor and Kara befriended you. They're something else, aren't they?"

He only nodded, not lifting his eyes from her fingers, where they rested on his forearm.

She let her hand fall and saw him shiver slightly, but he didn't move away. His hands were still stuffed in the front pockets of his jeans, as if he was unsure what to do with them.

"You really like this work, don't you?" she asked, hoping to draw him out once more.

"Yeah," he murmured, his gaze drifting to the distant hills. "I like all of it. I didn't realize how much I missed it."

They were near the corner of the house and right in the middle of the kids' chosen play area. As Monica tried to make eye contact with Jake, they were suddenly surrounded by running children who pushed them into each other as they dashed by. Feeling Jake's hard form against her sent a jolt of electricity slamming through Monica's body. Every nerve went on high alert, and although they barely touched before separating again, she still tingled everywhere they'd touched.

Their eyes collided and held.

"Hey, slow down!" someone that sounded like Shawn shouted. The giggling increased, as did their speed, Monica assumed, but she wasn't paying attention.

She couldn't pull her gaze from Jake and the mixture of dread and searing desire spilling from his eyes.

Her heart skipped a beat.

A sudden crash, followed by several frightened screams and a loud curse, sounded from the direction in which the children had just scampered. Jake took in the danger far more quickly than she did. His eyes widened in alarm as he looked up and then back to her, and she realized she was in harm's way.

One instant she was standing near the house. The next, her body slammed into hard muscle and they were tumbling to the ground as another much louder crash sounded directly behind her. Jake's arms wrapped around her, crushing her against him as they fell. His body twisted to take the full weight of their impending impact just before they crashed to the ground. He groaned when they hit, and Monica felt a twinge of sympathy.

A second later, his eyelids popped open and his concerned gaze searched her face.

"Are you all right?" he asked as his hand gently brushed her hair from her face, but Monica couldn't speak.

Since she had yet to find that one special man to have in her life, she relied on her memories to fill her need for intimacy. She had a wonderful imagination and plenty to recall, but that was nothing compared to feeling the real thing. This man's entire gorgeous body was solid, from the bulky thigh she now straddled, to the corded arms cradling her, to the broad chest supporting her. And every part of him was so damn warm! She stared down into his face, the heat creeping inside her, lighting a whole different kind of fire. This close she could see the tiny laugh lines at the corners of his eyes, the contours of his beard, and the golden tips of chest hair curling over the collar of his undershirt. His heart pounded against her breast, matching the wild pace of hers. His breath tickled her lips, so close—so *damn* close—but he didn't move.

She didn't either; she only stared into his eyes, unsure what he wanted, and strangely uncertain herself.

"Yeah," she said breathily, a little flustered by her own instant reaction to his nearness. "I'm okay. You?"

"Don't think I broke anything," he said with a slow smile, and his confidence seemed to come back to life.

Seeing both gave her a warm, fuzzy feeling that tightened her chest.

"Might be a little sore later, but..." He shrugged. "I can't say I'm sorry I did it."

"Me either." She smiled back and opened her mouth to speak again, but was interrupted.

"Are you two all right?" Shawn almost shouted in their ears. They both jumped at the intrusion.

"Yep," Jake said shortly, and the moment between them, the growing temptation to take the next step, disappeared.

"Yeah, we're fine," Monica answered a touch snappishly.

Shawn's crooked grin appeared as he tapped Jake's arm and gave him a blatant wink. "You can let her up now then, buddy," he joked, and then ran off to check on the others caught up in the minor calamity.

Jake's eyes locked with Monica's, shock and uncertainty radiating from him as his body stiffened with Shawn's words.

"Sorry," he mumbled as his arms fell away.

"It's okay," she said and glanced around, feeling oddly weighted down as she pushed away from him.

Shawn stood next to Kim, who was brushing dust off her shoulders. The heavy metal ladder she'd been standing on lay on its side, where Monica had been standing moments before.

"Kim?" she called. "Are you all right?"

"Yeah," Kim said, still swiping at her clothes. "I jumped before it hit the ground. I'm fine, just a little dirty."

"Are you sure?

Kim nodded.

"Anyone else hurt?" Monica asked, looking at Shawn.

He shook his head. "No, you were the only one in danger. Good thing Jake's quick on his feet." A crooked smirk bloomed on his face, and he nodded to the man standing beside her.

Jake shifted, and Monica could feel his unease at Shawn's teasing. She tilted her head and gave her foreman a knock-it-off glare. "What happened?"

Shawn's smile disappeared. "The kids weren't paying attention and running in the work area again," he said with a scowl directed at a group of youngsters nearby. "They knocked the ladder over."

"Are they okay?" Her gaze drifted to the children. They didn't look hurt, just scared. A little girl with blonde curls had her arms wrapped tightly around her brother's waist and was crying into his chest.

"I think so," Shawn said, but his tone sounded deep and serious, an indication of his annoyance and concern.

Monica raised her voice to the children. "Are any of you hurt?"

Obviously shaken up and worried about getting in trouble, the children answered her question with shaking heads and a chorus of "no."

"You're lucky," she said to the group, breathing a sigh of relief. "You all know better."

Now that she knew everyone was all right, her awareness of the man at her side came shimmering back to life. He'd retrieved his hat from the ground, and a grass stain marred the shoulder of his shirt, which reminded her of his quick reflexes.

"Thank you, Jake," she said, nodding toward the ladder that had been propped back up against the house. "I'm glad you were there."

He looked down at her. "Me too," he said. "I'm glad it wasn't worse."

She nodded, gazing at the children, making a note of the ones who needed reminding about safety and the consequences of breaking the rules. Some had wandered off to play, two or three were being admonished by parents who'd witnessed the scene, and a couple more were talking to Kim and Shawn, but Trevor and Kara stood by themselves. The boy was glaring at Shawn, and his sister was still hiding her face. Monica wondered what was going on there.

She made another mental note to have a talk with Rosa about it all later.

"You are okay, right?" Jake asked, and when Monica met his gaze, she read concern in his hazel-green eyes.

"Yes, I'm fine." Her lips curled upward. "You probably saved my life, you know," she said, hoping to tease another smile onto his lips. "Doesn't it say somewhere that I'm now indebted to you?"

His quiet chuckle was like music to her ears. "I don't know if I'd go that far. Besides, even if that were true, I'd say saving me from Darla's dungeon would make us even."

And just like that, his eyes became troubled, and a heavy weight fell between them, opening a wide gap that seemed impossible to bridge.

Damn Darla!

Right then, Trevor and Kara ran over to Jake, both of them throwing their arms around him, one at his waist the other at his thigh, burying their faces against his body.

Anxiety tightened Monica's chest. Did one of them get hurt?

"Hey, are you two okay?" he asked, ruffling their hair, then smoothing the strands back down in a tender display that touched Monica's heart.

They both nodded, but then Kara looked up with dire seriousness on her tear-streaked little face.

"We almost killed Kim," she said in a voice too serious for a child.

"Yeah," Trevor moaned. "And Shawn's gonna kill us."

Kara started crying.

"Oh, hey," Jake crooned as he crouched down to wrap them in his arms and hold them close. "Shawn's not going to kill you, but y'all know you're not supposed to be running around the worksite. Right?"

"Yeah," the siblings replied in unison as they nodded against Jake's chest.

"Have you apologized to Kim and Shawn?"

They both shook their heads, and Kara, having calmed a bit, hiccupped.

"He's not our dad," Trevor said defensively. "He's not even Sally's dad."

"He cares about both of you, Trev. Maybe you should give him a break, huh?"

Trevor didn't look convinced.

"Okay," Kara said and started crying again.

"How about you, Trev?" Jake said to the boy, as his arm tightened around Kara's tiny form. "Will you give Shawn a chance? He's really a good guy."

"You *like* him?"

Jake paused, taken aback, but Monica didn't think Trevor noticed.

"Yeah," Jake said, "Shawn's my friend, and so are you." He pushed them both back so he could look into their faces. "You want me to go with you when you apologize?"

"Yes!" Kara shouted, her tears dried up for the time being, but Trevor was still not convinced.

"Most of the other kids don't have to say they're sorry!"

Jake looked lost at that comment, and Monica jumped in.

"Oh, yes, they do," she told Trevor as she joined their little huddle. "Rosa and I will talk to their parents and make sure of it."

"He doesn't like us," Trevor complained again. "He's always yelling and telling us what to do."

"He does like you," Monica said, rubbing the boy's back and bumping into Jake's arm, still wrapped around Trevor. She glanced over at this smart, sensitive, wary man and found him watching her. The look in his eyes made her heart ache and flutter all at once, even more now than before he showed this new level of compassion for the children.

"You don't have to be afraid of Shawn, Trevor," Monica told the boy, sensing that his fear of letting another parent figure into his life was what kept him from accepting Shawn. He'd been reluctant to accept Kim at first too.

"He's just a big kid," she continued. "I'll bet he'd love to go out and play with you both every day if he could, but he has to make sure we all have a place to live and food to eat. Do you think he'd do all that if he didn't like you?"

"He only does that 'cause you make him," Trevor said looking angry, almost accusatory.

Monica blinked.

"That's not true," Jake jumped into the gap. "Miss Avery doesn't make anyone do things they don't want to do."

Monica stared at him, stunned, and wondered if he actually believed that—but she thought she read doubt in his gaze.

"He makes us do things we don't want," Trevor accused.

"That's because he cares about you," Monica said.

"Come on, Trev." Jake stood, gathered Kara in his arms, and, with a hand on the boy's shoulder, guided him toward Shawn and Kim, who were sending worried looks their way. "Let's go talk to them."

Monica watched them go with a lump in her throat and pain in her heart.

She knew how much Shawn wanted things to work out with Kim and the kids. He worried about them constantly and, lately, had been feeling a bit jealous of Jake's easy relationship with Trevor and Kara.

"That's because he's just their friend," she had explained to Shawn a couple of weeks ago. "He's not trying to be their father."

Now, she watched as Jake helped to forge a connection between the two orphans and another man who desperately wanted their affection.

Maybe the children sensed Jake was a lot like them, wounded by the harshness of this new world and afraid to be hurt more, and that's why they bonded with him so quickly. Whatever the reason, she suspected he would be the catalyst that fused those five people into a family, and he wouldn't even be a part of it with them.

The thought made her a little sad as she watched Jake acting as a buffer between the anxious children and Shawn.

Does he have a family somewhere? Someone he cares about? Someone he misses? She'd lost her own family several years ago. Their loss still hurt, but at least they'd died happy and free. And she had her friends to balm the pain. *Who did Jake have? Had he been living on his own all this time?* Again, she thought it might be time for her to find out more about this enigmatic man she kept wondering about, find out what else lay behind his wary gaze and the charm of his slow, compelling smile.

Be careful, her responsible side piped up. *You can't afford to save him or further alienate one of the most powerful women on the council.*

Yes, she knew all that, but her other side, the reckless one, wanted to know more—and when that voice spoke, she rarely ignored it.

10

MONICA SAT IN HER OFFICE, attempting to go over the ranch accounts, but she found concentrating difficult. Her mind kept drifting, distracting her with thoughts about Jake Nichols. She stared at a row of credits in her ledger and wondered how much more she would need to convince Darla Cain to sell him to her. The small amount she'd saved didn't seem likely to entice Darla, considering her possessiveness and treatment of him a few days ago.

Darla... Monica dropped her pencil and sat back in her chair. She gazed out her window at a patch of the afternoon's clear blue sky. *That damn woman is a menace.* Not only had she refused to lend Jake when asked, she had argued against the council when Angel intervened on Monica's behalf. Jewel, being an uninterested third party, had brokered the arrangement, somehow alleviated Jake's worry, and gotten him away from Darla. It pained Monica now to think about how afraid he must feel knowing he must eventually go back.

That didn't stop her from thinking about the possibilities though, no matter how unlikely a positive outcome might be. It also reminded her of Jake's condition when he first arrived. His body, too lean from hunger, had been filthy and covered with welts and bruises, but it was the look of unveiled terror in his hazel-green eyes that had struck a chord deep down inside her. She'd seen that look again when Darla tormented him in the dooryard, though she'd noticed anger in his eyes then too. Still, she desperately wanted him to lose the haunted expression that had been clinging to him since Darla's visit. She wanted him to feel safe and at home here. She wanted everyone to feel that way, but sometimes she wondered, despite their achievements of the last year, whether Angel's plan would succeed.

A knock at her door startled Monica out of her musing. She picked up her pencil, as if she'd been working, and called for whomever it was to enter.

"Hi," Shawn said, with his crooked grin firmly in place as he peeked his head around the door. "You got a few minutes?"

His too-eager smile made her suspicious. "For what?"

"I wanted to talk to you about something."

Monica sighed. She set the pencil down again, closed the accounting book, and pushed it aside.

"Well, come in then," she said, waving him in.

His brow wrinkled. "If you're busy…" he said, as if he hadn't noticed.

She held in an irritated sigh. "You know I am, but come in anyway."

He beamed at her again and closed the door behind him. Crossing the short distance, he flopped his lean form down in the only other chair in the room, opposite her desk. "Thanks."

Monica folded her hands in her lap. "So, what did you want to talk about?"

"Jake Nichols."

Monica almost groaned. Shawn was almost as tenacious as she was, and if he wanted to chat about another man working the ranch, there was either a problem with the man or Shawn was going to make one for her.

She raised her brows but kept a straight face. "What about him?"

"I want you to make an offer on him," Shawn said, and seeing her head drop and her shoulders sag in exasperation, he hurried on. "I know he'll be expensive and I know Darla will be difficult to convince, but he's worth the effort. His construction knowledge alone makes it worthwhile."

"I don't disagree," Monica said, "but you know we don't have the funds."

"We could make up a lot of the difference with what he knows. And," Shawn waved an arm toward the new pasture they planned to fence in, "he'll also be a major asset with the new livestock coming in next month. We could get by until we see a profit. We can find a way."

"Shawn," she said slowly, shaking her head, her heart heavy in her chest.

"There must be a way." Shawn sat forward in his chair and braced his forearms on top of her desk. "We can't let that woman take him back. Jake told me a little about what life's like with her, and after seeing what she tried to do to him here, I'm sure we don't know half of the abuse she torments them with." His hands curled in frustration. "Jake says she hates him. That she's just waiting to torture him again. We can't send him back." He pounded his fist on her desk. "We can't."

Monica rested her elbows on the desktop. "If I could help him, Shawn, I would."

Shawn nodded, but didn't give up. "All the more reason to find a way."

"Look, Shawn, I know he's a good guy, and I'd love for him to stay," she glanced at the desktop and her fingers began to fiddle with her pencil, "but I don't know how." She heard Shawn's chair squeak, and she suddenly realized her nervous fingers revealed too much of her own thoughts.

When she tossed the pencil aside and lifted her eyes to meet his gaze, Shawn tilted his head, sat back, and, crossing his arms over his chest, gave her a self-satisfied smile.

She'd seen that look before. "What?" she asked, a little hesitant to hear his reply.

"You like him."

Monica blinked. "Who?"

"Jake. You like him."

"I barely know him."

"Doesn't matter," Shawn said, a shrewd gleam in his eyes. "I know you. You like him, and it's about time too."

"Time for what?"

"For you to let someone back into your life."

"I don't have time for that," Monica said dismissively. The statement was true, but if she were honest—with herself, at least—she had stopped looking for someone with whom to share her life.

"You had time for Theo and you were basically doing the same job at Angel's, just on a larger scale."

Theo, she thought as she lowered her eyes to the desktop to hide from Shawn's too-perceptive gaze. Theo had been her last lover, more than a year ago. He was happily involved with his new partner, Peggy, now. Seeing them together, and the other couples on her own place, made Monica long for the same thing.

"I haven't been interested in Theo for a long time," she said. She and Theo had parted as friends and she liked Peggy a great deal too, but she couldn't keep from comparing the happiness they shared with the emptiness in her own life.

"I know that," Shawn said, dropping his hands to his thighs, "but you need someone special in your life, just like all the rest of us."

She nodded. She wanted someone special, someone she could trust to keep her secrets as well as she and Angel had kept each other's over the years. She wanted a man who accepted her, understood her, someone strong and kind who would be a lover and a friend and who she could give her heart to forever. In reality, she wanted everything she would probably never find, not anymore.

"You've been alone too long, Monica. It's not like you."

"I have other things to do," she said. Sitting up straighter, she pushed back the melancholy that threatened to lace her comments.

"You're lonely."

"I'm fine."

"Monica, don't lie to me," Shawn said in the big brother tone he used when he thought she was being unreasonable.

"I'm not lying, Shawn. I'm just tired of the flings." She'd grown tired of them because they were short and meaningless and had become her norm. She'd also tired of the stigma and loneliness that went with them.

"That doesn't mean you should stop trying. Like you said, Jake's a good man, and I think he likes you."

Monica shook her head. "He's too...broken right now to want anything like that."

"I think you're wrong. He lived a long time as a free man before they captured him, he knows what it used to be like. He might be a little screwed up right now, but he's still a man and he needs someone too."

"I don't have time for this, Shawn." She wanted to give in to the urge to discuss her feelings with her old friend, but she resisted. Instead, she pulled the account books open again and picked up her pencil, dismissing the conversation.

"You find him attractive." Shawn's blatant comment captured her attention once again, which, judging by the smug look on his face, it was clearly meant to do.

She frowned. "Who? Jake?"

Shawn grinned. "Yes, Jake."

"Yeah, I suppose he's an attractive guy."

"He seems to be a nice guy too. He's also my friend, and I don't want that damn woman to get her hands on him again."

Monica shook her head. "You're an impossible romantic, Shawn."

"Does that mean you'll try?"

"It means you're impossible." Monica smiled. "But I don't want him to go back either."

Shawn's eyes lit up, and he jumped to his feet with a loud "Yeehaw!"

"I didn't promise anything," she said in a grave tone.

"So I was right? I *knew* I was right."

"About what?"

"You like him." Shawn winked at her and went for the door. "I know you'll try. I know you'll find a way."

"How does your girlfriend put up with you?" Monica teased, shaking her head. Shawn's clowning personality hadn't changed much since they were kids, but when he wanted something, he kept after it.

They were a lot alike that way.

"She *loves* me," he said, dragging out the middle word like a mocking eight-year-old, but then he sobered. "And so do you."

"Yeah, yeah," she said, waving him away with a tolerant grin. "I love you too. Now get out. I have work to do." Though she knew it wouldn't be what she'd planned on accomplishing today.

Shawn was right. There had to be a way, and now, after Shawn's unusually serious request and her own desire to help, she'd be spending her time coming up with options to save Jake Nichols.

11

HE WAS ON HIS KNEES AGAIN. They had shackled his wrists behind him, attached them to his ankles, which were also bound, and anchored him to the floor. The stress position forced him to lean backward over his heels, and after being kept that way for well over an hour, he was exhausted. His arms and legs and abdomen were trembling from exertion and pain, but so far this was the only punishment they'd given him for his minor show of defiance.

The door to the small cell where he was chained squeaked open, and he felt the booster shot of the drug they'd given him start viciously pumping through him, intensifying his shaking.

As she entered the room, his Mistress spoke the words her slaves dreaded: "You've disappointed me, slave."

Jake kept his eyes shut and didn't reply. Speaking wasn't expected or helpful. He heard her cross the floor, the heels of her fancy dress shoes clicking on the stones. He sucked in a steadying breath, but it did little good.

"You like little girls," she accused from his side.

He jumped at her proximity, causing his spine to stiffen, sending tendrils of agony shooting through his overwrought muscles. He knew where this was going.

"Perhaps that little blonde is more to your liking than my guest was tonight?" She sounded conciliatory, but Jake knew better.

He shook his head. A tiny part of him longed to be free of his bonds so he could strangle this woman and keep her from hurting him, or anyone else, again. But the drug kept that part of him at bay and instead amped up his anxiety so all he could do was shudder and sweat.

It didn't matter what the woman who'd bought him for the night had done to him, what pain or humiliation or injury she had caused. The evidence was plain to see on his body, but his Mistress, this hated woman beside him now, didn't care. He'd broken one of her rules by offending her guest. Now, he would suffer for it.

"She's very cute, the little blonde," his Mistress taunted him.

She can't know, *he told himself as a knot of fear tightened his chest.* She can't... Please, don't let her know anything about Anna.

Her fingers traced over his clenched jaw, down his neck to his heaving chest.

A sour tang of disgust filled his mouth at her touch.

He despised these taunting games she played to torment her victims. He just wished she would punish him and get it over with.

"My guards have seen you talking to her. What's her name again?" she asked as her hand traveled over his twitching abdomen to settle between his spread thighs.

A wave of dizziness struck him, and a cold, heavy weight of horror settled in his chest.

He gritted his teeth. He didn't want to tell her anything, didn't want to speak, but no matter how hard he fought, he couldn't stop it.

"A-Anna," he croaked, hating himself.

"Ah, yes..." she said softly as her fingers fondled him.

He cringed with revulsion and his face flushed with shame.

"Very good, much better, but you have already greatly displeased me,"

his Mistress said, squeezing him until he thought he would vomit. "Whatever the reason for your disobedience, you must be punished." She released him and stood again.

He dragged in a ragged breath, fighting the nausea in his churning belly, knowing what was coming, knowing she would beat him for pushing the woman who had hurt him away.

The door opened again. "Get in here," his Mistress said, and someone else entered the room. Jake didn't dare open his eyes to see who. The footsteps were less noticeable than the heels of his Mistress, but he sensed the other person was much larger.

"Take this," she said, and Jake couldn't help but peek at them. Another male slave stood before him, as naked as Jake, holding a short, multi-thonged leather whip in his hand.

Jake's breath huffed out in rapid pants. Shit, shit, shit!

"Hit him," his Mistress said. "Hurt him."

There was no hesitation before the first lash slapped across Jake's pecs, nor was there any pause between blows. By the time his Mistress called a halt, the whole front of his torso was on fire, and he was screaming.

"You will obey," his Mistress said as she grabbed the collar around his neck and yanked him as far forward as his bonds would allow. He could feel her hissing breath on his cheek. "Say it."

Jake hesitated, fighting against the drug, and somehow managed to hold back.

Maybe the pain helped.

"Say it!" she screamed in his ear, and his entire body flinched. "Say it!"

He couldn't stop it this time. "I will—obey."

"Yes," she said, letting him go and sounding supremely satisfied, "you will... Hit him again."

"No!" Jake lurched into a sitting position. Sweat covered him, and his heart thumped out a rapid rhythm against his ribs. Looking around, he realized he was in his room at Monica's. He dragged in a deep inhale and rubbed at his chest.

No chains here. No beatings. No pain.

He was safe.

The dim light of early morning filtered through the window curtains. He would never get back to sleep again now, not after that. He threw off the damp blankets and swung his legs over the edge of the bed. Elbows on his knees, he sat with his head in his hands.

Even if her implications about his relationship with Anna were all wrong, how had Darla known about his association with her?

Had she only been guessing?

Did he reveal too much by admitting to knowing Anna's name?

He dug the heels of his hands into his eyes. *There's no way to know,* he thought, but it didn't make him feel any better. Anna had been depending on him, and he'd let her down, completely.

A growl rumbled up from his chest as he rose and began jerking on his clothes.

It was over. Nothing could change what had happened. He needed to concentrate on the present and stop dwelling on the past. That litany kept repeating in his head, but he knew himself well enough to know he would never forget what he had done.

* * *

Hours later, feeling stronger once again, his nightmare all but forgotten, Jake knelt beside the framework of the main house, with Trevor directly beside him, mimicking his posture. The sun was out, and puffy white clouds floated overhead. Some of the other children were laughing and playing nearby, while the older kids helped with the roofing preparations. A wide, smooth-topped rock sat between Jake and the boy. A small hill of bent nails—collected by Trevor, Kara, and the other youngsters—were mounded to one side of the stone, and a short metal pail sat on the other.

"It's easy," Jake said as he picked up a crooked nail and showed the boy how to roll it along the rock with one finger, while using the flat end of a ball-peen hammer to straighten it out.

"See," Jake said, holding the newly straightened fastener up. "Good as new." He grinned as he dropped it in the metal bucket. He gripped the hammer by the head and held out the handle to Trevor. "Think you can do it?"

"Yep." The boy grinned broadly and snagged the tool from Jake's hand.

"I want to try, too," Kara piped up from Jake's other side. He twisted, reached over, and pulled her into his lap, holding her close.

Kara squealed with delight at his attention.

"Of course you do, Squirt," he said, giving the girl a quick hug and then setting her on her feet. "Run over and ask Shawn to lend you his ball-peen hammer." He gave her a little shove, and she took off to find Shawn.

"Shawn?" Jake called across the distance as he stood up and brushed off his jeans. Shawn looked up, and Jake pointed at the fast-approaching little girl. Shawn smiled as she reached him, and he scooped her up into his arms, Kara already telling him what she needed and why.

Jake grinned as he watched his new friend with the little girl.

Tap, tap, tap. The sound of metal on stone sounded out beside him, and Jake glanced down at Trevor, already sitting in the dirt, hard at work.

"Looking good so far, Trev," he said to encourage the boy. Trevor grinned up at him briefly and went back to work.

Jake chuckled as he lifted his eyes...and froze. Monica stood no more than ten feet away, smiling.

"Hi, Jake," she said.

"Hi." He pulled his hat down low as she came to stand beside him.

"Looks like you've got a couple of good little helpers today," she said, smiling down at Trevor.

Jake nodded.

"Is that okay?" Trevor asked, holding up his first nail.

Jake leaned over to examine it. "A couple more whacks right here," he pointed to a slight curve in the shaft, "and it should be good to go."

Trevor went back to work.

"Do you have a minute, Jake?" Monica asked quietly after he'd straightened.

He nodded again and ruffled Trevor's hair. "I'll be back in a little while. You just keep at it. If you have any trouble, talk to Shawn."

The boy frowned across the yard. "I'll just wait for you," he said and went back to pounding.

Jake shrugged and lifted his gaze back to Monica. "What can I do for you?"

"Walk with me?" She pointed toward the river.

The idea of being alone with her made his heart beat wildly. His mouth went dry and his palms began to sweat. Whether it was from excitement or anxiety he wasn't sure, but he didn't see much choice either way. He nodded and waved a hand forward. "After you."

They ambled toward the river in silence, and Jake's mind wandered to the night in his room with his unwanted visitor. He had recovered from the stress of his encounter with the woman, but he didn't understand his reaction to her. He had never fought back like that before, and despite his situation, he would've attacked her if Monica hadn't appeared when she did.

Then there was the incident with Darla in the dooryard several days ago. Again, he had almost taken the situation into his own hands, but Rosa had saved him from himself. Standing up to Darla would've been a mistake he would've paid dearly for upon his return. Immensely thankful for Monica and Rosa's interference, he still cautioned himself about his behavior.

Damn it, you need to get ahold of yourself. If you're not careful and Darla learns of your actions...

A groan always followed that train of thought.

Should she find out he'd rejected a woman's advances, and violently at that, he shuddered to think about the merciless whipping Darla would unleash on him once he returned.

Still, ever since the incident with Kristine, he'd become more and more distracted by his present situation. His worries about Darla Cain—though not lost, as his nightmare that morning evidenced—slowly ebbed into the background, and Monica Avery began to take a more prominent place in his mind. He couldn't help but note that she was monitoring their work more frequently than before. Several times he would look up from whatever he was working on to find her eyes scrutinizing their work, but he always wondered if it was actually him she was studying. In spite of his wariness, he kind of liked the idea of her looking at him. Now, as they strolled toward the river, he found it strange that, though she still made him nervous, he didn't feel the same level of anxiety as he did with the other women who continued to ogle him from afar.

"You're very good with them, you know," Monica said, startling him from his thoughts. They had traversed the whole way to the water's edge, and he hadn't even realized.

"With who?" he asked.

"The kids. The workers. Everyone. They're all quite fond of you."

He shrugged. "I like them too." He didn't know what else to say.

She started strolling along the riverbank, and he hurried to catch up.

"You're doing a great job, Jake. I'm so glad we found you."

"Thanks," he mumbled. Her nearness and singular attention caused his stomach to twist into knots, yet pride swelled within him too. When she grinned over at him, he found himself grinning back as his heart sped up and a pleasant, almost forgotten feeling of anticipation fluttered in his chest. The sense of something different passing between them, something far more personal, alarmed him, but warmed him as well. Overtly aware of his attraction to her, however, he kept his captivation in check.

"Was there something you needed?" he asked, careful to sound curiously polite.

"Yes," she chuckled and stopped to face him, "there is something." She gazed up at him, her eyes roaming over his face as if searching for an answer to a question she hadn't yet asked. He shoved his hands into his jeans pockets and rocked on his heels, doing his best not to appear nervous or impatient.

The sun shone down on them, and a warm breeze lifted the ends of her honey-colored hair. It ruffled around her shoulders, and he squeezed his hands into fists in his pockets, fighting the sudden urge to run his fingers through the golden strands.

"I don't want to upset you by bringing it up," Monica suddenly spoke, "but I wanted to thank you."

Confusion rattled him, and he frowned. "Thank me for what?"

"For trusting me." Her eyes flickered between his face, the ground, somewhere behind him, and back again.

Running his hand over his face, he tried to figure out her meaning, but his frown stayed in place. He had no idea what she was talking about, but he didn't want to be rude.

Use your manners. He heard Darla's voice in his head and squelched it before the phantom pain of her whip could lance through his body. Darla and her damned training were the last things he wanted to think about right now.

He didn't want to ruin this moment.

"In your room, a while back," Monica said, as if he had a clue. Then, "I'm sorry." She sighed, apparently realizing he didn't get it. She reached for him and he trembled, but he didn't pull away. She cradled his hand between both of hers and looked up, her gold-flecked hazel eyes intent and sincere, as if about to make a solemn pledge.

"I wanted to thank you for trusting me. After everything you probably went through before coming here, I know talking about what Kristine did must've been hard for you. And after Darla the other day..." Her eyes dropped to their joined hands. When she looked up again there was sadness and determination in her gaze. "I just wanted you to know, I'm grateful for your faith in me and I'll do my best not to let you down."

He swallowed, hard, his eyes riveted on her face. His arm burned from her touch, and pleasant tingles prickled along his spine.

"I...appreciate that," he said, squeezing her hand a little. She smiled and he responded, feeling lighter and stronger somehow. A sense of belonging washed over him, and he shivered slightly. He wanted to slide his hands over the soft skin of her arms, touch her sun-kissed cheek, run his fingers through her silky hair, but he only stared at her stupidly.

Will I ever be normal again?

Will I ever get to hold her?

You will do whatever my guests require of you, Darla instructed in his head. *If they want you to scream, you will scream, as loud and long as they wish, or you'll regret your disobedience.*

He squeezed his eyes shut and shook his head.

"Are you all right?" Monica's voice sounded alarmed, and a second later, her free hand gently cupped his cheek. He jumped and reached to bat it away, while crushing the fingers on her other hand that he was still holding. His eyes flew open, and he instantly loosened his grasp when he saw the grimace on her face.

"I-I'm sorry," he stuttered. "I d-didn't mean to—"

"It's okay, Jake," Monica said, patting his chest. "I shouldn't have touched you like that. You just looked so pained; I thought you were hurting somehow."

"I was," he mumbled.

"Because I touched you?" An expression of what he thought might be self-recrimination crossed her face and she started to pull away, but he flattened his hand over hers to hold it in place against his body. Then his fingers wrapped around hers, and he lifted her hand from his chest. He considered kissing her knuckles, but he only gave her hand a gentle squeeze and let go.

"I don't mind...you...touching me," he rasped. "I'm just..." He swallowed again, unsure how to articulate what he was feeling.

"Good," she said, and her twinkling eyes filled his lonely heart with hope. "It's a place to start."

12

JAKE AND SHAWN RECLINED side by side on the gently sloping riverbank. Aside from managing their regular chores, everyone had the day off from work, and Shawn had invited Jake to go fishing with him and the kids. The children lost interest when the newness of baiting and casting their lines faded and the waiting became intolerable. They were now swimming in the shallows down river, which meant the men had little luck on the lines, but neither one cared. They'd been watching the kids playing, and they chuckled periodically at the children's antics, until Shawn caught Jake staring out at the jagged horizon.

"Gauging the distance to freedom?" Shawn asked, reading Jake's thoughts.

Jake glanced at his friend. "I was just thinking."

It wasn't a lie. Escape was a tempting proposition. The guards at Monica's home were more like extra cow hands, lax and almost nonexistent compared to Darla Cain's prison. He had thought often about running when he first arrived, but the urge had dwindled with time and with his growing affection for the people here. Since Darla's visit a couple weeks ago, though, the impulse had returned.

"The mountains are too far away," Shawn said. "You wouldn't stand a chance."

"Has anyone ever tried to run?"

"From other places, sure, but they didn't get far. Not from here though; life here's too good to risk getting caught by the Section Guard patrols, and they pay special attention to homes like this. They're just waiting for one of us to try to escape. You'd never make it. No one would."

The Section Guards were under Darla's control but were managed by a woman named Carrie Simpson, whom Jake knew far too well. He knew Carrie's proclivities, and he didn't want to fall into the hands of women who worked for her.

Running was not an option, but neither was returning to Darla Cain.

Jake merely nodded his understanding, and Shawn's mood brightened. He sat up suddenly and his eyes twinkled.

"How about we ditch the fishing and go play in the water with the kids?"

Jake grinned. "It *is* damn hot today."

Shawn smirked, and they both jumped up and headed for the screaming laughter.

The next week flew by. The exterior construction and the insulation for the house were almost complete. Jake didn't know where the supplies came from, only that they arrived each week on time when he asked for them. The work kept him busy and wore him out, so he spent less time worrying about his future.

Standing in the shade of the house on an early Friday afternoon, Jake was helping fasten the last few plywood sheathing boards to the back of the house. He had just finished nailing one in place when Rosa approached and called his name. He dropped his hammer in his tool belt and, wiping his forehead with the back of his arm, turned to meet her.

"Miss Avery would like you to join her for dinner," Rosa said, with no preamble.

"Is that an...order?" He shuffled his feet and glanced around to see if anyone else had overheard.

"No. It's an invitation. Haven't you learned the difference yet?" Rosa smiled.

"Oh, I see." Jake shoved his hands into his jeans pockets and rocked on his boot heels.

Can I really refuse the offer?

Do I want to?

"Don't look so worried, Mr. Nichols," Rosa said. "You're not in any trouble."

He nodded and turned back to the house, taking his hammer once again in his hand.

"She'll be expecting you in her office at six sharp."

He nodded, his back to her. "I'll be there."

Jake spent the rest of the afternoon working inside the house and trying to ignore the growing knot of tension in his belly and between his shoulder blades. A few times he heard Monica's voice and her musical laughter coming from the dooryard, and the memory of the day almost two weeks ago when he'd saved her from injury popped into his head. Having her soft body pressed against his, and the way she looked at him...

Damn it, I should've kissed her right then and there. But he had denied himself the pleasure. His gratitude for Rosa and Monica's intervention with Darla had left a soft spot in his heart for both of them, but his heart wasn't what had goaded him the afternoon of the ladder incident and every night thereafter; it was desire. His dreams were filled with Monica—when he wasn't having nightmares about being sent back to Darla Cain's.

What could a woman like Monica possibly want with me? Not that she had demanded much from him yet; he only hoped she wouldn't turn out to be as greedy as the last woman he was alone with. Or worse, like Darla or Carrie Simpson.

A few minutes before six, cleaned up and nervous, Jake knocked on Monica's office door. He held his straw hat in his hand and had to concentrate to keep from crushing the brim.

"Hi, Jake," Monica said as the door opened.

Jake looked up and froze.

Oh, God—damn, he thought as he stared, dumbfounded by the beauty before him. Her red button-up shirt, with its sleeves rolled back to her elbows, made her soft, sun-kissed skin glow. Blue jeans hugged her long legs, and black boots covered her feet. Her golden hair hung past her shoulders in waves, and the strength of the smile she beamed at him nearly stopped his heart.

"Come in," she continued, eyes twinkling. "You didn't have to knock."

He shoved aside his wayward thoughts about her beauty and how she'd felt in his arms as they lay in the dirt after he'd saved her from the ladder. He smiled a greeting but said nothing as he entered, too afraid his voice might crack.

Stepping inside, he glanced around at the small room, taking in the old wooden desk pushed to the far side, with some kind of silver serving tray and lid placed in its center, the short bookshelf below the window, and a small table, set with dinnerware, across from the door.

"I hope you're hungry," Monica said as she closed the door behind him.

With his stomach tied in knots, he wasn't sure he could eat, but he nodded anyway. "Yes, ma'am."

"Please, Jake, I told you, call me Monica." She smiled again, though with gentle encouragement this time.

"Yes, ma'am—" He stopped when she lowered her chin and gave him a what-did-I-just-tell-you look. "I mean, Monica." He spun his hat brim around with his nervous fingers.

She brightened again. "That's better. Please," she waved a hand at the table, "sit down. The cook sent over a feast."

He set his hat on the bookshelf and did as she asked. He felt as awkward as a teen on his first big date as he took a seat at the table. The moment she began setting out the food, which had been hiding under the silver lid on the desk, he stood up again. "I...I guess I should...help you," he stammered.

She smiled again, with gratitude this time. "No, Jake. Just sit. This'll only take a moment."

For a few minutes, they ate without interruption, with nothing but the occasional scraping of their silverware on the porcelain plates to break the silence. Laughter coming from the temporary dining hall not far away reached their ears, and though he exchanged an awkward grin with Monica, the merry sound, coupled with their quiet meal, increased Jake's anxiety.

"I noticed you made some changes to the house's construction," Monica said unexpectedly.

He nodded, his eyes flicking between her face and his plate. Her keen observation and construction knowledge surprised him, and he expected an admonishment, or worse, for making the upgrades without her approval.

"It should be much sturdier with the reinforcements you added," she told him with a smile that warmed him far more than it was supposed to.

"I'm glad you approve." His shoulders relaxed a little, her easygoing yet direct nature winning him over.

She asked what work still remained, and when the conversation wound down, she changed direction.

"So where did you get your ranching experience? You seem quite knowledgeable with that too."

He shrugged. "I'm not really a rancher," he confessed. "I just worked as a cowhand on a spread my friend Bret ran before the wars."

"Did you like it then as much as you do now?"

He stared at her, anxiety stirring in his gut. This was branching into personal territory he didn't want to discuss. But the curious expression on her face and the glow of interest in her eyes overcame his hesitation.

He started slowly, relaying his experiences working the Double H with Bret, before the war invaded and sent them running for the alleged safety of the mountains.

"Bret was the rancher, a real cowboy," Jake said with a laugh. "He could work with any animal and have it respond to him. He was good with his people too—managing the ranch and other cowboys, I mean. Not so much with people in general."

"Why's that?"

Jake glanced at Monica, startled by what he'd revealed.

"Well, he...he didn't trust easily, but he was a great friend once you got to know him. I'm not sure I would've survived living in the wild so long if not for him."

"You miss him a lot, don't you?"

"Yes," Jake answered and, before he thought better of it, he elaborated. "We'd known each other since we were kids. He was the only family I had left."

"I'm sorry you lost him, Jake," she said softly, her eyes earnest as she reached across the small table to squeeze his hand. "I hope you find him again someday."

His breath hitched at the brief touch, but before his anxiety could make him squirm, she released him.

"I don't," he answered with quiet conviction.

"You don't?"

He looked up from his plate to find her watching him. "No, I don't. Not if I'm still a slave. That would mean he was finally captured, and if I see him that means Darla has him. I can't want that. I hope he's far from here and in a better place with better people, if there are any."

Monica's shoulders drooped, and the look she gave Jake said his words cut her deep. "I'm sorry you feel that way," she murmured, dropping her gaze.

Seeing the light in her eyes doused by something he had said felt like a gut punch.

"I don't mean you," he said quickly, needing to reassure her that he knew she wasn't like Darla and Carrie. "You..." He paused when her gaze locked on his face once more. He took a deep breath and dived in. "Coming here...it's been the best thing to happen to me in...well, years."

The smile that lit her face set his heart to a galloping beat.

"I'm glad to hear it, and I'm glad you're here too."

Her simple words warmed him, starting in his chest and radiating outward as a grin spread across his face.

They continued their conversation, changing topics and direction several times. They talked far longer than he would've thought possible, but she put him at ease and made him feel more comfortable than he ever thought he could be with a woman again. She laughed at his stories and smiled at all the right places. She didn't inquire too closely about his private life, which allowed him to tell only as much as he was willing. They'd been chatting amiably for some time when Monica yawned and said they should probably wrap things up.

"What time is it?" Jake asked as he stifled his own yawn.

"After nine," she said, checking the clock on her desk.

"Nine?"

"Yep." She smiled.

"Wow, I didn't realize it was so late."

"Me neither, but I don't mind. Do you?"

She regarded him with tenderness, and alarms went off in his head.

Calm down, he scolded himself. *She's not doing anything. Just relax.*

He took a deep breath.

"No," he said with a timid smile, and found that he meant it. She demanded nothing from him; she treated him like a man, rather than a toy or a slave. Why would he mind any of that? He enjoyed talking to her. He enjoyed looking at her. And if she kept behaving the way she did tonight, he could see himself falling for her.

Maybe I've already started to. His heart briefly seized at the scary thought before stuttering back to life.

"I guess I should go now," he muttered, "unless you want me to help clean up?" A part of him hoped she would say yes.

"No, I'll take care of it. You need your rest. You look tired."

"Do I?" He chuckled. "I suppose I am."

She smiled. "Good night, Jake. Sleep well."

"Thanks...you too. Good night, I mean." He shook his head. *Why am I babbling now?*

She laughed. "I will." Something in the way her eyes looked at him, like a warm caress over his skin, shot straight to his groin.

Nervous again, he headed for the door.

"Jake?" she called as he reached for the knob and anticipatory prickles raced over his skin. He looked back over his shoulder. "I enjoyed dining with you."

His neck heated and he dropped his eyes, but he lifted them again a second later. Her hopeful expression made his chest tighten.

That's not the only thing tightening...

He tried to return her smile. "Me too."

"Would you mind meeting with me regularly?"

His eyes widened, but he fought down the instant surfacing of panic.

She's asking, not demanding.

"Ah..." He hesitated again, unsure what his answer would be, worrying her query was a command after all. "Is that a requirement?"

His eyes searched her face, locked on her mouth. Her lips kept distracting him. He couldn't stop looking at them and wondering how soft they were. *As soft as her hands?* He wondered how her lips would feel pressed against his own. *Soft and warm and supple? Eager for his mouth? His tongue?* Heat shot through his body. Then her lips moved, breaking his trance.

"No," she said, shaking her head. "It's a request. I had fun with you. That doesn't happen very often. Besides, you're responsible for all the work on my house. I thought, maybe, we could meet over dinner to discuss your progress and...whatever else may come up."

Something's coming up, he thought, and tried to imagine taking a cold shower. What was it about this woman that had his body responding while his mind was wracked with dread? He'd been fighting the allure all night, but she put him so at ease he didn't notice until now.

Jake stared at the floor, scenarios swarming through his brain, but when he met her gaze again, he still wasn't sure what he would say.

"I'd...like that," he answered, surprising himself. Monica appeared surprised as well, but she beamed at him and her whole face lit up.

My God, she's beautiful.

"Good," she said. "Monday, Wednesday, and Friday sound all right with you? Or is that too much?"

"Fine by me," he said, wondering what they needed to talk about that required meeting so many times a week. Then his libido responded, and he searched her face again. *Does she feel the same things I do?* She appeared to be pleased with his response, but he didn't understand why she would want him. He was only there for a short time. She didn't know he never intended to return to the hell from which he came; he would run for his life and gladly give it up before going back to Darla Cain. But everything in Monica's demeanor told him she wanted more from him than his construction skills.

He resisted an abrupt urge to touch her, to cross the short distance between them and kiss her. Normally, he didn't have to hold back. During his time at Darla's, he had to struggle to perform. But with Monica, he couldn't deny the desire was there. Yet instead of giving in to the powerful need, he simply smiled, his heart light and warm for the first time in a very long time, and left the room.

MONICA STOOD STARING at the closed door, trying to get her heartbeat under control and still picturing Jake smiling back at her. He was as kind as she thought he would be, funny too. Drawn to him in every way possible, she wanted more than anything to touch him again, be close to him the way they had been when he had saved her from the falling ladder. She wanted to be with him, but she sensed that if she pushed too hard, he would instantly pull back. That would be a shame, especially since he seemed to have come out of his shell. He had accepted her invitation to dine with her, at any rate, and he had been mostly comfortable with her tonight. It was a marked improvement from the stuttering, awkward conversations they'd struggled through before.

If his reaction to Darla's surprise visit and to Kristine's stupid ploy was any indication, Darla Cain had done a real number on him. Monica couldn't imagine what living under that woman's rule would be like, but she knew a little about the wicked and twisted games she played with her slaves. She had also heard about Darla's training techniques, which were nothing short of torture.

Pity constricted in her chest at the thought of what he'd be returning to.

Monica closed her eyes and concentrated on Jake's smile. Thinking about him suffering under Darla's depraved control was too painful to consider. He deserved better. But no matter how much she wanted him, she couldn't afford to wrest him away from Darla. Even if Monica did find the means somehow, Darla was notoriously reluctant to let any of her favorites get away from her. Judging by her hesitation to give him up voluntarily for only a few months, as well as her unheralded visit, it was clear Jake was one of her favorites. He must have done something to lose her favor, however, and Darla must want him to suffer for it. Whatever he had done, she hadn't forgotten yet. Her angry refusal to even discuss lending him to Monica implied that Darla planned to punish him more. Maybe he was to be an example to the other slaves. Monica made a mental note to find out.

She sighed and cleared their dishes from the small table while she continued to ruminate on her problem.

I could simply refuse to return him. If she offered a decent sum, she might be able to force Darla to accept. Though not an unheard-of tactic, it was unlikely in this scenario.

You can't save them all, Monica reminded herself as she gathered the last of the dishes for cleaning. She shook her head. *But I want to save this one.* More than anything, she wanted to take away his fear and the haunted shadows in his expressive hazel-green eyes. She wanted to soothe his pain and give him the security he needed to heal. If she allowed him to go back, he would never be whole again, and that knowledge weighed on her heart, tempting her to risk everything she had built to save him.

"Shawn's right about that too. You've been alone too long," she murmured to the empty room as she glanced out the window. Just catching sight of Jake as he returned to the bunkhouse, she sighed. *You stopped taking risks to take care of these people,* she silently scolded herself. *And now you're thinking of risking it all, for a man you barely know?* She sucked in another long breath, shook her head, and mumbled, "What *are* you thinking?"

The admonishment did little to temper her feelings. She realized she'd been considering taking a chance on Jake since the day he arrived. And the more she got to know him, the more she thought about giving up everything to protect him.

How can I let him go, when all I want to do is hold him close?

Dragging her eyes from the window, she set the last of the dishes in the tub. If there was a way to help Jake, she would, but she must consider the others under her care as well. They depended on her. If she started a civil war with Darla Cain, the fallout would affect them all.

You have time, she thought as she picked up the tub of dishes to take to the makeshift kitchen. *He agreed to meet with you, and Darla can't take him back for almost four months yet. You have time to work something out.*

Monica shook her head as anxiety tightened around her heart, and she said a quiet prayer that last part was true.

13

A FEW DAYS LATER, Jake once again sat across the small table from Monica in her office, listening to her talk about the cattle to be delivered in late July. Her excitement to finally have the animals on hand was a bit infectious. Her broad smile and dancing eyes made him grin, but he had reservations about her purchase. Jake understood a little about cattle—not as much as Bret Masters, but he certainly knew the trade better than the people here. He couldn't help but worry that the cattle would be sickly creatures they'd have to pamper and overfeed to fatten up for sale in the fall or to use for food themselves. When he mentioned his misgivings to Monica, she tried to allay his concerns, but he was not convinced. Not at first anyway.

"Angel wouldn't do that," Monica said.

"How well do you know this woman?"

"Pretty well, she's my best friend."

Jake grunted and took another bite of the incredibly tasty roast beef.

"She's trustworthy, Jake. Believe me."

"Business is different than friendship." His cynical response earned him a quizzical look.

"You're very distrustful. Do you think of me that way too?"

He met her gaze and paused, assessing her and weighing his answer, before replying, "No, I don't."

"Angel has her problems, but she's a lot like me. We can trust her. You can too."

"I trust what I know," Jake retorted.

"Well, then I'll just have to introduce you when we go to help with the harvest in August and you two can have a long chat."

He nodded and went back to eating, uninterested in spending time with a woman he didn't know.

"She hates Darla Cain with a passion."

Jake's head snapped up.

A small smile curved the corners of Monica's sweet mouth. "I thought that would catch your attention."

He couldn't help relaxing in the wake of her good spirits, and his frown eased. "Well, she can't be all bad then." He was only half joking.

"No, she's not. You'd like her, I think."

"Maybe," he muttered.

They finished their meal, and he stayed to help clean up.

"I'll take that," he said as he stacked the serving tray on top of the tub filled with their dirty dishes and picked them both up.

Monica chuckled. "Are you trying to impress me?"

He gave her a sly smile. "Maybe."

"Mr. Nichols," she said in mock shock, "I believe you're flirting with me."

He glanced at her and his smile faltered slightly, but he didn't shy away. "Maybe," he said again and headed for the door.

The night was cool as they walked through the darkness from Monica's office to the dining hall, which also housed the makeshift kitchen. The only sounds were the river rushing in the distance, the wind whistling over the valley, and an owl hooting in an evergreen nearby.

No one was around when they entered the hall, and Jake felt a surge of happiness that he would get to spend a little more time with Monica alone.

They filled one side the handcrafted portable sink with hot soapy water and the other with clear, and then Monica started scrubbing while Jake grabbed a clean towel.

"So," she said, drawing out the word as if unsure of herself, and Jake felt a stab of unease. "Have you ever been in love?"

Reaching for a rinsed dish, he stopped midair to stare at her.

"I don't mean recently," she said in a rush. "I mean..." She bit her lip and trailed off. Her eyes dropped to where her fingers brushed the soap bubbles in the sink. She shook her head, and pink tinged her cheeks. "I'm sorry, that was a stupid question."

She pulled one of the glasses from the tub at her feet and dunked it in the water.

Jake stepped up beside her. "No," he said quietly, and she turned her head toward him with what looked like hope in her eyes.

"No?"

"It's not a stupid question. It's just been awhile since anyone cared to ask me anything like that."

"If you'd rather talk about something else?"

He smiled and took the unrinsed glass from her hand and dried it. "I thought I was in love once, a long time ago."

"Did it last long?"

"No, not really," he said as he crossed over to the storage shelves along the far wall to set the glass in its proper place. "We were only together about nine months, but that was about five months too long."

"Why five months?"

"Once she met Bret, things started to go downhill."

"Bret? The cowboy friend you told me about?"

Jake nodded, and a fond smile touched his lips. "The same."

Dripping soapsuds from her wet hands, Monica bent over to grab a few more items from the tub, and Jake couldn't help admiring her backside while she did it.

"What happened? If you don't mind my asking?" She dropped the dishes in the sink, and Jake adjusted his gaze.

"Well, Bret happened," Jake said with a laugh, and when she only frowned in confusion, he explained. "Women seem to find him irresistible."

"Great friend," Monica muttered.

"It wasn't his fault," Jake said, snagging another item from the rinse sink. "Bret's a good-looking guy. He didn't have to *do* anything. And it wasn't as if he tried to interfere. He discouraged female interest, at least those who were supposed to be with me. But I still kept my girlfriends away from him until I felt a little more comfortable in the relationship. That particular one I was very wrong about."

"Did she break up with you?" She looked over at him, concern in her eyes.

He nodded.

"And did she date your friend afterward?"

"She tried, but Bret wouldn't have anything to do with her."

"Stupid girl," Monica said, shaking her head, her blonde hair falling into her face as she started scrubbing again. "Why would anyone dump you?"

Jake reached over and tucked the bright strands behind her ear. *Her hair is as soft as I thought it would be.* He purposely slid his fingers over the sensitive edge of her ear and brushed them along her neck. She trembled. He liked how she responded to his touch, and he grinned when she looked at him.

"Thank you," he said softly, and her eyes followed his hand as he went back to drying dishes. He wasn't looking at her anymore, but he could feel her watching him, and the temperature in the room seemed to go up several degrees.

"What about you?" he asked, suddenly uncomfortable in the long silence.

"Me what?"

"Have you ever been in love?"

Still staring at him as if in shock, Monica dunked her hands back into the soapy water. "Well, no, I—Ow! Damn it!" She stumbled back from the sink, holding her hand in front of her. Red-tinted soapsuds dripped down her wrist as dark crimson pooled in her palm.

"What happened?" Jake dropped the towel on the counter and carefully took her bleeding hand in both of his as a surge of worry and protectiveness tightened his chest.

"I think I sliced it on a knife." She wobbled slightly, he assumed with shock and pain.

"Here," he said, holding her hand by the wrist. He supported her with his other hand and eased her back to the sink. "Let's rinse the soap off and see how bad it is."

MONICA STARED AT HIS PROFILE as they stood at the sink. This was a change from his normal wary friendliness. He'd never voluntarily touched her before, but tonight he'd done it twice. And now, his hard body stood so close—his arm and shoulder brushing hers, his hip and long legs not quite touching her side—that her entire being was acutely aware of him.

She studied him while he gently rinsed off her bleeding hand. He seemed unperturbed by her nearness, but his close proximity made her shiver.

"Are you all right?" he asked as he lifted her injured hand with both of his.

She nodded and swallowed, still gawking at him stupidly.

Stop staring! she shouted in her head. *You'll freak him out.*

Her eyes dropped to her throbbing, aching hand, and she grimaced. A long ugly gash stretched from the meaty base of her thumb, across her palm, and ended below her pinky finger. Just seconds after he pulled her hand from the water, it welled with more blood, which blocked a clear view of the cut.

Jake leaned in close to examine the wound. "It doesn't look too bad," he said as he pushed her hand back under the water and grabbed another clean towel off the shelf to wrap around her hand, "but we need to stop the bleeding."

With slightly trembling hands, he put pressure on the wound, and Monica hissed through her teeth. His grip lightened, but not by much.

"I'm sorry," he said, glancing into her face. "It's the only way to stop the bleeding."

"No, it's fine. I just feel like an idiot."

"Why? I'm sure you're not the first person to cut themselves while washing dishes."

And I'm probably not the first woman to do something dumb because she couldn't take her eyes off you either.

She nodded. "I still feel foolish."

He smiled. "Don't. I've done dumber things than this."

"Like what?"

He straightened. "Where's the medical kit?"

"My office."

"Well, let's get you patched up, and I'll tell you one of my secrets." He winked at her, and heat unexpectedly vibrated through her body. She glanced down at his big hands almost engulfing her much smaller one, and she shivered again. Tiny sparks ran up her arm and straight into her belly. Her insides quivered, her breasts tightened expectantly, and she suddenly couldn't breathe.

With a curled finger, he tipped her chin upward, and her gaze snapped to his. The tenderness of his expression stopped her heart.

"Are you alright? Does blood upset you?"

She nodded mutely, then she frowned and shook her head as she stared wide-eyed at this beautiful, emotionally scarred man, astounded by his selfless care of her. Having his hands on her didn't seem to unnerve him either, which was the biggest surprise of all. Every time she'd touched him before, he'd stiffened. Granted, his adverse reaction seemed to be lessening with time, but still, all this attention focused solely on her seemed like a lot, especially for him.

"So you're okay to walk to your office? You're not going to faint or anything, and make me carry you?" He smiled.

Carry me? A part of her wanted to say she could take care of herself, thank you very much. But deep down, she knew she wouldn't mind having his arms around her. She didn't mind having him look after her either.

She chuckled at his teasing, shook her head, and then found her voice.

"No, I'm fine. The pain just shocked me that's all." The agony in her hand seemed to throb in time with the distracting pulse between her legs. The realization made her blush as he led her into the cool night air, his arm hovering behind her as if she might pass out before they reached her office.

As they walked, he told her a story about his first experience with horses: his first ride and his first fall. By the time they arrived, her hand still hurt, but her tense shoulders were loose and she was laughing again. She wasn't sure how much of his tale was true, but she appreciated his willingness to share it with her.

"There," Jake said a few minutes later as she sat in her office once more. He knelt on the floor at her feet and, after stemming the flow of blood with the towel, gently cleaned the wound again. He then swabbed antibiotic ointment on the cut and covered and wrapped it with gauze, all while Monica watched and tried to get her runaway emotions—not to mention her body—under control.

He looked up at her. "I think you should see the doctor in the morning just to be sure. It's probably fine, but the lower part looks a little deep to me, and I'd feel better if the doc took a look."

"I'll head over to Angel's first thing."

"Good," he said as he got to his feet. "Why don't you head in to bed. I'll finish cleaning up."

"You don't have to do that," she said, rising from her chair.

"I know." His voice sounded very close, and she looked up to find him so near she could feel his breath on her upturned face, and he was watching her. Her heart sped up from the look in his eyes—desire, pure and raw.

Heat flooded her body in anticipation, and she felt herself leaning ever so slightly in his direction.

Is he going to kiss me?

Should I kiss him?

He hovered there, gazing down at her hungrily, but then he swallowed, blinked, and it was gone. He stepped back and gave her a half smile.

"I'll walk you back to your room," he said, and her hopeful heart, dismayed by his sudden withdrawal, tumbled into her stomach.

14

AN ORANGE AND PINK SUNSET filled the early evening sky over the distant steel-blue mountains as Jake stood by the river, watching the sun sink toward the jagged horizon. He'd come out here after dinner to think about his future and go over his plans for saving himself.

He'd gone riding with Shawn and Rosa a few times recently to get a better look at the property and to aid his friends in deciding how to set up the hay fields for next year's crop. Jake helped them with their options as best he could, but the farming side of ranching was not his specialty and he once again thought of Bret.

Where was his friend?

Was he still alive?

Was he still free?

Jake crouched down on the riverbank and picked a long strand of grass. He stared down at the broad blade, his fingers tearing it into thin strips while he again considered his plans.

Despite his growing attachment to the people here and Shawn's warnings about persistent patrols, Jake wanted to scope out escape routes. He wanted a better idea of where he would go and how he would get there if a miracle didn't arrive to save him from returning to Darla's rule.

And he had found a way.

Whether the course he'd mentally mapped out through the foothills would be guarded or not, he had no idea, but he thought he had a good chance of getting away cleanly. Still, he had a backup plan should danger block his path.

But how long should I wait?

Instead of Rosa's usual friendly company, Monica had joined him and Shawn earlier today as they inspected the hay field and pasture locations. It was a study in self-restraint for Jake as he found himself being drawn in once again by Monica's direct gaze and brilliant smile. At times she had ridden so close that her scent—floral soap and sunshine—filled his senses. Every time the wind had shifted his way, her hair had furled toward him in a silky blonde wave, and he had tightened his grip on the reins to keep from reaching out to run his fingers through the soft, shimmering tresses.

"I'm so glad you're here, Jake," she had said softly while they rode side by side. Her knee had periodically brushed his, making his skin tingle and sending a rush of heat through his overly aware body.

He had only smiled and nodded at her comment, unable to articulate his own happiness at being with her. The way she looked at him, almost as if he was the most important person in her life, lit him up inside with joy—and apprehension.

This afternoon's ride had elevated his reluctance to leave to a new level, his growing feelings for Monica making him question his desire to run. Something sparked between them whenever they were together, and when they touched, each minor contact struck him like a mortal blow. He looked forward daily, almost hourly, to the opportunity to catch a hint of the sweet scent of her golden hair as she passed by or to feel the sensation of her silky-smooth skin against his.

The forgotten blade of grass dangled from Jake's fingers as he tipped his hat back and stared at the yellow orb winking from behind the mountain horizon. The sky was mostly lavender-blue now, the long, fluffy clouds still flushed with pale rose and bright amber hues. It was a lovely scene, one that inspired optimism and cheerfulness, but he didn't know how much of either he had left. He sighed and stood. His fingers released the tattered piece of grass, and it fluttered to the ground. He brushed his hands on his jeans, his body still reliving the afternoon a few weeks ago when he'd saved her from the falling ladder and the feeling of Monica's soft curves pressed tightly against him.

Too many years had passed since he had experienced the hot, tingling anticipation of being with a woman he coveted. For years, no one had triggered such an innate rush of sexual desire in him. Since his capture, he had usually needed a lot of cajoling and insistent stroking to have any reaction at all. But with Monica, even just one of her gentle smiles made his heart beat fast and instantly woke the long-untouched needs of his body. But if he gave in to his longing to kiss her, which he felt nearly every minute of the day, he worried that the heartache he'd suffer later might be more than he could bear.

Thoughts of Monica kept him awake at night, and his anxiety about returning to Darla Cain gave him horrible dreams. But all of his worries faded away when he and Monica were together. He trusted her, but he couldn't rely on her to save him. Not that he would ask; he simply didn't believe she could. He knew Darla held a great deal of sway in this area. He also knew she was ruthless, and she would not let him go easily.

"Hello, Jake." He jumped at the sound of Monica's voice, and when he spun around to face her, he nearly lost his hat in the river. Scrambling, he caught the brim just before the water could claim the whole thing.

"Sorry," she said, chuckling at his frantic display. "I didn't mean to startle you."

He grinned, happy to see her, as he straightened and jammed his hat back on his head. "What are you doing out here?" Self-consciousness about his prior thoughts made his reply sharper than he meant it to be.

"I could ask you the same question."

He stuffed his hands into his jeans pockets and kicked at a tuft of grass on the bank. "I was just thinking."

"Good thoughts, I hope," she said as she stepped beside him and sighed. "I love this view."

Jake followed her eyes, taking in the wide, darkening valley sprinkled with greens and browns and peppered here and there with colorful wildflowers. In the distance, rolling foothills led into the Cascade Mountains. Deep shadows from the setting sun, like craggy, creeping fingers, stretched toward them, and brilliant shades of blue, purple, and pink painted the cloud-dotted sky.

He glanced back at her profile and thought there was no comparison.

"Yeah, me too," he said.

She glanced at him, her eyes bright, and she smiled before turning back to the vista beyond the river.

They stood companionably side by side, letting the breeze ruffle their clothes and watching the light fade.

"I saw you out here when I left the office," she said and turned her head to gaze up at him. "I came out to see if you were okay."

He nodded and kicked at the grass again.

"No worries or issues?"

"No," he answered. "I'm fine. Just wanted a little time alone to watch the sunset."

"Oh." She blinked and turned to leave. "I'm sorry to interrupt. I'll leave you to it."

"No," he said. And as if it were the most natural thing in the world, he reached out to take her hand, stopping her retreat.

She stared up at him expectantly.

His mouth suddenly went dry.

"You don't..." He coughed to clear his constricted throat. "You don't have to go. Stay. Please?"

"I was going to go for a walk," she said, still gazing up at him. "Care to join me?"

MONICA WAITED ALMOST BREATHLESSLY for his response. He looked a little surprised by her request, but at least he didn't appear afraid, and he was still holding her good hand.

He smiled after what seemed an eternity, but which couldn't have been more than a few seconds. "Sure," he said. "Where do you want to go?"

"I usually just follow the river," she said, tilting her head away from the house and outbuildings.

"Lead the way." He gestured with his free arm; his other hand still hadn't let go of hers.

They walked slowly, neither speaking. Monica was just happy to be with him, to have him touching her, even if he only held her hand.

"So," she said, "you've told me a little about the friend you adopted as a brother, but you haven't said much about your mom or dad or real siblings."

His stride slowed, and she knew she'd asked the wrong thing. Or maybe his sudden frown was for how she had asked it.

"I'm sorry," she said. "If that's too personal—"

"No, it's fine. It's just kind of a sad story is all, and it's been a long time since anyone's asked about it."

"We can talk about something else. Or not talk at all..."

He glanced at her, and a soft smile curved his handsome mouth. She loved his mouth.

For a long heartbeat, she thought he wouldn't answer, and sadness sat like a weight in her heart.

"What would you like to know?" he finally asked, and she felt lighter again.

"Hmm...Do you know how your parents met?"

Jake chuckled. "Yeah, actually, I do. They met in college."

Warmth flashed through her body; she loved to hear him laugh.

She glanced up at him and her lips curved. "Study buddies or something?"

"Not exactly. My dad was a star receiver on the football team, and my mom was a science nerd. A friend of hers was a cheerleader and dragged my mom to practice one day. Dad ran her over on the sidelines trying to catch a pass. Broke her ankle."

Monica's eyes widened. "Oh, my! That's...terrible."

"She wasn't too thrilled either, but my dad always said he was smitten from the first moment he set eyes on her. He said he felt so bad about hurting the pretty girl in glasses, he stayed with her until the ambulance came."

"What about your mom? Was she smitten too?"

"No." He chuckled again, and a shiver shot down Monica's spine. "She thought he was a big dumb jock and was really angry about her broken ankle." He tossed a glance her way, smiling broadly. "It didn't last long though."

"He won her over?"

"Yep. He apologized, brought flowers to her dorm for days, did everything he could think of just to get her to talk to him."

"And she did?"

"Yeah, took a little while though."

"What finally did it?"

"She was in advanced chemistry, and he was barely a C student. In fact, he said he was close to losing his place on the team because of his chem grade. He asked his instructor to set him up with her as his tutor."

"And that worked?"

"Yeah," he said, laughing again. "Mom said once he started using his brain, she found him far more attractive."

"Cute story," she said with a smile. "Which one do you take after?"

"My dad, I guess."

"So you were a football star too?"

"No." He shrugged. "I played, but I wouldn't say I was a star. I just had more time with him is all. My mom died when I was almost fourteen."

She stopped to cradle his hand in both of hers. "Oh, Jake, I'm so sorry."

He met her sympathetic gaze. "Thanks," he said and squeezed her hand gently. They started walking again. "It was a long time ago, but I was pretty angry at the time."

"What happened?"

"Brain tumor. She went from being a brainy scientist to a frightened woman who sometimes couldn't remember who I was." He smiled sadly. "Not really something you want to deal with when you're thirteen."

"Or ever," Monica said.

He nodded. "Or ever."

"And your dad?"

"He was around until just before the war finally landed on our shores. Died of a sudden heart attack."

"Wow, I don't know what to say. I'm sorry always seems so...insignificant."

"It's okay. I appreciate the thought, but they've been gone a while now. I miss them, but I've come to terms with their loss."

"I'm glad to hear it." She smiled, and without thinking she hugged his arm. She glanced up at him, worried she might've upset him, and pulled back, but he just kept walking.

"What about you?" he asked.

"Oh, well, my parents met in their late thirties. Set up on a blind date by a mutual friend. They married a few months later."

"That was quick."

"Yeah, well, they both knew they'd found 'the one' almost from the start."

"And when did you come along?"

She narrowed her eyes at him for the quiet innuendo in his question.

His soft smile melted her heart, but she put a little tartness in her response. "Not for several years, thank you. For a long time, they didn't think they could have children. But here I am." She waved her arms expansively and grinned at him. But she didn't let go of his hand.

"And which one do you take after?" he asked.

"Both I guess. I'm impulsive and stubborn, just like them."

"I assume they're no longer with us either."

"No, we went to the mountains before the war hit hard. We were pretty happy there for a while. They both died within a few years of each other. My mom's the reason I'm here now."

"How so?"

"She wanted me to move back to society and make something of myself. To help others if I could. When I met Angel, well, everything fell into place."

His brows lifted in a quizzical look.

"It's a long story," Monica said, "but basically Angel wanted the same thing: to help people."

He nodded, but let the topic drop.

"Any siblings?" she asked. "Besides Bret, I mean."

"Oh, you mean 'real' siblings?"

The corners of her mouth pulled up, but she knew there was more behind his teasing. "I'm not belittling your connection with him. Just asking."

"No, I don't have any other siblings. Neither of us did. Maybe that was part of why Bret and I got to be so close."

She frowned, confused by his comment.

"We both needed something at the time. Someone outside our own immediate family. It took us a while, but we finally got past our own arrogance and mutual animosity. We basically stuck with each other after that."

She nodded. "I'm glad you had someone."

"Me too."

They strolled along the gurgling riverbank for a few seconds of comfortable quiet.

"How are you doing, Jake?" Monica asked suddenly.

He frowned at her. "How do you mean?"

She dropped her eyes to the ground, wondering where that question came from. "I'm not sure exactly, but you seem...different somehow."

She felt him shrug, and she glanced at him. "I'm okay, I guess. I feel better being here, but I'm still worried about going back."

"That's understandable."

He nodded, and they walked in silence again.

All Monica wanted to do was stop him in his tracks and kiss him. Or for him to kiss her. For something more to happen. She knew she needed to tread carefully with him, to let him set the pace, but she was beginning to wonder if he would ever take the next step.

I suppose the fact he's still holding my hand counts as something, she thought, but she wanted so much more. Wanted to give him everything.

He stopped suddenly and turned to her. She gazed up at him through the quickly diminishing light, and the need she read in his expression stabbed through her heart. Heat swept over her skin and her body came alive. *Finally*, she thought. *Finally, he's going to make a move.*

But after a couple of aborted movements, all he did was stare at her. She could feel his unease in the tautness of his body and the moistness of his palm as he tightly gripped her hand. She knew he was fighting something, but she didn't know how to help him.

"We should probably head back," Jake rasped, dropping her hand. Sadness and something else—*self-reproach?*—flickered in his eyes.

"Sure," she said, and to keep him from suffering any greater discomfort, she smiled—even though she wanted to scream from the overwhelming loss she felt at his withdrawal.

15

ANOTHER WEDNESDAY EVENING and he'd let everyone off early, as he usually did, but Jake hung back to check on a few things at the house before heading to his room to clean up for dinner with Monica.

He crossed the unfinished living room of the new house to the corner where another ranch hand had asked Jake to take a look at some installed electrical wiring. He crouched down beside a stack of tools and supplies to get a better look, as thoughts of Monica filled his head. He was tired of fighting the urge to discover what was hidden behind her eyes, of being afraid. It was time to take a risk, to show her how he felt. Yet the heartache he might suffer later still worried him.

Unable to stop thinking about her last night, he'd gotten little sleep. But this morning, as he dragged himself out of bed, he had smiled, relieved to have finally made a decision about Monica and his feelings for her. Tonight, he would push his boundaries. If Monica looked at him the way she did almost every time their eyes met, he would pull her against his body, wrap his arms around her, and kiss her with every ounce of the pent-up passion he'd been holding back. A delighted grin curled at his lips. He felt happy and hopeful, two things foreign to him only two months ago, and it was all because of one beautiful blonde who made him feel like a man again.

Kneeling in the corner, Jake inspected the wiring, pleased to find no issue. He wasn't expecting company, so when he heard soft footsteps on the floor behind him, he rose to his full six-foot-one height in a flash and spun on his heel to face the intruder.

The woman facing him now hadn't approached him since her last disastrous attempt to seduce him several weeks before. A smile adorned her appealing face, but the expression seemed more predatory than pleasant. Her soft, brown doe eyes raked over his body in an assessing way that made his skin crawl, but he suppressed the sudden urge to hide. Without a doubt, Kristine, with her tall, shapely frame and long chocolate-colored hair, was an attractive woman, but her attitude disturbed Jake. Rumors abounded about her persistence once she set eyes on something she liked. Worse, however, were the hints about why. From what Jake had heard, she wanted a child and was actively searching for a suitable sperm donor, willing or not.

In his case, he was absolutely not willing.

"What do you want?" Despite the tendrils of trepidation causing his heartbeat to race, he kept his tone neutral—no reason to create a worse enemy.

In the days after she surprised him in his room, she had given him several angry looks, and he worried she might do something worse. In his experience, too many women in this new world believed dominating a man was their right, which was all the more reason for the tingle of apprehension prickling his skin now.

Kristine crossed her arms over her chest, tilted her head, and lifted her chin. "I wanted to speak with you alone."

His stomach clenched. "There's nothing to talk about."

"Oh, I think there is." She stepped toward him, and he backed into the wall.

"No." He tried to move by her, but she blocked his path and he recoiled out of her reach.

One hip cocked out and arms akimbo, Kristine huffed, flicking her hair behind her shoulders and then spearing him with her eyes once more. "I wanted to apologize."

He frowned in suspicion. *What's she up to now?*

Dropping her arms, she took another step closer. He frantically searched for an escape route that didn't involve shoving her out of his way, but he was cornered and the woman blocked his only exit.

"I didn't mean to upset you. I only wanted to get better acquainted with you. You're an attractive man, Jake." Kristine's fingers brushed his forearm, and every muscle in his body tensed. "Is it so bad that I want to be with you?"

"I told you, I'm not interested." Jake jerked his arm away and his fists clenched at his sides.

Her brow furrowed. "Why?"

"I'm just not."

"You'd rather spend your time with Monica?" Her tone was biting.

He didn't respond.

"I get it. She's exceptionally pretty, beautiful even, but she's also very fond of men and popular with them as well. You do realize that, right?"

He still didn't reply.

She stood too close, and her words bit into him like a whip.

He was sweating again, his breath coming in short, fast gasps. Dread spiraled through him, and he didn't know how to stop it.

"She's had quite a number of male companions over the years," Kristine said as she turned to stroll along the row of supplies and tools stacked up to Jake's left; she stroked her fingers over a hammer and then examined a box of nails, as if fascinated. She had his full attention now, and he stood, riveted, as she continued. "You're only the most recent to receive her attention. Don't think it makes you special."

Pain shot through his chest. If she was trying to hurt him, she'd hit her mark. But after years of hiding his inner thoughts from Darla, he'd learned how to keep his face blank.

"She'll tire of you too," Kristine said, ambling slowly to her original position in front of him, all the while impaling him with her eyes. "When she does, I wanted you to understand you still have an option." She took another small step toward him.

He inhaled sharply and pressed back into the wall, hard. The framework creaked under the pressure, but the structure didn't give an inch. Unless he wanted to risk harming her to push her out of his way, he was trapped. *Why didn't I move when I had the chance?*

He trembled. Hysteria bubbled inside him like a pinball bouncing off electric bumpers.

"You'd be happy with me. I'd treat you well," Kristine crooned. "There's no reason to fear I'll have you beaten. I'd rather give you pleasure." She lifted her hand as if she meant to touch him.

"Don't touch me." He mentally hauled back on the reins of his runaway fear and wrestled back control.

"What's wrong with you?" she asked, a darkling glare marring her features. "You'd rather waste your time with a woman who'll discard you? Is it just me, or don't you like women?"

He shook his head, disgusted by her attempts to needle him.

"You spend an awful lot of time with Shawn," she tried again. "Is he more your type? What were the two of you up to all those hours alone together in your room? I could get into that. Maybe we—"

"Shut up," he hissed. He didn't like her implication. Not that he cared what Shawn or anyone else did in their private life, but he didn't like the idea of this woman fantasizing about it.

He didn't like her nearness either. She was too damn close!

He couldn't breathe.

If she didn't step out of his way, he would move her, and soon, it wouldn't matter how he did it.

He needed out of this small room, out of this house.

His chest hurt. His head hurt. He must get away...

Kristine leaned toward him. Her lips parted to verbally strike at him again.

"What's going on in here?" Rosa's voice broke the tension.

Kristine's eyes widened, and she spun on her heel, stepping away from him.

"Rosa..." she stammered.

"Kristine," Rosa said in a stern tone, "what are you doing? You were told to stay away from Mr. Nichols."

"I...I...We..." Kristine spluttered. "We were just talking. I...wanted to apologize. Isn't that right, Jake?" Her eyes held a dark promise as she glared at him over her shoulder: One word to Darla Cain and he would pay in blood.

He swallowed the lump of fear in his throat. "Yeah..." he murmured and lowered his gaze.

"I see," the head guard said, and then huffed out a breath. "Well, you had your say, Kristine. Now, be on your way. And in the future, keep your distance from this man. You've been warned, twice now. Don't make it three. Finding work in a decent place isn't as easy as it once was."

"Yes, ma'am," she grumbled and rushed past Rosa. Jake heard her footsteps cross the front porch a moment later and breathed a sigh of relief.

"Are you alright, Mr. Nichols?"

He met Rosa's frowning gaze.

"Mr. Nichols?"

He closed his eyes and took a deep breath, then let it out slowly, striving for calm. He looked up.

"I'm alright, ma'am."

Rosa tisked with a shake of her head. "Sure you are. What did she want?"

"Like she said, she...apologized."

"And what else?"

"It doesn't matter," he mumbled.

"Did she threaten you? Hurt you in any way?"

He thought of Kristine's description of Monica and his chest constricted.

"No," he croaked.

She eyed him askance.

"Very well," she said after a long pause. "If you don't have any complaints, I won't dig for one, but I know that young woman better than you and she didn't come here to apologize."

He dropped his gaze once more.

"Don't you have somewhere to be?" Rosa asked.

Jake suddenly remembered his dinner with Monica.

What if what Kristine said is true? It's not that he believed her exactly, but after everything he'd endured over the last two years, he couldn't discount her either. Maybe he'd been too optimistic about his connection with Monica. Maybe he'd just been naive. Either way, if Kristine was right that Monica—the only woman he'd felt any affection for in years—merely wanted to use him, Jake feared the heartache would destroy him. He couldn't take that kind of disappointment.

All at once, he felt lost, hollowed out, and so exhausted.

Rosa still gazed up at him.

"Would you please give Miss Avery my regrets," Jake said softly. "I won't be able to dine with her tonight."

"Why not?"

He should've expected the question, but his brain wasn't functioning fully yet.

"I...I just can't."

"What did Kristine say to you?"

He shook his head and looked away. It didn't matter what she had said. He would be leaving in a few months, and no one could stop it. When the time came, despite the dangers, he planned to run for the hills. He might make it, and maybe he would find Bret again. If he didn't—if they caught him—he would die slowly, painfully, either in the government prison designed for runaways or in the living hell ruled by Darla Cain.

"She didn't say anything important," Jake told Rosa, meeting her frowning gaze. He wouldn't risk any more trouble either.

"She said something to make you turn away from Monica," Rosa said. "Don't let her influence you, Jake. She's a selfish woman. She doesn't mean any real harm, but she's young and she doesn't take rejection well."

"I don't care about her. I'm just tired, and I need to check on the progress of the pasture fencing before turning in."

"Without something to eat? You must eat, Jake."

He didn't miss her switch to using his first name. Somehow, the change made her comments more personal, but he didn't think she consciously did it to manipulate him. She was genuinely concerned.

"I will. I'll pick up something on the way to my room," he said. "I'm just not good company tonight."

"She'll be disappointed."

He sighed. He also ignored the sudden desire to take back everything he'd just said.

"Please, Rosa, will you give her the message?" He used her first name on purpose.

A long pause followed his request, while Rosa stared up at him with narrowed eyes. She shook her head. "I'll give her the message, Mr. Nichols, but you're making a mistake."

"Thank you, Rosa. I appreciate it." He stepped by her and headed for the door.

"She likes you, Mr. Nichols," Rosa said to his back, and he stopped.

"She?" The question slipped out before he could stop it.

"Monica, she likes you. You're good for her. You make her smile. She hasn't done enough of that lately."

Warmth spread through his chest, and he squeezed his eyes closed. *You can't go there,* he told himself. *You were a fool to think you could. She can't help you. They'll be coming for you, and if you keep on the way you have been, leaving her will kill you. Don't go there!*

He glanced at Rosa over his shoulder and saw the look of concern on her tanned face. Her ebony eyes pleaded with him to reconsider.

He almost did.

"She's a fine person, Miss Santos," he said instead. "She deserves to be happy. I hope she will be."

16

JAKE WAVED A HAND in front of his face to disperse the swirling dust kicked up by the cattle that had just been driven into the new pasture. Since his most recent encounter with Kristine, he'd worked himself ragged on the house construction and the fencing for this enclosure. He considered the work a much-needed distraction and a blessing because it occupied his mind and exhausted his body. Lately, physical fatigue was the only reason he got any sleep.

The summer heat had dried the ground so much that the passing of the fat, healthy stock—and a damn fine breeding bull that had arrived earlier—over the sunbaked grass and parched soil had created a dirty mess. The evening sunlight filtered through the particles and gave everything a sepia hue as the animals milled around the field, getting familiar with their new home.

Angel Aldridge had sent several cowboys from her ranch to deliver the herd that evening. Her generosity—evident in the animals she sent—

impressed Jake, but he was less thrilled about the man who led the drive.

From his spot at the pasture gate, Jake clenched his jaw and eyed the tall blond man tying up his horse outside the barn. To Jake's annoyance, everyone appeared to be happy to have Theo Swenson there. Merry expressions lit every familiar face as each waved to the blond man, who, in Jake's opinion, grinned far too much.

Jake looked away from the scene, but he couldn't keep his eyes on the cattle in the field. His tense shoulders tightened further as his gaze was drawn back just in time to see the man approach a cheerful-looking Monica.

When Shawn had told him Theo—Monica's former lover—would be the one responsible for bringing the cattle to them, Jake had known he would dislike the man on sight. Now, as Theo shouted a hearty "hello!" to Monica and wrapped her in his arms, Jake's first impulse was to rush over and punch the man in the face. But he had no right to be jealous. No right to stake a claim on her. No right to dislike the man for being able to touch her the way Jake longed to every minute of every day. The combination twisted together in his gut and burned like acid.

"Theo's an easygoing guy," Shawn had said that morning as they chatted over breakfast. "I'm sure you'll get on with him as well as everyone else does."

Jake had only grunted in reply, but Shawn's comment, overheard by others at their table, brought up Theo's past involvement with Monica, which garnered several more praises that Jake didn't want to hear. The talk about Monica's previous relationship with Theo led to more sordid gossip, and the topic turned to the last foreman, whose death had brought Jake to the ranch. Several suppositions involved Monica and the previous foreman in some kind of lover's quarrel, which made Jake so uncomfortable that he left the table.

He hadn't felt much like eating anyway.

"Hey," Shawn had said as he caught up with Jake outside. He tilted his head in the direction of the dining hall. "Don't listen to them, it's all just talk."

"Then what really happened to your old foreman?"

Shawn shook his head. "It was an accident, but you'll hear lots of whispers about it. Hell, I've heard all kinds of crazy theories on what happened to Ed, everything from a love triangle and jealousy, like you just heard, to suicide, but none of them are true. Ed was never involved with Monica, and he was not suicidal. He slipped and fell, broke his neck with one wrong step, that's all. It was a very sad day for all of us."

Jake nodded, not missing the slight emphasis on the word "all," but he didn't pry further. Shawn took his silence as an opportunity to ring Theo's praises again, but Jake tuned him out as they strode toward the barn to finish their morning chores.

He had been unable to get Monica out of his head last night. Images of her with an unidentified lover had tormented him for hours and kept him from sleep. The idea of another man touching her made him sick inside and so angry he wanted to tear someone apart. But he'd made his decision to stay away from her, not to pursue the promise he read in her sparkling eyes and tender smiles. Not to create a bigger heartache for himself or Monica.

Now, he stared at the cattle, cataloging their needs and worth, while trying to ignore the happy reunion going on several yards away. He crossed his forearms over the top gate rail, propped his boot on the lower bar, and leaned into both with a heavy sigh.

You're kidding yourself, Nichols, he thought. *The animals can't distract you from her.* He wasn't even seeing the cattle, and he was so addled that he was getting nowhere with his calculations. Every cell in his body vibrated, sharply attuned to Monica's presence as she chatted with another man several yards away. All he could do was feign indifference while he struggled to control his raging jealousy and ease the hurt that had settled in his heart.

MONICA SMILED AS HER OLD FLAME dismounted from his horse

and headed her way. Theo Swenson's light-blue eyes seemed to glow beneath the brim of his tan cowboy hat, and his handsome Nordic features grinned back at her warmly. He looked good. But Monica knew his content, carefree demeanor had nothing to do with her, and the thought made her a little jealous. She pushed the feeling aside and smiled at him.

"It's good to see you, Monica," Theo said and wrapped her in a bear hug, swinging her around in a circle.

She laughed as he set her back on her feet. "You too, Theo. I'd ask how you've been, but I can see you're happy. How's Peggy?"

"She's better." Theo's face darkened.

"I was really sorry to hear she lost the baby." Monica touched his arm, and he gave her a tight smile.

"Thank you." He pulled his hat from his head and ran his fingers through his short blond hair.

"Are you all right? Is Peggy? I know how much you were both looking forward to having a child."

"I'll be okay. Peggy took it pretty hard, but I'll help her through it."

"I know you will. Does she need anything? Do you?"

"A visit would be appreciated, but we know you're busy."

"Yes, we are, but we can chat for days when we come over for the harvest in a few weeks."

"Whew," he said in mock relief, wiping his brow with the back of his hand and tugging his hat back on. "She'll enjoy that, and I'm glad too. We've got a lot of extra cutting this year." His tone sobered. "I understand a big portion is coming your way."

"Yep, part of the cattle deal," she said. Leaning over, she put a hand on his shoulder and murmured, "Give Peggy my love, will you?"

He smiled. "You know I will. She'll be glad to hear you're doing so—"

"Theo!" Shawn shouted as he rushed over. Theo turned to hold out his hand in greeting, a wide, toothy grin filling his face. Shawn clasped Theo's hand and shook it vigorously before pulling him into a quick, brotherly hug. "How you been?"

"Doing okay," Theo replied as he gazed into the distance toward the new house. "Looks like you've been busy. Did you find a replacement for Ed?"

"Yes," Monica replied and glanced around to locate Jake. She saw him in the distance, leaning against the closed pasture gate, his gaze angled in their direction. She nodded toward him. "He's over there."

"Jake!" Shawn shouted and waved his arm for Jake to come over.

Monica frowned when Jake shifted his gaze to the newly arrived cattle as if he hadn't heard.

What's going on with him now?

He'd stood her up for their last two dinners with an excuse about being tired, but she knew a lie when she heard one. Rosa had told her about his second encounter with Kristine, and Monica swiftly deduced the younger woman's jealousy. Monica had reprimanded Kristine and sternly reminded her that her role on the ranch in no way included harassing the men.

Jake had been sullen and distant ever since that confrontation, at least toward Monica.

"Jake!" Shawn shouted once more, and Jake glanced over at them. His shoulders slumped as he shoved his hands in his pockets, lowered his head, and slowly started their way.

To Monica he looked like a surly teenager being forced into something he didn't want to do.

Her frown returned.

"So," Theo leaned in, threw an arm around her shoulders, and asked in a low whisper, "is he as good at construction as Ed was?"

"Better." Monica grinned, thankful for Theo's good cheer. "And he knows about ranching too."

Theo's eyebrows climbed upward. "Well, lucky you. You think he could give *us* a few pointers?"

"I'm sure he could be persuaded."

"He's helped us a lot already," Shawn joined in. "Too bad he can't stay." He gave Monica a loaded look.

She shook her head at his less-than-veiled meaning, ignored Theo's quizzical glance, and turned to Jake as he approached.

Jake's eyes shifted over the group, taking in the scene, and narrowed when he noticed Theo's arm around Monica's shoulders. Monica tried to meet his gaze, hoping to figure out what his problem was, but he turned to Shawn before she could.

Theo glanced at Monica and raised one pale eyebrow in curiosity, but he didn't comment.

"Jake," Shawn said again, "I'd like to introduce you to a friend of ours." Shawn turned toward Monica and Theo and made the introductions.

Jake shook Theo's hand when offered, but his whole bearing seemed stiff and unfriendly.

Monica was beginning to feel the same way toward Jake. It was one thing to keep her at a distance; it was another to be rude to her friends.

"So, Monica," Theo said, and his arm went almost purposely over her shoulders once more, "you think I could get a tour of the new place?"

Jake's eyes narrowed again, and Theo's body tensed beside her.

What's that about? she wondered, at a loss to explain Jake's hostility.

Jake lowered his head and dragged his boot over the dusty ground.

Theo flashed her a broad smile and wiggled his eyebrows, clearly teasing her about something. But whatever it was, she didn't have a clue.

"Well, I think Jake would be the best guide," she said, frowning at both men's odd behavior. "Do you have a few minutes, Jake?"

Jake's head snapped up, his indignant gaze shifting rapidly between Monica and Theo—whose face now revealed a thoughtful mien—and back to Monica again.

She held her breath, once more taken aback by the look in his eyes.

A moment later, Jake's granite-like expression softened slightly, and he nodded.

"Sure." He shrugged. "There's not much to see."

"Don't be so modest, Jake," Monica said touching his arm, hoping to convey some comfort for whatever was ailing him. "You're doing a wonderful job."

He slowly pulled away from her hand but gave her a small, grateful smile. His eyes flicked to Theo's arm, still draped over Monica's shoulders, and his half-hearted grin disappeared. Then Jake turned and, with stooped shoulders and not another word, headed for the house.

17

MONICA SAT WITH ROSA, Shawn, and Theo through dinner, retelling old stories and laughing, but her heart wasn't in it. Her eyes kept drifting to the other side of the room, to the one man with whom she truly wanted to talk. Jake ate as far from the four of them as possible, occasionally glancing in their direction with lowered brows, while carefully avoiding Monica's eyes.

He had come to the dining hall almost an hour after everyone else and had appeared surprised to see anyone still there. He'd skimmed the uncrowded room, taken in the four of them together, and promptly averted his gaze. She knew something was bothering him, but she didn't know what. And though she wanted to discover the cause, she also knew it wouldn't help the situation to call him on his behavior. She'd decided to wait for him to come to her, but she was quickly losing patience.

"Well, I don't know about the rest of you," Shawn said, rising to his feet, "but morning comes early, and I've got other commitments to see to tonight."

"You finally found yourself a good woman, huh?" Theo said, waggling his eyebrows suggestively.

"I had to," Shawn replied, with his crooked grin firmly in place. "Couldn't let you one-up me on that score."

"We're keeping score now?"

"We're always keeping score." Shawn laughed. He placed a hand on Theo's shoulder and leaned toward him. "And for the record, I'm winning." He winked. "Good to see you, buddy." Shawn patted his shoulder and walked away chuckling.

Theo grinned and shook his head.

"I'm going to leave you too," Rosa said, also standing. "It's really good to see you, Theo. Give Peggy my best."

Theo nodded.

Monica said good night to her friends, but her eyes drifted back to Jake. She didn't realize how long she sat there in silence until Theo spoke.

"You should talk to him."

Startled, Monica turned wide eyes on her friend. Theo's usually smiling face carried a serious expression.

"What? Who?"

"You know who," Theo said, taking a sip of their precious coffee, so hard to come by since the wars, and then tilting his head in Jake's direction.

Monica's eyes flashed across the room and then down at her own mug. She sighed.

"He's interested in you," Theo said quietly. "More than interested, I'd say. And I'm more than certain you feel the same."

Monica's back stiffened, and she straightened her shoulders as she turned wide eyes on him. "What makes you say that?"

He leaned playfully toward her, bumping his thickly muscled shoulder against hers. "I know you, and I've been on the receiving end of your longing looks. That's not something a man forgets."

"I'd have thought Peggy erased all that."

"I love Peggy," Theo said, "but I wouldn't change the time I spent with you. We might've not been compatible as a couple, but we are still friends and I still care about you. Plus, a guy may fall in love with one woman, but that doesn't mean his memory fails. Not completely, anyway, but don't tell Peggy."

He winked and grinned, and Monica shook her head.

"Jake's been through a lot," she said, knowing the pointlessness of being evasive with Theo, "and he's only here for a few more months."

"So you've told him it can't be and now he glares at any man who comes near you?"

"No, I..." Monica frowned. "He...He *what*?"

"You didn't notice how much he disliked me touching you earlier?"

"That wasn't about you. He's been grumpy for a few days."

"Right," Theo straightened, shifting in his seat, his eyes drifting toward Jake across the room. "That's why he keeps looking at me like he wants to rip my head off."

Monica slanted a look at Jake, only to catch a glimpse of his broad-shouldered back as he left the room. "He does?"

"Monica, come on. Really?" Theo set his mug down with a soft thud. "If looks could kill, he would've skewered me right after I arrived. When I had my arm around you, I thought he might tear it off and beat me with it. The man's jealous. No doubt about it."

Monica stared at her friend as the pieces fell together in her mind, and then nodded. Hearing Theo voice what Monica should've guessed herself about Jake's odd behavior not only annoyed her, but gave her a little thrill of hope too.

"I didn't turn him away," she murmured, dropping her eyes to the mug of tea she cradled with both hands.

"*He* turned away from *you*? What's wrong with him?"

Monica chuckled. "I told you, he's been through a lot."

"Where'd he come from?"

"Darla's."

"Ah...Well, that makes more sense."

They sat without speaking while several other ranch members shuffled out of the building and the cleanup crew began their work. Theo glanced at her, but she didn't meet his gaze, not until he reached over and placed his big hand over one of hers and gave it a gentle squeeze.

"You're hurting, too," he said sagely. "I know you too well not to see it."

She nodded, still not looking his way. "We were doing fine. Then something happened and he just...stopped."

"Something?"

"One of the guards propositioned him...aggressively."

"Ah, Kristine's work I presume?"

Monica glanced at him. "How'd you know that?"

"She was a little," he tilted his head as if searching for the right word, "forceful with one of the young men at Angel's the last time she came over with you."

"Why didn't someone tell me?"

"Michelle took care of it."

"And Angel's head guard didn't see fit to tell either of us?"

"I don't know, you'll have to ask Michelle, but I do know she scared the pants off Kristine."

Monica stared, annoyed by being left out of the situation, but then she nodded, chuckling. "Maybe I should ask Michelle for some pointers when I'm there next month."

Theo tilted his head and shrugged one shoulder. "Couldn't hurt."

She laughed again.

"Look, Monica," Theo said as he pushed his empty cup toward the teenage boy who was clearing the table. "You do what you need to, but if you care about him, you should tell him before he explodes. The man's wound so tight he creaks."

"He won't talk to me."

"Then make him. You're direct enough, and I've never known you to lose a fight. Besides, he doesn't need to talk if you do it right."

"Right?"

"Remember the first time you approached me in the barn?"

Heat crept up her neck, and she dropped her eyes with a nod.

"You didn't have to say a word. I knew what you meant all the same."

"You weren't being difficult, as I remember."

"Doesn't mean I wasn't worried about the possible ramifications of getting involved with you. Especially if it didn't work out. But I didn't know you that well then."

Her brows lifted. "You were worried?"

He smiled and stood up. "You'll figure it out, Monica. You always do."

18

JAKE SPENT THE MAJORITY of the night trying not to picture Theo Swenson in Monica's bed. After a long night of tossing and turning, with very little sleep, he had finally given up and crawled out of his tangled sheets. The sky was still dark when he'd ambled out to the barn almost two hours ago. After letting the horses out and cleaning the stalls, he got started on feeding the cattle. Now, still alone in his work, he gripped the two strips of orange twine holding a bale of hay together. With a grunt of exertion, he hefted it and tossed it out the hayloft door and down onto the wagon below.

He stopped to wipe the sweat from his forehead with his shirtsleeve and, while adjusting his loosened gloves, heaved a sigh of frustration. The work kept him busy, but his brain would not stop torturing him with unwanted images of Monica with another man.

He didn't like Theo being so familiar with her. All through the short tour of the house construction yesterday, the man could not keep his hands off her: an arm over her shoulders, a hand on her back, leaning in to whisper in her ear. It was all Jake could do to keep from decking the bastard. Yet she didn't seem to mind Theo's attention. She had smiled at him far too often for Jake's taste, but, as he kept telling himself, he had no say in the matter. That didn't make him feel any less angry or frustrated though.

Unable to eat much at dinner last night, he'd picked at his food and done his best to ignore the good cheer of the four old friends seated together, chatting and laughing as if the rest of the ranch population didn't exist. He'd purposely gone in late, hoping to avoid seeing the one-time lovers together, but it had made no difference. Upon entering the dining hall, Jake had immediately noticed that Theo was sitting too close to Monica. In fact, the moment Jake had seen them together, he could've sworn Theo scooted in closer.

The memory made his stomach burn.

He clenched his gloved hands and turned away from his view of the empty dooryard. He climbed down from the hayloft and went outside to arrange the bales on the wagon. The sky was slowly turning from navy to azure, birds were singing nearby, and in the distance, the rush of the river mixed with the gentle wind in the trees.

As Jake arranged the bales, his thoughts turned back to Monica. Shawn had told him she and Theo had gone their separate ways, but that didn't mean they didn't still enjoy a physical relationship. Just the idea of the man touching her set Jake's teeth on edge and triggered an overwhelming need to claim her as his own.

You can't do that. He couldn't give her what she deserved, but he didn't like seeing her with anyone else either.

"Mornin'," a man said from behind him. Jake snapped his head around and his already sore jaw clenched again when he saw Theo Swenson approaching. Jake stifled a groan and turned back to the bales, hoping the other man would get the message and keep on walking.

No such luck.

"Need a hand?" Theo asked.

"Nope." Jake strove for a civil tone, but he wondered if the one-word response sounded as aggressive as he felt.

"I don't mind. Besides, I wanted to talk to you about the ranch," Theo said.

Surprised, Jake stopped positioning the hay to frown at the other man. "What about it?"

"Monica and Shawn both say you've been a big help in straightening out their setup."

Jake only shrugged.

"I was hoping to convince you to give us some pointers when you come to Angel's next month."

Jake's eyes narrowed further. "By the looks of those cattle you brought in yesterday, you're doing fine."

"They're not the only ones we have, and there are other issues we could use an experienced opinion on. We've done okay with books and guesswork, but we need to grow and be ready for lean years. As it is, we may not make it if something goes wrong."

"I'm not actually a rancher." Jake knew he sounded unfriendly, but he couldn't help it.

"Are you always this surly, or am I just lucky enough to catch you before your morning coffee?"

Jake glanced at him, saw Theo's open yet perplexed expression, and then dropped his gaze to the bales at his feet. He shrugged, annoyed with himself for feeling guilty about being so terse with Theo.

"I could take a look," Jake said, shrugging again. "Give you some pointers if I see anything."

"We'd appreciate any help you could give us," Theo said as he jogged into the barn and climbed up to the hayloft. "My wife would love it if I could be home more."

"Wife? You're married?" Jake stared up at Theo as he appeared in the opening above him, hauling another bale for the wagon.

Theo met his startled gaze and chuckled softly. "Well, we didn't exchange rings, sign any papers, or have a ceremony or anything. But, yeah, for all intents and purposes, Peggy's my wife."

Jake's puzzled frown didn't ease. "But I thought they didn't...?"

"Allow marriage?" Theo shook his head. "You mind?" he shrugged with the heavy bale and Jake got out of the way. Theo dropped it, and while he went back for another, Jake aligned the new bundle with the others and stepped back again. When Theo returned, he spoke again. "The council outlawed marriage years ago as an archaic tradition. But to us, marriage is a partnership. We share everything and take care of each other. Peggy's the best thing to ever happen to me."

Theo dropped the hay and went for another.

Jake nodded. He had a nagging suspicion his restless night had been pointless.

As they finished loading the last few bales in silence, some of the ranch staff began crossing the dooryard, heading for breakfast in the dining hall. A few waved, asking if they were needed, but Jake told them to eat first, and they continued on their way.

When Theo joined him at the wagon once more, he crossed his arms over the stacked bales and looked at Jake as he arranged the last two on the end of the wagon. Jake could sense Theo's assessing gaze on him, but he avoided the other man's eyes, still trying to process his earlier comments.

Theo sighed. "I'm sorry, Jake."

Jake's brows lifted as he looked up from his work. "For what?"

Theo tilted his head. "I shouldn't have tried so hard to push your buttons yesterday."

Jake froze. His lips parted to suck in air as he stepped back from the wagon. His stomach tightening, he met the other man's gaze with a frown. "I...I don't know what you're talking about."

Theo eyed him askance, but there was an upward curve to his lips. "I understand the appeal," he said as if Jake hadn't spoken. "I just wanted to be sure."

"Sure of what?"

Theo turned toward him, one arm still propped on the hay. He looked toward another group of ranch hands headed for the dining hall and lowered his voice. "Of how you feel about Monica."

Jake's eyebrows climbed toward his hat brim. He also glanced over his shoulder before speaking. "She's my temporary owner and I work for her, that's all."

"No, it isn't, but you don't have to tell me. I just wanted to find out what kind of man you are."

Jake's back straightened as he faced Theo. "And you think you've figured that out?"

He shrugged. "Well enough. Plus, Angel asked me to see how things were going here."

"Angel? Monica's friend Angel?"

"The one and only."

"What does she care?"

"She cares about Monica, the same as the rest of us," Theo said as if trying to convey a message.

Jake turned away and adjusted his hat, unsure what to make of Theo's comments and beginning to feel foolish for his prior notions about this man.

"What's she like?" He blurted out the question without thinking.

"Angel?"

Jake nodded.

"What has Monica told you?"

"Only that they're friends and that Angel's trustworthy."

"She is that," Theo said. "She's also a bit...complicated."

"Complicated?"

"She has her problems and she has a temper when provoked, but she's been more than decent to us, generous even."

Jake stared at the frayed end of a piece of twine, remembering Monica saying something similar. He met Theo's gaze and tilted his head to the side. "What kind of problems?"

Theo cleared his throat and glanced at him. "We..." He crossed his arms over his chest. "We don't talk about it...much."

"Okay. Forget I asked," Jake said, but his curiosity about this unfamiliar woman grew a little more. The amount of influence Angel seemed to have on Monica—and, hence, on the lives of everyone on Monica's ranch—made Jake uneasy.

"She's not a threat," Theo said, apparently reading Jake's thoughts. "*We* usually worry about *her*."

"I see." But he didn't see at all.

A long pause followed.

"Monica's a fine woman," Theo said suddenly.

"No argument here."

Theo smiled and patted Jake's shoulder companionably. "Good," he said as he headed for the dining hall.

Jake nodded and started for the barn.

"Jake?" Theo called, and Jake glanced over his shoulder. "Take care of her."

Jake frowned. "Who?"

"Monica." Theo's broad grinned flashed, and then he gave a little wave and disappeared into the dining hall.

19

JAKE NICHOLS WAS STILL AVOIDING HER. Monica stood in the shadows beside the barn and studied him as he talked with Shawn on the deck of her new home. He stood several inches taller than Shawn's wiry form and had much broader shoulders, but she suspected Jake didn't realize his allure. She, conversely, was all too aware of his attractiveness, sensing his presence whenever he was around. He drew her eyes right to him, and she felt an unmistakable pull to go to his side. She enjoyed looking at him, but she wanted more than that.

She felt certain his attraction to her was as strong but that he fought it. She recognized the signs. She also realized he was afraid, of what precisely she wasn't sure, but thanks to Theo's suggestion, she intended to find out. Since Jake no longer attended their dinners and seemed to dodge being alone with her, she had devised a way for him to join her away from everyone else—a change of scenery to make their time together about the two of them, not the ranch.

By midmorning, after they had completed the daily chores of feeding and caring for the animals, everyone took the rest of the day off—a reward, Monica said, for all their hard work. Shawn and Rosa had convinced Jake to go fishing with them upriver, and they were supposed to leave soon. From all reports and from the smile on his face, Jake was looking forward to the outing.

"Are you sure you want to do this?" Rosa's soft Spanish inflection interrupted Monica's thoughts as Rosa exited the barn through the rear door and joined Monica in the shadows on the far side. Monica glanced at her head guard. She'd known Rosa Santos for years, ever since her father had found Rosa half-starved and cringing with cold in a stand of bushes. Monica's family lived deep in the mountains by that time, and winter loomed right around the corner. If her father hadn't brought Rosa home, she would have died of exposure or starvation, a toss-up as to which would've come first.

After Monica's parents were gone, Rosa had returned to society with her and took on the role of head guard after Monica—with Angel's help—had purchased this land. She was a worthy ally and a loyal friend, and Monica trusted the older Latina woman with her life.

"Yes, I'm sure," she replied to Rosa's inquiry.

"He's damaged," her friend said, and Monica glanced at her again. Rosa's black eyes were worried when they met Monica's thoughtful gaze. "And unstable."

"He's been hurt, and he's afraid. I won't toss him aside for things he can't control. It's too late now anyway."

"There are other men," Rosa hinted, as she often did lately.

"I realize that."

"Then why this one?"

"I don't know why, but he's a decent man and when I look into his eyes, I see he has feelings for me. I can't ignore that, especially when my heart has the same feelings for him."

"You can't know that, Monica," Rosa said in a frustrated hiss. "How many men have you loved? How many have you wanted and taken to your bed? You will find another. It doesn't have to be *this* one."

Monica bristled. She understood Rosa's concern, but she didn't like the clear implication about her morals in the words her friend chose. *Then again,* Monica thought, *Rosa might only be worried about her.* Like a second mom, Rosa always worried about her "pretty, little girl."

"I've never hidden the fact I like men, Rosa, or that I enjoy their company," Monica answered in a quiet yet assertive tone, "and I'm not ashamed of those I have shared intimacies with, but I've never loved anyone. A few I hoped would grow into more, but they didn't. I cared for them, yes, but they were never a forever kind of thing. They all knew that, and so do you."

"Are you saying you love this man?"

Monica crossed her arms over her chest. "I'm not sure what I feel, but it is different. He's different."

"He's just another man."

Monica's brow furrowed. "No. He's *different.*"

"How?"

Monica tilted her head and took a breath before replying. "He's afraid, but he's willing to listen, to try. He wants to be normal, to have a normal life. He accepts me. He likes me for me, and he's never suggested by word or deed that I should behave in a way contrary to my nature. He likes me outspoken, even though I make him nervous sometimes, but he also worries about my safety. He wants to care for me. He *does* care for me, but he's holding back."

"Because of Kristine?" Rosa asked, her black brows arching upward. "I find that hard to believe."

"She may be part of it, but she's not the main reason." Monica met her friend's gaze again. "You've heard how Darla Cain treats her slaves, what she does to them. Can you blame him for being afraid?"

"No, but I can blame him if he hurts you."

"He's not going to hurt me, Rosa," she said as her eyes drifted back to

Jake.

"You don't know that either. Even with your hysterical-strength, he could easily overpower you before you could stop him. What if you kiss him and he freaks out on you too? Then what?"

"Then I slow down."

"And if he kills you when you're out there alone with him today? You're taking an awfully big chance with a man you barely know."

"I know enough. He won't hurt me."

"For your sake, and his, I hope you're right." Something in the tone of her voice made Monica stare at her old friend again.

"Do I detect a note of approval?" She grinned and then laughed at Rosa's exaggerated look of disapproval.

"I think he's dangerous, but you're also right. He's a good man and he deserves better than Darla Cain. I just hope you're right about the rest as well."

"I am."

Rosa glanced at the two men on the deck, then turned back to Monica again. "What about him?"

"What *about* him?"

"How's Jake going to feel when you must send him back?"

"I haven't worked that out yet," Monica said, and Rosa gave a derisive snort, "but I'll think of something. I don't want to let him go, but I'd rather someone else, who won't cause him more agony, take him than send him back to Darla."

Rosa's mouth fell open as her wide eyes stared incredulously.

"What?" Monica asked. She couldn't fathom what she'd said to make Rosa look so surprised.

"You're in love with him."

"I told you, I'm not sure."

"You are," Rosa said with finality.

Monica frowned. "And what makes you so sure?"

"Because you're willing to give him up to save him. Because the way you look at him is different from all the others. I've seen this, and I've worried."

"You knew all that and still you lectured me?"

"Someone needs to watch out for you." Rosa smiled. "You're too headstrong for your own good sometimes, and you don't always look before you leap. Your mother would want me to do this for you."

"Don't bring my mom into this."

"She loved you very much, as do I. We both want you to be happy, but we want you to be safe too."

"He won't hurt me," Monica insisted.

"I hope you're right."

"I am." Monica was absolutely sure. "And I'll figure out something to keep Darla from taking him back."

"Maybe Angel will help?"

Monica shook her head.

"She's helped you before."

"That was different, and she's done enough. She has her own problems. I won't ask her to take on more, not unless I have no other choice. Angel will only be my last resort."

Rosa nodded. She understood Angel's troubles too.

Silence descended between them as Monica's gaze fell on Jake once more and Rosa examined the sky, judging the time.

Monica took the moment to admire Jake. He had a rugged aspect, almost stern at times, but when he smiled, he took her breath. His physique was impressive, and his face matched the rest of him. His high cheekbones, straight nose, and hazel-green eyes, which she often got lost in, were all topped by sandy brows. His square jaw jutted a bit at his chin, and his full, chiseled lips tempted her from across the yard. He kept his hair cut ruthlessly short on the sides and in the back, but a little longer on top, revealing blond highlights intermixed among the butterscotch-brown depths. She longed to run her fingers through it, mess it up a little, test the texture, and smell its scent. But his hair was not all she yearned to touch. She hoped, someday, she would have the chance to explore all of him.

Several seconds passed during her perusal of Jake, and then her guard spoke again.

"Well," Rosa said, "if we're going to do this, I'd better get to it."

"Thank you, Rosa," Monica murmured before the other woman walked away. Tears glistened in Monica's eyes when Rosa met her gaze once more. "Thank you for everything."

"Oh, *mi hijita bonita.*" Rosa whispered the old endearment as she wrapped her arms around the young woman who'd become like a daughter to her. "I'd do anything for you. I just worry about you is all."

"I know," Monica said. "I love you too, Rosa."

They held each other for a moment longer, and then Rosa pushed back.

"You go," she said with a sniff, her eyes suspiciously shiny. "You must be gone before we reach the barn."

"I will be," Monica said with a smile. "Take care of him for me."

"He's in good hands, *niñita*. Now, go. Shoo." She waved Monica away, indicating she must hurry.

Monica glanced at the deck once more as she went to enter the barn and noticed that Jake and Shawn were no longer there. She didn't see them leave, but she assumed they'd gone to the bunkhouse to retrieve their things.

She smiled as she crossed the threshold into the barn. Dimmer inside, shafts of sunlight spilled through the cracks in the wood panels, creating slats of golden-yellow light on the dusty floor. The barn smelled like hay and horses and leather. She loved the combination.

Pleased to find her mount saddled, she said a silent "thank you" to her head guard.

Despite her arguments, Rosa liked Jake. She was right though; he was damaged, which made him a little unpredictable, but Monica would never get to know him if she didn't take a chance. She knew he could heal, but that certainty hinged on somehow procuring him from Darla Cain.

She led her chestnut gelding to the door and peeked out. No one occupied the yard. She heard voices talking and the laughter of children coming from the direction of the river. Everyone was enjoying the warm summer day, keeping cool by the water. The happy sounds gladdened her heart. She said another silent "thank you," to Angel this time, for helping her with this place and for giving her what she needed to keep these people safe. It fell on Monica now to make sure they stayed that way.

Jake was a complication she hadn't counted on, but she couldn't just forget about him—and she wouldn't let him accept his fate as Darla Cain's plaything. She would help him without hurting everyone else.

She must find a way.

JAKE RODE ALONG, listening to his two companions chatter ahead of him, without paying attention to their conversation. Sometimes they asked him a question—to keep him from feeling left out, he suspected. He responded when needed, but in general, he remained lost in his own thoughts. And those centered on a lovely blonde with tempting curves, a beautiful smile, and a light in her eyes that called to him.

You can't go there, he told himself for the thousandth time. *You're going back to Darla in a few months. Don't torture yourself.*

He forced his brain to concentrate on the work he had yet to finish, and avoided thoughts about what would happen when the project ended. Unfortunately, thinking about work as a distraction from his thoughts about Monic was a terrible idea. No matter what else he tried to focus on, his mind took him back to her.

He tried to think of the wiring that still needed finishing upstairs, and then he remembered the only room left was her bedroom. His mind envisioned Monica unclothed between white sheets, her long hair a golden halo around her head, her sun-kissed skin shimmering in the soft light of a lantern, and a bright, inviting smile on her face.

He instantly pulled back.

Don't go there.

He fixated on the still-unfinished bathroom plumbing, namely the tub and shower. Within minutes, he pictured Monica naked and wet, looking at him with those eyes that seemed to stare right into his soul. Longing tightened his chest, and need crushed his vitals.

Don't go there.

He considered how long it would take to complete the floors in the front room, and an image of Monica in something red, lacy, and revealing, lying on a rug in front of the fireplace bloomed complete in his mind. The vision flooded his body with another rush of desire so strong it stole his breath.

Stop it! Don't go there.

No matter what he thought of, her image invaded shortly after, usually dressed provocatively—if at all—and calling to him with her eyes, her mouth, her arms...wrapped around his neck, her body plastered against his, her lips searing his, her breasts...

Oh, God... Stop it!

He shook his head.

Damn it. His runaway thoughts were causing him physical discomfort. If he kept it up—he moaned as his mind put those words together—he would need to jump into the freezing river straight from the saddle to resolve his dilemma.

So distracted by his thoughts and the rising tide of longing assailing him, Jake was unaware the other two in his party had called out a greeting to someone already at the river. When the change in the tone of their voices finally registered, he looked up and groaned before he could stop himself.

Monica was there. The real, live woman, not a figment of his overactive imagination. His groin tightened almost painfully, and anxious flutters took flight in his belly.

What the hell am I going to do now? Just riding away might be construed as an escape attempt. Well, it would be, sort of, but not the kind normally considered by a slave. But his freedom didn't concern him right now. He worried about being close to his temporary Mistress and his body's inconvenient reactions to her.

He had stopped the dinner meetings partly because of Kristine's hints that Jake was just one of many men in Monica's life. But he had also stopped because all he could think about when they were together was kissing her. And he didn't want to get involved with her when he would be leaving soon.

Did he?

"Hi, Jake!" Monica shouted to him with a big smile on her beautiful face. Barefoot, her long hair pulled back into a ponytail, she wore cutoff jeans with a white tank top. The white strings tied around the back of her neck hinted that she also sported a bathing suit beneath her clothes. The amount of her silky bare flesh on display now was another hit to his continuously growing problem.

That's not funny, he thought when he realized the pun in his choice of words.

She waved at him, and he returned the gesture, pasting a grin on his face that he hoped looked more sincere than it felt. He rode forward to where Rosa and Shawn, still on their horses, were chatting with Monica.

"You don't mind if I join your group, do you, Jake?" she asked, and he stifled another groan of dismay. He didn't have a choice; the others had already agreed. What stupid excuse could he give to get away from her?

None, that's what.

"No," he said as he dismounted, purposely facing his horse when Monica came up beside him and wishing he had stayed home.

"I'm glad you came along."

He paused in unsaddling his gelding to glance at her. He focused first on her lips, and, imagining their softness, the tightness in his jeans swelled uncomfortably once again. She still had a beauteous smile on her face, and when his gaze met hers, her eyes stared up at him expectantly.

This time, his grin came without effort.

"Me too," he said and discovered he meant it. Something about her infected him, made him happy, proud to be in her company, and glad to be afforded the opportunity.

"Great!" she exclaimed and tapped his arm affectionately. "We'll have a wonderful time, you'll see. I—"

Monica's comment was interrupted by a horse neighing, a loud curse, and a splash, followed by the sound of rapidly departing hooves. They both glanced over and saw Rosa jump from her steed to help Shawn out of the river, where his now-missing gelding had tossed him.

"What happened?" Monica called as she went to assist Rosa.

Jake held back a groan, knowing he couldn't just stand there and watch from behind his horse. He quickly adjusted himself, willing his unwanted erection away, and, feeling incredibly awkward, followed Monica. Keeping his troublesome issue concealed until his discomfort ebbed was tricky, but getting splashed by the cold river water alleviated his problem as he helped pull a moaning Shawn onto the bank.

"Something spooked my damn horse," Shawn gritted out between clenched teeth. He had blood on his forehead and he favored his right ankle. "The cursed animal's probably halfway home by now."

"Let me see your leg," Rosa said, working his boot off.

Shawn grimaced but didn't argue.

Monica went to her saddlebags and pulled out a folded piece of cloth, which she used to clean the cut on Shawn's head.

Jake stood back out of the way. Their obvious concern for the other man surprised him. Jake hadn't received so much affection from anyone in years, and it had been longer still since anyone had treated him with true kindness. Not until he came to work for Monica, that is. He had actually started to feel safe in her home. He was still uneasy at times, but the outright fear was gone. No one had harmed him, and aside from Kristine's advances, no one had demanded anything of him either. He did his job and they left him alone, a wonderful change from the conditions he had endured under Darla's dictatorship.

"This head wound is fairly bad," Monica muttered. "I think you're going to need stitches."

She and Rosa exchanged a look.

"My head hurts like hell too," Shawn declared. "I think I hit a rock under water."

"We need to take him to the clinic in town," Monica said, and she sounded worried. "He might have a concussion."

"I'll take him," Rosa and Jake offered in unison.

Rosa reached out and patted his arm. "No, you stay, Jake. No reason to ruin everyone's day. Besides, you two can't go alone."

"I think we all—" Monica began, but Rosa interrupted.

"We can manage on our own. Right, Shawn?"

The injured man nodded, groaning with the movement, and lifted his pained gaze to his Mistress. "I'll be all right," he told Monica with his familiar crooked grin. "Just a little banged up. If someone will bring me a mount, I can ride back alone."

"You're not going anywhere on your own," Monica scolded. "Not with a head wound."

"I'll go with him," Rosa said.

"All right, but take my horse," Monica offered. "It'll be easier than riding double. I can ride home with Jake later."

Jake mentally shouted a string of curses. That's the last thing he needed right now. To have her soft body pressed against him in the saddle would drive him mad, but he could do nothing about it now. The decision made, Monica quickly fastened the saddle on her horse before leading the animal over to Shawn.

"Jake?" Rosa called. "Would you help me get him in the saddle?"

"Sure."

Safely seated on Monica's gelding a few minutes later, Shawn rode away with Rosa riding beside him. The man swayed a little but seemed solid enough in the saddle.

"I hope he'll be alright," Monica said at Jake's side. Her voice held a touch of anxiety.

"Rosa will take care of him."

"I know," Monica said, and then shaking off her concern, she smiled at him again. "Well, at least we can still have a nice afternoon." She turned and walked to the blanket she had spread out on the ground. "Lunch is served," she said, still grinning.

Jake almost groaned. How long must he endure being alone with her? Not that spending time with Monica was a hardship exactly—he craved her company—but what he wanted he could never have.

Shaking himself mentally, he forced his lips to return her smile, and though his stomach was too knotted up to eat, he sat down across from her.

"What do we have?" he asked, trying not to notice the smoothness of her thighs, the elegant curves of her neck and chin, or the way the sunlight caught in her hair, turning her locks from their normal golden color to pale, pale honey.

Oh, damn, he thought. *Who are you kidding?* He was already responding to her.

His heart pounded in his chest, excited by her nearness. *Stupid thing! Don't you know when to save yourself?*

She smiled at him again, and his heart stumbled before picking up the beat once more. *Apparently, not.*

He didn't have a choice. He would spend the afternoon with her, but he would offer nothing. He didn't want another uncontrollable reaction, especially not one directed at her. The last thing he wanted was for her to realize how she affected him.

You are a rock, he told himself mockingly. *Act like one.*

20

"ARE YOU ENJOYING your time with us?" Monica asked as she sat opposite Jake on a picnic blanket in the dappled shade of a honey locust tree.

Jake nodded, while snacking on the last of the homemade potato chips from their lunch and not meeting her gaze.

"Is everything going okay with the construction?" She leaned forward to grab a chip of her own. Jake snatched his hand back when their fingers brushed. His gaze flicked toward her, then instantly away again.

"It's moving along as expected," he answered in a bland tone, still avoiding her eyes. "Should be done on time."

Monica glanced up at the branches of the tree shading them and then back to Jake again.

"How long have you known your friend Bret?" she asked, shifting toward him slightly.

"A long time." He sat forward and rested his elbows on his knees.

"How long did you work with him on the ranch you told me about?"

He shrugged. "About...eight years."

Monica clenched her jaw and bit down on the inside of her lip. With jerky movements born of frustration, she began putting their empty dishes back into the picnic basket while trying to think of another question that might get him talking.

"Where'd you learn to read blueprints?" she asked suddenly as she set the basket aside and repositioned herself closer to him.

His eyes followed her movements warily, and when she settled closer to him, he leaned back, away from her, propping his weight on his straight arms before answering. "I worked in construction for four years and took classes for two before we moved from the west side, and two more after I started working with Bret on the ranch."

"Why did you leave?"

He shrugged again, his eyes on the river. "With the way the war was going, I wanted to get out of the city."

She turned away in exasperation, but out of the corner of her eye, she once again caught him sneaking a peek at her when he thought she couldn't see.

Monica released a silent sigh. She glanced at Jake, still ignoring her and gazing at the glittering pool of water not far from where they sat. Resolved to her course, she straightened her back, then stood up and removed her top.

"What are you doing?" Jake sounded alarmed.

She smiled as she tossed her tank top down on the blanket, along with her hair tie. "Going for a swim," she told him. She pretended not to notice his wide gaze dropping to her breasts as she worked on shimmying out of her cutoffs. "You should come with," she said. "It'll be fun."

His eyes skimmed over her, and her skin heated at his lingering perusal of her body. Her heart sped up. She smiled when his gaze flashed back to her face. He looked away an instant later.

So far, so good, she thought as she kicked her shorts on top of her tank and headed for the river. She wasn't looking forward to immersing herself in the small pool formed by the swirling power of the river, but she'd chosen this spot for its isolation and for the refreshing cold of the water.

The air temperature was enough to melt plastic in the dry, desert-like heat, but feeling Jake's eyes on her backside sent a pleasant shiver up her spine, her whole body aware of his stare. His gaze made her feel so overheated that she half-expected steam to hiss upward when her first step broke the surface of the chilly waters. She waded to her thighs and then glanced over her shoulder.

Jake sat where she'd left him, but instead of reclining back, he was now leaning forward, back straight, hands gripping his knees. His eyes, wide but shiny, were focused on her, and a flush rode high on his cheeks. The minute he realized she was watching him, however, his face changed. But his façade of disinterest didn't fool her. No mask of indifference could hide the desire in his eyes.

Monica smiled at him.

"Come on, Jake." She waved her arm toward the water. "Cool off a little." She dived under the surface and swam along the bottom to the other side of the pool.

JAKE GAPED AS MONICA DISAPPEARED beneath the water. A part of him sighed with relief, no longer assaulted with the need to devour her with his eyes. His more primal side, however, screamed for him to go after her.

Her white bikini left little to the imagination. He had fought to keep from staring, but it was all he could do not to drool. She was as beautiful as he had dreamed, real, and right in front of him, which made it harder for him to resist.

He waited several seconds for her to resurface, but she didn't. Several more seconds went by, and he began to worry. He rose to his feet and stared out over the rippling waters. What was taking her so long? Did she hit her head when she dived in? Did she get tangled in something at the bottom?

He stood at the edge, trying to locate her, but he saw no movement below.

He cursed and started to unbutton his shirt. The third had just slipped from its buttonhole when her head finally popped up above water on the far side of the pool. He sighed with relief.

Jake stood like a statue and stared as she brushed her golden hair from her face and stood up. This time he did groan at the wave of heat pulsing through him when he saw her trim, long-legged, near-naked body glistening in the sun. His skin tingled. His body burned. Every part of him demanded he go to her, but his mind said no. His hands dropped to his sides, but he didn't turn away.

He couldn't.

She smiled at him and waved. He only stood and stared. She had him wrapped in a spell he couldn't seem to break, and it would land him in trouble.

Shit, you're already in trouble.

She dived under again, and he spent several more seconds waiting to see her reappear. He wondered where she would pop up this time. He didn't have long to wait, as he saw her outline and the flash of her white suit coming toward him.

Go back and sit down! his brain screamed, but his body wouldn't move.

She emerged from the shallow water near where he stood, pushed back her lovely hair, and straightened up to face him. She was a vision, a goddess, and at that moment, he couldn't have stopped looking at her if his life depended on it. She could ask him to do anything right now, and he wouldn't be able to say no. The sight of her fed a part of him that had been starving for years, and he wanted to feed it.

He must.

"Come on in, Jake," she said as she sank back into the water and pushed out of the shallows. "It's not too bad."

He shook his head, but his fingers finished unbuttoning his shirt and pulled the tails from his jeans. His eyes never wavered from her.

"I just love the water," she said, moving toward the deepest part of the pool. Her golden hair floated around her shoulders and shimmered in the sunlight. She glanced at him, and her eyes held a promise that made Jake's heart slam into his breastbone.

The shirt slithered off his shoulders. Jake tossed it on the ground and then fumbled with his belt. He made it halfway through unbuckling it and then stopped to tug off his cowboy boots.

"It just feels so good sliding over your skin," Monica said in a sultry voice that caressed Jake's ears and burned into his chest, before heading straight south. He looked up as she turned her body to float on her back, every supple curve visible along the surface. Her sun-kissed flesh glowed like pale copper, her hair a honeyed veil around her head, as her slim legs moved up and down, propelling her slowly through the water.

"Mmm," she hummed.

Transfixed, Jake stood there with no shirt, his belt half-unbuckled and his boot held forgotten in his hands as he gawked at the glory in the water. He understood she was flirting with him, but his mind, too far-gone with longing, considered nothing beyond the vision in front of him.

The boot dropped out of his hands, and the thudding sound it made caused him to start as if something had bitten him. He was burning up—and not only because of the sun beating down on his bare flesh.

Fed by yearly snowmelt, the river had carved out this small inlet, which meant it wasn't all that warm, even in the hottest of months. Yet the icy water might work to cool the blazing need within him that grew fiercer by the minute.

"Are you going to join me?" Monica asked as she tugged at the top of her suit. She readjusted the material, but the motion caused her breasts to swell enticingly above the water.

Jake grunted at the jolt of passion flaring like a rocket to his groin. His limbs trembled with the rush of molten fire coursing through his veins.

His brain asserted itself for one last attempt at self-preservation. "The water's cold," he said and almost grimaced. *What a moronic thing to say. Of course it's cold, you idiot!*

"It's not bad once you get in," she told him.

"I don't have a suit," he muttered.

"Just go in your shorts, or your jeans if you're shy. Or strip down to nothing if you like. I won't watch...unless you want me to." She grinned, and there was something more suggestive than her words in the way she stared at him.

His fingers finished with his belt, made short work of the fasteners on his jeans, and in seconds, he was standing in his forest-green briefs, his hands unconsciously hiding his arousal. Their eyes met and didn't break contact until he hesitated at the pool's edge. She was still smiling, but her eyes drifted over him in an appraising way that made him sweat. His breath came too fast, like he'd just ran a marathon.

When Monica's gaze returned to his, her grin had turned into a full-blown smile. Her whole face beamed, and without thinking about it, he stepped into the shallows. The shock of the chilly water made him shiver, but it didn't stop him. A minute later, he was treading water beside her.

"See," she said when he faced her, "it isn't so bad."

He snorted. "It's *freezing*."

She slapped at the water and drenched him. He reciprocated, and she squealed. Bit by bit she helped him relax, until they were playfully chasing each other around the pool.

Jake hadn't felt this carefree since before the war. Hard to fathom now, but just over two months ago he had thought he would die in lonely darkness. Now, he was splashing around in a cold river-carved pool, under the summer sun, with a lovely woman—and he was happy.

Monica disappeared under the water, and Jake spun around, expecting her to show up behind him. Instead, something tugged at his ankle, and his head dipped under the water.

Her body bumped against his, setting off fireworks as they both resurfaced. She giggled, and he laughed with her. He automatically wrapped an arm around her waist to pull her against him, moving them both toward shore and solid ground. Her arms curled around his neck. When he could plant his feet on the rocky bottom, he stopped but held her up, the water still too deep for her to stand.

Still chuckling slightly, he looked into her face.

The air became thick and hard to breathe.

Jake swallowed as he stared into her eyes.

Her fingers stroked the back of his neck, ruffling the short hair at his nape, and he shivered with the sensation.

Her warm body pressing against him short-circuited his brain, and he was certain she must feel his arousal burning against her soft curves.

Her wide, hazel eyes stared at him as the laughter dwindled away and they swayed quietly in each other's arms.

Jake sucked in a breath, wanting so much to take the next step, but reality had crept back into his head. This wouldn't work. This path led to nowhere but heartache.

His mind said release her, but his body didn't listen.

At that moment, she leaned forward and pressed her lips to his.

At first, he didn't move. Every muscle tensed and he almost pulled away, but when her tongue slid seductively along the seam of his lips, the fiery eruption of desire took over. His arms tightened around her waist, molding her body against him from shoulders to knees. He slanted his mouth across hers. His tongue dived in to sample the hot nectar of her passion, devouring it, devouring her like a man possessed—but not too starved to savor the sweetness.

God, she tastes good.

Her hands caressed his back, his shoulders, his neck, and he loved it. Her hot, urgent tongue dueled with his, teasing him, taunting him, challenging him, and he wanted to accept. Her soft moans begged him for more, and he wanted to give it. He loved holding her, kissing her. But it couldn't be.

Jake jerked his head back with a gasp. His eyes squeezed shut, fear and suspicion filling his mind while he struggled to regain control of his breathing.

His whole frame tensed.

Was this another mind game? Like the ones Darla and her friends used to play with him.

Was everything she said and did designed to make him fall for her?

Was she different or just like all the others?

Monica moaned her displeasure at his sudden withdrawal, her arms tightening around his neck, but then she pushed back to look at him. When he met her gaze, a mixture of emotions he couldn't separate swirled in her eyes, and an avalanche of doubt crashed in on him.

He wanted to believe she was the sweet, beautiful woman he had always wanted. But he had experienced too much agony with Darla Cain and her friends to accept that was possible anymore.

He glared down into her surprised expression. "Why did you do that?" His voice sounded hoarse.

She took a deep breath as her eyes searched his face. She seemed afraid, but she didn't pull away.

"I..." she began but stopped. She swallowed and licked her lips. The small motion drew his attention, and then she tried again. "I thought...I thought you wanted me to kiss you."

Oh, God, yes, I wanted that, his brain seethed. *I* still *want it.*

His body tightened again, and he was suddenly so hard he thought he might burst. But then anger slashed through him as memories came crashing in, memories he didn't want but wasn't strong enough to stop. They flooded his brain, reminding him he couldn't believe her. Couldn't allow a woman to hurt him. Could not trust again.

21

JAKE'S ARMS DROPPED AWAY from Monica so fast she nearly sunk beneath the surface before her body reacted. He spun away, wading back to shore. She swore to herself and started after him. If she let him go now, she would never get him back.

"Jake!" she shouted as she neared him. "Jake, wait."

As she reached shallower water and her feet found solid ground, she grabbed his shoulder, but he shrugged her off. The motion and her overextended position caused her to lose her balance. She slipped on the rocky river bottom, stumbled back, and suddenly found herself sinking into deeper water. She cried out as she fell, and the icy river filled her mouth, blocking out the air. Her lungs felt the loss instantly. She didn't immediately know which way was up, and panic tinged her heart, but right then something snagged her wrist and hauled her upward. Her head broke the surface, and she clung to the first solid object she could reach. She sucked in a deep breath and heard Jake's voice in her ear.

"I'm so sorry," he mumbled. He sounded distraught and afraid.

She hated that he feared her.

"I didn't mean to hurt you."

She was in his arms again. The water lapped against his neck and shoulders, but he was standing, holding her against his warm, wonderful body. She loved being in his embrace, even if she had to almost drown to get there.

"Monica, are you all right? I'm sorry. Did I injure you? Talk to me. Please..."

The knowledge that he was worried about her warmed her insides, even as his body, so close to hers, warmed her skin.

She lifted a hand from his shoulder, where it had landed after he pulled her to safety, and placed it on his cheek. His body stiffened against her.

"I didn't mean to hurt you," he muttered again as he stared into her eyes.

She smiled, not understanding what it was about this man that touched her so profoundly, but she accepted the feelings without reservation.

"I know," she said. Her other hand slipped around his neck, and she leaned into him, wrapping her arms around him and holding him close.

His arms squeezed her, but then he pushed away again. He took several steps toward shore as he tried to evade her.

"Jake, *please*," she said. The water lapped against his pectorals now, and her feet barely reached the pool's slanted, rocky bottom.

He must've heard the desperation in her voice because he stopped trying to escape and stood still in the cool water. His arms went around her again to hold her up, their eyes on a level, but his body was as rigid as a board.

"Please don't run away from me. Don't shut me out again. Please..."

A pained expression crossed his face, and he turned away.

She tried again.

"You're attracted to me," she murmured, her gaze tracing the hard line of his stubble-darkened jaw.

His head whipped back toward her, and he frowned.

She read suspicion in his eyes.

"What do you want from me?"

"Your time. Your attention. Your friendship. I want to get to know you."

"Why?"

"Isn't it obvious?"

His jaw tightened, and he shook his head slightly. "Not to me."

Monica stifled her groan of frustration. "I think you're a very interesting man, and I would like to be better acquainted with you."

"A lot of women have given me that line. They only wanted one thing."

"Did they all hurt you?"

"Not all, but most."

"I'm sorry."

His eyes narrowed. "Don't pity me," he ground out, and, as impossible as it seemed, his body hardened further.

"It's not pity. I—"

"Forget it," Jake said as he lowered his head and sighed. His arms tightened as he took a deep breath and lifted her out of the water. Startled by the sudden movement, she slipped both of her arms around his neck, and he carried her to the shore. Once there, he hastily set her on her feet, turned away, and began grabbing up his clothes.

What just happened? she thought.

"Jake, I—"

"I said, forget it," he growled as he jerked on his jeans and wrenched on his shirt. "You should get dressed."

She frowned at the hard tone of his voice. "I don't understand..."

His head snapped up, and he glared at her with cold, flinty eyes. Then he grimaced, turning away as if disgusted. He pulled on his socks and, without sparing her another glance, reached for his boots. "Put your clothes on," he said slowly, then looked up again and tilted his head. "Or don't. I don't care."

Monica shivered at the coldness in his voice and had to fight to keep the tremor out of her own. "What's wrong? What happened?"

JAKE FROZE IN STUNNED AMAZEMENT. Heat pulsed through his body, and sweat started under his arms and along his hairline. He stared at her as his pulse pounded out the rhythm of his fury.

"What happened? You're just like the rest of them. That's what happened!" He shook his head. "Take what you want and fuck everything else." He yanked on his first boot and stamped down into it. "I should've known better," he grumbled to himself.

"That's not what I meant—"

"I don't care!"

"I'm not—"

"I said, I don't care!" he roared. He took one threatening step toward her, but something stopped him from taking another.

Monica stumbled back, her feet splashing into the shallows, staring at him as if he were a wild animal about to maul her. She shivered, and he wondered if it was because she feared him or if her hysterical-strength was finally kicking in.

It didn't matter.

He took a deep breath.

"You used my friendship with Shawn to lure me out here, didn't you?" he said, his voice hard and hoarse, but he didn't wait for an answer. "You wanted to get me alone, expecting me to just give you whatever you want?" He shook his head again and chuckled bitterly. "That's not going to happen. No one's taking advantage of me again. No one's going to hurt me again. I won't live like that anymore." He tore his eyes away. The muscles in his arms and legs quivered. He had to get away from her.

His eyes roamed around the clearing, took in the blanket and basket, her clothes still sitting beside it, the saddle resting on a fallen log nearby, his horse loosely tied just beyond it. His gaze fell on Monica again.

She stood, arms wrapped around her middle, teeth biting down on her lower lip, eyes wide and shiny as she stared back at him. She shook her head as if to deny what he had said, but he wasn't in the mood to listen.

"Jake..." she rasped and then sucked in a halting breath.

"I'm going back to the homestead," he said, grabbing his hat from the blanket and shoving it on his head. "I'll leave the horse. I'm sure you can saddle it yourself."

He started walking. A part of him wanted to look back, but his pride and anger wouldn't let him. As he crashed along the overgrown path, Jake called up every memory he could of what women had done to him over the last two years—every demeaning word, every humiliating or painful act—to fight the part of him that didn't want to leave.

But none of it erased the pain he'd seen in Monica's eyes.

22

JAKE POUNDED THE NAIL into the drywall so hard the hammer left deep, round indents in the wall. He knew he was using too much force, that the extra damage would cause them more work later, but he needed an outlet for the anger that still burned in his belly.

Two days had passed since Monica's attempted seduction by the river, and he still couldn't get the incident out of his head. Her beautiful body, the promise in her eyes, her teasing smile, the kiss.

The damn kiss. His hammer made another indentation in the drywall, and he muttered a curse.

All he had been able to think about as he walked home from the river that sunny afternoon was that he'd trusted her. He'd believed she was different from the others, that she saw him as a man and wouldn't try to use him the way so many had before. Those other women had hurt him, treated him like an animal, a thing, a slave. They didn't ask how he was, what he felt, or if he wanted them. They took what they wanted from him and expected him to obey their commands without complaint. Fighting any portion of that only made his life harder. When he'd finally stopped resisting, their treatment of him had improved, but only slightly. Yet Monica's actions now were worse. She pretended to show him kindness. She had all but convinced him she would never treat him like a toy or a slave. Instead, she had tried to seduce him into performing. It wasn't as unpleasant an experience as the others, but it cut far deeper.

He fished another handful of nails out of his tool belt, placed one against the drywall, and started hammering again.

He hadn't spoken to her since the evening of the disaster at the pool. He'd gone out to the river again that night, after dinner, to think, to let the sound of the water and the cool breeze calm the hurt inside him. Monica had followed him. He hadn't known what she wanted when he heard her say his name, but it didn't matter.

"Stay the hell away from me!" he'd shouted as he backed away from her.

She dropped her head and pushed her hands into the pockets of her lightweight denim jacket.

"Jake, I want—" She looked up and the soft sheen in her eyes almost made him listen, but then self-preservation won out.

"I told you, I don't care what you want. Just stay away from me and we won't have any issues. I'll do my job, you'll get that much out of me, but nothing else."

He'd stormed off without looking back.

She'd avoided him ever since. He still felt her eyes on him occasionally, at meals or when he went outside, but she didn't approach him again.

The problem now was that he was questioning his actions and having second thoughts.

Maybe he'd been wrong to jump to conclusions, to think Monica was anything like the others.

Maybe he'd overreacted to her advances.

Maybe he should apologize for screaming at her as if she were the enemy.

No longer certain his reaction was valid, his conscience warred with his past experiences, creating a wealth of frustrated confusion. More than once, he'd snapped at the other workers, grumbling and growling to the point that most of the crew was now avoiding him—so much so, in fact, he'd been working alone for the better part of the last two days.

He shoved his hammer into his belt and stomped outside to grab more drywall. The late afternoon sun shone brightly as he exited the shaded interior, and he squinted as he went down the stairs to the stack of drywall sheets waiting in the yard. He paused in hefting the weighty material as a gang of kids came tearing across the dooryard, laughing and screaming as they did almost every day. Unlike other times, though, seeing them having so much fun failed to lighten his mood. In fact, his irritation level went up a notch, even though they had nothing to do with his problem.

Once the kids had rounded the corner of the house, he lifted two sheets and carried them back into the house. He propped them against the wall and then positioned the first one on the framing, beside the last sheet he'd fastened. He dug another handful of nails from this belt and secured the next sheet in place.

He worked methodically: Pull nails. Hammer nails. Get more drywall. Repeat.

Working on the next sheet he'd hauled in, he was so completely wrapped up in his thoughts—angry at Monica, angry at Darla, angry at himself, angry at everything and everyone—he didn't hear someone calling his name. A pair of small hands pushed at his hips, right as he was preparing to slam a nail head with the hammer. He missed the nail altogether and smashed his fingers instead. He cursed loudly. The hammer and his handful of fasteners clattered to the floor. He shook his hand, then gripped his throbbing fingers with the other. He turned around shouting.

"What the hell? Are you trying to break my damn hand?" His eyes fell on the upturned face of Kara. A handful of wilting wildflowers were clutched in one tiny trembling hand. Her blonde curls bounced around her shoulders, her eyes wide, lips quivering. Fear for her safety, and his own unresolved frustration, caused him to react without thinking. "Damn it, Kara. You're not supposed to be in here. Get outside, now!"

The whole room went silent.

The little girl stared at him, and he realized what he'd done a half a second too late. He watched, disgusted with himself, as Kara's face crumbled and she burst into tears. The flowers in her hand tumbled slowly to the floor.

"Back off, Nichols!" Shawn shouted as he came forward to crouch down and gather the little girl against his chest.

"I didn't mean to—"

"Get out," Shawn ordered, a vein pulsing in his temple as he glared at Jake. "Wait for me on the deck."

"I—"

"Out!" Shawn shouted. "Now, Jake."

Jake unbuckled his tool belt and set it on the floor. Then, hunching his shoulders and feeling like the biggest monster on the planet, he did as Shawn said.

He caught sight of Trevor and some other kids near the door as he crossed the room. The other children ran off when they saw him coming, but Trevor stood rock still, fury painting his young features.

"You shouldn't yell at my sister," the boy said with hard eyes as Jake approached.

"I know. I'm sorry," he mumbled, but Trevor was no longer listening. He stabbed Jake with another accusing glare, and then ran to where Shawn still comforted the little girl.

Jake looked back at them over his shoulder.

Trevor positioned himself beside Shawn and reached over to rub his sister's back. Shawn lifted his eyes and opened his arms. Trevor hesitated, but only for a beat. The next instant he fell against Shawn, wrapped his arms around the man and Kara, and offered his own comfort for the girl's hurt. Shawn cradled them both, murmuring soft words to ease the damage Jake had done.

Kara's sobs felt like shards of glass digging into Jake's flesh, slowly ripping him apart.

"I thought he was my friend." Kara's cry, slightly muffled by Shawn's shirt, was still clear enough to reach Jake's ears. His chest constricted, and a thick lump formed in his throat. Jake averted his gaze, swung around with his head down, and shuffled outside.

* * *

"Follow me," Shawn growled as he stepped out onto the deck a few minutes later. He barely glanced at Jake before he stomped down the front stairs.

"Where are we going?" Jake asked, trailing behind Shawn like a beaten dog. He jumped back when Shawn unexpectedly spun around.

Face red, voice barely controlled, he said, "We're going somewhere quiet, where no one will hear me beat the crap out of you."

Jake recoiled and shook his head. "I'm not going to fight you, Shawn."

"Maybe not," Shawn replied, his fisted hands tightening at his sides as he leaned closer to Jake, "but you *are* going to tell me what the hell's got you so riled. Follow me. Now." He turned and started toward the barn with long purposeful strides.

Jake took a deep breath and, with heavy feet, went after him.

"Out!" he heard Shawn bellow from inside the barn, and two teenage boys hustled outside as Jake entered, ignoring their curious looks. He let the barn door slam closed behind him as his eyes adjusted to the dimness. Dust motes floated in the shafts of light piercing the slats of the barn walls. The mingled scents of hay, horse, and leather struck Jake the minute he entered. The mixture always brought a wave of calm and a sense of security he associated with his time at the ranch with Bret before the war—before everything in his life turned bad and then worse.

In the middle of the barn's central aisle stood a fuming Shawn, his legs braced apart, hands fisted at his sides, ready to confront Jake.

"What the hell is wrong with you?" Shawn nearly shouted. He yanked his hat from his head and ran his fingers through his short brown hair. "How could you do that to Kara?"

"I'm sorry," Jake said, though he knew it was inadequate.

"I'm not the one you need to apologize to."

"I know. I'll talk to her."

"I'm not sure I want you anywhere near those kids."

Jake frowned, his jaw dropping as he pulled in a breath through his mouth. His already aching heart hitched at the thought of losing his connection with the children, and his friendship with Shawn.

He dropped his gaze, uncertain what to say.

"I don't want them hurt anymore," Shawn said. "Kara is six years old! She lost everything she's ever known and everyone she's ever loved, except Trevor. She trusted you, Jake, and you just screamed at her for no good reason. It's going to take a while for her to forget that."

"I know," Jake said without looking up. "I didn't mean to yell at her. I'll make it right," he lifted his head slightly, "if you'll let me. I feel like a gigantic ass. I never would've done it if I wasn't—" He cut himself short. His gaze flashed to Shawn, then shifted around the open space before settling on the dirt below his boots.

Shawn sighed, then slapped his hat against his thigh and then pulled it back on his head. When Shawn spoke again, his voice was still tight but didn't sound as furious.

"What's up with you, Jake? You've been a bear for the last two days. Monica's been quiet, too, and that's scary. Did you two have a fight the other day?"

Jake closed his eyes and sighed. He struggled with himself, not wanting to open up again, but this was Shawn. He'd welcomed Jake, been a friend from the very first day.

"She...kissed me," he said softly.

"I'm sorry. She...*what*?" Shawn was closer now, his tone incredulous.

When Jake finally met his gaze, Shawn was standing a few feet away, his head tilted, eyebrows a dark V over his nose.

Jake flinched at the disbelief in his friend's brown eyes. He swallowed and tried again.

"She kissed me," he said louder, with a determination he didn't feel.

"She kissed you?"

Jake nodded.

"And you've been storming around, growling like a bad-tempered cougar for that?"

"She didn't ask. She just...attacked." Jake cringed inwardly. It sounded ridiculous when he said it out loud. Heat crept up his neck.

"A pretty woman kisses you and you think it's a threat? Isn't that what a man wants her to do?"

Jake shook his head and huffed out a breath. "You wouldn't understand, Shawn. You've never been a real slave. You don't know what it's like."

"You're right, I don't." He stepped forward and, hands on his hips, bent at the waist to catch Jake's eyes. "And the reason I don't," he continued, "is because of Monica. She's not like them, Jake. You should know that by now."

Jake swallowed, hard, and turned his head.

Shawn sighed. "That's it, isn't it?"

Jake flicked a glance at his friend but couldn't maintain eye contact.

He nodded.

"Monica kissed you because she's attracted to you. She's never been the type of woman to be coy. I'm surprised it's taken her this long to approach you—it's not like her. And I'll tell you something else. She took her time, waited until you felt more comfortable here, kept her own desires in check...for you, Jake, to give you time. Because she *cares* how *you feel*. Shit, if I'd known something like that would cause this kind of uproar, I would've never agreed to help."

Jake looked up. He'd suspected Monica had compelled Shawn to lure him to the river, but, stupidly, Jake never considered that Shawn had any say in the matter.

Shawn's lips thinned, and he tilted his head. "Come on. I'll admit I got a little over-zealous, but do you *really* think I just *fell* off my horse?"

"And Rosa...?"

"Yep." Shawn crossed his arms over his chest. "If you're going to be angry with Monica, you might as well be pissed at both of us too."

Jake shook his head, replaying the incident with Shawn at the river in his mind.

Shawn's arms dropped to his sides, and his tone gentled. "No one here wants to hurt you, Jake, and I really believed the two of you would be good for each other. She needs someone loyal and steady, and you need someone kind and understanding. Seemed like the perfect match to me."

Jake's cheeks were flaming now, and the enormous lump in his throat made it difficult to breathe. He closed his eyes and dropped his chin. He wanted the ground to open up beneath his feet and swallow him whole. Not only had he messed up by hurting Kara and Trevor, but he'd angered Shawn and pushed Monica away too.

Monica... Hadn't he been fantasizing about her—albeit reluctantly—on the way to the river that day? Hadn't feeling her lips on his stoked that same fire, almost to the point of an uncontrollable inferno? Didn't he dream about her, long for her, want her more than any woman he'd ever met? Yes, yes, and yes! But he'd messed that up too. He'd let his fear rule his head, and now his heart paid the price. A part of him knew Monica would never hurt him like the others had, but he'd been too afraid, too shattered, to let her prove it.

"Jake..." Shawn began, but Jake didn't let him finish.

"I know," he said in a low, apologetic voice.

"You know what?"

Jake met his friend's gaze. "Everything you said. I know it's true. I know I screwed up. I know I need to fix it." He sighed. "I just...don't know how."

"Well, you can start by apologizing to the crew," Shawn said. "You've been impossible to deal with."

Jake nodded.

"And then Kara and Trevor, but you'd better be careful what you say to them. We're friends, Jake, but I won't let you hurt them again."

"I won't. I swear. I'll take care of all that, but..."

"But what?" Shawn sounded exasperated.

"What do I do about Monica?"

"What do you want to do?"

Feeling his face heat again, Jake dropped his eyes and shrugged.

"Well," Shawn said, "you best get your shit together and figure it out."

23

MONICA ROLLED ONTO HER BACK and glared at the faint light seeping through the window curtains in her bunkhouse room. She groaned softly, yanked the blankets over her head, and then pulled a pillow up to cover her face. She did not want to tackle another day pretending everything was okay.

Just as it had every morning for the last five days, her mind began to comb through the events that had transpired between her and Jake at the river. She'd done the same thing a million times, trying to decipher what had happened, what she'd done wrong, why he'd gotten so angry, and how she felt about it all. She analyzed her actions and reexamined the signals she thought Jake had been giving, but the actual cause of his reaction—though she could guess at least part of it—remained a mystery.

As much as it hurt for him to refuse to talk to her, his hostility and defensiveness angered her too. She'd seen him justifiably lose his cool with Kristine, but Monica had never expected him to treat her the same way. Is that how it would be if they found a way to be together? Would she always be on edge, worried about him losing his temper, worried she might say or do the wrong thing to set him off? Which man was the real Jake Nichols? The kind one who'd bandaged her hand so tenderly when she'd cut it doing dishes? Or the angry, bitter man who'd stalked away from her at the river without a backward glance? And why had he pulled away that day? He knew she wouldn't harm him. So why did he treat her like an enemy? Why wouldn't he at least listen to what she had to say?

Her chest tightened with aggravation and exasperation. Eyes squeezed shut beneath the pillow she gripped over her face, she sucked in air through the layers of cloth and screamed out her frustration. The muffled sound fell flat inside the walls of her room. The act only made her feel marginally better, but it was enough to get her out of bed. Tossing the blankets off, she threw the pillow aside and got up to dress.

Jake's rejection after she kissed him had hurt, but the words he had said were far more painful.

You're just like the rest of them, he'd said, sounding immensely sad and profoundly furious all at once.

Those words, coming from him, had broken her heart that day. But as she rode home alone, anger at the way he'd treated her swirled around the hurt in a confusing mix of emotions.

Had she really misread him so completely?

For a moment, just before he'd raged at her for attempting to take advantage of him, she'd thought he was going to attack her. His eyes had looked murderous, but something had flickered in them and he'd stopped. She'd been too shocked by his reaction to speak, too appalled by his accusations to defend herself. She'd tried approaching him later—wanting to clear up the misunderstanding and apologize for her clearly too-forward behavior—but he wouldn't listen. Fury and pent-up aggression had radiated off him like a man severely wronged, but she hadn't mistreated him. At least, she didn't think so. But after two days of his dark looks and avoidance, she'd begun to question herself.

Now, almost five days since their afternoon at the pool, Jake appeared to have calmed somewhat. Though anger still stewed in his eyes, it seemed to Monica that something about his manner had changed in the last few days. She couldn't place just what, but she wouldn't attempt to question him. She didn't want to cause him any more distress, and, if truth be told, she needed a little time to cool off too.

Pulling her hair up, she used a hair tie to whip it into a quick, messy bun. Loose tendrils framed her face and curled along the back of her neck, but it was good enough for the day she had planned. Shawn had asked her to go fishing this morning after chores, and, not wanting to give in to the sadness clawing at her or allow her anger to rekindle, she had agreed. Maybe it would take her mind off her heartache for a few hours.

Grabbing her straw hat, she opened the door to find a small bouquet of bright, freshly picked wildflowers, tied with a piece of twine, lying on the floor just outside her door. For the last three mornings she'd found just such a surprise waiting for her. She glanced down the hallway—one way, then the other, as she'd done on the other days—but no one was there.

The flowers were a rainbow of purples, pinks, and yellows, the ends trimmed neatly and the stalks arranged in a pleasant display. The first time she'd found them three days ago she'd been surprised, and her inclination—her hope—was to believe Jake had left them as an apology. But seeing him in the dining hall a few minutes later had changed her mind. He'd been sitting with the other workers, a dark frown on his face. He wouldn't meet her gaze, and it didn't seem possible to Monica that this sullen man had secretly left her flowers.

Today, as she had done the other mornings, she gathered up the flowers and carried them to the dining hall.

As she entered the crowded room, she couldn't keep her eyes from seeking out Jake. She saw him on one knee in the corner, head bent, looking very somber as he talked to a little blonde girl sitting on a chair. Shawn was hovering nearby, watching, with the girl's brother by his side. The little girl—Kara, she remembered—appeared upset. Her eyes were downcast, and her arms were wrapped around her middle. Monica didn't know what was going on there, but she was glad when Kara smiled and looked up at Jake with shiny, adoring eyes. The girl nodded eagerly, blonde curls bobbing around her face, and then leaped off the chair to wrap her arms around Jake's neck. He hugged her tight, whispered something that made her giggle, and then let her go. Jake's show of affection with Kara was quickly followed by a grudging handshake with Trevor and a much friendlier one with Shawn, who grinned and slapped Jake on the back.

Monica observed the whole scene from the kitchen, where she stood with her bouquet, unable to look away. There was something very sweet and tender about the whole exchange, and she couldn't help but feel a little pang of jealousy for their easy interactions with Jake. If only he would talk to her and look at her like that again.

She turned away before he could notice her staring and went to collect a vase. She put the wildflowers in water and left them in the hall for everyone to enjoy. She had no idea who had given them to her, but she'd finally decided that Rosa and Shawn must be the culprits. They both knew how much she loved the wildflowers growing around her home, how she'd learned all their names when she was a girl hiking through the hills with her mother, who had loved them just as much. Her two oldest friends had to be the ones leaving the bouquets, probably in an attempt to raise her spirits. Nothing else made sense, and hoping for something different would only cause her heart to break a little more each time.

* * *

"Come on, Monica. Hurry up!"

Shawn was in a joyful mood as he steered his horse along the overgrown trail. He'd been teasing her since they'd left the house about being a sad sack and dragging everyone else down. She'd only glared at his nagging and then smiled when he winked at her. She knew what he was doing, but she wasn't ready to be cheered up. Not completely anyway. She couldn't get Jake's angry words or the horrid look on his face when he had screamed them at her out of her brain.

"What's the hurry?" she called after Shawn, who grinned back over his shoulder at her as he rode ahead and disappeared behind a copse of pine trees and sagebrush. Not in any rush, she kept her mount to a walk and admired the foliage on the surrounding hills. Spires of purple lupine dotted the landscape, and the wildflowers outside her door that morning popped into her head. Tired of the guessing, she decided to ask Shawn about her morning gifts when she caught up to him.

"I'm just anxious to get started!" Shawn's voice shouted from somewhere up ahead. "I promised the cook I'd bring back enough to supplement dinner."

"We'll have to be out here all day to do that!" she shouted back.

"That *was* the idea!"

Monica chuckled.

Shawn's curse rang out from up ahead. She heeled her horse to a faster gait, worried her friend might be in trouble. She rounded the thicket of trees and brush he'd passed a minute before and rushed into the clearing—the same clearing by the pool where she and Jake had gone swimming.

Her chest tightened, and her stomach churned.

Why did he bring me here? she thought, realizing she should've been paying attention to where they were headed. This was the last place she wanted to be.

"What's wrong?" she asked Shawn, forcing her own hurt and anxiety to the back of her mind as she surveyed the glade, looking for the danger she was certain must be nearby. But Shawn was alone and unharmed, standing beside his mount and rummaging through his saddlebags.

"I forgot my hooks," Shaw replied as he dropped the flap on his saddlebags. He kicked the dirt in frustration and then yanked his hat off to run his fingers through his hair, appearing completely put out. He looked up at her. "I'm sorry, Monica. I've got to run back to the bunkhouse." He pulled his hat back on and kept talking as he mounted up. "Stay here. I'll be right back."

"I can ride with you."

"No." The denial was loud and sharp, and she frowned at him. His horse sidled as if unnerved by his rider, but Shawn calmed him easily. "You've been stressed all week," he said. "Just stay here. Lay on the blanket. Take a nap. Relax. I'll be back as quick as I can."

He didn't wait for her to reply. He simply kicked his heels, and the gelding bounded back down the path.

Monica stared after him, considered following, and then shrugged. There was no reason she shouldn't enjoy this spot. She'd always loved it here, and she wasn't going to let Jake Nichols and his unpredictable, hurtful behavior ruin it for her. Instead, she dismounted and unsaddled her horse, then slung her saddlebags over her shoulder, planning to cross to the shady area a few yards from the river.

When she turned, her heart stopped and she gasped.

A man stood in the center of the clearing. A slight smile curved his mouth, and his eyes gleamed at her from beneath his straw cowboy hat.

"Jake?"

"Hello, Monica," he said, and his sexy little grin faltered slightly.

Her eyes drank in his long-limbed form, and her heart gave a little flutter at the tender expression on his face. The vulnerability she saw there stunned her. She shook her head. She couldn't believe he was standing there, staring back at her. "What are you doing here?"

"I came to see you."

"You...? To see *me*?"

"Yeah."

Okay, what? Confusion numbed her brain, and she babbled the first thing that came to mind. "But Shawn will be right back."

"No," Jake said, shaking his head, "he won't."

"He won't?"

"No." He took one step toward her, seemed to think better of it, and stopped.

Monica bit her lip. *He's here to see me?*

Suddenly the day seemed brighter, the air warmer, and the birdsongs a little sweeter.

"I'm so glad to see you," she said.

"Me too."

He pushed his hand into his jeans pocket, and her eyes dropped to the one thing about him she'd overlooked. In his other hand, he held a large bouquet of wildflowers, exactly like those she'd found outside her door. Her gaze lifted to his face. He seemed to be watching her, waiting for something. She searched his eyes for the anger she was sure would still be there, but all she saw was uneasiness.

The night, weeks ago, when they'd walked along the river and Jake had told her the story about how his parents met—about the flowers his father brought to his mother as an apology and his persistence in pursuing her—ran through Monica's mind. A little grin pulled at the corners of her mouth.

"Are those for me?" she asked, tilting her head to indicate the flowers.

He nodded. "I wasn't sure you'd stay long enough for me to give them to you."

"Why wouldn't I?"

"Because I..." He stopped, rubbed his free hand over the back of his neck, and shifted his feet before looking at her again. "You didn't keep any of the others," he said.

"I did. I just shared them with everyone. They were too beautiful, too thoughtful, to hide in my room."

He smiled and stood a little taller. "I thought you gave them away."

"No." She returned his smile, feeling giddiness bubbling in her chest, but a part of her was still anxious and angry. If he thought he could gain her forgiveness with flowers alone, he was mistaken.

Jake turned to the river, and she followed his gaze. The sun glittering on the greenish-blue, undulating surface was almost blinding.

"I'm sorry," he said softly, and she turned back to him, hope filling her chest. His strong jaw was set, and his whole body looked tense, ready to bolt. He ran his hand over his face, his fingers brushing along his neatly trimmed beard. "I'm sorry for being such a complete jackass the other day. I shouldn't have screamed at you like that. Should've never said any of those things. None of it was true, I just...panicked, and I'm so sorry."

Monica's breath caught at the heartfelt tone of his words, but they were just words. "Thank you. I'm really glad you said that, but...how do I know it won't happen again?"

"Give me another chance and I'll prove it to you," he said, his earnest eyes locked on hers. "The other day," he shook his head, "that wasn't me. I'm not like that. I don't lose control and shout at good people for no reason. I know you care, Monica, and I...I'm learning to trust you. I'm just asking you to let me prove you can trust me."

She searched his face, wanting to believe him. Worried he might break her heart again, she hesitated. But then she mentally shook her head. It was already too late to fret over the possibility of a heartache.

The breath she didn't realize she'd been holding whooshed out through her parted lips. Warmth tingled in her heart, and she felt lighter, as if she could float on a breeze.

She smiled, all the fear and irritation draining from her body as she crossed over to him. She took the flowers from his hand—her fingers lightly brushing his sent tingles up her arms—and buried her nose in their foliage. Lifting her face to his, her grin broadened. "You're forgiven."

Jake exhaled in a rush, and his shoulders relaxed. His whole bearing seemed to shift and brighten before her eyes as a lively grin lit his face.

"You don't know what that means to me."

"Tell me."

He sighed, and worry wrinkled his brow. His eyes clouded again, and he looked alarmed by the idea of expressing his inner thoughts, as though by doing so, he might lose the resolve that had brought him out here. Fear that she'd said the wrong thing, yet again, settled in Monica's stomach like a rock. But in the next instant, Jake's back straightened, and he seemed to gather himself up, as if drawing from the deep well of courage she knew he had inside him.

"It means everything," he said, his eyes soft and glowing and his chin set in valiant determination. "It means I wasn't wrong about you. That you are different from the others. It means I don't have to be afraid of the things I'm feeling."

"And what are you feeling?" she asked, almost breathless.

His throat muscles worked as though he was having trouble swallowing. Then he took a deep breath and gave Monica her second pleasant shock of the morning.

"Like I want to try to be the man I used to be. I want to stop being afraid. But I'm not sure how."

24

THE ALMOST DESPERATE LOOK on Jake's determined face tugged at Monica's heart. There was so much more in his eyes she couldn't put a name to, but she thought she understood. He wanted to work past what remained of his fear, not just of women but of physical closeness as well. His fortitude impressed her, yet again, and she felt a swell of pride for his accomplishments—and for the man he was. Her first impulse was to hug him, but she stopped abruptly after thinking better of it. Instead, she ran her hands over her hair and settled for vocal encouragement.

"I think you just took the first big step," she said as her arms dropped to her sides. "But before we go any further, I need to apologize too. I could've...I should've done things differently. I'm sorry I tricked you into coming out here the last time. I'll be more up front in the future."

His eyes and his smile were full of tenderness and gratitude. "Thank you. I appreciate that."

"You're welcome." She returned his smile, wanting to jump up and down from the bubbling excitement swirling in her chest. "Now that we have all the apologies out of the way," she said, the corners of Jake's mouth curving up a bit more as she spoke, "that leaves one more question."

The humor in his expression slipped into a frown as he cocked his head. "And what's that?"

"Why are we out here?" Monica said, still grinning.

He blinked as if stunned by her question. Then he surveyed the area around them, looking more nervous than before, and took a deep breath.

"I thought..." He looked down, shuffled his feet, and tucked his hands into his pockets before meeting her eyes again. "I thought, maybe, we could...pretend this was our first time here and...pick up where we left off."

"You mean go for a swim?" She grinned as she tossed the saddlebags in the direction of the shade and began pulling off her boots. Shawn's insistence that she wear her bathing suit made perfect sense now. And spending the day at the river with Jake was a promising proposition.

He smiled at her enthusiasm and nodded toward the river. "That water's pretty cold."

"We'll keep each other warm."

His mouth flattened, and the joy in his eyes turned bleak and distant.

Too much, Monica thought as she noticed his discomfort. She dropped the bouquet into one of her boots and moved toward him, placing a hand on his arm.

To his credit, he didn't pull away.

"Let's just have fun," she said.

The shadow in his eyes disappeared, and, though slightly dimmed, his sunny expression returned.

A few minutes later, they were splashing through the shallows.

"Damn, this water's *cold*!" Jake had his arms folded tight against his chest, shoulders hunched, knees slightly bent, shivering in his gray briefs like it was thirty below. She had tried not to stare as he got undressed, but she'd been unable to keep from sneaking a peek or three at his glorious physique. Now, her eyes caressed the firm lines and solid muscles of his body as she attempted to ignore the burning need in her own.

"It's not that bad," Monica said, and then purposely dived into the deeper water. When she surfaced, she playfully splashed water at him.

"Hey!" he shouted, feigning irritation. "Keep it up and I'll go back to shore."

"Big baby," she teased. "Come on, just bite the bullet and get in."

He tilted his head and gave her a peeved look, then raised his eyebrows and took one exaggeratedly small step deeper.

She laughed and swam away, but she kept glancing back as, bit by bit, he made his way to the drop-off.

He's so adorable, she thought fondly, and she smiled at his playfulness.

As he took another step, Monica's eyes drank in his brawny arms and his wide chest. She bit her lip and enjoyed how his gray cotton briefs hugged his lean hips and how they did little to hide the tempting bulge between the long, thick muscles of his thighs. He made her mouth water. What she wouldn't give to have him smile at her while she ran her hands over those broad shoulders again. She wanted to rake her fingers through the soft mat of hair on his sculpted chest, feel his body harden and respond to her...or simply have him hold her close once more.

Take it easy, she cautioned herself. *He's not ready for brazen Monica. Not yet.*

He was up to his belly button and shivering when she returned to splash him again. This time, when she tried to dart away, he dived in after her, dragging them both under.

"Are you *trying* to drown me?" she spluttered as they resurfaced. She rubbed water out of her eyes to glare at him in mock aggravation.

"Just giving you some of your own medicine."

She groaned and splashed him again.

"Hey!" He ducked and then reached out to pull her close. Her hand clutched at his shoulder, and one of his arms automatically circled her waist, while his other arm cut back and forth through the water to keep them afloat.

The mischievous mood evaporated as their bodies converged and sparks of passion burst to life, igniting the air around them. Every tiny hair on Monica's body seemed to stand at attention all at once. Her skin grew hotter despite the chill of the water.

She got lost in his hazel-green eyes staring back into hers. His expression looked so...vulnerable. Her heart ached for him, but she wouldn't let it show.

He shuddered and licked his lips.

"I don't know if I..." he began, but his words faded.

She ran her fingers along his clenched jaw until her hand came to rest on his neck. His rapid pulse thudded against her palm. She frowned and took a deep breath.

"I understand," she said. Unable to take the ghost of anguish in his gaze, she dropped her eyes. She didn't want him to see how much his pain affected her. "I wish you hadn't experienced their cruelty, Jake," she said softly.

She felt him tense against her, and she looked up once more.

"It's not pity," she said in a rush. "I just wish I had been there to help you. I wish..."

"You wish what?"

"That I'd met you first."

"Wishing doesn't change anything." He shifted and kicked toward shore, and Monica sensed he was angry again. Not like he was the last time they were here, but still annoyed.

"No, it doesn't," she said hurriedly, allowing him to drag them both through the water, "but that doesn't mean we can't enjoy something now."

He stopped, and she could tell he was standing, even though the water still lapped at his neck and shoulders. His eyes were hard when he turned his face back to her. "And what can we have now?"

She shrugged. "Whatever you want."

"What *I* want...?" His brows lifted, and he sounded stunned.

"Yes, Jake. I'm not going to force you into anything."

He frowned again and stared at her as if she were a strange bug he had never seen before.

Dread balled up in her stomach. Had she misread him again?

"You said you wanted to stop being afraid." She said it like a question.

He nodded slowly.

"So, start with me." Her voice cracked. She'd known this would be difficult, but she didn't expect to suffer such and overwhelming sense of desperation. "I like you, Jake," she said, holding his face in her hands while his arms kept her afloat, and she gazed into his eyes. "I think that's obvious, but I don't want you to think you don't have a choice. You do. If you want to get to know me, if you want to hold me and kiss me, you may. But if you don't, if you'd rather finish your job with nothing more between us, you may do that too. I'll be disappointed, but I'll understand."

He was still frowning, and although he appeared calm, his breathing was heavy.

Monica searched his face, but all she saw was anxiety and suspicion. She smoothed her fingers over his brow, and he swallowed hard. She brushed his hair from his forehead, traced the shape of his ear with one finger, and then ran her palm over his neck. His skin felt warm and smooth.

He swallowed and then shivered. Something that she couldn't quite place flashed in his eyes.

"Jake?"

"You're giving me a choice?" The question was laced with disbelief.

"Yes. It isn't a command or a requirement."

"I'm a slave," he rasped.

"No, Jake, you're a man. And I'm just a woman who finds you interesting. If you don't feel the same way about me or if you're not ready to, that's okay."

He snorted, and she smiled. She already knew he found her attractive.

"Do you feel the same, Jake?"

He gazed at her with lowered brows but didn't reply.

"Jake...?"

"What happens later?"

"Later?"

"Yeah, in a few months when you're obligated to send me back?"

"I can't make you any promises, Jake, as much as I'd like to. But I can try."

"There's nothing you can do," he said bitterly. "When the time comes, you'll send me back and then forget I ever existed."

Her hands clutched his shoulders, and she shook her head. Clearly, he needed more time for his mistrust to dissipate, even with her. She ignored the irritation tightening her jaw and shook her head.

"I won't forget, and I don't want to send you back," she said, unable to conceal the despair in her voice.

"But you can't keep me either. You can't afford me, and it wouldn't be fair to risk everyone else back at the ranch. Miss Cain is a vicious enemy," he said, unconsciously slipping into the respectful form of address his real Mistress required of her slaves.

Monica stared at him. He was right. If she did that, if she kept him without Darla's approval or some kind of adequate payment, there would be consequences for them all.

Her chest constricted painfully. She wanted to cry, and she never cried... Well, almost never.

"I'll think of something," she said, her voice choked with emotion.

Jake didn't reply. He only stared back at her, worry on his brow.

She pressed her hand to his cheek and swept her thumb slowly over his lips.

"You're an attractive man," she unintentionally mumbled aloud. Then she sucked in a breath as her eyes snapped up to his, afraid he'd release her and retreat.

Instead, his eyebrows arched up and he looked at her as if she'd lost her mind.

Happy he didn't pull away, she sighed and, with an inquisitive grin on her face, cocked her head at his quizzical look. "What? Do you think I'm lying?"

"I think you need your eyes checked."

She laughed, glad he was joking with her again.

"Humble too," she said, her thumb sliding over his lips once more. "You're an interesting man, Jake Nichols. Do you know that?"

"You may have mentioned it before."

She returned his grin and brushed a gentle kiss on his lips. He didn't resist. Though she could feel the tautness in every part of him she touched, he didn't move, only held her. She pulled back but hovered close enough for her breath to warm his cheek.

"I promise you, Jake," she said, her thumb once again sweeping over his mouth, "I won't forget you, and if you do end up with Darla again, I won't stop trying to get you back...for good next time. I swear."

He held his breath, and Monica could feel his heart thrashing in his chest.

"God, you're so..." he said and shook his head as if at a loss for words. His searching eyes delved into hers. For a long minute, her breath seemed to halt, and all time ceased with it. His pupils dilated, the irises darkening to forest green flecked with amber. Her heart stuttered. Raw desire filled his gaze, burning out every other emotion in the changing hazel depths. She couldn't blink, couldn't look away from the dazzling transition. Trapped by the expression of naked need now etched on his face, she hoped she would never escape.

One instant, he hesitated. The next, his restraint broke. Heat shot down to her toes as his head lowered to hers. She barely had time to suck in a breath before he kissed her. Not a soft, gentle pressing of his lips, but a hard, needy conquering of her mouth. Her lips parted eagerly, allowing his demanding tongue to capture and ravage the moist cavern. He tasted faintly of coffee. His beard felt course against her cheeks, the mustache part of his goatee tickling her upper lip. His musky scent surrounded her, filled her senses. His lips were firm and warm as they moved over hers, inviting the response she was only too happy to give. She moaned into his mouth.

Her body melted into him. Her arms circled his neck. She pulled herself closer, giving him everything, every ounce of the passion surging through her. His arms tightened, crushing her breasts into the broad expanse of his chest, but she didn't care. She wanted this. To have him kiss her as if he'd die if he didn't. To hold her as if he'd never let her go. She used the fierceness of his embrace to mold herself more completely against him, shifting to give him better access to her mouth. She surrendered completely to the intensity of his ardent kiss. Anything he wanted from her right now he could have. She was eager to please him, but worry that he might pull away again pecked at a tiny part of her mind.

His calloused hand skimmed over her back, setting off a wave of prickles along her skin as he continued downward to her hip, her thigh. She automatically lifted her legs and wrapped them around his lean waist. She thrust her hips forward into the hard shaft barely contained by the thin cotton of his briefs. Instinctively, she ground her softness against him, and he moaned with pleasure.

Thrown off-balance, either by Monica or the swirling current of the river, Jake stumbled over the rock-strewn floor but then righted himself.

Their lips never parted.

The warm sun was a welcome sensation on the chilled flesh of her back and shoulders as she clung to him. She couldn't get close enough to him. Couldn't get enough *of* him. She slipped her arm between their bodies, her hand sliding down over his belly button, searching for the hot, thick rod she wanted so badly to free from the confines of his underwear.

His fingers combed through her hair, once, twice, and then he clenched the soft tresses at the back of her head in his fist, holding her fast.

He started to shake in earnest.

A thrill of excitement shot through Monica. *Finally! He's opening up, about to share all of himself with me. There'll be no going back after this.*

She didn't want to go back. She wanted this. She wanted him.

His trembling worsened, and he moaned deep in his throat, not a cry of passion or joy this time, but of torment. In the next instant, his lips ripped from hers and his arms released her. He disentangled her legs from around his waist, pushed her back with gentle urgency, and then turned away.

Monica stared dumbly at the shifting muscles of his exposed back as she swept her arms through the water and kicked to keep from sinking. Several long white marks marred the strong planes of his back. She hadn't noticed them before, maybe because there'd been too much going on. This time, however, she couldn't help but see the fading proof of the torture inflicted upon him. The welts and bruises he'd arrived with had healed, but these scars would take years to diminish. She started to reach out, to trace the damaged flesh, but she pulled her hand back before touching him. Her throat thickened, and she swallowed a knot of sorrow for the agony he had suffered. Suspecting he wouldn't take kindly to the sympathy she felt for him, she remained silent.

He made no move to go to shore; he just stood, shaking, his head down, one arm braced against a protruding boulder.

"Jake?" Her soft inquiry made him jump, but he didn't reply. She heard him pulling in deep breaths, saw his back heave as if in great distress.

Alarmed by his reaction, she swam around to his front. The slanting floor of the pool, higher on the shore side, enabled her to stand and face him.

He wouldn't look at her. He trembled uncontrollably, and she could swear he was crying.

Maybe he is. The thought frightened her. What other terrible things had happened to this strong, intelligent man to make him weep?

"Jake?" She reached for him and touched his arm, but he flinched away and she dropped her hand.

"I ca-can't..." he stuttered. "I can't...can't..." He still wouldn't meet her eyes.

"Can't what? What is it?"

He heaved in a deep breath and then words tumbled out of him. "I can't do this. I can't do this with you, with anyone. I'm s-sorry. I-I can't." He squeezed his eyes closed and sucked in air through clenched teeth, but he said no more.

"My God, Jake, what did they do to you?"

He gave a stuttering chuckle that contained no mirth, only despair.

"Look at me, Jake," Monica ordered, her voice sharp from the anger she felt over what they'd done to him. He balked at her tone, and she deliberately softened it. "Please, Jake, look at me."

He dragged his fingers over his eyes, pinched the bridge of his nose, and wiped at his face before his hand dropped to his side. He hesitated, but, at length, he met her gaze.

"We'll go slow," she told him and reached for his hand. He flinched again at her soft touch, but he didn't pull out of her grasp. "I won't make you do anything you don't want to do. I told you, Jake: I won't hurt you."

His eyes shifted from her face to their joined hands and back again, but he remained silent and shuddering.

"Right now," she said as she gently pulled on his hand, encouraging him to step closer, "let me help you."

His hand rested on her hip now, and one of hers slid over his hard muscles up to his shoulder. Her other hand cupped his cheek.

He stared at her in disbelief, fear and self-loathing clear in his eyes, but something else lingered there too, a need for consolation, for understanding, for love. Monica silently vowed to give him everything he needed, and more.

"Please, Jake, let me care for you."

His expression crumpled, and he leaned into her. He buried his face in her damp hair and his arms circled her waist. His body shook with his quiet sobs as she held him, murmuring soft words of comfort and reassurance.

They stayed that way for several minutes, until he seemed calmer. He was still trembling with shock and fear and shame when she leaned back against the strong band of his arms, still encircling her waist, and held his face in her hands.

"Hey," she said with a smile, "let's get you out of this water. I can't tell if you're shaking because of me or the cold."

He chuckled and nodded. His arms dropped away, and she took his hand to led him onto the shore.

Monica grabbed her saddlebags. Reaching inside, she yanked out a quilt from one side, which she tossed to the ground, and two towels from the other, handing one to Jake.

"Dry your hair," she said and went behind him to wipe down his body. "Let's warm you up."

She enjoyed pampering him. It gave her a reason to touch him, although she was careful and tried not to notice the assorted scars all over his body. She dried him off and then wound the long towel around his lean waist, tucking the end in to hold the cloth in place. He made no move to stop her, but he watched her every action with hooded eyes. He was still partially aroused—it was hard to miss the thick stiffness jutting against the wet cotton of his briefs—but she didn't comment. His physical reaction, however, gave her hope that the wounds inflicted on his mind would heal.

She took the other towel from his hands, quickly dried her own hair, and then draped it around her body like a sarong.

"Stay here a minute," she told him and went to spread the quilt out beside a tree. She situated the coverlet so the majority of it was still in the sun, and sat down on the edge closest to the tree trunk. She motioned for him to come over. He did, and she asked him to lie down. "The sun and the blanket will warm you up."

"What about you?" It was the first words he'd spoken for several minutes, and she smiled.

"I'll be fine for now," she said and waved a hand at the quilt.

He obeyed without another word.

When he lay back, she rested his head on her lap. He resisted, but with a soft word from Monica, he allowed her to cradle him on her thighs.

His shivering had not dissipated, and she wondered if he shook because he was still distressed, or if the chill of the water had seeped inside him—or both.

When he lay on his back, his big hands resting on his chest, she reached out and pulled the other end of the blanket over him. He was a tall man, but the wide blanket covered his long body down to his toes.

Jake closed his eyes and swallowed as she stroked his hair, massaged his temple, and traced the edge of one ear. He shivered, and she wondered if it was from fear or from the familiarity of her touch.

At least he isn't running away, she thought

She glanced at his face. Except for his occasional quaking, he looked peaceful, as if he'd fallen asleep. She hoped he had, if only to relax a little and find a bit of peace.

She wondered what had brought on his sudden panic attack and his withdrawal from her. Was it holding her, kissing her? Or was it her kissing him? Touching him? Was it that those actions generally preceded intercourse, and the possibility of that act, even with her, frightened him? And if so, why? Did she remind him of the women who had hurt him? Did he see Darla or her friends in his mind while kissing her? Did she remind him of someone he hated, or someone he lost? Or was it something else altogether?

Monica turned her head to gaze at the river, wishing she could ask Jake what had been done to him, ask about the internal pain he clearly had endured. Maybe if she could get him to talk about what tormented him she could help him overcome it—but she feared doing so would only chase him back into hiding.

A soft snore drew her attention. She glanced down at Jake's slumbering face and smiled. He twitched slightly as if reacting to a dream, but he didn't wake. Gently, she brushed his hair back from his forehead once more, glad he'd found a little escape and pleased that he felt safe enough in her company to fall asleep.

She sighed and rested her head against the tree trunk behind her. The only way she could help him was to be patient and understanding. To let him know he truly could trust her, to allow him to heal at his own pace. And the best way she could do that was to give him a permanent home. She'd already written out a list of options, and they rolled through her mind on a regular basis. She shook her head, feeling overwhelmed by the task, as she did every time she thought about it. But she wouldn't give up. She couldn't. She would save him. There had to be a way.

25

HE COULDN'T MOVE. Steel shackles encircled his raw wrists, and the hard metal gouged into his chafed flesh as the chains held his arms wide. His ankles were similarly bound to anchors in the stone floor, imprisoning him completely. He couldn't protect himself, couldn't forget what had happened, couldn't stop what was coming next. The chains clinked softly as a tremor shook him. A vise of hopelessness crushed him as he stood, naked and defenseless, before his tormentor.

"What's the first rule, slave?" Her voice slithered over his battered flesh, reached inside him, and gripped his terrified heart.

He squeezed his eyes closed.

His jaw clenched.

Sweat slid down his chest, over his ribs and belly, while he battled with the drug surging through his veins.

"Answer me!" she screamed and struck him.

His body convulsed from the pain she inflicted, and the hated word burst from his lips. "Obey."

"Obey who?"

"You, Mistress... Y-You," he panted.

She continued to grill him about her rules, and he answered with a quivering voice he couldn't control. When he stumbled over a response, she hurt him, over and over again.

"P-Please," he finally begged, knowing it would do no good, but unable to stop himself. "Please, stop. P-Please...no more. Please..."

"Jake..." Another voice called him. "Jake!"

"No!" he screamed, pain cutting through him. "No!"

"JAKE?" MONICA SHOUTED as she wiggled her legs out from under his head and gently lowered it to the blanket. Then she sat back on her heels while he thrashed in his sleep. She'd been happy to let him rest, but now she wondered if letting him drift off had been such a good idea. Afraid of touching him again and making his distress even worse, she knelt beside him and held her fisted hands in her lap. "Jake, wake up. Please wake up!"

His arms waved erratically through the air.

His eyes popped open.

He pushed up onto his elbows, seeming disorientated as he glanced around.

"We're at the river," Monica told him, and his panicked gaze locked on her. "You fell asleep. You were dreaming."

He cursed and closed his eyes as he collapsed onto his back once more. He wiped the sweat and tears from his face.

Her aching heart squeezed a little tighter.

His hand covered his eyes. He looked mortified. The tenseness in his jaw said he was also angry.

Another tremor rocked him, and Monica touched his cheek.

He flinched and dropped his hand.

"You're safe, Jake," she whispered, and his eyes opened. He looked up at her with a blank expression, the gentle soul of the man inside him shuttered from her view.

She smiled tremulously, uncertain if she should speak again.

He looked away, and she settled her hands back in her lap as he stared up into the branches of the tree shading them. Studying his profile, she thought he still seemed haunted by the nightmare, reliving whatever horror he'd once suffered. She wanted to help him, but she knew she could do nothing beyond being there when he was ready for...whatever he needed.

Wondering if he would emotionally and physically retreat from her again, Monica glanced out at the slow-running river where it fed into the small pool, while she sat quietly beside him. Allowing him to recover from whatever tormented him, she stared at the greenish-blue water swirling over rocks and against the banks, making tiny whitecaps as it slowly made its way downstream. After a few twists and turns, the watercourse would eventually reach the small town where Darla Cain lived.

Determined to give Jake however much time he needed, Monica waited while she watched the water roll by, and her mind returned to how she might convince Darla to give him up. Though there were several scenarios, she was beginning to think only one was a viable option.

"I'm sorry," he mumbled, interrupting her musings.

She turned her head to look down at him, but he was still staring at the leaf-laden branches overhead. "For what?" she asked.

"For..." He waved his arms frantically through the air as he had while asleep, still not looking her way. He took a steadying breath. "I hope I didn't frighten you."

"A little," she admitted, "but I was worried for you. Was it another nightmare about...Darla?" She knew she was pushing, but he'd said he wanted to work on his fear, and trusting her was part of that.

He inhaled deeply, as if priming himself for a difficult task, and let it out in a rush. "Yes."

"I'm sorry." She pressed her hand to his shoulder, and he turned his head to meet her eyes. He appeared less distant, and she read insecurity and doubt in his expression.

"Do you really...care about me?" He sounded like a lost little boy in need of love and reassurance, and her throat grew tight at the look in his haunted eyes.

"Yes, I do," she said without hesitation, and then tilted her head curiously. "Why is that so hard to believe?"

His gaze returned to the leafy branches overhead. "Because they tortured all the trust out of me."

Her heart split apart at the bleak tone of his voice.

"That's not true," she said, and his eyes were sharp when they met hers again. She gave him a gentle smile and traced her fingers along his clenched jaw. "You're trusting me now."

He held her gaze for a long moment before saying, "You're...different."

"How?" she asked as her brows drew together.

Again, he paused. A muscle in his jaw twitched, and she could tell he was fighting an internal battle.

She saw the decision to speak in his eyes before he opened his mouth.

"I want to trust you. I *want* to believe you."

Even as her heart jumped with joy at that revelation, her chest ached at the earnestness of his words.

"That's what I want too."

"You want more than that."

Her brows went up this time. "Don't you?"

He averted his face and lay with his head beside her knees, his expressive eyes closed once more. "Yes..." His reply was so soft she almost didn't hear him.

"That's a good thing, Jake," she said as her fingers caressed his furrowed brow.

His lids lifted, and his head swiveled toward her. "But I'm not sure if I can ever..." His voice faded, and he swallowed, shaking his head slightly. "After what they did, what they made me do... I don't know if the memories will ever leave me, if I can let it go." He made a frustrated noise in his throat as he kicked the blanket away from his legs and sat up to face her. He took her hands in his, rested them on her thighs, and stared gravely into her eyes.

On his knees in front of her, he looked so big and capable, his bare chest and muscular legs so strong and very male, but as he shared his fears, his expression was utterly vulnerable. "If I go back," he said slowly, "they'll destroy the little bit of me that's still left. If I stay, I may never be able to give you what you want, what you need, what you deserve."

His concern for her and her feelings told Monica everything, and her resolve to help him intensified.

"I deserve the man I want," she replied as a desperate need to protect and support him swelled within her. "And I want you, Jake. I will find a way to make Darla let you go. And you will heal. I can wait however long you need."

His hands tightened around her fingers, and she realized her whole body was shaking with the strength of the emotions surging through her.

"You're trembling," he said quietly, his troubled eyes searching her face.

She nodded. "You do that to me," she said with a shaky smile.

He shifted their position by sitting with his back to the tree and pulling her into his lap. Then he wrapped her in his arms and pressed a light kiss to the top of her head. "I didn't mean to upset you."

She rested her cheek on his shoulder, her forehead nestled against his neck, and listened to the steady beat of his heart. Inhaling deeply, she closed her eyes and soaked in the warmth of his body, his musky, masculine scent, and the wonderful feeling of him all around her.

"That's not what I meant." She tapped his chest and tilted her face toward his. "It's not a bad thing, Jake."

His lips curved up in a shy yet knowing smile, and he lowered his chin in a brief nod. His arms gave her a quick squeeze as he rested his cheek on top of her head once more. "I'm glad."

They stayed that way for some time, talking and laughing. Then, because no one was expecting them back at the ranch, they went for another swim, played, and enjoyed each other for the rest of the afternoon.

After their talk beneath the tree, Monica sensed a change in Jake. He seemed calmer, more at ease than before, and the idea filled her with hope.

When the sun sagged toward the distant mountains, it was time to go, and they packed up unenthusiastically. Since Shawn had apparently ridden off with Jake's gelding, they would have to ride back together on Monica's horse. As Jake saddled up, Monica approached him from behind, and he turned to face her. His expression seemed uncertain, but then determination tightened his features. He reached out to run his fingers through her damp hair, stepping in closer as he did so. She allowed her head to tilt back with the slight tug of his hand, loving the small sensation. Staring into her eyes, he wrapped his arms around her, pulling her against him. She went willingly, biting her lip with anxious anticipation. *Was he finally making the first move?* Was he going to kiss her again?

Oh, please kiss me again!

When his head lowered to hers, Monica got her wish. His lips were still cool from the water, his skin and clothes a bit damp, but she didn't care. His mouth was hot, and the fresh sent of the outside lingered on him. He held her a little too tight, almost desperately, while his mouth ravaged hers with heated urgency, but she didn't mind. She was right where she wanted to be.

The basket she was holding dropped from her fingers as one of his hands delved into the hair at her nape. The other slid down her back, drawing her fully against him. Her heart seemed to swell with the surge of joy and desire his tender actions aroused in her. A heatwave washed through her body, and prickles ran down her spine to settle low in her belly. Shuddering with the force of her emotions, she surrendered to him as he gently bent her backward over his encircling arm.

He had touched her periodically over the last few hours, testing himself and her. She didn't press him for more, only smiled at him as heat radiated through her with every small contact. She couldn't remember smiling so much in one afternoon. But this! This was what they'd been working toward: Jake taking control of his fears and opening himself to her, trusting her, taking the next physical step to conquering the ghosts that still haunted him.

She clung to him as his lips lingered on her mouth, and every second her admiration and affection for this man grew tenfold. Without a doubt, his fear still hounded him, but he was trying. He would never have pushed himself this far otherwise.

The idea warmed her more.

When he ended the kiss, he rested his forehead against hers, gasping like a field runner after a race. He was trembling, but she didn't sense apprehension or regret.

"I've wanted to do that for months," he said, his breath warm against her face.

"Me too," she replied, then leaned back a little. "Are you all right?"

His hands cradled her face, and a tender, sweet smile tugged at the corners of his mouth.

"Better than you know," he said and placed another quick kiss on her lips before releasing her. "We should go."

He jammed his hat on his head and mounted the gelding. Once he was seated, Monica handed him the basket, and he tied it to the saddle. Then he jerked his boot free of the stirrup and reached down to help her mount. She put her foot in the vacated stirrup, and he hauled her up behind him. Wrapping her arms around his middle, she snuggled up close to his hard back. His free hand came to rest on both of hers as he heeled the horse into motion. His whole body seemed to relax, melding with hers as they swayed together in the saddle. She peeked over his shoulder, curious to see his expression, and was pleased to find that a sunny smile adorned his lips as he directed the horse down the path home. Seeing him so cheerful made her grin too. She sighed as she laid her cheek against the hard warmth of his back, happy and content for the first time in far too long. If only every day could be like this.

Maybe for a little while, she thought with a giddy little thrill, *it will be.*

26

WHEN MONICA AND JAKE RETURNED to the homestead, Shawn's overly interested gaze had followed them. He stood on the main house's new deck, nodding sagely and grinning like the Cheshire cat as they rode toward the empty barn. At the time, Monica had been thankful he didn't make any further comment. The next morning at breakfast, however, was another story.

The dining hall was mostly empty as Monica and Jake sat side by side, comfortably enjoying each other's company. They were discussing the next steps in her house's construction when Shawn slid into the chair next to Monica. With a wide, mischievous grin, he unceremoniously pushed so far into Monica's space that he practically shoved her into Jake's lap.

"You know," he said in a conspiratorial whisper only she and Jake could hear, "you two can sit a little closer now. Don't be shy."

Jake's face reddened as he glanced around at the few people still in the room, but he only glowered at Shawn.

Monica was more direct.

"Damn it, Shawn," she scolded, pushing against his chest. "Stop clowning around. Don't you have work to do?"

He grinned, got up, and, with his brown eyes twinkling, patted Jake's shoulder. "Good work, buddy," he said and then strolled off.

"Jackass," Jake grumbled under his breath, but there was no heat in it.

Monica looked at him. "What's that about?"

He shrugged. "Nothing, he's just being an idiot."

Monica lowered her chin. "I'm sorry about that."

Jake reached under the table to squeeze her hand. Her breath caught at his touch, and she lifted her gaze.

"Don't worry about it," he said with a soft smile. "It's not like he shouted across the room. He's just Shawn being Shawn." He glanced over his shoulder as he squeezed her hand again, then brushed his lips against her cheek. Stunned by his open show of affection, she, too, quickly scanned the room, but no one appeared to have seen a thing. Though she trusted most of the people here, Monica knew they must be cautious in revealing their budding relationship, especially to strangers. It wouldn't do for a stray word of their involvement to reach Darla's ears. Jake knew that as well as she did, yet his act warmed her. A lot. Though he was still somewhat hesitant, he seemed more willing to touch her now, and he didn't balk when she touched him.

As she watched Jake leave the dining hall, her mind turned again to their time at the river the day before. When she had kissed him, he'd seemed as excited as she had been, but something happened. Maybe her over eagerness in kissing him set him off. Could it be the simple act of *her* kissing *him* in the first place? He hadn't seemed troubled when he initiated their ardent embrace just before they mounted up to head home. Maybe her aggressiveness is what triggered him. If she was going to avoid upsetting him again, she needed to know. She could ask, but even if she had been at fault, she suspected he would only deny it to spare her feelings. Maybe she should be more reserved in showing her affection and pay more attention to his reactions. Maybe she should just ask his permission next time and see if that made a difference. If it did, she could work with that. If not, then she'd have to try something else.

After he had broken down at the river and allowed her to comfort him, Monica felt closer to him than ever. Her eyes regularly sought him out, and just looking at him made her heart rate kick up. Whenever their gazes collided, his expression softened and his eyes lit up—that look could only be classified as longing, and it always set off excited butterflies in her belly. Scorching heat would sweep through her, leaving her tingling in all the right places, and her skin became so damn sensitive she could almost feel his eyes caressing her.

Despite the sensual sparks that zapped between them, or possibly because of them, Jake seemed a little unnerved by her presence. He didn't avoid her as he had previously, but he sometimes seemed more restless than usual. He had even jumped once when she approached him with a question. She wasn't sure if his nervousness was because of her or something else altogether, but either way, when she did catch his eye, he would nod and return her smile, and that was enough for her.

One evening, almost a week after their day at the river, Monica asked Jake to give her a tour of the nearly completed aqueduct system. Everyone else had finished work and gone to the river to cool off, so they were alone.

As he escorted her across the yard and around the project area, Jake walked her through the new watercourse's design. He explained how they used the natural landscape to ensure the water wouldn't cause backflow or stagnate when the river ran low, but she hardly heard a word he said. As he spoke, he guided her around with his hand resting familiarly on her back. All she could think about, while the inviting heat of his palm burned through her shirt and spread over her flesh, was what it would be like to have that warm, calloused hand sliding over her bare skin. When he touched her, her blood heated, and she found it hard to breathe. She tried to read him for signs of what he was feeling, tried to follow his words as he explained the project, but her attraction to him only grew worse the longer he touched her. All she wanted to do was plaster herself against him, draw his head down, and once again press her lips to his.

"Hey," he said, stopping their forward progress and turning her to face him. His hands gently gripped her shoulders as he searched her face. "Are you all right?"

Silently cursing herself, she looked up into his concerned eyes. The scent of him filled her nose, and she was suddenly assaulted with a desperate desire to taste him. All of him, not just his wide, firm mouth, but his entire hard body.

"Monica?"

She trembled, and his hands tightened on her arms as his thick sandy-brown brows drew down over his nose.

"What's wrong?" He sounded worried now too.

"Nothing," she blurted out, still a bit shaken by the surge of desire that rocked her moments before. "I...I was just...distracted."

He smiled softly, his eyes filling with understanding, and Monica's heart fluttered.

"Me too," he said as his big, rough-skinned hands slid up and down her arms in a slow, comforting caress that she enjoyed a little too much. Studying his expression, she thought he really did know what had caused her to shiver, and he hadn't been unnerved by it. The realization heartened her.

He released her, and they started walking again. His hand, once again, casually rested on the small of her back, and another round of sparks shot straight to her core.

"Hey, Jake," Shawn's teasing voice sounded from only a few feet away. "Go ahead—give her a kiss, no one's looking."

Jake and Monica both jumped when Shawn spoke. They glanced at the jokester and then around the empty yard, as if they'd been caught doing something wrong.

"Two little love birds sitting in a tree..." Shawn sing-songed the childish rhyme only loud enough for them to hear as he wrapped his arms around their shoulders and inserted his face between them. He made smooching noises and winked at Monica, a toothy grin splitting his handsome face.

"Love you," he crooned in a joyful tune. He placed a quick peck on Monica's cheek, swung his head to smirk at both of them, and then dashed away toward the river.

Monica silently cursed Shawn for the interruption. His antics, however innocent, caused Jake to drop his hand from her back and increase the distance between them as they strolled toward the river to join everyone else.

She would have to wait for another day to discover more about this man she couldn't stop thinking about.

FISHING THE FINAL NAIL from his tool belt to secure the room's last piece of drywall, Jake pounded it in and paused to mop his sweaty brow with the back of his forearm. Working alone upstairs today, he had little distraction, so all day his thoughts had been on Monica. In his mind, he saw her pulling off her tank top by the river, shimmying out of her cutoffs, revealing her wonderfully feminine curves. But in his imaginings, she didn't stop there. She stared at him with those twinkling eyes of hers as she slowly pulled on one end of the strap that held her suit-top up. His heart tattooed in his chest and his breath caught as he pictured her suit dropping to the ground, baring the luscious bounty of her creamy breasts with their rosy pink tips for him to savor. She smiled at him with that knowing look of hers, as if completely aware of what she was doing to him with her little show. And he loved it!

Then the vision changed. They were in her bedroom—the room in which he now worked—and she was still smiling at him. She slowly walked toward him, her beautiful breasts swaying slightly with every step...

He groaned and tried to remember what he was supposed to be doing. He wanted to keep thinking about her—hell, he never wanted to stop—but his fantasies were not only distracting him from his job, they were also causing some physical discomfort in his body's lower regions.

He banished the image and shook his head. He needed to get out of this bedroom before the erotic images dancing provocatively through his brain drove him mad.

Earlier that morning, he had remembered how she'd trembled at his touch as they strolled around the yard the day before. That recollection started his mind down the paths he couldn't seem to avoid.

"I was just distracted," she had said. Heat and a feeling of bubbling joy had exploded inside him at those words. He'd wanted to pull her into his arms and kiss her, but he hadn't. They were out in the open where anyone could see, so he'd settled for placing his hand on the small of her back again as he continued his explanation of the new waterway. He was thankful for that choice when Shawn had showed up to harass them. But Monica's words had made the ribbing worth it.

That memory led him to the other one he couldn't stop thinking about either.

A little over a week had passed since Jake's interlude with Monica at the river, since she'd seen a small part of his torment and hadn't turned away from him in disgust. He'd been so embarrassed by his emotional breakdown and then by the nightmare that he'd wanted to crawl into a hole and hide from the revulsion he expected to see on her face. But, instead, she had treated him the way she always did—like a man, a person. He'd felt more comfortable touching her since that day, and, as he had in the yard yesterday, he took the opportunity whenever he could, even if somewhat slyly.

He'd also quickly discovered after their return from the river that, though Shawn approved of Jake's interest in Monica, the man was relentless in teasing him about it—though, thankfully, he'd been discreet so far. Yet at first, Shawn's jokes had made Jake uncomfortable, but after days of it now, he'd become somewhat used to Shawn and the situation—if still a bit uneasy about how much Shawn seemed to know or guess. There were times over the last several days, however, that Jake had shaken his head at Shawn's antics. He'd even wondered aloud whether his friend would ever mature past eight years of age. Shawn had merely grinned, gave Jake a wink, slapped him on the back, and justified his question by jokingly replying, "Wouldn't you like to know!"

Jake shook his head again now and chuckled at the memory.

Ever since their afternoon at the pool, and every smile, touch and tiny connection since then, Jake couldn't get Monica out of his head. Being in her soon-to-be bedroom only made matters worse. Sensual images of what the chamber would look like with her in it and what they might do here together someday kept filling his head.

Yeah, right... he thought cynically. *Someday. If by some miracle I'm allowed to stay.* He shook his head in defeated disbelief, and regret swept through him as he stared at the unfinished floor. *And if I can ever forget what I did.*

A woman's weeping resonated in his head.

Anna...

He pictured Anna's soft brown eyes, wide and shiny with tears.

Just do it... That short, bitter statement echoed in his mind, and his chest grew heavy, his breathing rapid and shallow. He squeezed his eyes shut as remembered pain sliced through him.

Mentally recoiling from the scene in his head, he looked out the open French doors at the distant mountains, using the view to drag himself back to the present. A gentle breeze swept in and tugged at his pale-blue chambray shirt as he focused on the dark emerald of the evergreens blanketing the hills, the lawn behind the house, the deck just outside the door...Monica's bedroom.

Slowly, his breathing and heartbeat returned to normal.

Monica. His heart lightened, and the iron bands of guilt and sorrow loosened around his chest.

I deserve the man I want. Her words, spoken with such conviction as they talked beside the river, had broken through his walls of suspicion and doubt, gotten him thinking about a life that he'd probably never get a chance to live. But despite his worries, he couldn't stop thinking about it, about her. He couldn't keep from hoping for that shiny, possible future.

During their day by the pool, he'd allowed himself to explore not only physical closeness with a woman he actually felt attracted to, but also emotional affection—for the first time in years. It wasn't exactly intimate, aside from the few hugs and kisses they shared, but it had felt that way. Better still, their interactions made him optimistic that, someday, he might be normal again. His willingness to push his boundaries with Monica proved that one day he could be with her without the demons of his past rising up to haunt him.

"Hi, Jake."

The hammer, still clutched in Jake's hand, slipped and clattered to the floor. His heart skipped a beat, then thudded double-time to catch up. A sigh escaped him as he realized who spoke, and he glanced at her over his shoulder.

Monica's eyes shined as she seemed to glide into the room. She swiveled her head, taking in the installed drywall, and then met his gaze again.

"All done, I see," she said as she stopped beside him. Her attention turned to the view outside, and she sighed appreciatively.

"We still have quite a bit of work to do," Jake said as he bent over to pick up his hammer and tuck it into the loop on his tool belt, determined to act like a normal man instead of the nervous fool he felt like inside.

"Yes. Mudding, and sanding, and painting, and flooring, and trim, and more." She grinned at him, and he swallowed.

"Is there something you needed?" He didn't mean to sound annoyed, but it came out that way.

Her brow furrowed at his tone, and she tilted her head, her eyes oddly troubled. "Are you okay?"

"Yeah." He sighed. "You just startled me."

Her expression relaxed but now appeared contrite. "Sorry about that. You did seem deep in thought. I should've knocked or something."

He shook his head and chuckled, realizing his day seemed so much better with her standing beside him. "It's good to see you."

"You too," she said, brightening with his words. She patted his shoulder, letting her fingers trail over his arm as she moved away. Then she strolled around the room with her hands clasped behind her back, as if inspecting the work.

He ached to pull her back, closer than before, and savor the silkiness of her hair as he combed his fingers through the gilded strands.

"You know," she said, scanning the area around them and dragging him from the daydream he'd momentarily drifted into, "there *is* something you could help me with."

He heard the playful note in her voice, and though he had no idea what she was up to, the possibilities made him smile. "What's that?"

She spun around to face him, swinging her arms out from her body, and grinned. "Help me decide where to put everything."

Her teeth bit into her lower lip, and his eyes were drawn inadvertently to the tiny action. His breath caught as memories of claiming her mouth replayed in his mind. He wrenched his gaze back to hers.

"Everything?" His brain wasn't working correctly.

"You know," she said in that same playful tone as she strolled back to him, her eyes locked on his as she took his hand and began to lead him around the room. "All my things. For instance," she waved a hand at the wall beside the bedroom door, "what do you think of putting my dresser over there?"

He blinked. *She's asking me for decorating advice?* His head pivoted from her, to the wall, and back again.

"Well..." he said, rubbing at his forehead and then tugging his earlobe, unsure what to say. "I...don't..."

She suddenly released his hand and sashayed to the far side of the room.

"What about my chest of drawers here?" Facing the drywall, she flattened her hands over it and bent at the waist. She skimmed her palms back and forth in an expansive movement over the surface, while her backside swayed seductively in tight-fitting jeans. The subtle sweeping sound made him think of her hands sliding over his chest, and as his eyes dropped to the prominent curve of her shapely ass, he felt himself flush.

She dropped a sultry look over her shoulder and lifted one eyebrow suggestively.

With his heart slamming against his ribs now and his loins responding to her display, he wiped his hands on his jeans and took a tentative step toward her, her direct stare luring him in.

A slow smile spread across her face, and then she danced to the outside wall directly between the set of French doors.

"What about here?" A twinkle of mischief lit her eyes. "What shall I put here?" She leaned back against the wall, legs braced slightly apart, while her hands brushed over the surface and her gaze seemed to devour him. "Do you think the bed should go here?"

His whole body tightened.

Just as he had so many times before, he instantly imagined her wrapped in nothing but smooth, white sheets, her eyes soft, her smile inviting—the way she was looking at him right now.

He tried to swallow, but he couldn't.

"You're...You're flirting with me," he rasped almost accusingly.

Her head slanted to the side and she shrugged, her gaze seeming to study him closely. "A little." She pushed away from the wall and sauntered seductively toward him.

A tingling heat flashed over his skin, then coalesced into a hot, yearning throb in his groin. She stopped inches from him, so close the tips of her breasts brushed him when she breathed, tantalizing his overloaded senses.

"Do you mind?" she whispered as her hands flattened on his chest and slowly slipped up around his neck, while her eyes delved deeper into his.

He unconsciously licked his lips and then shook his head.

Her hands grazed down his arms and lifted his trembling hands to her hips before encircling his neck again. His fingers tightened around her waist as she rubbed her cheek against his left pec.

"May I kiss you, Jake?" Her voice was a breathy whisper.

His knees felt rubbery.

She lifted her face, her lips slightly parted, and need struck him like a body blow, clamping down on his vitals so hard he nearly cringed.

There was a moment of doubt as he stared down at her, dumbfounded by her beauty and the proximity of her luscious body, but lust burned it out.

"Yes," he growled, and then his hands squeezed the soft curve of her hips and he pulled her flush against him. He wrapped his arms around her, drawing her closer still, and she smiled as he lowered his head.

She tasted like honey, sweet and natural.

She smelled like sunshine and roses.

She felt like pure heaven in his arms.

Her back arched as she went up on her toes to deepen the kiss.

She moaned and slowly slid a hand to his waist, his thigh. The slight pressure of her fingers crept upward again, and he shuddered.

His past invaded his mind.

The young woman's weeping vibrated through the desire infusing his brain.

He stiffened.

He tried to make the sound go away, but it wouldn't leave.

A part of him wanted to run, but he refused to break away from Monica.

His arm constricted around her, and his hand, molded to the back of her head, squeezed tighter.

He had said he wanted to be the man he used to be, that he wanted more. Well, this is what he wanted. To show her what he was feeling. To have every part of her against him. To taste her, smell her, *be with her*.

Monica pulled back and looked up at him with questioning eyes.

Uncertainty made him pause. Had he hurt her? In his urgency, did he squeeze her too tight, kiss her too hard? His arms loosened, and he took a small step back. He'd only meant to show her how much she affected him, but instead, he feared, he'd practically mauled her.

A wholly different kind of heat crawled up his neck.

"Are you all right?" he asked dreading her reply.

The corners of her mouth quirked up. "I'm fine."

"Did I...frighten you?" His face felt warmer than ever.

She rocked her head from side to side as if weighing her answer. "Maybe a little, but I'm not afraid of you, if that's what you're asking. That was...*much* better than...before, but I do have a question."

He tensed, preparing for an accusation, but tenderness was all he saw shimmering in her eyes. She hadn't pulled away. His fingers still lightly clasped her waist, and her hands rested on his arms. It was a cozy scene and—despite the images that filled his head when he tried to be intimate with her—he loved having her this close.

"What would you like to know?"

"Well, when we were kissing just now...everything started out great, but then your whole body tensed. Was that because of me? Did my approach upset you?" She pressed her lips together, as though anxious about his reply.

He stuttered out a breath and dropped his head. "No." He looked up. "It's not you."

"So, it's not because I came on too strong?"

"No." He grinned. "I liked that part. I liked it a lot. If I wasn't so messed up..." He shook his head again. "The rest is on me."

"No, Jake, it's not." The tone of her voice was soothing as her small hand pressed against his cheek. She went up on her toes again and, leaning into his chest, brushed another soft yet ardent kiss on his lips. The light caress felt like a thunderbolt had struck him. His body quivered, and his groin, already very aware of her, grew harder still. But that was all. No images in his head. No sad, frightened weeping. Cautious relief welled up within him, and a heavy weight lifted off his shoulders.

Monica's eyes glowed when she pulled back to look up at him again. "You're doing very well," she said with a little grin that made his heart stutter. "We'll have to keep practicing and see what happens."

He could only stare at her. She was so damn beautiful. But more than that, he admired her tenacity and that she defended him, even from himself. He liked that she knew what she wanted, and—though it made him nervous sometimes—he loved that she wanted him.

She seemed to be studying his face, a little nervously too, though he didn't know why she would feel that way. Maybe his reactions—his uncertainty when he tried to be intimate with her—bothered her more than she let on. He opened his mouth to ask about it, but someone calling for her from the stairwell dissuaded him, and he snapped his jaws closed once more.

Monica's expression dimmed, and he had no trouble interpreting why: she was annoyed by the interruption. He wasn't too thrilled about it either.

Her eyes still locked with Jake's, Monica pressed her hands against his chest as if consoling him in some way. The heat of her palms swiftly sank through the thin cotton of his shirt to his skin. The gesture made him feel a little better.

"Monica?" Rosa's voice called down the hall. "Are you up here?"

"Yes, I'm here," Monica replied as she stepped away from Jake and walked to the hallway. "What's the problem?"

"The construction supply delivery," Rosa said as she approached. She gave Jake a quick gesture of greeting and then focused on Monica once more. "They shorted us on the remaining flooring totals, and they're claiming that's all we ordered. You need to speak with them. They're not listening to me."

Jake, who had turned back to his work while the two women talked, glanced over his shoulder. He saw Monica nod, and then she turned to him. A gentle smile brightened her face as she met his eyes, and the tenderness he read in her gaze was like a balm for the torment in his soul. That look told him without words how she felt. The knot in his chest loosened a little more, and he returned her smile with a grateful one of his own. She may not know what haunted him—and he wasn't sure he'd ever be able to share that disgrace with her—but she wasn't condemning him either. Not yet anyway.

She turned to Rosa. "All right, I'm coming," she said and then glanced at Jake once more. "I'll see you later, Jake. Thanks for the...chat."

He chuckled at that. "Sure, any time."

She gave him an appraising look for the innuendo in his statement. Then she lifted her hand in a little wave and disappeared down the hall, leaving Jake with a warm, buoyant feeling that spread through his whole body and curved his lips into a slow, confident smile.

27

MONICA COULD FEEL Jake's gaze on her. She'd seen him at breakfast that morning, but they didn't get much chance to talk. Over the last several days, his increasing desire for her company had only amplified her feelings for him. So much so that going the better part of a day without his company made her lonely in a longing sort of way.

Maybe that explained why she was always so aware of his presence.

The August weather had turned from a desert-like heat to what she not so affectionately thought of as surface-of-the-sun, and for the last few hours, she'd been sweating in the sweltering interior of the house, helping Shawn. They were in the process of mudding and sanding the newly installed drywall in what was to be her bedroom. She'd just finished covering a line of nail heads—lost in the memory of the staggering kiss she and Jake had shared a few feet away only days before—when she felt a familiar prickle on the back of her neck. She used her bare forearm to push her hair back from her face, then turned her head in anxious anticipation, knowing what she would find.

She was not disappointed.

Across the room stood Jake, shoulder propped against the doorframe, idly flipping a drywall nail between his fingers. He was staring at her with smoldering eyes that seemed to see straight into her soul. He didn't smile or give any other indication of his mood, but the look he gave her was enough.

She gazed over her shoulder at the quiet man observing her a few feet away. Her pulse sped up and she inhaled sharply as his eyes traveled over her in a long, deliberate perusal. When his gaze met hers again, a slow, sensual smile pulled at the corners of his mouth. In his eyes she saw the fire that had been ignited during their last encounter in this very room, and her skin flushed at the expression on his face. What she wouldn't give to have him touch her again.

She looked down at her disheveled state. Drywall mud coated her hands. Dust covered her jeans and blue work shirt, and tendrils from her loose bun hung around her face, tickling her nose and sticking to her sweaty cheeks. She looked a sight, but when she lifted her eyes again, Jake's gaze said otherwise. He looked at her like she was something precious, something treasured—like she was the most beautiful woman in the world and everything he wanted.

The notion made her heart flutter.

"How's it going in here?" he asked as he dropped the nail into a pouch on his tool belt and pushed away from the doorjamb.

Monica opened her mouth to respond, but Shawn beat her to it.

"Doing good," Shawn said, turning from the wall. "Should be ready for paint tomorrow."

"Great," Jake replied, and his intense regard shifted to Monica. "Anything you need from me?"

A tingle prickled Monica's flesh at the innuendo in his words.

Is he flirting with me in front of Shawn?

Standing a few feet away, Shawn must've noticed the tension between them because he went momentarily quiet, shifting a curious glance between her and Jake. "Well," he said as if considering his answer, and she prayed he wouldn't make some childish joke about love or some such. "I wouldn't say no to a few more helpers."

Monica breathed a sigh of relief and then turned a mock frown on Shawn. "Are you saying I'm too slow?"

"No, no, no," he replied a little too quickly, shaking his head and holding his palms up toward her in a placating gesture. "I'm not saying anything. Just thought a little more help would be good."

"I think you're secretly complaining," Monica teased.

Shawn shook his head once more.

"You're doing fine, Monica," Jake said. His gentle praise held a hint of something deeper, as if he was sending her a message, telling her that things between them were better than he'd ever hoped. Her heart sped up, and she took a deep breath as she faced him again.

"Thank you," she replied. Not wanting to encourage Shawn's teasing by saying too much to Jake, she turned a triumphant smirk on Shawn.

He only shook his head again, a good-natured grin tugging at his lips as he replied. "It still wouldn't hurt to have more help."

"As it so happens," Jake said casually, "there are a couple workers who need something to do." He waved his hand behind him, and Trevor and Kara ran into the room, each holding a putty knife. They looked ready to work, huge grins on their eager faces.

Monica smiled. "Hi, you two. So, you're going to help us?"

"Yeah," Trevor said, nodding his head so enthusiastically his wavy brown hair bounced on his forehead and around his ears.

"Jake said we can put mud on the walls." Kara's big grin was infectious, and her denim-colored eyes sparkled.

"Well, get over here then," Shawn said, also grinning. "Let me show you what to do."

As Shawn explained how to apply the spackling compound, Monica glanced at Jake to find his gaze on her again. A smile still curved his tempting masculine mouth.

She got to her feet and crossed the room. With a hand on his arm, she led him into the hallway.

"You did that for Shawn, didn't you," she whispered.

He shrugged. "Trevor's been less resistant to Shawn lately. I thought he might respond well to a little more time together."

She peeked around the corner and saw Trevor following each direction Shawn gave him. They were both smiling.

She turned back to Jake as her heart filled with warmth. She gripped his forearm and leaned toward him. "You're a good friend, Jake."

He shrugged, and a light shade of pink spread over his cheekbones. In the next instant, he smiled and lifted a hand to brush a stray strand of hair from her cheek.

"I'd like to kiss you right now," he said quietly as he cupped her jaw. Her skin tingled beneath his palm, radiating outward, sending prickles of gooseflesh down her arms. His thumb slid over her mouth, and she felt suddenly light-headed.

"I'd like that too," she answered, lifting her chin and breathing in his manly scent, "but I'm covered in drywall dust. It might be a little gritty."

He leaned toward her until their mouths were almost touching, and her breath caught in her throat.

"Just a quick one then," he said and brushed his lips against hers.

The second his mouth landed lightly on hers, her knees went weak. Still, she rose up on her toes, instinctively begging for more. Her hands slipped up his chest, reveling in the hard muscles under his shirt. She wanted to hold him. She wanted his arms around her. But before hers could curl around his neck, he pulled back.

Her whole body aflame, she moaned in complaint as her lids fluttered open to gaze into the blazing heat of his eyes.

He glanced around the empty hallway before he turned back to her again. Then he smiled and dropped his hands from her face.

"We've got to get back to work," he said, but he sounded reluctant.

She licked her burning lips and resisted the urge to pull him back. His eyes dropped to her mouth, and her ache to touch him again tripled. But when he looked up, she dug her fingers into her thighs to keep them still and only nodded.

Jake smiled at her again and then turned away.

Pressing her cool hands to her hot cheeks, she inhaled, trying to get her heartbeat under control as she watched him saunter—in that sexy, almost-cowboy-way of his—back down the hall.

* * *

The hot sun blazed in the clear azure sky as Monica relaxed on a small grassy knoll near her home. The whole population of the ranch had turned out for the first summertime game of kickball. As usual, Shawn was the instigator and had planned it over the last week or so. He and Monica both loved to get everyone together for a game once in a while, and this year it was long overdue.

"Come on, Trevor!" Jake shouted encouragement to the boy from the rock that represented third base, while Trevor waited at home plate for his final pitch. "Get us home!"

Those not participating in the game sat on blankets along both baselines bracketing home plate. For purely selfish reasons, which had everything to do with Jake Nichols and their burgeoning romance, Monica had chosen to sit in an open space between third base and home plate. In shorts and a tank top, like most everyone else, she chatted with the other spectators and cheered the players on, waiting for Jake to return from the field.

Watching the game brought back memories of playing it when she was about Trevor's age, before the war started and everything went bad. Unlike the well-maintained, green field where she played as a child, this meadow was uneven and dotted with patches of dirt, tufts of sagebrush, and yellowed grass. The first and third bases were marked with stones. Someone's shirt represented second, and, thanks to Jake, a pentagon-shaped piece of drywall—now cracked in places from being stepped on—signified home plate.

Monica had joined in for a while, but, like many others, she eventually bowed out to allow all the kids more time to play. Jake currently had a grinning Kara clinging to his back as they waited to dash for home. He seemed to be having as much fun as the kids—they all did—and Monica delighted in the happiness radiating from their faces.

Though their relationship grew steadily closer, she knew Jake wasn't ready to do anything too physical with her sexually, but he seemed to be heading in that direction. The soft brush of his lips in the hallway a few days ago, while Shawn instructed the children on spackling, was not the first or last time he'd stolen a quick kiss. There'd been instances in the barn, in the fields, and by the river at night during the walks they'd made a habit of taking. She never knew where he might show up.

The thought made her smile.

In fact, just a couple of days ago, at the end of the workday, Jake had made another advance toward their developing romance.

She had been thinking about him as she started down the unfinished upstairs hallway of her new home, headed for the bunkhouse to clean up for the evening meal. She'd been lost in thought, her stomach quivering in anticipation of seeing him soon, when someone tapped her on the shoulder. Startled by the unexpected interruption, she wheeled around but relaxed instantly when she saw Jake grinning at her. He slanted his head to indicate she should follow him, and he then disappeared inside the room.

Curious and excited, she followed. As she entered the empty room, a hard arm snaked around her waist, and solid heat pressed her into the unpainted wall. She dropped the bucket she'd been carrying, and the tools inside went clattering across the floor. She squeaked in delighted surprise, and her heart, already beating rapidly in expectation, pounded harder against her ribs.

"I missed you today." Jake whispered in her ear and then nibbled at her neck, teasing the tender skin below her ear.

"You're lucky I like you," she teased as she tilted her head, exposing her tender throat to his lips. Her hands clung to his shoulders.

His chuckle sent a shiver racing up and down her spine. "You *more* than like me."

"Yes," she said in a hushed voice as his free hand skimmed upward from her hip. "I *much* more than like you."

"Mmm..." he hummed against her neck, and goosebumps danced across her skin. His hand cupped her breast, and she sucked in a breath, both amazed and excited by his boldness. Her nipple responded instantly to his touch, pushing into his palm through the thin layers of her clothes. Her head dropped back, and her fingers dug into the hard muscles of his back.

"Jake," she breathed as his thumb brushed repeatedly over the responsive tip of her breast, and his head lifted. His ragged breath warmed her cheek as he stared down into her face. His eyes, dark emeralds flecked with amber, were filled with the same hunger she felt gnawing at her body. "Kiss me, Jake. Please..."

Something flickered in his eyes—need, fear—but his hesitation didn't last long. His mouth descended on hers, and her lips parted instantly. Their tongues touched, searched, demanded. His hand squeezed her breast, taunting the hard little nub at its crest with his fingers, and she moaned a little louder.

Her hands slid down his back to the firm, round curves of his buttocks. She gripped him, pulled him tighter. Seeming to know what she wanted, he pressed himself against her, wedging her tightly between the wall and his firm torso. She squirmed in response, grinding against the thick shaft of his desire.

She wanted so badly to touch him, to feel the velvety softness of the steel-cored rod jutting against her belly. She wanted to taste it, taste him. She reached for the button of his jeans, her hands shaking and fumbling.

His mouth traced searing kisses over her cheek, down the delicate column of her neck, and she moaned—a pure, raw outpouring of need. She wanted him, so hungry for him she didn't care who might hear or walk by. No one else existed. It was just her and Jake and the wonderful things he awoke inside of her.

His button came loose, and she pulled his shirt out from inside his jeans. Her fingers rushed inside, greedy for the satiny feel of his hot flesh. Work-hardened muscles contracted as her fingertips brushed over his abdomen. Eager for more, she reached for the waistband of his briefs. She'd barely touched the elastic when his body stiffened, but after the briefest of pauses, he resumed nuzzling her neck. His hand—under her T-shirt now—tightened once again over her bra-clad breast as if eager to continue. Still, his whole body—pressed against her from shoulders to knees—felt taut, as if ready to fight a fierce battle...or flee.

Too much, she told herself as her sanity returned. *You're pushing him to fast. Get a hold of yourself!* She hadn't meant to go so far, but he'd surprised her. And his kisses—not to mention that big, warm, calloused hand brushing over her sensitive flesh—sent her brain on a temporary vacation. He still wasn't ready, she could tell, yet it seemed he was valiantly trying to push through whatever tormented him anyway, to please her. She was sure he wanted her as much as she wanted him, but she wasn't willing to cause more harm to his already damaged psyche.

Monica moved her hands to his sides and stepped back. As much as she wanted to be with him, she didn't want to push him too fast. He got the message and lifted his head. His face was flushed, his lips slightly parted, and his eyes were still dark with desire, but a touch of dread swirled in those hazel depts.

"Jake," she said, sounding out of breath as she looked up at him. "We need to stop." She tried not to notice the way the tension seemed to leach from his body with those words, but even if he argued, she wouldn't let this happen, not yet.

"Are you sure?" he asked in a rough voice much deeper than his regular tones. He wasn't asking for himself, she knew.

"Yes," she said. "It's not time."

He looked a little sad at that—a little relieved too—but he let her go and stepped back.

A burst of male laughter rolled up the stairs from somewhere below, and booted footstep echoed on the hardwood downstairs. Both sounds reminded Monica that they were not alone.

"Besides," she joked as she straightened her shirt, "someone might see us. I'm not really into exhibitionism." She grinned and was pleased to see a smile spread across his face too, but there was a shadow of something in his eyes. He blinked once, and it was gone.

"Me either," he replied.

Despite Monica calling a halt a couple of nights ago, he'd still found time since then to sneak quick kisses. He'd risked another one by the river last night while they walked. Though it was short, it was so sweet her toes had curled in her boots.

Now, sitting in the shade, enjoying the fun and camaraderie around her, she remembered the feel of Jake's warm lips on her flesh as his big hand cupped her breast, and little shivers of happiness washed through her.

"Are you ready, Trev?" Shawn asked, set to roll the ball toward the boy waiting behind home plate.

Trevor, frowning in serious boyish concentration, gave a nod.

Shawn, with ball in hand, hauled his arm back and bounce-rolled it in an underhand fashion toward Trevor. The boy started running before Shawn released the ball. In a display of youthful skill, Trevor caught up to the ball in midstride and kicked it high into the air. It flew directly between second and third base, sailing past both basemen and bouncing in the outfield before the fielder could get beneath it.

The crowd erupted in cheers as Trevor headed for first and Jake—with Kara shouting "Go, Jake, go!" on his back—took off for home. The ball flew toward home plate, but it was too late. Jake and Kara shouldered past Shawn, who was waiting for the fielder's toss, and stomped across home for a run.

Watching him jubilantly bounce Kara on his back and shout "Good job!" to Trevor, Monica felt another surge of affection for Jake. He swung

Kara down from his back and laughed as she hugged his leg. She graced Shawn with a little girl high-five and then took off at a run to sit with her new mom and sister, asking them if they had seen her and Jake score.

Jake chuckled as he crossed over to the shade where Monica sat alone. He walked straight up to her small cream-colored blanket and plopped down beside her.

"Hi," he said, as if they hadn't spoken just twenty minutes ago. "You having fun?"

She smiled. "Yes, I love this. Everyone always has such a good time."

"But you're not playing anymore."

"It's still fun to watch. I don't want to take a spot from one of the kids. Plus," she said, leaning toward him conspiratorially, "it's really hot out there."

He laughed. "Yeah, it is much cooler in the shade."

"It *was*," she murmured so only he could hear.

He glanced at her, and a boyishly lopsided grin pulled at his lips. "Maybe I should go sit with Kara." He lifted a questioning eyebrow even as she scowled at his suggestion.

"Don't you dare," she said in mock severity.

Surprising her again with an open show of affection, he wrapped his arm around her shoulders and moved closer. The heat from his body seared her side, and his proximity made her heart beat a little faster.

"I wouldn't think of it," he whispered in her ear, his hot breath making her shiver. He dropped his arm as he straightened, but he didn't move away.

He threaded his fingers through hers, and she butted her shoulder into his biceps. "Good," she said.

He grinned and squeezed her hand.

"Have you thought any more about the trip to Angel's for the harvest next week?" she asked evenly, broaching a tricky topic they'd discussed for the first time several days ago.

"Yeah," he said and turned his head toward her, "I have." His eyes had turned serious, but she didn't read any reluctance in his gaze.

"Did you decide what you want to do?"

"About the harvest or about sharing a room with you?" His response was soft, barely loud enough to reach her ears, and somewhat playful.

"The room." She cringed inwardly at the eagerness in her voice. Since their afternoon at the river weeks ago, she'd thought a lot about his difficulties with intimacy, particularly what she might have done to upset him. The problem didn't seem to be her flirting with him, nor her innocent caresses—her fingers on his arm, her palm on his chest, holding his hand—and she didn't think their steamy make-out sessions were an issue either. He'd responded eagerly to all of that, but something happened when they were more intimate. After carefully considering his reactions, she wondered if her interest in the more private parts of his body was what troubled him. And she feared the reasons why that might be.

Jake looked back at the players as another teen kicked a long ball straight out to the center fielder, who caught it for an out.

"We don't have to try this yet," she said carefully, not wanting to press him into anything. "I can wait."

He shook his head and looked down at their clasped hands. Then he lifted his gaze back to her. The self-assured determination she saw in his expression gave her goosebumps.

"I don't want to wait. I told you I want to get over what happened to me, but I also want to be the kind of man you deserve. I can't do either of those things if I keep playing it safe." He paused, his mouth slightly parted, his breaths rapid as he stared back at her.

"You don't have to prove anything to me," she said. "You've already impressed me, Jake. Forcing this isn't necessary."

"It is for me," he replied, then glanced around them and leaned a little closer. "I want to be with you, Monica, and I know you want the same thing. It's been long enough."

"So, that's a 'yes' then?"

His slow smile as he straightened once more made her heart do flip-flops in her chest.

"Yes." He squeezed her hand again for emphasis.

They turned back to the game as one of the other kids prepared to kick. Jake shouted encouragement to the adolescent girl lining up for the next pitch. She waved her gratitude and then directed her eyes to Shawn.

Monica couldn't concentrate fully on the game. She still laughed and cheered with all the others, but she kept thinking about the man beside her. His bravery made her feel inadequate, though not in any of the stereotypical female-questioning-her-worth sort of ways. No, she was in awe of his willingness to face his fears, and flummoxed by his inability to see how courageous his actions really were. If the situation were reversed, she didn't know if she could be so strong.

"Jake?" she said impulsively, surprising herself.

He looked over at her, his expression open and trusting, which made her feel protective of him and of their growing affection.

Her eyes made a swift sweep to ensure no one was close enough to overhear. Then she turned back to Jake and cleared her throat, feeling suddenly nervous. "May I ask you something...very personal?"

His sandy-brown brows drew down slightly and his shoulders tensed, but he lowered his chin once in acquiescence.

She took a steadying breath, still unsure if she should ask her question, knowing this would push him, hard, and dig into places he may not wish to go.

"What happened to you...before...at Darla's. I...know they hurt you. I know they forced you to..." She paused, her eyes wide on his now shuttered countenance—no emotion showed through the veil shrouding his face. She took another glance around and then focused on him again. "I'm sorry," she shook her head in self-disgust, "this isn't the time to ask you this. Forget I said anything."

Jake sighed, and she couldn't tell if it was from relief or annoyance at her curiosity. He stared out at the players, once again running the bases. Trevor was finally on third.

"I had sex with some of them," Jake said very quietly, and she focused on his face again, "and many of those...hurt me, yes, but that's not the only reason I have problems being..." He glanced at her, and the hurt in his eyes broke her heart. "Being with you—" He hesitated. "They did terrible things, but...I've done things too, and *those* things are what I can't forget."

Monica frowned, confused by his explanation, but concern for him filled her with dread. "Do you want to...talk about it?"

Another sigh escaped him as he faced the ballfield once more. He hung his head a moment and then he turned back to her. His hand tightened on hers, and she squeezed back, letting him know she was on his side no matter what. The blank expression on his face made her heart ache all the more for the pain she knew it concealed. She started to tell him not to worry about it, that she didn't need to know, but then the corners of his mouth tipped up ever so slightly in a tentative smile, and the mask hiding his inner thoughts from her dissolved before her eyes. She saw trust and something more shining back at her now, and her throat grew thick with emotion at the sight.

"Thank you, but, no," he said, "not right now and maybe not for a long while. But someday, I don't know when, I'll share it with you. I only hope you'll still look at me the same way after I do."

A loud cheer erupted from the families and friends surrounding them, effectively ending their conversation. The girl's kick had sent the soccer ball bouncing into the outfield, and Trevor headed for home. The noise increased as the fielder launched the ball toward home plate, but the boy was quicker.

"Way to go, Trevor," Jake said in a congratulatory tone as Trevor ran toward them. The boy was all smiles as he stopped to slap a grinning Shawn's outthrust hand, paused to give Jake and Monica both another high-five, and then ran over to his sister and their new family for more celebration.

Monica purposely banished the host of new questions swirling through her mind after Jake's last admission.

He would tell her his secrets when he was ready.

The rest would take care of itself.

28

JAKE MET MONICA'S EYES the moment he entered the dining hall for breakfast. She smiled at him, but her eyes held the same questions they had last week when he made his confession during the kickball game. He'd been extremely grateful she didn't press him for an explanation about his revelation. More than thankful, because even though he trusted her, he couldn't talk about it with anyone.

His belly tightened as he stared at her across the crowded dining hall, but he returned her smile before going to collect his food.

He had thought he could kiss her, hold her, be normal because he didn't fear what she might do to him if he disappointed her. But apprehension still filled him every time her deft fingers reached inside his jeans. When she moaned her pleasure, in his mind he still sometimes heard another woman weeping, still felt pain slicing through him. He kept trying to forget about those terrible moments, about his shameful surrender to the pain. He had managed to push past them in the last few weeks, broaden the boundaries that had once inhibited him. Unfortunately, when things got a little too intimate, the images from his past returned and were so strong, so real, his body would involuntarily stiffen when they bloomed to life in his mind. And Monica, sensitive woman that she was, picked up on it every time.

He wanted her. No matter what may come, he wanted to be with Monica, wanted to hold her, kiss her, make her scream his name, but the memories, thus far, wouldn't let him move beyond heavy petting. Still, he was determined to try. He would just have to live with the embarrassment of his abnormal behavior—and her acceptance of it—until he could get past his issues completely.

If he ever could.

He took his plate to the table where Monica, Rosa, and Shawn were in what appeared to be a deep yet heated discussion. Instead of sitting in what had become his normal place beside Monica, he positioned himself beside Rosa on the opposite side of the table.

"I still say her actions are severe and extreme," Shawn was saying as Jake walked up and sat down. "Good, another man to join my side. Back me up here, Jake."

He glanced around the table, unsure what he'd just walked into.

"Enough, Shawn. Just drop it." A warning tone imbued Monica's voice and set the hair on the back of Jake's neck on end.

Shawn glanced at Monica—who widened her eyes, giving him a significant look—then back at Jake, before guiltily averting his gaze.

"What're we talking about?" Jake's eyes scanned between the two.

"Nothing important," Monica said, but Shawn, despite Monica's warning, had another opinion.

Shawn lowered the fork he'd used to stab a piece of sausage, and his eyes narrowed. "Men being enslaved and how they are treated *is* important."

"That's not what I meant, Shawn, and you know it."

Shawn huffed and shook his head but didn't reply.

Annoyed by their obvious overprotectiveness, Jake's brows twitched together when Monica's apprehensive gaze met his. He appreciated their sensitivity to his situation, but he wasn't a child or made of glass, and he didn't want to be treated as if he were. "Don't let me stop you," he said with a headshake. "Spill it."

Monica met his resolute gaze with an equally resolute frown. Seeing he meant what he said, she sighed. "We're theorizing why Darla Cain hates men," Monica said bluntly, though her expression turned worried, as if mentioning the other woman's name would send Jake running from the room.

He shifted in his seat, comprehending, now, why she'd been hesitant, but she needn't have been. "Actually, I've wondered about that myself," Jake said, then popped a bite of pancake into his mouth. The burst of maple sweetness from the homemade syrup erupted on his tongue, and he closed his eyes briefly to savor it. When he focused on the group again, he saw Shawn jut his chin at Monica, a smug grin on his lips. She smacked Shawn's arm like an annoyed sibling, but her attention never left Jake.

"You've actually thought about it?" Amazement filled her question.

"Well...yeah," he said with a shrug. "It's kind of hard not to speculate why someone you've never met wants to hurt you for no reason other than she can."

"My point exactly," Shawn said in triumph.

"Shut it, Shawn," Monica said in the same sharp tone she'd used earlier.

"It won't make what she did better or change my opinion about her, but it might explain a few things to know why," Jake said, his eyes locking on her face once more.

"There's no excuse for what she does," Monica replied, while staring at her plate and pushing the food around with a fork. "But there are stories." She met his gaze.

"What kind of stories?"

"Does it matter?"

"No, but I'm curious."

"Me too," Shawn added.

Monica cast a dark look in Shawn's direction but didn't chastise him again. She turned a quick glance at the oddly silent Rosa. The nod the older woman gave Monica made Jake frown, but Monica only returned to staring at her plate again and sighed.

"I don't know how true they are, and I've only heard them third- and fourth-hand." Monica shrugged.

"So, share with the rest of the class then," Shawn said, and Monica glared at him.

"You're too cocky for your own good, Shawn."

"Tell me something I don't know." He grinned, but she didn't respond.

She looked at Jake. "Do you really want to hear this?"

He nodded and took another bite of his breakfast. Shawn mimicked Jake's head movement, but Monica ignored him.

"All right," Monica said as she set her fork down and rested her hands on the table. "Well, as I'm sure you know, Darla hates men, and she enjoys hurting them."

Jake nodded again; he had firsthand knowledge of that fact.

"She's also extremely jealous by nature, which should explain why she doesn't let anyone go easily and why she dislikes me and Angel so much."

"Why you and Angel?" Jake asked.

"Because we're not like her, and Angel interferes with her plans as often as she can."

"How?" Jake's eyebrows furrowed.

"Angel's outbid her at auction more than once to keep her from taking a man she'd obsessed over. Angel also argues against her treatment of slaves and fights to change the laws. When I get on the council, which should happen in the next year or so, I'll do the same thing, and Darla knows it."

Jake nodded. Knowing Darla, Monica's explanation made sense.

"Anyway," Monica continued, "there are several rumors about why Darla acts the way she does. Angel overheard one conversation that seemed the most probable. From what she heard, it sounded like Darla had been abused as a child, then repeated her mother's mistake and married young to an abusive man."

"That doesn't absolve her of her crimes now," Shawn said heatedly.

"No, but the possibility does make some sense of her behavior."

"We don't even know if it's true. Maybe the wars and hysterical-strength just gave her the excuse she needed."

"True," Rosa said, finally joining the conversation, "but being abused at any point in a person's life can change who they once were. Not everyone will become a sadist like Darla. Some survive, others become terrified of their own shadow."

"You're defending her?" Shawn's voice rose, and his fingers balled up on the table.

"No," Rosa said. "I'm saying you don't know what women lived with—for centuries—before discovering we were strong."

Jake glanced at the older woman. He sensed something more lay beneath her words. Her whole body had tensed at Shawn's comment, and her voice was far harsher as she spoke than her normal sedate tones. But Shawn wasn't done.

"What could possibly be bad enough to justify Darla whipping and beating men or letting them die in their cells?"

Jake's heart stuttered, remembering his fear of suffering the same fate.

"I didn't say it did," Rosa said. "As I said, I'm not defending her. I simply meant our lives weren't all rosy either. Besides, this is all just conjecture anyway. No one really knows anything."

"What happened to you?" Jake asked her softly. He might be off base with his inquiry, but something told him he wasn't. When Rosa stiffened and inhaled sharply, he knew he was right.

She glanced at Monica before meeting Jake's gaze.

"My husband beat me for years." Her face held no emotion, and her voice fell flat. Across the table, Shawn straightened up as if she'd slapped him.

"I wanted to leave," Rosa continued, her eyes still locked on Jake's, "but by the time I realized what he was, I didn't feel I could. I had no self-esteem left and nowhere to go if I did leave." She dropped her eyes to the empty plate in front of her. "After a while, I was too scared to try."

Jake nodded in understanding, her story reminding him of Bret and his family.

"How did you get away?" Shawn asked quietly, clearly stunned by Rosa's disclosure.

"I didn't," Rosa said without raising her eyes. "When the war finally struck home, we ran for the mountains like everyone else. We had nothing, and being the bully he was, he tried to steal food from a woman we came across. But she wasn't like me. She fought back. She took her share of hits, but she eventually killed him with a rock. Her name was Joan and she helped me after that, but she died the next winter." She looked up at Monica, whose eyes looked suspiciously shiny as she gazed back at the older woman. Rosa gave her a tight smile. "Monica's family took me in a short time after that."

"I'm sorry," Shawn said, reaching across the table to squeeze Rosa's hand. "You never said anything before. I had no idea."

Rosa glanced at Jake, then focused on Shawn again. "I've always been too ashamed to talk about it."

"Don't be," Jake said. He hadn't meant to say anything; it just popped out. Considering his own situation, he felt like a hypocrite for saying anything at all. He met Rosa's surprised gaze and realized he needed to say more. "What your husband did is on him, not on you."

Rosa's eyes narrowed as she scrutinized his face, and he felt heat crawl up his neck.

"You speak from experience," she said.

"Yes," Jake shrugged, "I've been affected by my recent experiences." He gave her a half-smile. "But I was also talking about someone I was close to once, who lived a similar story. What you went through"—he paused and glanced at Rosa—"what *we've* gone through," he corrected, "didn't turn any of us into cruel people. You're still a good person, Rosa, and so are many others who've been abused. I know that's how it worked for my...friend, and it seems to be the same for you."

Rosa nodded, but she didn't comment further and wouldn't meet any of their eyes for several seconds.

They all fell quiet while the other ranch members chatted and laughed and forks and knives clattered on plates and tables around them.

"Well, that turned into a morbid conversation," Shawn said suddenly.

Monica chuckled and bumped his shoulder with hers. "You were expecting cheery?"

"Nah, I just didn't expect it to go"—he glanced at Rosa—"where it did. But I agree with Jake. Rosa's a good person, even if she scolds me about my humor."

"It's okay, Shawn," Rosa said with a smile, while temporarily ignoring his dig about her scolding. "I am a good person, but I'm also a much different person now too. No one will make me feel the way my husband once did. I won't allow it. And," she smiled slightly, "you need someone to keep your clowning in line sometimes."

"I agree with that," Monica said emphatically as she leaned over her empty plate. "And as for the rest, I, for one, am glad you are who you are, Rosa."

"Me too, mi niña." She smiled and then sighed and picked up her coffee mug. "So, is everything ready for tomorrow?"

"What's to get ready?" Shawn said, clearly happy to let the last topic drop, even though he had been the one to start it. "We just ride over. No big deal."

"What's tomorrow?" Jake asked, searching his memory. Then he remembered, and his shoulders slumped. "Oh, right, the harvest."

"Yep," Shawn grinned again. "Should be fun."

"Sweating in the sun is fun to you?" Monica's eyebrows climbed upward, and Jake nodded in approval of her question.

"Not really, but hanging with Theo and Peggy should be fun. Kim and the kids are looking forward to it." He stood up. "But I suppose I should make sure everyone who's not going knows what they're doing while we're gone." He looked at Jake. "I'll see you at the house?"

Jake nodded, and Shawn grinned as he gave a little salute and took his dishes to the kitchen.

"I have things to check on too," Rosa said as she picked up her own plate. "I'll make sure everything's ready for your departure tomorrow and give you a report after lunch," she said to Monica. She gave Jake a long look and then smiled at both of them before walking away. Her lengthy glance held all kinds of questions, and Jake wasn't sure how to feel about that exactly. Sharing a small piece of his past with all of them had come easily because he'd wanted to make Rosa feel better. But even though he'd come to trust them all, their curiosity about his story didn't sit as well with him—maybe because there were things he was still too ashamed to even consider himself, let alone share with anyone else.

Once she was gone, silence blanketed the table while Jake ate his breakfast and Monica drank her coffee. He glanced at her and she smiled.

"I sent Darla a request about selling you," she said as she set the empty mug on the table.

Jake choked on his pancake and then coughed to dislodge it. He took a gulp of his lukewarm coffee. "What?"

"I asked Darla what she wants for you."

He lowered his eyes to his meal. No longer hungry, he pushed the plate away and shook his head. "Don't waste your time. I told you she won't let me go."

"It can't hurt to ask," Monica said as she scooted over and settled into the chair Shawn had vacated. "And I can't just sit back and wait for something to happen." She glanced around, then leaned forward and lowered her voice. "Or for you to take matters into your own hands."

He focused on her, his breakfast churning in his stomach, but didn't remark on her last statement.

She tilted her head and reached across the table to squeeze his fingers. "It's worth a try," she said in a cheery tone. "Maybe we'll get lucky."

Though he appreciated her optimism, Jake snorted. "I seriously doubt it."

He glanced at Monica and lifted a corner of his mouth in a half-grin to soften his comment, but inside, he knew he was right. He hated to think about leaving here, leaving Monica, but he was far better acquainted with Darla than anyone else here, and she'd made no secret about her plans for him. When the time came, she would come for him; that was an absolute certainty. The only question was, whether he would still be here to be taken.

29

"I CAN SEE YOU WORRYING, JAKE," Monica whispered as she rode beside him on her chestnut gelding. He glanced at her, and she smiled in her knowing way, which sent his anxiety level up another couple of notches. He tried to return her smile, but she saw right through him.

"Angel's going to like you, Jake. Trust me." She reached over and rubbed his arm. An unexpected rush of warmth flooded his body, and he had to adjust his seat as she rode ahead to speak to Shawn.

After breakfast and chores, all but a few members of the ranch had mounted up for the journey to Angel's house. They were cutting through the hills to keep their ride a short, less than an hour-long trip, and so Monica could show Jake more of the area.

The horses kicked up dust from the trail as they climbed the ridge above the green, open space of Monica's homestead. The higher they climbed, the more bluffs of jagged basalt jutted between the knurly trunks of soaring pines. Patches of grass bleached by the sun and low-growing weeds with tiny yellow flowers and emerald-colored leaves dotted the landscape.

When they reached the top, they came to a clearing with the long-dead remains of a tall wind-twisted Ponderosa pine clinging to the loose soil along the cliff's edge. Beyond, the verge dropped away to reveal a panorama of rich summer colors. The gray craggy rock face yielded to more evergreens, before the sloping ground flattened into a wide, green valley and then on to more lavender-gray ridges on the cloud-dappled horizon.

Jake sighed, moved by the beauty of the sight. He enjoyed the landscape and Monica's company but wished for a little more privacy. He'd tried to catch her alone for another kiss that morning, but the bustle of preparation didn't allow it. Instead, he had to settle for the happy light in her eyes when she smiled at him and the pressure of her fingers when she squeezed his hand.

Now, as he rode along the trail with the others, Jake couldn't keep his eyes from Monica's shapely form a few yards in front of him. His fingers caressed the leather reins in his hand as he gazed at her golden hair billowing out behind her with the wind. Imagining its texture and scent stirred up his desire, which was always brewing just beneath the surface. The first chance he got he would kiss her again, caress her soft skin, and make her moan his name. He wanted to push his boundaries a little farther, but afraid of the memories and his reaction to them, he refrained from even the most innocuous show of affection in front of an audience.

Even though they had tempered their escalating relationship around others, Jake recently overheard a conversation that made him understandably nervous. He'd been making his way out of the barn a few days ago when he heard Kristine Collins' voice on the other side of the door.

"It's not fair," Kristine had complained to an unknown companion. "I approached Jake first."

The comment made him pause inside the barn.

"He should be mine," Kristine continued in an angry yet possessive tone. "Monica just warned me off so she could have him all to herself."

Jake's hackles prickled. He should've guessed she would notice him spending more time with Monica.

"You know that isn't true," another voice said, and Jake's shoulders sagged with relief when he realized it was Rosa.

"I know the rules don't apply to *her*."

Kristine's peeved reply annoyed him, and he was grateful to hear his own irritation reflected in Rosa's reply.

"Of course, they do. It's not her fault the man didn't choose you. Stop acting like a child."

He heard Kristine huff and stomp off.

Grumbling to herself, Rosa almost walked right into him as she entered the barn.

He grinned when she met his gaze. "Thank you."

She narrowed her eyes. "Just be good to Monica, Mr. Nichols," was all she had said before stepping past him into the building.

Swaying in the saddle as they descended the ridge, Jake had to chuckle softly. Kristine didn't join them on this trip, and he was certain he had Rosa to thank for it. Despite her sometimes standoffish behavior, Rosa seemed to like him and he returned the sentiment, but she acted like a mother hen when it came to Monica's well-being, though he didn't begrudge her. He appreciated that she would be there to look after Monica when the time came for him to return to Darla or run for the hills.

Angel Aldridge was a completely different story.

Through his numerous conversations with Monica, he'd come to learn she and Angel were more than close. A strong bond existed between them, and he suspected they kept secrets for each other. Due to this, Angel having a high opinion of him became of paramount importance, at least for Jake.

Excited to introduce Jake to her friend, Monica practically bounced in the saddle, and her excitement increased his need to make a good impression. When Monica had asked why it was so important to him, he was slow to answer. Hesitant to admit how much he cared about her, even to himself, he skirted his real reasons by simply saying he wanted Angel to think favorably of him for Monica's sake. He mumbled a few other noncommittal comments before he stopped entirely. She seemed to understand his dilemma and didn't demand he tell her everything, which he was thankful for, but he was still nervous. He felt like a man confronting a formidable mother-in-law-to-be for the first time.

Considering his situation, his feelings for Monica were stronger than they should be, but he wouldn't have it any other way. He felt safe with her, wanted to make her happy and see her smile, but fear of his real Mistress haunted him.

"I wish I could just go with you," Monica had said as they strolled by the river after dinner one night. "If I didn't have so many responsibilities, I would."

His gut clenched, and his eyes widened in surprise. "Go with me?"

She glanced up at him with her eyebrows lifted. "When you run."

Jake stared in disbelief. Was he that transparent? Seeing no point in denying his plans to her, he groaned and shook his head. "You can't do that. You'd have nothing then, and these people would lose the security you promised them."

She hung her head. "I know. I just wish there was something more I could do now besides wait."

He could see her frustration in the rigid set of her jaw. He stopped and turned toward her. With his hands on her shoulders, he looked deep into her eyes, as if urging her to believe his next words. "Monica, soon you'll have a seat on the Section Council. You can make a difference then. I know you want to. I know you'll try. If you give everything up for me, you're condemning all those people currently being held and any others who haven't yet been taken prisoner."

"I know," she had repeated, but she still sounded dejected.

They started walking again.

"Besides," Jake said, intending to add another barrier to her leaving, "living in the wild is no picnic."

She stopped and frowned up at him. "You think I can't handle it?" An odd note crept into her tone. It set him on edge, almost as if she was trying to impart something to him without saying it outright. He searched her features for some sign, but he found nothing in her eyes other than the question she asked.

"I don't know," he said, "you probably could, but I don't want to find out. I don't want to drag you off into the mountains to struggle and starve."

"You wouldn't be dragging me anywhere, Jake," she said, her attitude screaming frustration. "I'd be dragging you. I don't want you to go back to Darla, and I don't want you risking your life by going off alone."

"And what if we got caught?" he demanded. "They'll kill you, Monica! How do you think that would make me feel?"

"And if you run, what do you think they'll do to you?"

"They won't murder me for being a traitor."

"No, but they might whip you to death as an example."

"Better me than you."

She had stared at him after that. Her mouth—left hanging open in shock—snapped closed, and her face softened.

"I don't want that," she said and reached for his hand. "I know all the reasons I shouldn't leave, but I want you safe and with me too."

"Ditto," he replied and gave her hand a little squeeze.

"I don't want to argue about hypotheticals," she said, pressing her other hand against his chest. Her eyes were shiny when she looked up at him. "I'm just worried."

He pulled her into his arms, cradled her against his body, and rested his cheek on her head. "Me too," he said, her hair tickling his lips.

They had spent the next hour walking, talking, and enjoying their time alone. He still fretted about what Monica might do, but until they heard from Darla, his plans would remain the same. Even if Monica insisted, he would not allow her to give up everything for him or endanger her by allowing her to run away with him. Moreover, he didn't belong to her, so she couldn't be forced to sell the rest of her people because of his departure, as would normally happen to an owner if a slave escaped. If Darla refused to relinquish him, he would leave, disappear into the night, and take his chances getting to the mountains alone.

When they finally reached Angel Aldridge's homestead, Jake was stunned by its size. Monica had described the place to him more than once, but seeing it in person was an experience he could not have imagined. The fifteen-foot-tall concrete wall surrounding the homestead was a feat, considering the lack of construction machinery available nowadays, and he studied it as they approached.

The main house was huge. Designed in an old farmhouse style, the two-story, white structure rambled at least half an acre, with an expansive front deck spanning the width of the house. From his discussions with Monica, Jake knew that, like Monica's home, this building, almost twice as long as wide, boasted an oversized kitchen and an enormous dining hall at the back of the house, where the population gathered for meals.

Two other buildings bracketed the dooryard in front of the big house. One of them looked similar to the bunkhouse apartments at Monica's, though this building was larger and looked like it had been built in the last year. The one opposite the bunkhouse was of the same design, but older and constructed like townhomes or condos.

Several barns sat inside the homestead's wall, with long paddocks stretched out behind them. In three of them, horses grazed. As Jake and the others rode in, some of the animals came to the fence to watch them, their heads up and ears pricked forward alertly; a few nickered a greeting. They were all splendid looking animals, but the most stunning horse Jake thought he might have ever seen ran along the fence line. Tossing his head and tail high, a tall black stallion, fierce and proud, neighed a demand for a response from the newcomers. Jake only got a short gander at the majestic creature, but it was enough to be impressed.

"That's Ebony," Monica told him when she saw his rapt interest.

"He's beautiful," Jake said in a hushed tone.

"He's Angel's horse. Well, he will be. He's a bit headstrong."

"I hear stallions are like that."

Monica chuckled. "Yeah, well, Angel fell in love the minute she saw him. Bought him cheap from his last owner because Ebony wouldn't let anyone ride him. He's been more gracious with Angel, but they're still getting used to each other."

A small orchard of fruit trees stood behind the house, near the wall. Beyond that, past the river that snaked around the homestead and atop a grass-covered hill, Jake spied the most enormous weeping willow he'd ever seen. Its limbs extended at least twenty-five feet in every direction. It seemed to reach almost to the clouds dotting the vast blue sky, and it threw an undulating shadow over the entire hilltop. As he stared, the long boughs swayed in the wind, their tips brushing the grass at its feet. Jake couldn't explain the odd sense of melancholy that washed over him as he gazed at the ancient behemoth, but something about the tree felt sad and beautiful at the same time. His eyes kept being drawn back to it as they rode into the dooryard, until the house finally blocked it from view.

Jake and Monica dismounted near the front door while the others rode off to join a large group mingling at the barns. Monica tied her horse to a deck post in the shade, where the gelding could graze on the short-cropped grass, and motioned for Jake to do the same. He trailed Monica up the front steps, across the deck, and stood behind her as she knocked on the door. She waited, then turned the knob and entered with a loud but friendly "Hello?"

Jake followed her inside and closed the door behind them. As he did, a high-pitched squeal that sounded like an excited teenage girl erupted behind him. When he spun around, unsure if friend or foe had generated the noise, he saw a short, voluptuous woman with long, curling black hair and startlingly blue eyes hurrying down the hallway toward them. She wore jeans and a blue work shirt, and her brilliant smile radiated happiness.

Monica, squealing just as foolishly, met the other woman in the center of the foyer, where they embraced.

"Ah, it's so wonderful to see you!" the woman cried while hugging

Monica.

"You too," Monica replied.

Jake grinned at the heartwarming scene.

"I'm glad you could make it," the brunette said, pulling back and releasing her friend.

"I didn't have much of a choice."

"Of course, you did. I wouldn't have held back the hay, even if you didn't show up at all."

"I wouldn't do that and you know it."

The other woman laughed. "It's really great to see you. I've missed you," she said, and Jake caught a hint of...what? Sadness? Loneliness? Something else altogether? He wasn't sure. Maybe she really meant what she said, but he sensed more underlying her simple statement.

"Same here," Monica replied. She took her friend's hand and turned to smile at Jake.

His previous nervousness—forgotten during the women's animated display—abruptly twisted his stomach into knots.

"There's someone I'd like you to meet," Monica said as the other woman joined her, facing him with a curiously blank expression. "Angel, this is Jake Nichols. He's with us for a while, taking over for Ed Sterns. Jake, this is Angel Aldridge."

"Ah," Angel said as another bright smile transformed her face and her eyes skimmed him from head to toe and back. "You're managing the new construction then." She held out her hand as she spoke, and he grasped it, feeling awkward. "I hope you're doing good work for my friend here."

"I'm trying to, ma'am," he said and released her hand. She was a pretty woman—if not as breathtaking as Monica—and agreeable enough, but his nerves were on edge all the same.

"Call me Angel, please. May I call you Jake?"

"Yes, ma'am...I'd like that, Angel. Thank you." He shifted his feet nervously.

Angel smiled again. "So, how's the construction going?"

"It's coming along," Jake said, unsure of what else to say.

"Well, be careful," Angel advised. "After Ed's fall, I would hate to hear about another accident."

Jake frowned, unsure what that was supposed to mean.

"He's doing a wonderful job." Monica beamed.

"When everything's done, you'll have to invite us over so we can judge for ourselves." Angel smiled at Jake, but he was still frowning. He tried to straighten his face before Angel perceived his discomfort, but the curious look she gave him said he had failed.

"I'd love for you to come over anytime," Monica said, apparently missing the exchange between him and Angel. "You don't have to wait for the house to be finished. In fact, it's almost done. Right, Jake?"

His gaze shifted between the two women and then he shrugged. "Yeah. We've got a few more things to do, but it's basically livable now."

"See?" Monica turned to her friend again. "You should come over after the harvest and bring Theo with you. Jake could teach him some of the ranch stuff he's helped Shawn with."

"That's right," Angel said and placed a hand on his arm. "Monica wrote that you're a rancher too."

"Sort of," he admitted while trying not to squirm away from her touch. "My buddy was the rancher. He taught me what I know. What I remember anyway."

"Well, that's convenient," Angel remarked. "May—"

A knock sounded at the door. Monica was the closest and went to open it. While she was busy talking to Shawn at the door, Jake felt Angel eyeing him, and his heart stuttered out a nervous beat. Reluctantly, he turned his head to meet her gaze. The assessing look on Angel's face made his stomach churn in earnest.

Was he imagining the seductive glint in her eyes?

He frowned, but she only tilted her head, and her lips curved upward ever so slightly. He opened his mouth to speak—he needed to know why she seemed to be watching him like a cat does a mouse—but he didn't know what to say.

He didn't get the chance anyway.

"Shawn says it's time to go," Monica said, already on the front deck and descending the stairs with Shawn.

Jake stiffened as Angel looped her arm around his and led him outside, her small, warm body too close to his.

"There's a million things I'd like to try," she murmured as they headed to the dooryard. "We must have a chat later."

He stifled a groan as his suspicions increased.

She released him, patted his arm familiarly, and then gave him a smile that appeared friendly but made the hair on the back of his neck stand on end. Frustration and annoyance filled his chest. Maybe it was just his experiences at Darla's, or his anxiety, or perhaps he was simply mistaken, but Angel's smile—her interest and intense regard—seemed to insinuate that she wanted far more from him than just a chat.

That's great... Monica's best friend... Shit.

Mounting his horse to follow the others out to the fields, Jake silently strung curses together, damning himself and his luck.

Then he prayed fervently he was wrong.

30

MONICA AND ANGEL SAT alone at a small table on the wide front deck of Angel's home, sipping hot tea and watching the children play after dinner. They all had spent the majority of the day cutting and raking hay in the fields, but somehow the kids still ran and played noisily, like they could go all night. But mothers and fathers soon called them to come in for bed, perhaps because the parents were as exhausted as Monica. She smiled as the children said their goodbyes and followed their parents inside.

"The rebels attacked a small transport from Yakima last week," Angel said, continuing the conversation they'd started earlier. "Got some supplies and killed one of the drivers."

Monica's heart stuttered with the news of the rebels' seeming return to activity in the area. She cocked her head and lowered her brows. "And we're just hearing about it now?"

"Things aren't as fast as they used to be."

"Yeah, I know." Monica groaned, silently wishing they at least had telephones again. "Has anyone looked into the attack?"

"Yeah, Carrie sent a group of Section Guards down there to help," Angel replied. "But, right now, we've got enough to worry about with food and trade and keeping the electricity running consistently, though Carrie's still refusing to allow her people to assist further."

Monica nodded. The engineers they'd found to repair the war-damaged power grid were, unfortunately, owned by Carrie Simpson. "What's her deal, anyway? Why be all anxious to help and then back out?"

"Who the hell knows? Carrie's not the most stable individual around. But if you ask me, Darla had something to do with it. Probably to inconvenience me, but then, maybe I'm just being paranoid."

"I doubt it. Darla hates you."

Angel huffed out a short chuckle. "The feeling's mutual."

They quietly sipped their tea and gazed at the darkening sky as the sun disappeared.

"So, do you think the rebels will start attacking homesteads again?" Monica asked.

"I don't know, possibly, but if they do, I have my doubts it'll last long. They've always been too disorganized in the past to be much of a threat to anything. My guess is they're still as much of a chaotic mess as they've always been. The attack on the transport was just a means to acquire food or other supplies one of the factions needed, not a sign of coordination."

"Any news from the rest of the world?"

Angel laughed. "Sure, we got a report on the satellite phone just the other day."

"No need to be sarcastic."

Angel tilted her head and gave Monica an apologetic look before supplying the serious answer. "Aside from the information about the raid near Yakima and some correspondence from the west side, there's still been nothing from anywhere else."

Monica nodded and glanced at the empty, shadow-draped dooryard. "Do you still believe there are others out in the world like us?"

"Sometimes..." Angel answered. Her shoulders slumped as she stared at her hands. "I have to believe, if someone other than Darla Cain had organized this section, circumstances here might've been different. So, I hope there are more like us."

"You don't really believe that though, do you." Monica knew her friend well enough that she said it as a statement, not a question.

Angel shrugged. "Not really, no. It's probably just my pessimism showing, but I still fear that women like us are outnumbered everywhere. I hope I'm wrong."

They fell quiet again, both drifting in their own thoughts. Monica's, of course, turned to Jake.

After cleaning up in the guest room before dinner, Jake had escorted Monica to the dining hall. He, Shawn, and, astonishingly, Theo had chatted about cattle, horses, and ranching, while Monica talked with Angel and her head guard Michelle. The men were no doubt discussing the same subject even now down at the barns.

After a hesitant start, Jake appeared to be enjoying himself. His genuine smiles and calm, confident demeanor made Monica happy. She had hoped he would take to the people here, and he did, with a surprising readiness—even with Theo, which she'd been worried about after Theo's comments a few weeks ago. It seemed that the longer Jake was with her, the more he opened up, turning into an even better man than she had expected.

"Jake seems like a nice man," Angel said.

Monica smiled and looked down at the teacup wrapped in her hands. "He is."

"He's also quite attractive." Angel lifted her eyebrows as she gazed pointedly at her friend over her own cup.

"Yes, he is." Monica sipped her tea and then smirked. "He's a great kisser too."

Angel laughed as she placed her teacup on its matching saucer.

"I *thought* he was your newest conquest."

"I wish you wouldn't call him that."

"What? A conquest? That's kind of what they are, the men who fall for you, though it's been awhile since you've taken one in."

"You make it sound like I compel them, but I don't."

"You don't have to try, Monica. Men just fall at your feet."

"Not true," Monica said, straightening her spine. She shook her head and leaned forward. "They don't fall at my feet. Besides," she sat back again and picked up her cup, "it isn't as if men don't check you out with longing in their eyes."

"Ah, but the difference is, even if they do, which I doubt, I don't encourage them. I don't want a man in my life, not anymore."

Monica sighed, and the porcelain rattled as she set her teacup back on its saucer. "How many people do you have here now? A little over a hundred? More?" Angel nodded at the last, and Monica continued. "Dozens of men are in your life, Angel," she pointed out, "all around you every day. You should encourage one, at least; maybe having someone to lean on would help."

Angel's lips pressed together, and she shook her head, a frown marring her brow. "I'm not interested. I've told you that."

"Yes, you did, but I truly think if you'd open up a little you might find life more worthwhile."

Angel's chin lifted, and she glared at her friend. "As I've said, many times before, having a man in my bed does not give my life more meaning."

"All right, all right." Monica waved her friend's angry retort off. Angel's take on her comment was not what she meant, though she didn't think a physical relationship with a man would hurt the other woman in the least. Still, she dropped the topic. She didn't want to argue with Angel tonight, and the subject of her self-imposed celibacy was a sure way to start a quarrel.

"So, are you going to tell me about him?" Angel asked a few minutes later.

"What do you want to know?"

Angel's cerulean eyes glinted mischievously.

"I can tell there's something between you. It's obvious in the way you look at him, and he appears quite taken with you too. But I get the sense this is more important than a summer fling. So, what's going on with you two?"

"How could you tell?"

"You told Michelle to set him up in the guest room tonight. I assume you're not sleeping on my couch," Angel said conversationally, as she lifted her cup to take another sip of tea.

Monica shifted, oddly uncomfortable with Angel's casual comment, and she felt her cheeks warm. Angel glanced over her teacup. Seeing Monica's embarrassment over a topic she was normally comfortable with made Angel's eyes widen, and she choked on her tea. After she regained control, Angel stared at her friend, dumbfounded, and Monica felt her face heat even more.

"Monica, you're blushing!" Angel said in disbelief. "You! Are blushing! What the hell is going on?"

Monica sipped her tea to give herself a moment to think. She swallowed and met her friend's gaze.

"He's a good man," she said, "and I enjoy his company."

"But it's more than that. I'm not surprised you slept with him, but I—"

"I haven't slept with him." Her quiet denial cut Angel off cold.

Angel didn't reply, only stared in stunned stupefaction.

"Don't look so shocked. It's not as if I sleep with every man who passes my way."

"I never said you did," Angel said gently. "I didn't mean to imply it either. You're healthy and still young enough to delight in being with a man. I don't think badly of you for those you do enjoy. I just worry about you that's all. I don't want you to get hurt."

"You don't have to worry about that." Monica tilted her head, considering her friend closely. "And I could say the same thing about you. Enjoying a man, I mean."

Angel gave her a meaningful glare, and Monica shook her head.

"All right, all right," Monica said again. "You're fine and I'm fine." She didn't really believe that though. Not in Angel's case anyway.

"Your reaction a minute ago says otherwise."

"I'm sorry about that. I shouldn't have snapped at you. I know you don't think of me that way."

"But the implication still bothers you. Is it because of Jake? Did he...?"

"No," Monica declared emphatically. "Jake has been wonderful. He is...wonderful."

"I see."

Something in Angel's tone made Monica sit back and cross her arms over her chest. "What do you see?"

"Nothing," Angel answered, and, seeing her friend's dark frown, she elaborated. "It's just that after everything you've told me about him and his situation, I can see you're worried about him."

After Jake had arrived on her ranch, Monica sent Angel a message to thank her for her help. She wrote again later to inform Angel that everything was working out, but in it, she also said she had some details to explain. That was months ago, and so much had happened since then.

Monica sighed and dropped her arms. She hadn't intended to share that story with Angel right away, but, aside from simply refusing to tell her now, it didn't seem like she had much of a choice.

While Angel listened without interrupting, Monica detailed Jake's condition when he arrived, his obvious terror, and how long it had taken him to relax. She didn't reveal everything that had happened between them, but she did disclose his fear of being intimate.

"What could Darla have done to make a man afraid to be touched?" Monica asked.

"I don't know." Angel's eyebrows knit together.

"She was angry we forced her to let him go, if only for a few months. Now, she won't respond to my request for a meeting. I tried riding over to her house to pay her a visit in person, but they told me she wasn't there.

She won't even talk to me." Monica hated the desperation in her voice.

"I'm sorry," Angel said. "I wouldn't wish her on my worst enemy."

"He doesn't want to go back."

"I don't blame him."

"I don't want to let him go either." Monica tried to hold them back, but tears filled her eyes and her voice cracked.

"Oh, honey." Angel reached over to take her friend's hand. "How can I help?"

Monica pulled her hand back and sat up straight. "I want to try to work a deal out with Darla myself first."

"She's difficult."

"That's an understatement, but I still want to do this myself if I can."

"And if you can't?"

"Then I'll hold you to your offer."

"You really like him." It was not a question.

"Yes," Monica choked and cleared her throat. "Like I said, he's a good man. He's kind and sweet and funny and he likes me too. Me, brazen, outspoken Monica. I don't know why I was so drawn to him in the beginning, but..."

"You mean besides his great body and handsome face?" Angel teased.

Monica rolled her eyes and gave her friend a mock glare, then shook her head. "It's more than how he looks. He makes me happy, and thinking about sending him back to Darla makes me sick to my stomach." She stared down at her hands wrapped around her nearly empty cup.

"I'm so sorry." Angel reached for her hand again.

"I just wish this was easier."

Angel slouched back in her chair, her arms wrapped around her middle. "Loving someone these days is never easy."

A weight settled in Monica's chest, and she looked up at her friend. "Oh, Angel, I'm so sorry. I know what you've gone through. I shouldn't be whining to you about this."

Angel stood and ambled over to the deck railing. She crossed her arms and leaned back, facing her friend once again. "And why not? I'm more than just your friend, Monica. The things and people I've lost don't change that. I want you to be happy. If this man makes you happy, then I'll do what I can to help you. If that means only listening, then there's no reason for you not to talk to me."

Monica went to hug her, grateful to be part of Angel's life; since that rainy night three years ago, she couldn't have asked for a better friend. There was nothing she wouldn't do to help Angel heal, but so far, all of Monica's attempts to pull her away from her lonely despair had been useless. Fate and this screwed-up world had taken too much from Angel, and she was afraid to let chance take any more. Now, she was offering to take on Monica's pain as well.

"I appreciate that," Monica said, then pulled back and smiled. She opened her mouth to say more, but footsteps on the path to the house stopped her. Monica stepped back, and they both turned to see Jake approaching. Monica's heartbeat sped up, and a thrill flashed through her at the mere sight of him.

She glanced at Angel, who was smiling, her eyes twinkling again. She winked, and Monica's face heated.

Angel grinned wider and then turned her attention to the man mounting the front steps. "Evening, Jake."

"Evenin'," he said, returning her smile.

When Jake reached the deck, Angel yawned and crossed to the door. "I'm heading to bed," she said. "See you in the morning."

"'Night," Monica and Jake said in unison.

When they were alone, Jake's hand curled around hers, and she lifted her eyes to find him watching her.

"Did you have a nice chat?" he asked. "You two looked pretty cozy before I walked up."

"Yes," Monica answered with a sly smile. "We were talking about you."

His lips quirked, but there was hesitation in his eyes and he made no further comment.

The sun had disappeared behind the mountains some time ago, and the evening sky turned from indigo, to lavender, to slate gray, and now midnight blue. The dooryard lay in shadows, which grew darker by the minute as the last light of dusk dwindled into full night. A coyote barked in the distance, and somewhere closer, an owl hooted.

They stood on the deck, side by side and hand in hand, listening to the nighttime quiet.

"Are you worried?" Monica asked, glancing over at him.

"Worried?"

"About tonight. Us, together in one bed." Having far more privacy in Angel's guest room than the bunkhouse at home had been part of the reason Monica had broached this topic with him before coming here. He'd been consistently adamant in his answers, but looking at his tense jaw now made her question if he was truly ready to take this step.

"Oh..." His eyes turned back to the dooryard. He shrugged and met her gaze again. "A little, I guess."

"We could wait. Find another bed for you..." She hated having to offer that, but she didn't want to push him either.

"No," he said, his shoulders straight and a gleam in his eyes. "I don't want to find another bed. I want to be with you, Monica. I want to try."

"Me too," she said with a soft smile. "Shall we go to bed then?"

He waved his arm toward the front door. "After you."

31

JAKE JAMMED THE PITCHFORK into the wheelbarrow filled with straw. He forked a huge clump and tossed it through the open doorway of the barn stall he'd cleaned earlier that morning. He repeated the action until the floor was covered and then moved on to the next, all the while ruminating on the colossal disaster he'd made of his relationship with Monica.

Ten days had passed since their arrival. The last of the hay had been cut, raked into rows that stretched across acres of fields, and left to dry in the sun for collection in a day or two. The long week and a half they had spent preparing the bales and stacking them in the barns and storage buildings had worn everyone down, and Angel decided they needed an extra day off. As soon as she made the announcement, most everyone congregated by the river flowing through Angel's property—the same watercourse that crossed Monica's land downriver. The kids splashed in the shallows while the adults joined them or gathered in the shade of the nearby fir trees.

Jake was the only one not with them.

"Why don't you come down to the river with us?" Monica had asked earlier that morning. "We could sit, relax, and...talk?" She sounded so hopeful, but he blew that opportunity too.

"I...can't. I promised Theo I'd cover his chores so he could spend some time with Peggy." The pretext was mostly true, but Jake had finished the work in about two hours. He could have said he would meet her later, but he didn't.

Monica knew he was avoiding her; he saw the knowledge in her eyes. He had also seen her disappointment this morning when he told her about his promise to Theo.

He'd seen a lot of that in the last several days.

On their first night here, they had gone up to bed together, optimistic and excited. The minute he closed the bedroom door behind them and set the lantern on the nightstand, Monica was in his arms, kissing him with pent-up passion. He remembered being thankful for the sexual anticipation this beautiful woman stirred within him, rather than the fear and expectation of pain, and for a while their interlude had gone well.

Her deft fingers made short work of the buttons on his shirt and roamed freely over his back as he removed his boots. He stood barefoot and bare-chested as he stripped Monica down to her pretty, electric-blue underwear. She was even more beautiful than he imagined, and he took a moment to take in every gorgeous detail—her long legs and trim waist, the swell of her luscious breasts stunningly displayed by the delicate material of her bra, her blonde hair that fell in waves around her shoulders, the eager smirk on her soft lips, and the heat of desire burning in her eyes.

Their day by the river notwithstanding, he had imagined a lot, but nothing like the real woman before him. While he gawked, she reached behind her back and unhooked her lacy bra. She shrugged, and the flimsy garment fell down her arms to land with a soft thump on the floor.

Jake's breath caught. Like a starving man who'd just been offered a banquet, his eyes devoured the sight of her. She took his hand and brought it to her breast. The nipple hardened and nudged readily into his palm. His groin tightened painfully, and he groaned. He met her warm gaze, and his rapidly thumping heart pounded more strenuously against his ribs at the desire—*and something infinitely more*—he read in her eyes. She smiled as her hands slipped up around his neck, and he pulled her against him again.

She reacted to his every touch, clung to him as if she feared to loosen her grasp, afraid he would run if given the chance. But as much as she responded to him, she also held back. He hated that. Not her hesitancy, but that she kept her own desires in check to keep from upsetting him. He didn't want to inhibit her. He wanted her to be happy, to experience everything the way she was intended to, but for reasons he knew all too well, he couldn't make himself tell her to let go and enjoy herself.

Slowly, as if expecting him to balk, her hands slid from his neck and down his chest to unfasten his jeans. His body tensed as she slipped her hands around his waist and beneath the denim. He didn't try to stop her. He wanted this. Wanted her ardent hands on him. Wanted all the unbridled passion this bold, tender woman could give him.

He wanted to enjoy himself too.

This time would be different. This time he wouldn't break down, wouldn't disappoint her, or himself.

She kissed her way over his chest and abdomen, giggling when the curling mat of hair tickled her nose, as her hands worked his jeans down his legs. He stepped out of his pants and kicked them out of the way. She smiled up at him again as she stood, trailing her fingertips along the outside of his legs and over his hips. The hard heat between his thighs was almost unbearable, but he liked what she was doing.

Encourage by his lack of objection to her advances, her fingers dipped inside his underwear, splayed out over his buttocks, pulled his hardness closer to her softness. Her hips ground against his, her taut nipples poked into his chest. One hand slid from his ass, up his back, and slipped behind his head. She rose up on her toes as she tugged him toward her waiting mouth.

He kissed her, wrapped his arms around her, and held her closer still, hoping her warmth would melt the chill that started the moment her hands took hold of his backside.

Iciness coiled in his belly, a poisonous snake waiting to strike, and he shivered with dread. *Monica won't hurt you*, he screamed inside his head, but the reassurance made no difference.

Both of her hands were inside his underwear again, kneading him, holding him. He shivered as one of her hands inched forward.

You want this... You want her! He held on to the cliff of his resolve by his fingernails, fighting to keep from falling into the abyss of memories he wished he could forget.

He trembled harder still as her fingers wrapped around his rigid, heated flesh. Her touch felt like heaven. His swollen shaft pulsed with ardent enthusiasm in her palm as her fingertips gently brushed along his length, and...

The door in his mind crashed open.

Suddenly, a different woman cringed in his arms, open and vulnerable beneath him. She was blonde, too, but younger and terrified. He remembered her terror as if it was his own...

No...

Wait...

It *was* his own.

He couldn't help her any more than he could help himself. The searing pain of a whip slashed across his back, his ass, his legs, over and over, as he held the young woman under his naked body, protecting her from the lash as much as he could...

"No..." The strangled shout tore through his throat as he pulled himself out of Monica's grasp and turned away. He tried to hold it in, to not make a bigger fool of himself, but a sob escaped him anyway.

"Jake?" Her soft voice broke into his private torture chamber. His brain remembered where he was, who she was, and he groaned, struggling to control his breathing and himself.

He mumbled a curse, wiped at his face, and then slammed the side of his fist against the wall. He leaned into it, resting his forehead on the plaster, willing his quaking to stop, refusing to let any more of the long-held emotions escape.

"Jake, are you all right?"

Hysteria made him want to laugh and scream. He wanted to shout at her, ask her why she cared, but she was not at fault.

Anger swept through him, hard and hot and all-encompassing. He wanted to blame her, blame Bret, blame everyone.

He blamed himself.

He had hurt Anna.

He couldn't protect her, and she died.

He deserved to suffer.

He deserved to make all those who caused his pain, and Anna's, to suffer.

He didn't deserve to be happy.

He didn't deserve Monica...

Cool fingers on his shoulder startled him. He jumped and spun away from the gentle touch. With his back pressed against the wall and his mind in turmoil, he tugged his underwear up into place and stared at the woman who faced him a few feet away.

He felt like an utter fool. What was he thinking? He knew this would happen, and now she would ask—no, demand—that he explain. He couldn't tell her what he had done, what had happened because of him.

She stared at him as she would a rabid animal. Wary and a little afraid, trying hard not to show her apprehension, she took a single step toward him. "Jake...?"

He flinched and slid a few more inches away, the ability to articulate anything intelligible still completely out of his grasp. Normally, he kept his fear and doubt trapped, bottled up deep inside him, within the same container into which he now struggled to shove the overwhelming storm raging through him. But he couldn't figure out how to sift through the tangled mass of emotions, to separate the bad from the good. They all bubbled and swirled around inside him like something in a witch's cauldron, a potion that turned him into the crazed beast Monica was gaping at with a mixture of uncertainty, fright, and sympathy.

He wasn't sure which sentiment he hated more. He didn't want her to fear him or feel sorry for him. He wanted to be normal, damn it! To hold her, make love to her like a man, not some sniveling coward standing pressed against the wall, shaking like a leaf, afraid to move or speak. It's not as if he was under the influence of the drug.

What the hell is wrong with you? he shrieked inside his skull. *Say something! Tell her you're sorry. Tell her you love her. Tell her something, damn it! Don't just stand and stare at her.*

A quiet knock at the door nearly gave him a heart attack.

"Monica?" Angel's soft voice rang in his ears like a fire alarm. Her bedroom was next to this one. He must have awakened her when he hit the wall.

Good job, jackass! Now, you'll have to deal with both of them, when you can't even get yourself together.

"Monica?" Angel called again, and the doorknob turned. "Is everything okay?"

Monica ran to the door to keep her friend from entering. They exchanged lowered whispers and then Monica shut the door.

Meanwhile, Jake took the opportunity to grab his things off the floor. He couldn't stay here now.

Not after all that.

Not after totally embarrassing himself...again.

Not after the way she looked at him.

"What are you doing?" Monica asked when she turned to find him across the room, pulling on his shirt.

"Leaving," he finally croaked out. *Thank God. Now, if I could just stop trembling.*

"No." One word, spoken in an utterly flat tone, which should not have sounded commanding, but it did.

In the process of shaking out his jeans, Jake froze and peered over at her as she approached the bed. She frowned and shook her head again.

A long pause followed, and they stared at each other. Jake couldn't stop quaking. He worked moisture into his too-dry mouth and shoved another word through his obstructed throat. "W-What?"

"You're not leaving," Monica said. "I won't let you run away from me this time."

He shuddered as the winter storm inside him blazed into a blizzard. The damage had been done, but he still couldn't stuff the mess inside him back into the bottle it came out of.

What does she expect me to say to that?

She had never demanded more from him than he could give. Is this where things changed? When he discovered what an idiot he was for believing she was different? When he learned he could be as stupid about a woman as Bret had been over the one who'd betrayed him and enslaved Jake?

Panic welled up inside him. His eyes darted around the room before settling on Monica again. Her satiny skin glowed in the flicker of the lantern's light as she frowned at him from the other side of the bed. She looked beautiful...and dangerous. His very own femme fatale.

Jake still hadn't moved. His white work shirt hung open from his shoulders, and he stared at the woman refusing to let him leave. She moved around the bed toward him, and his trance broke. He shuffled back a couple of steps and hit the wall. He considered diving over the bed, and then she stood in front of him. She grabbed his jeans, pulled them out of his hands, and tossed them away. Her brow still furrowed, she gazed up into his face, and he closed his eyes and turned away.

He pressed into the wall. His breath halted, and sweat beaded his brow as he waited for the inevitable.

When nothing else happened for several long seconds, he peered at Monica from the corner of his eye.

She stared up at him as if she were studying an unusual but interesting creature. She didn't appear angry—frustrated, a little confused, but not angry.

"Look at me, Jake." He recognized a command when he heard one. He didn't want to obey, but he inhaled deeply, gathered what courage he could, and faced her anyway. If her act as his benevolent, temporary Mistress ended here, he wanted to know...now.

As soon as he decided to confront her, his shoulders eased a bit, but he was far from relaxed.

"So this is it, then," he said and couldn't keep the sadness from his tone. *I trusted you. I love you*, his heart cried. *How can you do this to me?*

"This is what?" she asked in a quiet voice, still gazing up at him, unmoving, her face almost wholly in shadow.

"This is where you take what you want from me," he answered bitterly. "What's your command?" His voice sounded hollow and forlorn. "What do you want me to do?"

Her shoulders sagged, and she seemed to shrink, as if she folded in on herself.

Unable to meet the terrible blankness staring up at him, he lowered his eyes like the obedient slave they all expected him to be.

They stayed that way for several lengthy seconds: Monica gazing into his face, Jake staring wretchedly at the floor. The shaking still plagued him.

Maybe it will never stop, he thought. He had seen other men suffer from uncontrollable body tremors caused by long-term use of the drug. Like the horrible images that tortured his overwrought mind, he wondered if his body's reaction would be persistent.

He waited for Monica to speak, his nerves taut, his breathing fast and shallow, panic brewing just below the surface. He waited for her to break his heart, to shatter him into tiny pieces.

When at long last she gave him a command, her voice, though gentle, struck him deeper than any whip ever could.

"I'd like you to go to the bed, Jake," she said, "pull back the covers, and sit down...please."

Choking down the knot in his throat, he sighed and did as she ordered, knowing far too well what happened to slaves who did not obey.

He kept his head down, his eyes on the floor.

She moved toward him a moment later. Through the gloom, he saw her small feet halt on the hardwood a few inches from his. His hands clutched the edge of the mattress.

"Take off your shirt, please, and lie down," she said. "Tuck your feet under the sheets so they don't get cold."

He squeezed his eyes closed and shuddered. The realization of how wrong he was about her made him sick inside. His stomach was so tight and roiling with disappointment that he wanted to retch, but he did as she directed.

When he lay on his back, head on the pillow, legs pushed under the covers, he risked a quick peek at her face. The light sat opposite her now, and though the illumination flickered dimly, he could make out her features—the lovely curve of her set jaw, her luscious lips pressed together into a thin line. A frown still marred her brow as she looked down at him.

His heart stuttered, and his lids closed again. He didn't want to see her like this. If he didn't look at her, he could pretend she was someone else, for a little while, at least.

Again, minutes stretched into infinity while he waited for her to claim his body with her demanding touch, her next command.

The blanket moved, and he braced himself for the coming sexual task he was not ready to provide. He expected to feel her weight on top of him at any moment. Instead, the soft, clean-smelling sheet and quilt dropped over his chest. Surprised and confused, he glanced down at his cloth-draped body and then looked around for her.

He followed her with his eyes as she rounded the end of the bed. When she reached the other side, she pulled back the covers and stood, gazing at him expressionlessly.

His fists grasped the fitted sheet below him, and he silently screamed for her to hurry up and get it over with.

Something crossed her face. It was hard to tell at that angle in the low light, but to Jake, it looked like...pain.

He averted his face and closed his eyes again.

All the better to pretend, he thought.

The lantern light went out. He sucked in another deep breath as his fists tightened on the sheet.

The bed moved with her weight.

The blankets shifted.

Sweat sheathed him from head to toe, and his muscles twitched. Heartache consumed him. He wanted to scream.

"Good night, Jake." He heard her words distinctly, despite her voice being soft and muffled. Stunned, he turned his head and, squinting into the darkness, barely made out the outline of her back...

...That was ten days ago.

He had lain awake for hours after her even breathing told him she had fallen asleep. He was half-afraid she was playing some cruel game and half-furious with himself for doubting her. Mostly, he suffered from bone-deep mortification. He still did. He'd not only broken off his best sexual encounter in years, he had treated Monica—lovely, sweet, kind, patient Monica—like the Mistress he feared.

How could I do that? The question still plagued him days later, and so did the shame.

She hadn't joined him to share the guest room again, and he'd been avoiding her ever since. It was cowardly, yes, but he couldn't make himself bring up the events of that night, mainly because, beneath the frustration and disappointment he detected in her, he also sensed anger. They still spoke—it was impossible for him to shun her entirely, nor did he want to—but the connection between them, the warmth, the certain something that made time with her special, was missing.

Now, once again working in Angel's barn, he hefted another pile of loose straw with the hayfork and tossed it through the open stall. Lost in his thoughts about Monica and how to repair the damage he had caused, he didn't notice another person enter the barn behind him.

"I'm not sure this barn has ever been this clean," a woman said, surprising him. He spun around on his boot heel, his nerves so on edge his heart climbed into his throat. The hayfork slammed into the doorframe and jerked out of his hands. He let it go as he stumbled over his own boots, corrected himself before falling over the wheelbarrow, and stopped to stare at the small woman confronting him.

Angel smiled and tilted her head. "I'm sorry. I didn't mean to startle you."

"What do you want?" He ducked his head and sighed. "I mean, what can I do for you?"

She chuckled and moved closer. He stood very still, waiting, as she examined the results of his efforts.

"You do good work, Jake," she said turning to face him. She stood three feet away, her gaze very direct. She was so small; her head barely topped his shoulder, but something about her set him on edge.

Angel smiled again, and a chill went down his spine.

"You may saddle two horses and take a ride with me."

32

THEY RODE FOR HALF AN HOUR before Angel broke the long silence. "It isn't far now," she said, staring straight ahead.

Jake nodded. She hadn't told him where they were going when she instructed him to saddle the horses, and he hadn't asked.

They traveled northwest, heading to a higher elevation through dense pale-green underbrush and emerald evergreens. It was a steep climb over sometimes loose, rocky terrain, but Angel, plainly not in a hurry to reach wherever they were going, set a slow, steady pace for the horses. The trees thickened, their gnarled trunks growing taller and broader as Angel and Jake rode, and though the temperature remained quite warm, the air cooled somewhat beneath the boughs of the soaring conifers.

At length, the trees thinned a bit, and more deciduous brush, saplings, and deadfall, gray and sun bleached, began to appear in the openings.

"Here we are," Angel declared a few minutes later as they broke into a small clearing at the top of a high ridge. She reined in her horse and sighed as Jake rode up beside her.

He stopped and stared. The spectacular view before them was nothing less than stunning. The tree-speckled ridge they had climbed, and the fuller one opposite, curved into a crescent shape, overlapping and turning back on themselves for miles, and in the gorge between them stretched a long, narrow blue-green lake. Cloud shadows dotted the lake and far ridges, and in the distance the white tips of the Cascades extended across the horizon, the topmost peaks touching the puffy clouds littering the bright blue sky.

"I love this place," Angel said.

"It is beautiful."

She grinned at him. "Yes, and quiet too." She dismounted and tied her horse in the shade, where the mare could feed, and walked farther into the clearing. She climbed up and sat down on a huge fallen log, nearly as big around as Angel was tall. Jake followed her example, still not speaking. He leaned back against the same enormous tree trunk and crossed his arms over his chest.

"I come here sometimes," Angel said. "Not as often as I used to—not enough time—but I try. This is the only place I can be completely alone."

"I can see the appeal."

"So can I."

Jake saw her looking at him and turned his head to meet her measuring gaze. She lifted an eyebrow, and her mouth pulled up in a slow smile. The question in her expression made him grit his teeth. He averted his narrowed gaze and sat up a little straighter. Tightening his arms around his chest, he concentrated on appearing as unapproachable as possible, while monitoring her for movement from the corner of his eye.

An instant later, she chuckled.

"You're a nice-looking man, Jake, but I'm not hitting on you. I'm not interested in that in any case. Not with you or anyone else."

When he faced her again, her teasing smile and the twinkle in her eyes threw him for another loop. He frowned, trying to piece together her meaning. Between her earlier comment and her assessing study of him, he was certain she planned to pursue him for sex. Add in the fact that she hadn't given him a choice about joining her on this little excursion, and he marked one more check in the making-Jake's-life-hell column. What better place to force an affair with your best friend's man than far from prying eyes and ears?

But then she laughed at him and denied any interest. *What's she playing at?*

Seeing his bewilderment, she explained. "I was referring to Monica's attraction to you."

"Oh," he stammered.

"Yes, 'oh'. You didn't think I knew about that, did you?"

"What did she tell you?"

"Not much, but she didn't have to *tell* me anything." Angel's reply was sharp. "I saw the way you two looked at each other the first day. Her interest was obvious to me, but then, Monica and I know each other pretty well. She likes you. She *more* than likes you. I'm assuming the feeling is mutual?"

He glanced at her again, wondering if she actually knew anything or if she was fishing. Monica had said Angel was trustworthy. Did he believe that?

"It's not a trick question," she told him. "I'm not trying to trap you or anything."

He searched her azure eyes and found no indication of deceit. No internal senses warned him not trust her. His instincts said he could, so he went with his gut...and Monica's word.

"Yes, the feeling's mutual."

"I thought so."

"Does it matter?"

She chuckled again. "No, it doesn't matter to me, as long as you're both happy."

He avoided the apparent opening in her statement by scrutinizing the landscape. The variations of blues, greens, and browns offset by pale-yellow flowers and the white clouds floating by overhead made the view truly lovely.

"What are you afraid of, Jake?"

He faced her again. "Nothing."

"Well, that's not true," she said with more than a hint of sarcasm. "We're all afraid of *something*. Is it Darla?"

"I'd be an idiot not to be afraid of her."

"No argument here, but the real question is, what did she do to you to cause you to feel that way?"

He chuckled bitterly. "It would be easier if you asked what she didn't do."

A long, uncomfortable pause followed as they both appreciated the panorama before them and let the topic pass.

"I'm sorry," she said. "I'm terrible at this. I'm not as bold as Monica."

"At what?"

"At prodding into other people's lives." She turned her head toward him. "What I'm trying to get at is... What happened with Monica?"

"What do you mean?" He didn't want to talk about this with her. He should talk about it with Monica, but he couldn't do that either.

"Come on, Jake. You were all smiles the first day, but ever since you've both been...withdrawn."

He sighed, unable to hold her gaze, and they sat for several minutes, both staring out at the passing clouds. His eyes spotted a bald eagle circling overhead.

"I screwed up," he finally confessed as his gaze trailed the predator in the sky.

"How?"

Again, he didn't speak for a while, still uncertain about telling this woman anything.

"Jake," she said quietly, "you can talk to me. I'll be here anytime you need me, and I won't lie to you or betray your confidence."

He lowered his gaze to hers. "Why?"

"Because Monica cares about you and I care about her."

His eyes narrowed, and he stared across the short distance between them, a liturgy of scornful thoughts running through his mind.

"Okay," he responded, intending to test her commitment to the truth, "then tell me—can Monica afford to buy me from Darla?"

A mantle of sadness dropped over Angel, and her lips parted to pull in a breath. "No," she answered softly.

"I didn't think so."

"You're avoiding my question," Angel accused.

"I don't want to talk about it."

"You don't want to talk about how you screwed up?" She tilted her head, her expression bemused. "Because you don't want to look foolish or because you're mad at me for asking?"

He scoffed. She was more audacious than she realized.

"No," he said. "I'm not worried about looking foolish, and I'm not mad at you for asking."

"Then what's the problem? Talk to me, Jake. Maybe I can help."

He kicked at a tuft of grass with his boot. He sighed, and his arms flexed as he tightened them over his chest once more.

"I...kind of...freaked out a little." His shoulders drooped. How could he think Monica would be anything like Darla Cain? How could he treat her that way?

"I know," Angel said, and when his head snapped toward her she quickly alleviated his distress. "Don't look so alarmed. I heard part of it through the wall."

"Oh," Jake muttered. "I'm sorry about that. I didn't think..."

"Not a big deal," she told him. "I'm more worried about you and her."

"Monica and I—we shouldn't have done this."

"Done what?"

"Gotten together, talked about a future, acted like we could make one."

"And why not?"

"Because I've got to go back." Jake shook his head. "Monica can't afford me, and Darla won't sell me. She wants me to suffer."

"Why? I mean, why you specifically?"

He glanced at her. His lips thinned, and he turned away without speaking. Should he tell her? It's not as if she couldn't find out. His actions weren't a secret; everyone at Darla's dinner party had witnessed and undoubtedly shared the story about his attempted attack and the brutal beating that had followed, before the guards dragged him out and chained him up in the darkness. Uncertain about how Angel would react to what he'd done, he hesitated.

"What did you do, Jake?" Her quiet inquiry rang with a hint of understanding.

He sighed. "I...attacked her," he mumbled, staring out over the landscape, his gaze following the eagle again. "I tried to anyway. Didn't even come close, but it was enough to scare her; I saw the fear on her face." He turned to Angel. "If I had reached her, I would've killed her, and she knew it."

He waited for the shocked gasp, the harsh chastisement, but neither came.

"She must've hurt you terribly."

He looked away again. "Yeah, she did."

"I'm sorry you had to go through that."

He shook his head and cleared his throat. "I can't go back there. I'll run first."

"They'll kill you."

He shrugged. "Better than living in hell. Going back to life with Darla would be the worst kind of torture after being with Monica and seeing sights like this again." He waved his arm toward the narrow valley before them. "If I go back, she'll murder me slowly. I'll die in the dark, chained to a wall...alone."

Angel nodded but didn't speak.

Jake wondered if he'd gone too far in telling her his plans. Would she stop him? Would she tell Darla?

"Is that why you're angry with Monica?"

"What?" He met Angel's concerned gaze with a puzzled frown.

"She thinks you're mad at her. Is it because you think she can't help you? Or that she won't?"

"I'm not angry with her. Why would I be? She's the one who has every right to be angry with me."

Angel stared at him as the wind whistled through the trees. And then she laughed—a happy, joyful chortle.

"What's so funny?"

"I'm sorry." She sat up, cleared her throat, and pushed her curly mane of ebony hair away from her face. "I just thought this conversation would be very...different."

"What does that mean?"

"Monica thinks you're upset with her because she pushed you too hard, too far, too fast."

"Did she ask you to talk to me about this?"

"No, I just listened to her. When she said you were upset with her, I knew I needed to help."

Heat crept up his neck. "What else did she tell you?"

"Just what I said: she's afraid she 'pushed you too hard, too far, too fast.' I didn't ask her to elaborate. I can guess, but it's none of my business. I only brought it up in case you understood what she meant. Do you?"

He stared at the ground and attempted to dislodge a rock with the toe of his boot.

"Yes," he said, "but that isn't what happened. It wasn't her, it was me."

"You should tell her that. Why haven't you talked to her?"

"I'm not sure. Cowardly, I guess."

"You're far from a coward, Jake. Most men wouldn't have even tried to attack their abusive Mistress, especially loaded up with the drug all the time."

He sighed, and his shoulders curled in a little more. "I wasn't brave. I was desperate. I didn't give a damn about anything, except making sure they didn't use me as entertainment again."

"At one of her *dinners*?"

His gut clenched, and he glanced at her. "You know about those?"

Lips compressed, she wrinkled her nose. "Unfortunately."

He nodded and relaxed a little. Then he shook his head, trying to push the memories away.

"I witnessed a lot of those," he said, staring at the ground, "and experienced the pain and humiliation when they made me the main event once." He shivered, banishing the images from his mind as an aching lump formed in the back of his throat. "That almost destroyed me. I won't let her do it again."

"I wish there was more I could say besides 'I'm sorry.'"

"There's nothing else *to* say."

Another long pause unfolded as clouds drifted over the sun and a breeze ruffled their clothes. The eagle was closer. Jake could see its telltale white head and tail clearly as it surfed the updrafts near the ridge.

"You need to talk to Monica," Angel said. "She's miserable."

Jake glanced at her and then back to the majestic bird. He admired the creature, how the raptor seemed so carefree, powerful, and in control. He wondered if he could feel that way again, if he could find the courage to share even a portion of his pain with the woman who'd helped him start to heal. And he wondered if she would look at him the same way once he had.

33

MONICA STEPPED OUT onto Angel's front porch, her eyes sweeping the dooryard, searching for the two people she couldn't seem to find. She closed the door a little too hard and wrapped her arms around her middle as she stood on the porch. *Where the hell are they?*

Monica had been sitting by the river with the rest of the ranch population, enjoying the sun and her friends' company when Angel had excused herself, saying she needed to return to the house to take care of some things. Monica thought nothing of her departure at the time, but three hours had passed since then. They were now about to sit down for dinner, and Angel was nowhere to be found.

Jake was also missing, but he might just be avoiding her, as he had been for the last week and a half.

Thanks to Darla's legendary cruelty, his reaction to Monica when they first tried to be physical had frightened her but did not surprise her. Whatever that woman had done to him was horrible enough that it tormented him still, months later, and caused him to mistrust not only her, but all women. Monica knew this, but his presumption that she would demand he perform for her sexually when he was not ready to—the way Darla would—hurt Monica more than she thought possible. She had been prepared for him to back away, and though stopping would've been hard, she would have let him go. But she had not expected him to treat her like an enemy to be feared.

She should have consoled him that night in Angel's guest room. She should've told him she understood, but words, for the first time in many years, eluded her. Due to her confusion and the ache in her heart—and maybe a little bit of wounded pride too—she could not form a coherent thought that night. She had wanted to hold him, stroke his hair, his back, and tell him everything would be all right, but she feared touching him again. She didn't want to make his plight worse.

Then he had tried to leave, but she couldn't let him. Where would he go? He had said he would run away before being taken back to Darla. What if he had tried to escape that night, thinking Monica was the same kind of woman as Darla Cain? She couldn't risk that, so she refused to let him walk out. Instead, she sent him to bed.

Since then, she had tried to talk to him, but distance stretched between them now, a vast abyss far wider than the three empty feet separating them on the bed when they had finally gone to sleep that first evening.

"I'm sorry," she'd apologized the next afternoon. "I did—"

"Don't worry about it." He cut her off gruffly and appeared so uncomfortable, she dropped the whole thing. She tried to talk to him about normal things, but his manner, though less brusque, was still reserved. Shortly after, he began avoiding her in earnest.

His aloof behavior cut like a knife slicing through her heart. His anger was obvious. That he blamed her appeared just as obvious, but no matter how she approached him, she could not get past the icy barrier he'd erected against her.

Why didn't I go more slowly? she thought, berating herself for the umpteenth time as she strode down Angel's front porch steps. *I should've held back. I should've let him lead.* But she'd never been timid when it came to men and sex. Still, Jake had come to mean so much more to her than any other man she'd known. That night in Angel's guest room, she'd gotten so wound up in him, so excited by the hunger he awoke in her and his apparent approval of her actions, that she'd stopped being careful. Emboldened by his responses and his lack of retreat, she'd let go and unleashed her full desire in all its brazen glory. *I am such an idiot! He deserved better from me and I let him down. I only hope he'll give me another chance...*

As she crossed the lawn and headed toward the barn, she wondered what was occupying Jake all day. She'd seen him at breakfast when he declined the invitation to join her at the river, but she hadn't seen him since. She hoped he was all right, that he'd at least had a good day. Another little pang struck her heart. She hoped he would allow her to spend time with him again.

Rounding the corner of the bunkhouse, she froze as she saw Jake and Angel riding toward the horse barn.

Monica Avery was not an insecure woman. But because of the new distance between herself and Jake, seeing her best friend riding into the barn with the man she was infatuated with—after an absence of several hours—set her on edge. She trusted Angel. Well, she thought she did. After everything they had gone through and all they'd built together, she thought their bond stronger than the pillars of heaven. But the columns of her faith were shaking.

What if he had moved on? She pushed the thought aside. Angel's heart was still buried in the past. She wouldn't be interested in Jake or anyone else. Still, the muscles in Monica's shoulders tightened as she approached the open barn door. Her stomach clenched, and suddenly she couldn't breathe.

Stop freaking out, she scolded herself. *Everything's fine.*

Her eyes adjusted to the lower light as Angel came out of the tack room at the back of the barn.

"Monica," she said cheerily, "I was just thinking about you."

"Hi, Angel. Considerate of you to let someone know you were leaving with one of my people." She cringed inwardly. She sounded like a jealous girlfriend.

"I told one of the kids to let Michelle know," Angel said, her eyebrows scrunching together. "She didn't tell you?"

"Michelle didn't know where you were either."

"Oh. Well, I guess Nick got sidetracked," Angel said, referring to one of the older boys living on the ranch. "I'm sorry about that. I'll be sure to deliver the message myself next time."

"I'd appreciate that," Monica said as she followed Angel to the stall where the chestnut mare she'd ridden was munching fresh hay. Angel picked up a brush near the door and began grooming the horse.

"Anything important happen while we were gone?" Angel asked.

Monica heard footstep returning from the tack room and bit down on her lower lip. Tingling raced up and down her back and her stomach tightened as she waited to see if Jake would enter the stall. She wondered if he would speak to her. But when he didn't appear, her shoulders sagged a bit and her hand pressed on her belly as she fought down the disappointment. She strained for any sound of what he was doing next door, hoping he would approach them when he finished with his horse.

"Monica?" Angel's voice garnered her attention once more, and she quickly replayed Angel's last question.

"Not really," Monica said in response. "Unless you count Theo getting dragged into the river fully clothed."

A soft chuckle vibrated through the wall, and warmth flushed over Monica's skin.

"What? Why?" Angel was frowning at her over the horse's back.

Monica swallowed before she answered. "Apparently, he lost a bet. They were playing some game and the loser got dunked. They put on quite a show, especially when he tried to walk out with his boots full of water.

He kept falling back in. The kids thought it was hilarious."

Angel chuckled at the image.

"I felt a little sorry for Theo though," Monica said. "I don't care how hot the weather is, the river is still cold."

"It certainly is."

Monica spun around at the sound of Jake's voice. Her heart thudded in her throat as their eyes collided. Arms crossed, he leaned a shoulder against the doorframe and gave her a crooked grin. A shot of something warm and fuzzy exploded inside her, and although her heart settled back into her breast, it didn't slow down.

He was smiling. At her. And she held no doubt he hinted at their own private swimming excursions in the natural pool near her house.

She glanced at Angel, who was still brushing down her mare, to find the other woman scrutinizing her and smiling. She winked and spoke before Monica could ask what was going on.

"I'm going to be a while," she said offhandedly. "Jake, why don't you and Monica take a ride up to the north pasture after dinner? You'll find a beautiful spot to watch the sun go down up there."

"Sounds like a good idea," Jake said, and then he looked at Monica. "You up for it?"

Stunned by the sudden change in his attitude toward her, Monica didn't reply right away.

His grin faltered a little.

When it finally sunk in that he was asking her to be alone with him, her mouth curled up at the corners and she couldn't respond fast enough. "Sure."

His smile brightened. "Would you like me to escort you up to the house?" he asked, a glimmer of mischief in his hazel eyes.

She glanced at Angel.

"You go on ahead," Angel said as she ran the brush over the same spot on her horse's flank that she'd covered three times already. "I'll be along shortly."

Jake stepped out of the doorway and gestured for Monica. "Shall we?"

Something in the tenor of his voice worked its way inside her and sent little shivers dancing through her body. His intense gaze seemed to burn as it swept over her, and when his eyes locked on her face, she went unexpectedly weak in the knees.

Am I reading him right? she thought. *He ignores me for days. Now he's being gallant and looking at me like that again? Has he forgiven me?*

Mouth dry, heart thumping in her chest, Monica followed him. He held out his arm for her to loop hers through, and when she did, he pressed his other hand over hers and led her from the barn.

"The two of you have a nice ride?" she asked him to fill the silence.

He nodded. "It was...beautiful and...interesting."

"Interesting?"

"I'll explain later," he said, flashing her the cutest boyish grin she'd ever seen.

If I weren't already in love with him, that grin would've sent me over the edge.

Her heart continued to hammer out a rhythm on her ribcage, and her stomach fluttered, as if filled with a kaleidoscope of monarchs all flapping their wings at once.

What's wrong with me? I don't have these kinds of reactions.

She had never been shy around men. She was always the one in control, but this time was different. This *man* was different.

Wait... What?

She stumbled over her own feet when her earlier thought came back to her: *If I weren't already in love with him...*

He stabilized her with his free hand, his long fingers gripping her waist. "You okay?" he asked.

"Ah... Yeah. Fine. Just clumsy, I guess," she stammered. She took his arm again, and he continued around the house to enter the dining hall from the back.

Am *I in love with him?*

Is it love or lust?

Monica snuck a peek at his profile, and the rapid tempo in her chest picked up. She could sense the power in the muscles of his arm, in the hard biceps that rubbed her wrist, and in the strength of his forearm beneath her hand. His whole body was solid and so warm. She thought about running her fingers through the soft, springy mat of brownish-blond hair on his chest, and another little thrill shot down to her toes. She thought about being alone with him again, and her tender emotions increased. As she envisioned his smile, his laugh, the sound of his voice, the heat in her chest dived southward and she realized he turned her on just by being him. He didn't need to look at her, didn't even need to speak. He was only walking with her, but all she could think about was sneaking off into the bushes—or better, the guest room—and kissing him breathless.

Then she thought of him leaving, and her heart drummed a slow, hard, repetitive beat. Tiny fissures splintered through it, and she felt like every part of her would shatter if she lost him. The sensation both alarmed and exhilarated her. Her breathing slowed and her hands inadvertently clutched at his arm, but she loosened her grip before he noticed.

She inhaled and concentrated on the moment—Jake walking beside her, both of them happy—and the heavy weight in her chest dissipated.

She had been attracted to other men, but not like this, never this completely or so deeply. She'd never felt like she needed anyone, but with Jake... She didn't want to live without him. She tightened her hold on his arm and rested her head against his shoulder, thankful to have him close once more.

I love him, she thought, a blissful grin splitting her face and buoyant happiness filling her heart. She could handle anything with him by her side; even his fear of intimacy couldn't faze her now. She loved him, and everything else would come in time.

34

MONICA BREATHED A QUIET SIGH of relief when they finally reached the north pasture. Aside from occasionally commenting on the beauty of the landscape, both she and Jake had remained silent during the ride. Her insides felt fluttery the whole way there, and now her palms were sweaty and her heart was pounding, hard. She looked around the clearing while Jake tied the horses nearby and loosened the saddle girths. When he returned to her, he carried a pair of thin blankets in his hands.

"Thought it might get a little chilly," he said as he draped one over her shoulders. The green wool was soft against her skin as it brushed her neck.

"Good thinking," she said over her shoulder. His hands lingered on her arms, and tingles flashed over her body. "Thanks."

"No problem," he responded as he spread the second blanket, this one red, next to a boulder jutting out of the ground like the hump of a giant camel. He motioned for her to sit, and once she did, he set his hat on the blanket and joined her.

They sat with their backs to the rock and their legs outstretched. Monica's hands rested in her lap, and Jake's arms were crossed over his chest. His shoulder brushed hers as they sat watching the sun lower toward the craggy, tree-topped horizon.

Admiring the pink and orange clouds highlighting the gradually darkening sky, Monica bit her lip and dried her clammy palms on her jeans. Then she took hold of the blanket's edges and wrapped her arms around her to keep her fingers from fidgeting, but her mind wasn't as easily restrained.

A minute swept by, two.

Was he ever going to speak or give some sign as to why they were sitting here?

He was quiet so long she eventually sighed and decided to break the ice herself.

"Jake?"

"Hmm?" he turned his head to look down into her face.

"I'm sorry about the other night," she said. "I didn't mean to upset you..."

He started shaking his head before she finished speaking, and her words faded away.

"It wasn't you," he said. "You didn't upset me."

"Then why were you so angry with me?"

"I wasn't angry with you. The whole thing was my fault." He lowered his head and sighed. "There's something I need to tell you, but I'm not sure how to, and I'm not sure I can."

"Just tell me, Jake. Nothing you say will change how I feel about you." Knowing the kind of man he was, she felt safe in that assessment. She only hoped those were the right words to say.

His eyes sought hers. "I'm glad to hear that," he said as he took her hand in his and rested them against his thigh. "What I have to say is hard for me. I'll tell you as much as I can, but I'm not promising I can share everything. I need you to understand that."

She nodded. "You can tell me anything, Jake."

His smile returned momentarily, and he squeezed her hand before looking away. He remained quiet for several long seconds, considering his next words, and when he spoke, his voice came out low and tentative.

"You know Darla, what she's like with her slaves?"

Monica nodded again.

He met her gaze, and her heart throbbed with grief at the bleakness she saw on his face.

"Have you ever been to one of her dinners?" he asked.

"No, but I've heard about them, the ones where she forces her slaves to perform in one way or another for the crowd."

"Those are the ones," he said. "Life there is bad for her slaves. She toys with us, tortures us for fun, starves us... At first, I thought I could handle anything they threw at me, fight off any amount of beating or humiliation, and I did. I told myself pain and starvation were better than giving in to her warped desires, that I'd survive and escape." He hung his head. "I was a fool..."

He took a deep breath, still holding her hand but once again staring at the ground somewhere to her left. A gentle breeze ruffled his shirt and blew Monica's unbound hair into her face. She reached up and tucked the strands behind her ear as he spoke again.

"It took a little while, but I began to realize I would never escape from there. I tried to force my way out once, and they punished me severely for that. I was lucky I didn't seriously hurt any of the guards. I hate to think what would've happened if I had... I didn't try that again, but I kept looking for a chance to run.

"When Darla started to pay attention to me, to use me as a breeder, things got so much worse. She hurt me in ways I won't describe, and her friends were almost as bad. Carrie Simpson was one of the worst." His voice had grown increasingly raspy as he spoke, and it cracked on the last word.

Monica noted that his breathing had increased, and his hand, palm damp from sweat, unconsciously crushed her fingers.

Silently, he stared out at the shadow-draped valley. His body trembled. He squeezed his eyes closed and took a deep breath. He opened his mouth to speak, but a grunting sob escaped him instead.

She reached over and placed her hand on his cheek, turned his face to her, and smiled when his lids lifted. The pain she read in those hazel-green depths stabbed straight through her heart.

"You don't have to go on," she whispered.

"Yes, I do. I need you to know this, at least some of it. I need you to understand..."

She understood, but she only nodded, her heart breaking for him, and waited for the rest of his story to unfold.

JAKE TOOK ANOTHER DEEP BREATH, trying to still his shaking and calm himself a little more before he spoke. Then, in a gravelly voice he could only partially control, he revealed to Monica the sexual amusements Darla and her friends had forced him to engage in, how they abused his body and tortured him worse if he refused them. He spoke of the mental games, the way Darla pitted all her slaves against each other not only for her entertainment but to keep them from uniting against her.

A select few of the men she owned were shown an overabundance of favoritism and got away with much more than Jake ever dreamed of trying. They did her bidding and not only took advantage of the other slaves, but mistreated them as well.

Jake would not join her favorites in harming the weaker slaves, and he often stopped them from doing so. This made him very unpopular, which resulted in additional beatings from her favored pets, on top of the agony inflicted by his Mistress and her friends.

He explained the ache of starvation when they withheld his food as punishment.

The freezing chill of the shackles on his wrists, ankles, and neck.

The forced labor and the searing heat of the summer sun.

The rattle of the chains.

The shuddering winter cold.

The soul-stealing darkness in the tiny cell Darla banished him to after he attempted to attack her.

He had started talking, and now he couldn't stop the words any more than he could keep his voice steady. He talked until he sobbed, but he did not tell her everything. He couldn't tell her about Anna.

He didn't want to think about the young woman he had saved, only to utterly fail her later. Anna was gone, and her death was his fault. He hadn't killed her, but would Monica see it that way? He wouldn't risk losing the one person he could rely on, the woman he now loved more than his own life. No, he would not tell Monica his most devastating secret. Not now, maybe not ever.

"There are scars," he murmured hoarsely. "You may not have seen them because the room was dim the other night and too much was happening, but they are there." He took a shuddering breath and finally met her gaze. "There are others. Deeper scars you can't see. Those are the ones I can't get past. They caused my crazy reaction the other night, not you. You didn't do anything wrong. You did everything right. I just can't forget what they did to me—what *I* did—and it comes back when I get close to a woman, to you. I can't—" He choked on his words again, and suddenly she was straddling his lap. Her arms went around him, and she pulled him against her, cradling his head on her shoulder.

He pressed his face into the curve of her neck and hugged her to him. She was so soft and warm, and she smelled sweet, like outside and floral-scented soap. She swayed ever so gently as she murmured kind words of comfort.

He realized he was crying. His scalding tears dampened her neck and the collar of her red work shirt, but he couldn't stop. Embarrassed, he tried to pull away, but she wouldn't let him go.

"Jake," she said, cupping his face in her hands. "Jake, look at me."

He felt like an idiot. He had already made a fool of himself by sobbing like a child. She'd heard his blubbering; he didn't want her to see the evidence on his face.

"Please, Jake, look at me." Something in her plea made him lift his head to meet her gaze, and he was surprised by tears shining in her eyes, gliding down her cheeks.

"You're crying." He sounded as shocked as he felt.

She nodded, chuckling nervously as she wiped at her face.

He only stared, too distraught to think straight. He had trusted her with his pain, most of it anyway. What would she do with it now?

"I know there's more you're not telling me," she said, staring directly into his eyes while her thumb slowly brushing along his cheekbone. "Something so terrible it broke something inside *you*. I wish I could fix your hurt, or at least make the pain less, but I can't. You don't have to tell me, not now or ever, if you don't want to, but you need to know, it won't matter."

"It won't matter?" he echoed, his thoughts still running a half-mile slower than the conversation. He sounded drugged, even to himself.

"It won't change anything," she said with a little shake of her head. "I want you with me. I want you safe."

"I don't deserve you," he said at length.

"I deserve the man I love, Jake."

"You...*What*?"

"You heard me," Monica said. "I love you, Jake Nichols. I have for a while now. And you need to know, I don't care what you did or didn't do. I love you, and right now, that's all that matters. So no more talk about who deserves what. I intend to make you love me back, and that's all there is to it."

Jake gawked at her like a child staring at a much-wanted toy out of his reach.

"But I can't even... I mean, we haven't..."

"What?" she asked, sitting back on his thighs. With her hands resting on his shoulders, she tilted her head. "'We haven't even slept together.' Is that what you were going to say?"

Heat burned his face, and he knew a deep red had tinted his cheekbones. He tilted his head and shrugged.

She threw her head back and laughed. The joyous, full-bodied, infectious sound made him chuckle too. Then she met his gaze again and sighed.

She cradled his face with her hands. "Oh, Jake. Does it really matter?"

He thought about it for a moment and lifted his shoulders again. "No, I guess not."

"You *guess* not?" She swept her fingers over his forehead, brushed the side of his ear, and settled her palm over the pulse point on his neck. "Come on, you can do better than that. I said I love you, Jake. Do you think I'd say those words if all I wanted was to sleep with you?"

He shook his head. "I didn't mean it like that. I meant we haven't shared everything, been that intimate. I'm not even sure I can again."

"We've been close enough," she said, taking his hand in both of hers. She lifted it and kissed his knuckles, sending warm tingles up his arm. "Besides," she continued, "I don't need sex to tell me how I feel. I love you, and sex, when we get to it, will be all the better because we'll have the emotional attachment."

"But what if..."

"You will again. You proved it the other night. You've already said you want to be with me. We just have to move slowly. You're more than worth the wait, Jake. I'll be ready when you are."

He shook his head. "I'm not usually so lucky."

"You are now." She lifted his face in her hands. "I'm going to kiss you, Jake. Stop me if you need to."

For the first time in a long time, his initial sensation was not panic. Instead, he enjoyed the gentle press of her mouth, the hot moistness of her tongue as she traced the contours of his lips, the softness of her cheeks as they brushed against the rough stubble of his beard. His mouth opened and met hers, drawing her into him, deepening the kiss. She moaned, and her arms slid around his neck. His hands cupped her buttocks and hauled her against him. He wanted her, to be inside her, to love her as he meant to do before. He wanted to show her how he felt...

You haven't told her how you feel yet, jackass.

He jerked back and stared up at her, his breath and hers both coming in fast little gulps.

"I love you." He swept her hair behind her ear. "I love you too, Monica."

She smiled and touched her forehead to his, brushing her fingers over his cheek.

"Good to know, Cowboy," she said with a hint of humor in her tone that warmed his heart.

"Cowboy?" he asked, taking her by the arms and holding her away from him. "Where did that come from?"

"You worked a ranch," she said with a playful smile, "they had cattle. You're helping on my ranch and I have cattle. You're a cowboy."

He chuckled. "Okay, if it makes you happy, I'll be a cowboy for you, but I'm not. Not really."

"Close enough for me," she said and kissed him lightly, teasing him, encouraging him to respond.

And he did.

35

JAKE WAS TOO HAPPY to think much beyond the wonderful, beautiful woman in his arms. She loved him! With all his screwed-up problems, she loved *him* and would give him what he needed to heal.

All he needed was Monica.

Her mouth opened to his, and he took it like a thirsty man in a desert oasis. Her smile, her laugh, her touch revived him, rejuvenated his lust, and gladdened his heart. Her arms snaked around his neck, and her fingers raked into the longer hair on top of his head. She clung to him almost desperately before she relaxed, and he felt her pause, slowing her movements and holding her passion in check.

He broke the kiss.

"What are you doing?"

"Kissing you," she replied, breathless. Her face was flushed and her eyes were bright, but uncertainty clouded the amber-flecked hazel depths.

"I don't want you to hold back," he told her. "I want you to enjoy this the way you normally would. Completely, with no hesitation."

"I don't want to upset you," she said, touching his face. "I want to go slowly, for you."

"I don't want slow, Monica, I want you. All of you. I want to be inside you...now."

"Are you ready for that?"

He took her hand and pressed it over the hard bulge straining beneath the fly of his jeans. "I'm very ready," he said with a roguish grin.

"That's not what I meant."

"I know what you meant."

"Are you sure?"

"That I won't see horrible images inside my head? No, I'm not sure, but I'm positive I want to be with you."

Her eyes were grave as she delved into his, searching for what, he wasn't sure. Then she gave him an impish smile and stood up.

"All right, Cowboy," she teased as she unfastened her jeans and pulled off a boot. "I'll take a chance with you but"—she paused to pull off her second boot and toss it away—"if you need to stop, you must tell me. No running away. Let me hold you until it passes. Agreed?"

His gaze swept over her, lingered on her breasts rising and falling beneath her shirt, and traveled to her open jeans, where he could just make out something pink and lacy inside. His eyes loitered there before returning to her face.

Her brows lifted.

"Anything you say, baby," he said with a crooked smirk.

"I'm serious, Jake."

"So am I." He held out his hand to her. "Come back to me."

She shook her head. "Uh-uh, not yet."

Her expression turned from solemn to sultry in an instant. Her hands clasped the waist of her jeans, and wiggling her lovely backside, she quickly shimmied the denim down her legs and tossed the jeans aside. Next, she started on the buttons of her shirt, one after the other, bit by bit, working them open, smiling at him the whole time.

"Monica," he ground out, "come back here. Now."

Her lips stretched a little farther as she sauntered toward him. Her long, trim legs gleamed in the sunset light, and the round curves of her breasts peeked at him as her half-open shirt shifted with her movements. Her pale-pink panties looked like cotton candy against the creaminess of her skin. She stood above him, straddling his legs, and then dropped to her knees, settling herself in his lap.

He groaned again and reached for her, tugging her closer. Fascinated with how her vibrant blonde hair changed color when it caught the evening sunlight, he reached one hand up to comb his fingers through the strands.

"You are so beautiful," he said as he kissed the hollow at the base of her throat and felt her shiver.

Her hands slipped up his muscular arms and over his broad shoulders. She moaned as he continued nibbling the tender column of her neck, unable to get enough of the taste of her skin.

She rested her cheek on the top of his head. "You're not so bad yourself, Cowboy," she purred.

His fingers finished the buttons on her shirt, and he pulled the edges apart. He pushed her back a few inches to admire her further.

"I *am* a lucky man," he said as his fingertips traced the straps of her cream-colored bra up to her collarbone. Plain, with a bit of lace adorning the deep V-front, the undergarment had a convenient front closure. He smiled up at her, a mischievous glint in his eyes as his fingers trailed back down the straps and over the lacy edge to the clasp in the center. "I am so—very—lucky."

"WE BOTH ARE," she panted and then gasped as her bra cup dropped away from her breast, only to be replaced by the scorching sensation of Jake's mouth. Her back arched, and she threw her head back, loving what he did, loving him loving her. She giggled softly at the tickle of his beard brushing her sensitive skin, but inhaled sharply as his tongue flicked expertly over her straining nipple. His hand covered her other breast, and he teased it in similar fashion with his fingers, alternating back and forth until she was so turned on that a soft, constant keen emanated from her lips.

She was unaware of the sounds she made, too absorbed with how he made her feel. She wouldn't have cared even if she knew.

Heat was building between her legs; moisture stained her lacy pink underwear, and a swirling need brewed low in her belly. All she could think about was Jake touching her, Jake kissing her, Jake filling the wildly growing need inside her.

Her hands started on his shoulders, but now one splayed out over the back of his head, his hair tickling her palm as she held him to her, demanding more without demanding at all.

He lifted his head, one arm curling around her back, the other hand cradling her head as he pulled her down into another long, yearning kiss.

She took the opportunity to tear at the buttons of his shirt and then tugged the ends from the waistband of his jeans. Once his shirt was open, she said a silent prayer of gratitude that he wore no undershirt as she combed her fingers through the golden-brown mat adorning his torso. Her nails flicked over his nipples, and elation filled her when he moaned and they instantly hardened. She flicked them again and slipped her fingers down over the flexing muscles of his belly to the button of his jeans.

His hand tightened on the back of her neck, his arm around her waist contracted, and his body tensed as his fly opened and her fingers slipped inside. She touched him, her hand molding over the hot, firm shaft, and squeezed gently.

He jerked away with a gasp and gripped her upper arms, holding her back. Her hand slipped free of his jeans and she stared into his face. His eyes were closed, and his breaths came in huge, heaving gulps.

He was panicking. She could feel his distress in the sudden surge of heat from his body, the sheen of sweat on his brow, and the quake racking his frame.

"Jake?" she called, cradling his face. "Look at me, Jake. Look at me."

His lids lifted, and he frowned at her, still panting, still shaking.

"It's me. Monica. I'm not going to hurt you." She took hold of his wrist, tugged until he released her arm, and then pressed his hand against her chest, directly over her heart. She did the same to him. "I love you, Jake. Can you feel my heart in your hand? I can feel yours." She applied a light pressure on his chest. "My heart, all of me, is yours. We can stop now if you want. I will still love you."

He shook his head. "No," he rasped. "I don't want to stop. I just need a minute." He sucked in a few deep breaths and looked at her again. "Will you stand up for a second and help me get these jeans down? Ordinarily, I'd do it myself, but I'm feeling...a little shaky."

"Okay," she said, but didn't move right away. "Are you sure?"

"Yes, I'm sure. I want you, Monica. I might be a little awkward, but I want this. Now, please, help me get my pants off."

She smiled and couldn't help teasing him a little. "How can a girl refuse a sweet-talker like you?"

He chuckled as she lifted herself off him and tugged at the legs of his jeans as he lowered the denim off his hips. His underwear, navy blue this time, slid half off as his jeans lowered to his thighs, and Monica admired the view.

Broad shoulders, a wide, furred chest, hard abs, narrow hips, and a tuft of golden-brown pubic hair curling over the elastic of his underwear were all prominently on display. Her eyes lingered on his body, leisurely making their way back to his face. When she met his gaze again, he appeared embarrassed by her prolonged perusal.

"I'm impressed, Cowboy," she said as she knelt over his lap. "You are gorgeous. Do you realize what you do to me?"

Apparently that was the right thing to say, because Jake smiled and relaxed a little.

"You're the only one to ever think so," he said, his cheeks reddening a little more.

"I seriously doubt that," Monica replied. She brushed her palm over his muscle-hardened belly and up his chest, then along his neck to rest on his cheek. "You are handsome, Jake, but there is so much more to you than that. To me, you are everything."

Something flashed in his eyes, doubt, maybe, or disbelief, but it vanished. A long second passed, and then his face lit up. The searing heat emanating from his gaze reached inside her, warming her heart and igniting her body.

The back of his fingers brushed her cheek and she trembled, as turned on by looking at him now as she had been by his actions before he had stopped so abruptly.

Please, God, she prayed, *don't let him stop again.*

"I love you," he whispered as if in awe. "I really do love you."

"I know," she said, sitting very still, waiting for him to make the first move.

He took her wrists and placed her hands flat on his chest.

"Touch me," he said. "Kiss me." He leaned toward her, and she eagerly complied.

"Awkward" was the last word she would use to describe what he did to her. He seemed to know every one of her secret places, where to caress or kiss to drive her wild, and he attacked them with a tender passion that left her breathless.

Her hand slipped inside his briefs, seeking the pulsing heat within. He stiffened as her fingers closed over him.

"I love you, Jake," she whispered in his ear, and he relaxed, pulling back and peering up into her face. She stroked him lightly while she held his gaze and eased his underwear out of the way until he was free and open to her touch.

His hands rested on her thighs, his fingers constricting and releasing as she fondled him. He groaned and closed his eyes. His head dropped against the boulder behind him and he stayed that way, breathing, trembling a little, while her hands kneaded and caressed him.

Worried she was losing him to painful memories, she leaned forward and kissed him tenderly.

"Are you still with me, Jake?" she whispered against his lips.

"Yes," he responded as his hands, in one swift motion, slipped over her thighs and around her hips to cup her backside. His fingers tightened on her buttocks, and he hauled her against him. "Only with you, Monica."

A surprised squeak escaped her as she released him and gripped his shoulders for balance. She glanced down to meet his ardent gaze, and the tension in her belly convulsed pleasantly at the desire she saw there.

"I want you," he said in a strained, husky voice. "I want you now." He emphasized his need by tightening his grip on her hips, pressing downward, and grinding against her softness. The resulting friction sent a blaze of fire through her whole body, devouring everything in its path: fear, hate, worry—anything that might come between them. She cried out at the sudden burst of excitement within. The flames he ignited melded around her heart as her love for this man swelled beyond her body and mind, beyond anything she had ever experienced.

Her hands clutched his shoulders. Her head dropped back as her eyes closed and her spine arched. She moaned.

"Yes," she murmured, "yes, now."

Their bodies trapped his erection between them, and its long length throbbed against her core until her sex beat in time with its hot insistence. Using his grip on her rump and the pressure of his arms alongside her hips, he moved her body in a swirling motion, pressing in and downward, rubbing his blistering need along the silky fabric covering her hot, wet opening and the tingling bud that craved him.

She was ready for him to enter her, but he held back, driving her mad by teasing her with his nearness. She wanted to yank her panties out of the way and push him inside her, ride him, pleasure him, make him cry out the way he had already made her moan with need.

But she couldn't do that. She must let him guide her. If she rushed him, he might pull away, and she could not stand that again, not after coming this close. She had a suspicion their union would be better than she ever imagined, and she wanted to find out.

His fingers found their way downward, inching between her thighs. He no longer moved her hips. She did it herself, grinding against him, sliding the sizzling heat he created in her along his shaft. He tugged her panties aside, and the pad of his thumb repeated the swirling motion, only in a much smaller, more direct area. She shuddered, and the pressure increased.

"Oh, Jake," she moaned again, head still back, eyes still closed, her whole body tense with wanting, captivated by the things he did to her and the way he made her feel.

"Monica." It was a hoarse whisper. "Monica, look at me."

Her eyes opened, and she lowered her head to meet his gaze. The love shining back at her tightened her chest. She kissed him, clutched him to her. His chest hair, slightly abrasive against her breasts, was as much of a stimulant as his mouth and fingers.

She kept moving, sliding against his shaft, while she kissed him.

His thumb plied her sensitive flesh, and her body convulsed. Her hands clutched his shoulders, and she sucked in a deep, preparatory breath. She cried out as the tension inside her broke and waves of pleasure washed over her.

In that instant, while she was dazed and vulnerable, he took over.

His large hands gripped her hips, lifted her up. She felt a momentary sense of anxiety, and her lids popped open. Her hands scrabbled at his shoulders, trying to hold on, unwilling to let him go as he moved her.

"No," she cried as their bodies separated. "Please, Jake, no..."

"Yes," he growled as he shifted, positioning her over him and then, once again tugging her panties aside, he pulled her back down onto his lap and his waiting cock.

"Oh! Oh, yes," she cried, sighing in relief and gratitude and a whole lot more as he slid inside her, hot and hard, filling her, warming her. Abrupt though his entry was, it was not unwanted nor was she disappointed. She had wanted this for so long, wanted him, and now she had him. She meant to make the most of it.

Evidently, so did he.

No longer hesitant, his hands roamed everywhere. He sucked on her breasts, kissed and licked and nibbled every part of her he could reach, and seemed eager for the rest. But she would not stop her insistent motions. Not yet anyway.

Her hands gripped his shoulders, while his hands slid over her body. Her knees dug into the ground as her thighs did all the work. Up and down. In and out. She rode him with amorous abandon, excited by his breath coming in hot little puffs against her neck. He nuzzled her throat, groaned expectantly as his tongue traced her collarbone. The tension built again, far more rapidly than the last. Her internal muscles tightened around him. She knew it was coming, knew the release would be nothing like the first, nothing like anything before, and she surrendered to it. To him.

The orgasm, when it came, blinded her in a searing white blast of sparks. She got lost in it, abandoned everything else but Jake. Wanting him to reach the same heights, her thighs continued to pump. Rising. Falling. He cried out and seized her, held her to his chest as his body convulsed around and inside her.

They slowed to a stop, both panting from exertion, both fulfilled.

It took a moment for Monica to notice he was shaking, and another to realize it was due to something other than post-coital bliss. She tried to sit back, to see his face, but he would not release her. The more she struggled the harder he held her. She was not afraid of him or that he would harm her, so his actions didn't trigger the hysterical-strength to fight him, but that didn't mean she wasn't worried.

"Jake?" she said. "What's wrong?"

He hugged her close, and then his arms dropped and his hands came to rest on her hips.

She sat back in his lap to search his face, but his head was down. She placed her palms on either side of his face and tilted his chin up. Amazement rocked her when she saw the glisten of tears in his eyes.

"What's wrong?" she asked, suddenly terrified she had hurt him. Had he wanted to stop, but she wouldn't let him pull away? "Did I hurt you? Are you all right? Oh, Jake, please tell me you're all right..."

He cupped his hand around the back of her neck and gently tugged her forward, kissing her softly.

"I'm fine," he said as she sat back again. His fingers brushed her cheek, caressed her jaw, her neck, and came to rest on her shoulder.

"Then why...?" she started, uncertain how to question him without embarrassing him.

"After...everything..." he said haltingly, then cleared his throat and spoke more smoothly, "I didn't really believe I'd ever be able to do that again. To *enjoy* it again. I don't think I could've without you."

"Oh, Jake." She kissed him, her own tears welling over, sliding down her cheeks.

He brushed them away.

"I meant it when I said I love you, Monica. I would do anything for you. Even things that frighten and haunt me wouldn't stop me from being with you again. I want you to know that."

"Are... Were they still there?"

"Yes," he murmured, but his voice grew stronger, "but you were here to hold on to, and you kept the horror from taking over."

"I'm not sure what I did," she said quietly, and felt a little overwhelmed with the emotions stirring in her chest.

"You love me," he said, pushing her hair back and cradling her face. "You showed me you love me. Nothing else matters after that."

"I do. And you're right, nothing else matters," she said with a smile and tilted her head into his palm.

She glanced at the clearing around them. The sun had set behind the mountains, and night was falling fast. "I love you a lot," she said, patting his hand, "but we'd better get back before it's too dark to see where we're going. I don't know about you, but I don't remember this area well enough to find Angel's place without light."

His hand dropped, and he made the same perusal of their surroundings.

"You're right," he said and then grinned, "but don't think this is the last of this conversation. Now that I know I'm still capable of enjoying sex, and a beautiful partner, I'll be insatiable."

"Good." She winked at him. "I'd hoped you'd feel that way."

"You're incorrigible," Jake teased as Monica stood up and began to dress.

She hooked her bra together and gazed down at him.

Unconcerned with his state of undress and in no hurry to adjust his clothes, his eyes drifted over her from head to toe and back in a slow study of her form.

Her hands went to her hips, and she faced him as if annoyed.

"And you like it, Jake Nichols. So don't pretend you're displeased by it."

"Never," he said, his hazel-green eyes hungry as he stared back at her.

"That's better," she said, working the buttons of her shirt. She glanced at him again. He hadn't moved. "Are you going to sit there and let the mosquitos devour you or get dressed and head back with me? We have a soft bed waiting and a door that locks."

Jake stood up so fast she almost thought he jumped, and he began putting himself in order.

"The mosquitos can't have me," he said with a silly sideways grin as he buttoned his own shirt and tucked it in. "I'm only for you, baby."

A pained looked flickered in his eyes and was gone.

Jealousy and protectiveness flashed through her. *You're mine, Jake Nichols. No one will take you away from me now.*

36

October 8th

MONICA SAT IN THE OFFICE of her newly completed home and reread Darla's long-awaited reply: *The slave is not for sale. He will be collected promptly tomorrow morning at eight o'clock. Make sure he is ready for my guards.*

Monica growled as she crumpled the paper in her fist and tossed it across the small room. It bounced off the bookcase against the wall and clattered to the floor. *Make sure he is ready* meant she wanted Jake restrained with chains, the way he had been when he arrived six months ago.

Clearly, Jake was right. Darla's hatred of him ran deep, and she wanted him to suffer for as long as possible.

Monica flattened her trembling hands against the polished surface of her new oak desk to keep herself from destroying something else in her fury. Her seething thoughts suddenly locked on a memory, an image of

Angel curled up in her bed for weeks at a time. It had taken months for her to trust Monica enough to share a portion of her pain. Now, Monica knew most of what had happened three years ago to cause Angel's despondency. The thought of experiencing the same fate herself terrified Monica.

I made her a decent offer, Monica thought, *and my arguments for his purchase were valid. She doesn't need a man with his skillset, but she completely ignored all of that and only replied with three blunt lines about returning him!*

Panic bubbled inside her, but she held it in check.

She groaned again and pushed away from the desk to pace the small room. She tried to come up with some other option, but she could only think of one that remained to her...to them.

She halted in the middle of the room. Her fists, hanging at her sides, tightened.

Her only recourse now meant asking for more help. It meant letting Jake go, letting someone else have him—he would live somewhere else, at least for a while. But she would make that choice; the outcome was far more acceptable than sending him back to Darla Cain for more abuse.

She cringed, remembering when he first arrived at her ranch. How starved he had looked, how terrified.

She recalled Jake's statement by the river months ago: *If I go back, they'll destroy the little bit of me that's still left.* The words had upset her back then, but now, hearing his stricken voice echo those words inside her head...

A sob burst from her chest, emotion strangling her throat as useless tears pooled in her eyes. Her knees trembled as devastation ripped through her heart. She would rather he live somewhere else—anywhere safe—than allow even a tiny part of the man she loved to be extinguished by Darla's cruelty.

Monica spun on her heel and hurried from her office in search of Jake.

"I TOLD YOU she wouldn't let me go," Jake said, his head down as he kicked at some straw on the floor. He'd ridden in from checking fences about ten minutes ago, intent on having a hearty dinner, only to find Monica rushing out to the barn to give him the bad news.

Monica moved closer and gripped his arm. "I won't let you go either, Jake."

He shook his head. He wouldn't allow her to give up everything for him. She didn't have a choice now, any more than he did. Their time of reckoning had finally arrived.

"I don't' see how you can stop her—"

"Shhh..." Monica whispered as she rested her finger on her lips. "Someone's here." A heartbeat later, she stepped into the aisle.

"Hi, Kristine," Monica said pleasantly, and Jake held back a groan of distaste. "Have a good time in town?"

"Yes," Kristine said as she quickly unsaddled her steed.

Monica glanced at Jake. Her lips were pressed together, and a frown marred her pretty features.

He shrugged.

"Everything okay here?" Kristine asked as she carried the heavy saddle to the tack room. As she passed, she looked over at Jake standing just inside the stall. He was thankful she didn't acknowledge him beyond one of the swift, assessing glances she saved for him whenever her superiors were around.

But her appraising eyes still made his skin crawl.

"Yeah, fine, nothing serious," Monica said.

Jake shook his head at her words as he threw his saddle on another horse, preparing to make his escape.

Kristine didn't comment.

"You must get to Angel's," Monica said in an urgent whisper as she stepped into the stall and stood next to him.

"I'll get there," he said as he threaded the cinch strap. "You should—" He stopped abruptly as a commotion erupted from the dooryard. A moment later, Jewel Stewart from the Section Council dashed into the barn, her gray-streaked black hair a tangle around her shoulders and an anxious look in her amber eyes.

"Hello, Jewel," Monica greeted with a stiff-looking smile and a hard edge to her voice. "To what do we owe this honor?"

"I got a message this evening concerning this man," she said without preamble, nodding toward Jake, and he stopped adjusting his saddle's girth to stare back at the newcomer.

Kristine went to her own animal to feed and brush her, giving every indication of disinterest, but Jake knew better.

"My contact came to see me a short time ago," Jewel said almost breathlessly. "Darla is sending guards to pick him up tonight."

"What?" Jake said.

"Why?" Monica asked. "They're not supposed to come until tomorrow morning."

"Apparently someone heard he was planning to escape."

Out of the corner of his eye, Jake saw Kristine freeze, and the grooming brush slipped from her hand.

I'll run before I go back to Darla, Jake remembered saying to Monica more than once, but they had always been alone. Or, at least, he'd thought they were alone.

"Now, how would she hear that?" Jake demanded, his eyes cutting to Kristine.

"Don't know," Jewel said, "but whoever it was reported Mr. Nichols' plans to Darla, and she sent a party, with orders to punish him here tonight and then bring him back immediately for more."

Jake felt the blood drain from his face. His heart stuttered at the thought of what they would do to him if he was still here when they arrived.

His gaze snapped to Kristine again.

Her eager expression turned blank as she stared back at him.

"Finish saddling your horse, Jake." Monica's voice was tight with fear. She seemed completely unaware of his suppositions about Kristine, and with no solid proof, now wasn't the time to discuss it anyway.

"Whatever you're going to do, do it fast," Jewel said as she shuffled back toward the door. "I saw the riders coming on my way here. They were only about fifteen minutes behind me when I arrived. You have maybe a ten-minute head start if you leave right now." She wished Jake good luck and hurried out of the barn. The sound of her mount's hooves rang out a moment later.

"Go, Jake," Monica rasped. "There's no time to waste now."

"Come with me," he said as he finished with the saddle and faced her again.

"I can't." Monica sounded so miserable his heart clenched. "I have to stay. I have to slow them down, keep them from following you."

"We can beat them," he said, leaning in to take her hand.

"No, we can't, and we don't have time to argue about it," Monica said, her words running together in her haste to hurl them out. "Do you remember how to reach Angel's place? How far it is? The direction? You can get there without getting lost, right?"

"Yeah," Jake muttered. "I'll find it."

"Then go. And don't stop for anything. Remember what I told you: Go straight to Angel and tell her you have a message from me. I don't have time to write one now, so tell her..." She paused as if at a loss or to catch her breath, Jake wasn't sure which. She sucked in a deep breath and resumed her rapid-fire speech. "Tell her 'I'm holding her to her offer.' She'll understand. Now, go!"

With one last glare at Kristine, Jake quickly wrapped an arm around Monica's waist, dropped a desperate kiss on her trembling mouth, then vaulted into the saddle and heeled his steed into motion. The gelding leaped into a gallop, and Jake directed him for the shortcut over the ridge leading to Angel's ranch.

37

JAKE RAN HIS GELDING the whole way to Angel's front door. During the desperate ride, his mount skidded around oversized obstacles and vaulted over fallen logs as Jake peered into the growing gloom and dodged hanging branches—until he didn't drop down fast enough, and a thick tree limb caught him in the forehead, almost knocking him from the saddle. Lying on his back over the cantle, his horse still bounding wildly beneath him, stars danced before his eyes. A deeper blackness than the impending night encroached on the edges of his vision. He blinked at the forest canopy above him and clung to the saddle with his legs and one hand. Thankful he still had hold of the reins, he struggled upright to regain his seat. Shaking his head to clear the threat of unconsciousness, he leaned low over the horse's neck, encouraging speed.

The yelling of Darla's guards and the beat of their steeds' hooves on the ground behind him rang in Jake's ears. They weren't too close, but they were gaining.

He breathed a sigh of relief when the lights of Angel's homestead came into view, but he didn't slow his mad dash until he raced his gelding through the open gates and pulled the animal up short, right outside her front door. He leaped out of the saddle, not bothering to secure the reins, hurdled the front porch steps, and skidded to a stop at the entry. He pounded on the wooden panel, praying Angel was there, that she was the woman Monica—and Jake himself—believed her to be. Monica had said her friend could save him, and he wanted to believe that too, but he severely lacked faith in his own salvation.

Although the dooryard was deserted, it was not overly late, so someone should be around. They might even be finishing the evening meal.

Jake's stomach growled. He had skipped lunch while out in the fields, and after the long hours of working and then the strenuous ride here, he was famished.

He hammered his fist against the door again, eyeing the knob. Maybe he should just go in. Darla's guards would be there soon, and he felt too exposed standing out on the front porch. At least inside he would not be readily visible. He glanced apprehensively over his shoulder toward the front gate. The tall wall surrounding the homestead ensured that his pursuers could only arrive from one direction, and there was no sign of them yet. But they were coming.

His gaze fell on his exhausted mount, which added another twinge to his growing list of unease. Not only had he overworked the poor horse to get here ahead of his pursuers, but the sweaty animal was a neon sign screaming "*Jake Nichols is here.*" He didn't have time to hide the gelding though; he didn't want the guards to catch him in the barn—out there he'd be away from Angel and her aid.

What the hell is taking them so long? The lights are on, so someone must be here.

He lifted his fist a third time, about to slam his knuckles harder on the wooden surface, when the door swung open. His nerves, strung-out as they were, caused him to jump back from the rapid movement of the door, and he took a second to catch his breath.

He knew the tall, fit strawberry-blonde woman who stood in the entryway from when they had come to help with the harvest.

"Michelle," he wheezed to Angel's head guard as he stopped to take another breath. "I need to see Angel. It's urgent." He peeked over his shoulder again to ensure he was still safe and then refocused on the woman at the door.

"What are you doing here, Jake?" Michelle asked, following the path of his frantic glances with a frown and obviously noting he was unaccompanied. "What's wrong?"

"I need to see Angel. Now!" He knew demanding anything was risky, but he couldn't waste time. The women on his trail wanted to whip him and drag him back to hell...in all probability, to his death.

"Please," he breathed.

Her eyes skimmed over his disheveled appearance—the sweat and blood on his face, his shaking, the way he fretfully shifted from one foot to the other—and stepped back.

"Come in," she said.

He hurried over the threshold, and she closed the door behind him.

"My horse needs to be hidden," he muttered as he stepped inside.

"Jane," Michelle called to a woman standing off to the side—the housekeeper if he remembered correctly. "Tell one of the hands to take Jake's horse to the barn. And tell them it's urgent." Michelle turned to Jake. "Stay here," she said and rushed upstairs.

Jake trembled uncontrollably as he waited in the foyer, his eyes darting everywhere, his ears straining for the sound of horses approaching. He wiped the cold sweat and blood from his head with his forearm, pushed his hair back from his face with his hand, and shifted his feet. He tried to ignore the icy chill of terror creeping up his spine. Outside he had felt exposed. Inside he felt trapped. If the guards came now and forced their way in, he was done for.

Turning to his right, he risked a peek into the living room and through the huge picture window overlooking the dooryard. Still no sign of Darla's guards.

Noises came from the dining hall at the back of the house. Apparently people were still eating or the staff was cleaning up. Dishes clashing with silverware, soft voices, and laughter echoed down the hall. The cheerful sound grated on his resolve.

Seconds seeming like hours ticked by, and he peeked out the front window once again.

As he paced the foyer, the smell of food made his stomach rumble, even as it roiled with dread.

Footsteps thudded down the upstairs hall. His pacing halted, and he looked up. When Angel appeared, coming toward the stairs, Jake almost broke down and cried.

"Jake?" Angel rushed down the stairs to his side. She looked very pale. "What's wrong? Is Monica all right? Are *you* all right?"

"Monica sent me," he said in a shaky voice. "She said for me to tell you: 'She's holding you to your offer.' She said you'd know what that means."

Angel gasped. "Darla's coming for you?"

"Yes," he said through his clenched jaw.

"When?" she asked as she touched the growing bump on his forehead.

He flinched. "Now."

As if that one word had called them forth, horses thundered into the dooryard.

"All right," Angel said and stood a little taller. "I'll take care of this, and then we'll take a look at your head."

"How?" he blurted. "How will you take care of it? Darla won't let me go, and I don't want to cause you trouble—" His voice hitched. He swore viciously and ran his fingers through his hair, realizing he had lost his hat when he hit the tree limb. "I shouldn't have come here."

"Yes, you should've," Angel said. "Don't worry, Jake. I *will* take care of this." She turned to Michelle. "Take him up to my room. Barricade the door and don't let anyone in but me. I'll be back as soon as I can." With that, Angel slipped outside to confront the angry posse at her doorstep.

"Come on," Michelle ordered as she grabbed his arm and tugged him toward the stairs.

He followed blindly. Iron bands of anxiety constricted around his chest, and his lungs felt starved for air as she hurried him down the hall and through a door on the left. The lit lantern on the bedside table illuminated the spacious room, revealing the biggest four-poster bed Jake had ever seen. It was enormous, but his gaze didn't linger on the unusual antique for long.

Michelle dashed to the far side of the room and picked up a straight-backed chair. She brought it back and braced it under the entry's doorknob. The obstacle wouldn't keep anyone out indefinitely, but it would slow them down. The head guard then went to the French doors, which led to a large private deck overlooking the backyard, and opened them to the chill night air. She crossed her arms beneath her breasts, leaned against the frame, and cocked her head as if listening.

Jake stood frozen in the middle of the room, watching her. The sound of shouting came from somewhere outside. The voices compelled him to the doorway, and he leaned against the opposite side of the frame, mimicking Michelle's posture, as the yelling momentarily ceased.

He let his eyes drift over the wall, past the river and up the distant hill to the huge, ancient weeping willow he'd noticed on his first visit. Through the gathering shadows of dusk, he saw its limbs sway languidly in the cool autumn breeze.

The shouting picked up. The words were unclear, but the screaming voice sounded like Darla's.

His skin prickled.

Michelle turned her head toward him, and he met her frowning glare.

"I hope you're worth it," she said, her pale blue eyes boring into his.

"Wha-What?" His voice shook.

"I hope you're worth the expense and the trouble this is going to cause Angel, and the rest of us too."

Jake blinked. Then his shoulders sagged, and he stared at the hardwood floor beneath his feet. He hoped for a whole lot more than that.

They waited in silence for what seemed like hours while the shouting continued. Gradually the yelling diminished until they could no longer hear anything. Jake listened to the endless ticking of the grandfather clock near the bedroom door and wondered what was happening outside. The timepiece had serenely chimed the quarter hour three times since they had come in here—twice since the shouting had stopped—but Angel still had not returned to tell them what happened.

Just when he was about to ask Michelle if she would see what was going on, a light knock sounded at the door. Jake jumped and his hands clenched into fists, prepared to fight. But Michelle simply crossed over to the entry and demanded, "Who's there?"

"It's Angel," a soft voice answered. "Open the door, Michelle."

The apprehensive expression on Angel's unusually pale face when she entered made Jake's anxiety level skyrocket. From all appearances, something had gone very wrong. He opened his mouth to ask what, but nothing came out.

Angel met his fretful gaze and tried to smile, but her lips barely stretched.

"Is she gone?" Michelle asked. Angel's eyes shifted to her head guard and back to Jake.

"Yes," she said softly.

Why does she look so nervous? Jake stared at her, unable to move. Standing by the open doors, the cool breeze chilling the sweat still beading his flesh, he couldn't help hyperventilating. He also couldn't stop the flood of questions firing in his mind.

When is Darla coming back?

Is she going to punish me now? Or does my torture begin in the morning?

What about Monica?

Angel touched his arm. "Monica is fine," she said, and Jake realized he'd vocalized his last thought. "I sent one of my guards to inform her you're here and to ask her to come. They'll use the road, as it's too dark now to take the shortcut, so they'll be a little while. But if I know Monica, she's on her way."

While she spoke, Jake's eyes darted between the small woman before him and the open bedroom door, expecting to see Darla's guards appear with chains in their hands. He already felt the cold, heavy weight of the shackles binding him once again.

A chill prickled over his flesh, and he stifled the fearful moan that tried to escape.

Only a few seconds had passed since Angel had entered the room, but to Jake a year seemed to crawl by with every tick of the grandfather clock. Sweat dribbled down his spine, and his body still quaked. *Why the hell won't she tell me what happened?*

"She won't let me go, will she?" Jake asked, finding his voice.

"We talked," Angel began, obviously choosing her words with care, "and came to an agreement."

"What's it going to cost us?" Michelle asked.

"A lot," Angel answered, and her eyes returned to him, "but I think Jake's worth it."

His breath clogged in his throat. *What the hell did* that *mean?*

She must've seen something on his face because she stepped closer and gazed up at him with earnest azure eyes.

"You're safe, Jake," she said, squeezing his arm, and Jake nearly tumbled to the floor. But doubt crowded out any sense of elation.

"Wh-Wha-What?" he stuttered out in disbelief and then swallowed, hard.

Darla Cain wanted him to suffer.

She wanted to hurt him, break him for his attempted attack.

She would never give him up. Never.

He couldn't have heard Angel correctly.

"I purchased your slave papers from Darla," Angel said, still staring into his terrified, skeptical gaze. "It will be finalized when I send payment tomorrow. You're safe, Jake."

He stood like a marble statue for a few heartbeats while her words sunk in, and then his legs crumpled and he landed on his knees. A sob ripped from his chest, and he could suddenly breathe again.

I'm free! he thought, panting with desperate relief. *No more Darla Cain and her twisted games, no more pain.* He could live with Monica now without fear. He didn't have to run, would never have to make the choice to leave her behind. *Oh, thank God!*

His thoughts had turned inward with Angel's revelation, and nothing else registered for a while.

Laughter brought him back to reality, a hoarse, croaking, almost hysterical chortle. A second later, he realized that fanatical chuckling was coming from *him*. On his hands and knees, he stared at the lavender rug next to Angel's huge bed, laughing so hard his sides ached. Tears streamed down his face to drip from his chin, and he couldn't distinguish whether they were due to his happiness or his utter relief.

He decided it didn't matter.

Angel knelt beside him, her hand on his shoulder, murmuring words of comfort and waiting for him to calm down.

She must think I've gone insane, he thought with another chuckle as he tried to collect himself. Slowly, the mania dwindled and his laughter ceased.

Hurriedly, he wiped at his face, embarrassed for his breakdown and his emotional display. When he had settled, he sat back on his heels and met Angel's worried gaze with a timid smile. "I'm sorry," he murmured.

"It's okay," Angel told him, her hand rubbing his back and shoulder. "I imagine getting away from her is a tremendous relief."

"You have no idea." Jake shook his head.

"There's more I need to tell you if you're ready to hear it."

He nodded, but she made him wait a little longer to get him up off the floor. She steered Jake toward her giant bed and eased him down until he perched on the edge of the mattress. She sat down next to him and regarded him kindly.

She still looks worried, he thought, *and not about my sanity.*

"Tell me," he said, though fear of Darla Cain stirred inside him.

"Darla required me to consent to some things before she would agree to sign you over to me."

"What things?" *What could that bitch want from me now?*

"First, you must stay on my ranch unless accompanied by me specifically." He frowned, but she kept talking, not giving him a chance to interrupt. "And I cannot sell you...to anyone, for any reason, for a period of three years."

"Three years?" Jake asked, and a wave of dizziness washed over him. He was grateful to be rescued from Darla, but this was a stipulation he hadn't anticipated.

"Yes," Angel replied quietly.

Jake got to his feet and took several paces before turning back. "But I have a home... a... a place...I need to be there."

"I understand, Jake, but on that one thing, she would not give. She wanted to make you wait five years, but I convinced her to take three." Seeing the desperation on his face, she hurried on. "It's not ideal, but it's better than the alternative. If I didn't agree to the terms, she would've taken you and I wouldn't have been able to stop her. I could not let that happen."

He nodded at that, knowing the outcome could've been far worse, but he still felt dazed by everything. He lowered his head and stared at the floor. The French doors still stood open to the night, the cold breeze chilling the room, but Jake didn't feel it. He was already frozen inside.

"It won't be as bad as it seems," she told him, trying to cheer him up.

Again, he nodded without looking up, but his thoughts were on Monica.

Angel must've guessed this as she continued. "Monica's close, and you'll see her as often as we can arrange and as work allows. No one will hurt you here, and we can use your experience on our ranch too."

"I'm just a hired hand," he said. He took two steps and then dropped down on the bed again, his head in his hands. He stayed that way for some minutes, his elbows on his knees, eyes staring holes in the floor as his brain tried to come to terms with everything that had just happened.

The next thing he knew, Angel was wiping the blood from the small gash on his forehead. He brushed her hands away and looked up. She handed him a small towel and antibiotic cream. As Jake rubbed the cream into the wound, Michelle ambled in through the bedroom door with a kitchen towel in her hands. Jake hadn't even been aware of her leaving. She held out the cloth-wrapped ice pack to Jake. He took it and pressed it against the large bump on his head. He grimaced and hissed through his teeth at the pressure.

"Come on, Jake," Angel said as she curled her small hand around his biceps. "Let's get you comfortable." She urged him to stand, using a slight upward pressure on his arm, and he complied. Still holding the ice to his head, he swayed slightly when he reached his feet, and she wrapped her arm around his waist to steady him.

"Okay?" she asked, and he nodded. "I don't think you have a concussion, but I'd like Dr. Beck to examine you tonight," she said as she walked him down the hallway to the guest room he and Monica had stayed in several weeks ago.

Jake didn't argue.

The room's walls were a pale azure, and a large window overlooked the backyard. End tables, a long dresser, and a queen-sized bed dressed in assorted shades of blue filled the room. It smelled clean and looked as neat as it had the last time he stayed here. For some reason the combination of the memories of his last visit, the cozy room, and Angel's kindness made his eyes burn.

He wouldn't be sleeping in the same bed with Monica tonight, as he had almost every night for the last six weeks. Well, he might if she was able to make the trip in the dark, but at some point, she would be back at home and he would be stuck here. *But I can think of worse places to be trapped in.*

Angel escorted him to the bed, propped up the pillows behind his back, and told him to relax.

"Someone should be up soon with some food for you," she said as she glanced at his still-booted feet on the clean quilt.

"Thank you," he muttered as he dropped the ice and shifted to tug off his boots.

"Would you like some help with those?"

"Nah," he responded with a slight shake of his head as the first boot came free. "Thanks though." He grinned and dropped his footwear on the hardwood, then made quick work of the other. He reclined back on the pillows again and picked up the ice.

Angel fidgeted and glanced around the room. "You'll stay here for now," she said as if nervous. "We'll get you set up with your own room out in the bunkhouse in the next couple of days."

"Miss Aldridge—"

"Please, Jake, call me Angel."

"Okay...Angel," he said tentatively. "I didn't say it before and it may seem as if I'm not, but I am truly grateful for what you did for me. I hope I didn't cause you too much trouble."

"No—" Angel began but cut herself short when footsteps came barreling down the hall and into the room.

"Jake!" Monica shouted. Flushed and out of breath, she rushed to the bed to sit and take him in her arms. "Are you all right?"

"I'm fine," he said hugging her back. "I am now anyway."

"I told you everything would be all right," she gushed, and Jake chuckled. She'd said nothing of the kind, but he didn't want to argue about it.

"I'll leave you two alone," Angel said from the door. "The food should be here soon."

"Oh, Angel!" Monica disentangled herself from Jake's arms, jumped to her feet, and hurried to her friend. She crushed the smaller woman in a grateful bear hug. "Thank you so much for doing this. I know it was a lot to ask, but—"

"Don't be silly," Angel said and smiled back at her friend. "I'm glad to help."

"I'm not sure how I'll ever repay you."

"I'll think of something." Angel gave her a playful wink.

Just then, Michelle showed up with a heavily laden tray of food, which she took directly to the bed.

Jake's stomach growled again when the scent of roast beef struck him, and he eagerly sat up to eat his first meal since breakfast early that morning.

"Really, Angel, tell me," Monica said as Jake prepared for his meal, "how bad was it?"

"We'll talk about it tomorrow," Angel replied as she followed Michelle out into the hallway. "Get settled. I'll send the doctor up in a little while to havc a look at the bump on Jake's head."

"Bump...?" Monica questioned.

Jake chuckled.

"Good night, you two," Angel said, reaching for the doorknob.

"'Night," Jake retorted for both of them before taking his first bite. He moaned his pleasure as the flavorful meat and gravy coated his tongue.

The door closed, and they were alone.

"Are you hurt?" Monica asked, coming back to the bed. "Oh, you are!" She gently touched the purplish lump, a worried frown marring her pretty face.

"I'm fine," Jake told her between mouthfuls. "Doc's only going to check me out to be safe."

Monica sighed as she eased onto the mattress, careful not to disturb his food.

"Did you know I wouldn't be able to come back when you sent me here?" he queried between bites. He didn't plan to ask that question right now; it just came out.

"I knew it was probable," Monica admitted, frowning at the floor and avoiding his gaze. "But I would rather let you go to live here with Angel than allow Darla to have you one more second."

Jake sat motionless, his fork forgotten in his hand as he stared at her profile. "Let me go...?"

She turned her head, and her eyes widened at the dread and anger he knew she could read on his face.

"I meant to live, Jake," she said. "I'll never let anyone else have you. I trust Angel with you. I wouldn't have sent you here if I didn't. You can trust her too."

He nodded and went back to eating.

Monica sat quietly while he ate his meal. When he finished, he rested back on the pillows.

"Will you stay tonight?" he asked, and she smiled at him.

"Yes."

"Then come here," he said, holding out his arm.

She quickly pulled off her own boots, moved the food tray to the dresser, and crawled over his lap to curl up beside him. They held each other for some time before Monica broke the silence.

"I'm going to miss you."

"Same here," he told her, hugging her close to emphasize his words.

"I love you, Jake."

He smiled, kissed the top of her head, and rested his cheek on her hair. "I love you too." It was the truest statement he'd ever uttered, but even though he was free to care for her now without reservation, he couldn't wholly banish the heavy weight of loss that had settled on his heart. Three years seemed like an eternity, but she was willing to wait for him. He would suffer anything if it meant they would have each other in the end. He only hoped nothing else got in the way.

38

JAKE LAUGHED OUT LOUD as Esther, the house cook, delivered the punchline of her ribald joke. When he first met her, he would've never pictured the grandmotherly woman telling dirty jokes, but she seemed to have a fondness for them, and quite a collection too.

Living on Angel's ranch for the last six months, he'd gradually become familiar with the people, the animals, and the work. Never having been in charge before, Jake felt a little overwhelmed in the beginning, but Bret had been an effective foreman for several years and what Jake had learned from his old friend benefited him now.

Monica visited as often as she could, but spring and summer were busy times of the year on a ranch, and her visits became less and less frequent. They exchanged regular correspondence, but he missed being with her all the same.

Angel's demeanor had worried him a little after he first arrived to live on her ranch last October. She'd seemed quieter, more withdrawn, than the woman Monica had introduced him to at harvest time only two months before. Even though Angel had told him she had no interest in him sexually, he still wondered if her behavior had anything to do with him. He had thought about asking what was bothering her, but if she'd seemed like she was in need, he would've felt obligated to try to help—and he was unprepared for that. The only aid he was willing to give her was with the ranch. Still, only partially due to Monica's encouragement, he'd kept an eye on her last fall and through the winter, noting Angel's sullen silences, lack of appetite, and decreased interaction with the other people on the ranch. She often left the daily affairs to him and Michelle, but as the holidays ended and spring neared, Angel's melancholy mood had faded and she spent less time alone.

Despite his horrific experiences and his lingering wariness, he'd come to like Angel and had grown more at ease in her company over the last six months—enough to be willing to offer support if she needed it. But so far, Esther was the only one with whom he truly felt comfortable, and he enjoyed the easy friendship he shared with the older woman.

Like many days lately, he had arrived home late and, after taking care of several details in the barns, came in for dinner after everyone else had finished. As she always did, Esther saved him a heaping plate of the delicious meal she and her crew had prepared. Now, Jake sat on a bench at the long wooden table in the corner of the kitchen to dine, while Esther puttered around the kitchen, chatting with him while he ate. He appreciated her company and her jokes.

"That was a raunchier one," he said of her latest humorous offering, still chuckling.

"I have all kinds," she said. "Did I ever tell you the one about—"

Esther fell silent as a loud thump followed by a piercing scream ripped through the air, and both of them automatically lifted their eyes to the ceiling. Their gazes collided again as alarm took hold and Jake's heart seized. In the next instant, his fork rattled onto his plate as he ran for the stairs.

More cries reached his ears as he sprinted up the steps to the second floor and pounded down the hall. He found Michelle outside Angel's bedroom door, shouting and shoving at it with her shoulder while twisting the handle. But her feminine form, though strong, wasn't heavy enough to move the solid oak panel. She glanced at Jake as he hurried up to her side, the obvious question on his face.

"Someone's in there with her and the damn door won't open," she said as another high-pitched, agonized scream rattled their eardrums. They both stared at the door, momentarily stunned, then Michelle turned to him once more. Panic and fear for her friend filled her eyes, but, impressively, she maintained outward control.

"It's been braced from the inside," Jake said, stating the obvious, the pulse of fear thumping in his throat. Although he didn't know her well yet—thanks mostly to his earlier reservations and to her inclination to keep to herself—Angel had saved his life. Whatever was going on in there, she was in terrible danger, and he would not sit by and allow it to happen. "Let me help you," he said to Michelle as he gestured to the door.

Violent noises still radiated from the other side of the door, but the screams had weakened into short whimpers of fear and pain. His heart slamming in his chest and sweat prickling his brow, he joined Michelle as she moved to one side to make room for him at the door. Hastily, he turned the knob and they both rammed their shoulders against the door, putting all of their combined weight into the blow. One. Two. Three. Four times, they slammed against the barrier before it finally swung open and Jake stumbled into the room, with Michelle right behind him.

When Jake regained his balance, he stared in disbelief at the scene before him. Angel sprawled on the hardwood floor. Her clothes were gone, her hair a wild halo around her head and shoulders, and one arm lay twisted and useless. A man held her other wrist pinned above her head, and his body lay heavily on top of her, holding her down.

Jake didn't care about the "who" or "why." He could see that the other man's attentions were unwelcome. He didn't think at all. He simply rushed over, gripped the assailant by his hair and the waistband of his open jeans, and yanked him away from Angel. Jake then shoved him, hard, across the room, where the man slammed into the wall. As Michelle rushed by Jake on her way to Angel's aid, he turned from where the assailant lay slumped on the floor and took in the scene. What he saw rekindled the fury boiling in his veins.

Blood and bruises adorned Angel's pretty face. Her blue eyes were wide and terrified, and she held her right arm protectively against her chest. She trembled uncontrollably, whether more from the assault or the adrenaline surging through her, Jake wasn't sure. Michelle covered her friend with a blanket she'd pulled from Angel's bed and tried to help her sit up.

Angel screamed in pain and clutched at her arm. At the same time, Jake sensed movement behind him. He tore his eyes from the injured woman and spun around to see the man striding toward him. The oil lamp burning on the nightstand illuminated his features, and Jake recognized him immediately: Toby Lonset. He had come to Angel's ranch a few months after Jake did. Not overly friendly, at least not with other males, Toby paid a lot of attention to the women, especially Angel. Jake didn't like him, but he hadn't thought much about Toby before now.

Jake took in his appearance as they stood facing each other. Angel had not gone down easy. Bruises and scratches adorned Toby's face, and blood gushed from his broken nose.

Good job, Angel, Jake thought, and pride for the small woman's courage filled his chest. A heartbeat later, Jake's protective instincts—jacked up to high upon seeing what Toby had tried to do—kicked in and rage surged through him as Angel's injuries fully registered. Angrier than he'd been in a long time, Jake bared his teeth at the other man and glowered threateningly. Toby responded by barreling headlong into him with a snarl on his lips and a deep growl rumbling from his throat. His lunging tackle took them both to the floor, missing Angel and Michelle by inches. They rolled around, exchanging blows before snapping apart and regaining their feet.

With a need to protect Monica's friend—and maybe to repay her, if only a little, for what she'd done for him—Jake attacked Toby with every ounce of fighting skill he had gained in his youth. Although not as adept at brawling as Bret, Jake was still a much more accomplished fighter than his current adversary. Toby landed a few strikes, but Jake's relentless assault overpowered him. Soon, Toby lay on the floor, with Jake's fingers fisted in his shirtfront as he pummeled Toby repeatedly in the face.

"Jake." Angel's gentle voice broke through the haze of red wrath engulfing him mind. "Jake, stop. Stop! Please, you're going to kill him."

Jake dragged his eyes from his target and settled them on Angel. For a second, nothing registered in his head; he simply stared hard and breathed briskly in and out. In and out.

Angel touched his shoulder and spoke again. "Please. Stop hitting him."

He gawked at her for several more seconds before his fingers opened and Toby's unconscious body thumped to the floor. Jake dropped his arm, turned away, and stood up, fighting to subdue the seething anger coursing through his heated veins.

Michelle pushed past him to check on Toby, but neither Jake nor Angel paid any attention to the man on the floor.

"Thank you, Jake," Angel murmured in a shaky voice, and he looked into her bruised face.

Damn that bastard, he silently stormed, rage flooding him once more.

"How bad is it?" he asked her, his tone far too assertive for a slave, but she didn't seem to care.

"Bad enough," she said, cradling her right forearm against her chest and grimacing. The blanket Michelle had brought to her was now wrapped around her body like a full-length sarong.

"Did he...?" Jake started to ask, but he couldn't force the rest of the words out.

She looked away, but she understood and shook her head. Her trembling became more prominent, and a tear streamed slowly down her nearest cheek. Without thought, he reached over and brushed it away. She cringed, and her eyes flashed to his.

"I'm sorry," he muttered and lowered his gaze. Reminding himself that this woman's attitude was vastly different from the cruelty he'd known, he flicked a quick peek at her face. His eyes locked on hers, and something in her fearful expression changed. The dread melted away and she smiled.

"You have nothing to be sorry for, Jake Nichols. I should be showering you with praise for coming to my rescue."

Jake winced and stared at his boots once more as he awkwardly shoved his bloody fists into his jeans pockets.

"My hero," Angel said, and he glanced at her again. Her eyes twinkled, her broad grin teased him, and somehow her levity loosened the tension bunching his shoulders.

"I'm no hero," he argued and returned her smile. "That would be Bret."

"Who?"

"A friend of mine. I'll tell you about him sometime."

"I'd like that," Angel responded, and just like that, Jake felt as if he had finally come home, as if he'd found a permanent place and people who would care about him the way he would for them. He had no clue what caused the sense of security and contentment that unexpectedly washed over him, but the sensation felt...wonderful.

All that's missing is Monica, he thought.

With help from Theo and a couple other cowboys Michelle had rousted out of their beds, they'd bound Toby hand and foot and locked him in a small storage shed by the barn. Guards were posted to keep watch on him for the night, while Dr. Beck checked Angel's injuries. Once Toby was out of the way, and on the doctor's directive, Michelle drove Angel to the hospital in town. Angel asked Jake to join them. He didn't need a doctor, but the protective side of him needed to ensure she would be all right. A few minutes later, he climbed into the rear cab of the old four-by-four Angel kept locked away most of the time, and they were on their way.

At the hospital, when the doctor called for X-rays of Angel's swollen arm to verify her spiral fracture diagnosis, Jake was stunned. He hadn't expected to see modern technology anymore, but they had quite a setup, though it was limited compared to what hospitals once were.

Angel surprised him again when she asked the doctor to check his injuries as well.

"That's not necessary," Jake protested.

"Let her check you out," Angel said, then she softened her voice. "Please, Jake. I need to know you're not hurt more seriously than you look. Do it for me. Please?"

His brows lowered, but he didn't reply.

Angel bit down on her lip and tried again. "Have some mercy, man. If Monica shows up and sees those bruises on your face, she'll kill me if I don't make sure you're cared for. Please?"

He gave a soft snort and grinned. "All right, Angel. Whatever you say."

Aside from the contusions on his face and hands, a split lip, and bloody knuckles, the doctor gave him a clean bill of health. When Angel returned and heard the doctor's report, Jake gave her a see-I-told-you-I-was-fine look. She merely smiled with gratitude in her eyes.

Once the X-rays confirmed Angel's fracture, the doctor put a temporary splint on her forearm and told her to return in a week for a full cast. She gave Angel some medicine to help with the pain, and then they were on their way home.

"You need to sell Toby," Michelle declared firmly as they drove back to the ranch.

"What?" Angel actually sounded surprised.

"You heard me: *sell* him."

"I don't sell my people," Angel snapped, but her words held no bite.

"The people you help don't usually attack you," Michelle countered.

"He's just confused."

"He's an asshole."

They went back and forth on this for a while until Michelle sighed in frustration. "Look, Angel, I know you don't want to and I know why, but he's dangerous. Not only to you but to everyone else too. What do you think will happen if he tries again and Jake's not there to break the door in? What if he really hurts you? What if you don't recover? What happens to all the rest of us then? What if he hurts someone else?"

Angel didn't respond; she only sat quietly in the passenger seat and stared out the windshield. Michelle chanced a couple of quick peeks at her silent profile and sighed again.

"Jake, what do you think?" Michelle asked, her eyes finding his in the rearview mirror.

Jake shifted uneasily. "I think you're right," he said at length, and Michelle flashed him a brilliant grin in the mirror.

"About which part?" Angel asked, startling the smile off Michelle's face. The head guard glanced over at her employer, up at Jake in the mirror, and then back to the road.

"He *is* an asshole," Jake answered honestly, and Angel chuckled, but he wasn't done. "He's also dangerous."

"How so?" Angel was being stubborn—he could tell by the tone of the question and the way she held her shoulders. Michelle's irritated huff said she detected Angel's obstinance too.

"Toby tried to rape you in your own bedroom—with your head guard, who could probably take him apart by herself, right down the hall, and more help in the barracks only a short run away. He must've thought of all that because he took the time to barricade the door, but he didn't care if anyone heard. If he did, he would've waited until you were alone and isolated from everyone else. He just didn't want to be interrupted. He wanted you, and he clearly didn't take no for an answer. A man like Toby won't stop. He knows you don't punish your slaves, but if you show him mercy, if you let him stay, he will try again. And the next time, he will be more careful and infinitely more dangerous. Michelle's right. You should get rid of him as soon as possible."

An uncomfortably long silence followed Jake's little speech as they continued down the road. The longer the quiet lasted, the more uneasy he became.

I knew I should've kept my mouth shut. It was not his place to tell Angel what to do, but he worried if Toby stayed he would eventually get what he wanted. He might even kill her. Jake didn't want to think about what would happen to him if that occurred. He made a mental note to ask Monica the next time they spoke.

His opportunity came sooner than he expected.

Monica was sitting in the front room, chatting with Sam, the assistant head guard, when the three of them walked into the house.

"Angel!" Monica gushed as she rushed into the foyer and, being careful of Angel's injured arm, pulled her friend into a protective hug.

"I'm all right," Angel said, hugging her friend in return.

Monica pulled back and cradled Angel's battered face in her hands, shaking her head. "Yeah, you look just dandy."

"The only serious injury is my arm, and that's going to be fine in a few months."

"Angel," Monica scolded as she stepped back and jammed her hands on her hips, "I know you don't want to hear this, but you *will* sell that man and I don't want to hear any arguments about it."

Angel gave her a sad stare and then glanced at Jake and Michelle before setting her eyes back on Monica.

"There seems to be a consensus," she said, and Monica frowned in confusion. She turned her attention to the other two people in the room and gasped.

"Oh, my God, Jake! Are you all right?" She went to him.

He brushed her hands away. "I'm fine."

"That bastard," Monica hissed. She spun back to Angel, glaring for all she was worth, and then echoed Michelle and Jake's comments from the truck.

Angel shook her head, glanced at the floor, and shifted her feet. Monica opened her mouth to continue her lecture, but Angel surprised them all with her soft reply. "I think Carrie Simpson will take him as soon as I send word he's available."

Jake saw Monica and Michelle exchange a look before Angel lifted her head and met their startled faces.

"What?" she asked the room in general. "You two," she pointed at Michelle and Jake, "harped at me the whole way home and now Monica makes it unanimous. Are you going to shout at me when I agree with you too?"

"Of course not, honey," Monica said gently as she put her arm around her friend. "But I know you and I thought persuading you would take...more convincing. I know how you feel about selling anyone."

"What can I say?" Angel said with a shrug. "Jake made some pertinent points and Michelle did too. I don't disagree with any of your assessments; I just hate to think of what will happen to him at Carrie's."

"Whatever it is," Monica growled and tightened her hold on Angel's shoulders, "it won't be enough."

"Don't be so dramatic, Monica," Angel said wiggling out from under Monica's arm. "I *can* take care of myself, you know."

"Yeah, Michelle taught you well, but even with the boost of hysterical-strength he still broke your arm."

"Next time he might break your neck...or someone else's," Jake heard himself say and then promptly snapped his teeth together when they all turned his way.

"I know," Angel whispered, drawing their attention from Jake. "That's why I've decided to sell him."

"Good," her three friends said in unison.

Angel laughed, and to Jake's dismay, she diverted the conversation by telling Monica about what Angel called "*his daring rescue*." Shuffling his feet and shoving his hands in his pockets, Jake quickly minimized his part in the scenario, but then Angel playfully called him a hero again and heat suffused his cheeks. The delight on Monica's face as she gazed up at him only made his discomfort worse.

He dropped his eyes and muttered, "It wasn't a big deal."

Monica patted his cheek and spoke as if he hadn't. "I'll have to show him later how very grateful I am to still have my best friend alive and relatively unharmed."

Feeling awkward, and positive his whole face was beet-red, Jake frowned at her.

Monica's grin broadened.

"I'm heading to bed," Michelle announced after rolling her eyes at Monica's blatant statement and starting up the stairs.

"Me too," Angel said, but she reached for Jake's hand. "Thank you again, Jake. What you did, and the fact you cared enough to give me your honest opinion when we asked, means a lot to me. Please remember that."

A lump formed in his throat as she stared up at him, and his heart thumped a few heavy beats before he acknowledged her with a nod.

Angel released his hand. "The guest room is available if you want to stay, Monica. Feel free to use it *however* you like. 'Night," she said and followed Michelle's path upstairs.

Jake caught the hint of innuendo in her lighthearted invitation, and his face grew hotter than before. Yet he was thankful not to have to take Monica to his small room out in the bunkhouse, with its thin walls and his single bed. If any of the other cowboys saw Monica—or worse, heard her cries of pleasure, since he had no doubt there would be some—he'd never hear the end of their teasing. The guest room was the far preferable option.

Angel's cheerful invitation also made him wonder at her fortitude. That she could suggest they enjoy their time together tonight despite what had happened to her only hours ago showed her own inner strength and her natural disposition to see those she cared about happy.

When they were alone, Monica wrapped her arms around Jake's neck, pressed her body into his, and pulled him down for a long, heartfelt kiss. He didn't fight her and would happily give as good as he got for as long as she wanted.

When she broke the kiss, she held her forehead to his and sighed. "Thank you, Jake," she said, her breath warm against his face. "I'm glad no one was more seriously hurt."

"Me too."

"Are you feeling fit enough for some grateful attention from your woman?" she asked as she leaned back, a smile brightening her face.

"My woman," he repeated and grinned. "Hmm, I like that. I could definitely use some attention from her. I've been going through Monica withdrawal."

She laughed. "Have you? Well," she took his hand and led him up the stairs. "We'll have to see what I can do about that." Halfway up, her gaze whipped around when Jake abruptly stopped. A worried frown marred her lovely features.

"I've really missed you," he said, and his breath hitched with the sudden ache in his chest.

She smiled and stepped down until their eyes were level.

"I've missed you, too, but let's not stand here wasting time. I want to hold you tonight, Jake, and make sure you're okay."

"I *am* okay."

"Come on and prove it then." She tugged at his hand again, and he followed without resistance.

Happiness welled inside him, warming his chest and spiraling downward in quickly tightening rings that vibrated along his growing erection. He watched the sultry sway of her hips as she led him by the hand down the hall to the guest room, unable to keep the broad, enthusiastic smirk off his face.

I love this woman, he thought as he followed her into the room, and after the door closed, he proceeded to show her precisely how much.

39

"I DON'T NEED YOU to tell me what to do," Angel snapped, sitting up straighter in one of her deck chairs. Brows drawn down, she glared across the small table at Monica as a soft breeze swept through the valley, tempering the heat of the warm mid-August evening.

"I wasn't trying to tell you what to do," Monica replied. "I just said you might be happier if you stopped being celibate."

"I don't want to talk about this."

"You're lonely, Angel, everyone can see that."

"I said I don't want to talk about this." Angel's voice turned dangerously soft, and Monica sighed.

Jake shifted his hips as he leaned against the deck railing across from the two women. It was their last night together after this year's final harvest. They were all tired, but Jake hadn't expected to find the two friends at odds when he returned from the barn. Hands stuffed in his pockets, he avoided eye contact and remained silent, after unknowingly walking in on their argument.

Angel had grown increasingly more irritable as the summer wound down, and she quarreled with Michelle more often than not. Now, it was Monica's turn, and her tenacity in confronting her irate friend amazed Jake.

"Angel," she said in a gentle tone, "I love you and you know I'd do anything for you. Please, don't make me watch you keep doing this to yourself."

Jake nodded. He didn't like seeing Angel sad or upset either.

"You can go home," Angel said, slouching back in her chair. "Then you won't have to watch anything."

"That's not fair."

"Life isn't fair."

Jake's heart clenched at the pain in Angel's voice, and he met Monica's gaze.

"I am aware," Monica responded as she glanced at Jake. She gave him a quick smile and he reciprocated.

Angel saw the exchange, and when she met Jake's gaze, several emotions shifted in her eyes, too fast and complicated for him to discern. Then her shoulders sagged, and she appeared to shrink.

"I know you mean well," Angel said, staring at the tabletop, tracing her finger through the fine layer of grit coating it. "I just... I can't."

Monica reached for her friend's hand. "I know that too. I just worry about you, that's all."

After Monica's comment, the whole argument dropped, and they were soon talking about the upcoming calving season as if hard words had never been spoken.

Jake wondered at their conversation. He'd asked Monica about Angel's odd moods and behavior the year before, but all she would say was: Angel's hurting.

* * *

Almost a month later, Angel sat motionless behind her big oak desk and stared at her hands, pressed flat and splayed open on her desktop as if memorizing every line and curve.

Jake shifted in the straight-backed wooden chair on the other side of her desk, distracting himself by straightening the brim of the felt cowboy hat he held in his lap. This was not the first time she'd summoned him to her office, but, though he'd come to like Angel, her behavior lately had become unpredictable. He changed position again to ease the stiffness in his leg muscles from sitting for so long on the hard surface. He glanced out the window and took a deep breath. Rousing his courage to speak, he turned back to Angel.

"Is there anything else you need?" he asked.

Angel's head snapped up and she looked...scared. He could think of no other word to describe her expression, but he didn't understand why she'd be afraid. He'd certainly done nothing to frighten her, but something had.

"I'm sorry," he said. "I didn't mean to startle you. I thought—"

"It's okay, Jake." She sat back in her chair, an almost identical match to the one he occupied, and cleared her throat. "I did want to tell you something, but I'm not sure how."

He shrugged. "I've found straightforward usually works best."

Now you're giving advice? he silently wondered at himself, but no condemnation came from Angel. Instead, she smiled at him sadly and folded her hands in her lap. She took a deep breath, sighed, and turned her face toward the window a few feet from the edge of her desk.

"I know you'd rather not be here, Jake, and I don't blame you. If I could, I'd send you back to Monica, but I can't."

He nodded.

"I do have to say, however, I'm glad you're here."

Jake's belly tightened, and he sat up a little straighter.

"You've been tremendously helpful here," she continued as she slumped in her chair and stared out the window with a faraway look in her eyes. "I've come to rely on you quite a bit and you've never let me down.

I've also..." She paused and glanced at him, then lowered her head to focus on her hands clenched together on her thighs. "I've also grown very fond of you."

Oh, no... his mind groaned. In his role as her foreman, they'd spent a lot of time together over the last several months. He'd grown to care for her, but in a friendly way, nothing more. He sat up straighter, and his fingers clutched his hat brim, wrinkling it again. The chair creaked when he pressed back, inadvertently putting more space between them, and the sound drew her attention.

Alarm wrinkled her features, and she sat forward abruptly. "Is something wrong?"

He swallowed and dropped his eyes, unable to meet her gaze. He shook his head. *Please don't let this be what it sounds like.*

"What happened to straightforward, Nichols?"

At first, her comment sounded angry, but when he looked up, she was smiling. He frowned, and her smile broadened.

"Monica said you worry a lot," Angel said as if she were teasing. "I'm beginning to see how much. So, the question here is: what are you worrying about right now?"

He shrugged again.

She studied his face, and he forced himself not to give in to his discomfort by squirming in his seat.

"I'm not like *her* either," Angel said and sat forward to brace her elbows on her desk. "I'm not Darla. I told you I'm not going to expect sexual favors or anything like that from you, Jake. Not...ever."

He nodded, breathing a sigh of relief and feeling like an utter fool. "Sorry," he muttered.

"No harm done," Angel replied, and then it was her turn to sigh heavily.

Silence descended. When a full minute had passed and Angel still sat wordlessly staring at her hands, folded on the desk this time, Jake broke the shroud of quiet. "You were saying?"

Again, she appeared startled and then smiled woefully. "Yes," she said at last and slouched in her chair once more. "I was trying to say something, but I was doing it badly."

"I'm sorry I interrupted you."

One side of her mouth quirked up a little higher. "I understand your concern, Jake, but your fear is needless with me."

"I know, I just... My experiences the last few years haven't been the best, at least not until I met Monica...and you. It's hard to forget..."

Angel shook her head while waving a hand in dismissal. "You don't have to explain. I get it, but to go back to what I was trying so poorly to say. I'm glad you're here and I feel comfortable relying on you with the ranch, but I need something more."

"What's that?"

She tilted her head. "What has Monica told you about me?"

He frowned. "How do you mean?"

"Has she told you I have...trouble sometimes? Mainly in the fall?"

"All she said was you're hurting." He didn't offer his opinion, though he had a strong suspicion about what ailed her.

"Yes," Angel said as her cheeks pinkened. "I guess that's the best way to put it. Did she tell you I get...difficult sometimes?"

"She may have mentioned something about that too."

Angel glanced out the window again. "Before last year, Monica took care of me when I couldn't take care of myself." She glanced at him and then lowered her gaze. "She kept me going. Kept me from giving up."

He didn't comment, only waited for her to continue.

"I miss her," Angel mumbled to herself, staring at her desktop once more. Then she looked up and spoke more clearly. "Right now, I miss her terribly. The people here are great. Michelle does a wonderful job for me, but Monica thinks they're not enough. She says I need you."

Jake's brows drew together, and his back straightened away from the chair. "Sorry?"

"I need you to tell me when I'm being stubborn and unreasonable, Jake.

I need your help to get through the next several months. I need you not to fear me, to trust I'll never hurt you." She chuckled lightly but without mirth. "I may not listen, I may argue, I may even act crazy angry, but I'll never punish you for doing what I'm asking of you...or for anything else either."

He sat mutely for a few seconds, stunned by her request. "Why me?" he finally queried. "Why not one of the others who've been here longer?"

"Monica said I could trust you and you've proved it," Angel said, honesty shining in her azure eyes.

A memory of Monica telling him the same thing about Angel echoed in Jake's mind.

"Plus," she continued, "you have a lot of responsibility here, Jake; the people are starting to look up to you. You're more involved with what's going on than anyone else. You're the best person *to* do this."

He sat staring down at his wrinkled hat, his fingers idly straightening it, while he considered her request. She was right—he was the best person, but despite his position on the ranch and his newfound affection for everyone there, he still had misgivings. When he finally looked up, he found Angel watching him. He met her gaze evenly and told her the truth. "I don't know if I can. Darla's training was...thorough. I'm not sure I can move past it."

"Darla is sick," Angel said. "I'll never treat you the way she did, Jake. And if it's within my power, I won't let anyone else hurt you either. If not for your sake, then for Monica's. I love her. I owe her everything. She's my family, and now, so are you. You can get past Darla's disgusting abuse—you've already started to—and I'll help you in any way I can."

That had been in mid-September. Jake had said he would try to help her, but he promised nothing more and Angel seemed to accept his limitations.

He had no idea what he was getting into.

Over the next few weeks, she grew more sullen and distant. At times, "difficult" didn't begin to describe her, and he often backed down or said nothing at all. He still struggled with trusting that she wouldn't hurt him, but he kept trying because he wanted to believe her.

By late October, he realized how much she truly needed his guidance. Using the example of Monica's gentle persistence with Angel last summer, Jake learned how to get her to respond.

"You need to eat!" he heard Michelle say loudly as he entered Angel's room, drawn by their shouting.

"I told you, I'm not hungry!" Angel sat in the middle of her huge bed, the blankets around her waist, her arms crossed over her chest, and her chin tilted belligerently. "You can just take that tray back to Esther and tell her to stop pestering me."

Michelle inhaled and opened her mouth to reply, but Jake interrupted what looked like a brewing battle.

"What's going on in here?" he asked.

Michelle turned to him. "Angel's refusing to eat again."

"Ah," he said. Then, gesturing toward the food, he whispered to Michelle, "Let me try."

Clearly frustrated, she willingly handed him the tray. Neither of them knew why, but they were both aware that Angel responded to him more readily than Michelle.

"I'll leave it to you then," Michelle replied quietly and, after a slanted glance at Angel, left the room.

He went to the bed and sat down beside Angel, then placed the tray carefully on the mattress.

"Why aren't you hungry, Angel?" he asked gently.

"I'm just not."

"You didn't eat lunch today either."

She narrowed her eyes. "Esther's been tattling again."

"Don't blame the cook," he said. "She's worried about you, and so are the rest of us."

Angel looked away, her jaw clenched, but he'd seen guilt shift in her eyes. She didn't like being the cause of their worry.

"You know I can't let you sit up here and starve yourself."

"I'm not *starving* myself. I'm just not hungry and I want to be left alone."

"I thought you liked talking with me."

She glanced at him. "I do." She shook her head. "It's not you, Jake. It's not Michelle either. I just..." She fiddled with the edge of her comforter as she stared at her lap.

"You asked me to do this for you," he reminded her.

She heaved a heavy sigh and nodded.

"I want you to eat at least half of your dinner, and I'm not taking no for an answer."

She looked up, then down at the tray and sighed again.

"Please, Angel."

Her lips pressed together briefly and he thought he might have a more strenuous argument on his hands, but then she reached for the fork.

It wasn't always so easy to convince her of anything in her current state, but Jake kept trying. By November, he ate meals with Angel every day and attempted to persuade her each morning to climb out of bed. Sometimes he convinced her to ride out to the fields with him. On their first ride, he began telling her stories about his assorted adventures with Bret to entertain her. Angel smiled at first, but after a few tales of their misadventures, she started asking questions. She didn't volunteer anything of her own, but Jake's tales seemed to be the only thing that held her interest.

After the events with Toby last spring, Michelle had insisted Jake stay in the guest room until the other man was sold a few days later. Angel then had Jake build an attached apartment off the kitchen so he could have his own living quarters but still be close to the house. Despite the distance from Jake's apartment to the upstairs bedrooms, when Angel began waking at night with terror-filled screams, they rang out clear enough to rouse him downstairs and send anxiety sliding through his veins. The first time he woke to her cries reverberating through the walls, he threw on his clothes and ran barefoot up the stairs to find Michelle trying to comfort an extremely distraught Angel.

"What happened?" he questioned as he entered her room.

"N-Nothing," Angel stuttered as she sat in her bed with her arms wrapped around herself, shivering. "I'm f-fine. It's j-just a nightmare."

He glanced at Michelle to find her staring at Angel with her mouth drawn down and her lips a thin line. Jake didn't believe Angel either. By the look on her overly pale face and the tremors that wracked her body, it was far more than a simple bad dream, but he made no comment.

The same situation repeated itself several times over the following days, and he checked on her every time. Usually, the only way to get her to calm down was for Jake to talk to her. At first, he thought it was simply the sound of his voice letting her know she wasn't alone, but a different pattern soon emerged.

One night, he scrambled out of bed to find Angel and Michelle standing halfway down the staircase.

"I must find...! Let me go!" Angel screamed at the top of her lungs as Jake came barreling into the foyer. Dim light filtered in through the living room windows, and a burning lantern sat at the top of the stairs as Michelle struggled to convince a very distraught Angel to go back to bed. When Michelle spotted Jake coming toward them, her eyes locked on him. He raised a brow in question at the red handprint on her cheek, but Michelle shook her head.

"She doesn't know what she's doing. I can't get through to her this time; you need to try."

He turned to Angel, who had gone quiet and now stared blankly at nothing.

"Angel?" he called and gently folded her hand in his. "Would you like to hear another story?"

She jumped when he spoke, and her eyes drifted to him. When she met his gaze, she smiled, but then her head rolled back and her knees buckled. Jake caught her limp form and lifted her easily against his chest. She didn't regain consciousness again until he laid her down and tucked the covers in around her. She looked like a small child curled up on her side under her comforter, and he cringed inwardly at the almost desperate expression in her eyes when she looked up at him. He sat down beside her, and she reached for his hand. He let her take it and smiled at her when she peered up at him shyly. Angel seemed calm and far more aware than she had on the stairs, but the shame and pain he read in the blue depths of her eyes made his heart wince.

"Was I screaming again?" she asked softly.

"Yes, and you slapped Michelle too."

Angel flinched and then stared up at him again.

"Why are you all so good to me?" she asked in the same quiet voice. "I'm so awful sometimes, and everyone's always kind."

He thought for a moment and smiled. Several reasons came to mind, but he went for the one he had realized weeks ago. "You remind me of someone."

"Who?"

"A friend of mine."

"The cowboy? Bret?"

"Yes." He smiled again, fondly this time.

"Tell me more about him," Angel said, and he cocked his head to the side and flashed his most charming grin.

"You like my tall tales?" he asked, and her lips quirked.

"They keep me from thinking." She sighed. "And I feel better when you talk."

Jake found her interest in his long-lost friend curious, but he obliged.

"What was Bret like?"

"Ahhh..." Jake sighed. "He's a complicated man."

"How so?"

"Well, for one, he wasn't the most trusting person. We didn't get along too well when we first met."

She yawned. "Why not?"

"He was cocky," Jake said with a short laugh, "and I was a very angry young man."

"Angry?" Her brows knitted together. "You don't strike me as an angry person, Jake."

"I'm not. Not anymore, but I lost my mom to cancer shortly before I met Bret, and I was pissed at the world."

She reached out from the covers and squeezed his hand. "I'm sorry, Jake. I didn't know."

He shrugged. "It was a long time ago. I've changed, but back then I was in no place to deal with a smart-ass kid with a bad attitude and..." He paused, debating how much he would tell her, and then smiled and shook his head. "We eventually got past all that."

"Must be hard knowing he's out there somewhere." She waved her hand toward the French doors beside her huge four-poster bed.

Jake nodded.

"Do you think he's still free?"

"I hope so. I don't like thinking about what might happen if he wasn't."

Angel yawned again and blinked at him slowly. "What was his family like?"

Jake peered at her sleepy face, again not sure how much of that tale he should disclose. He decided to share just a little and replied, "His mom was great. She kind of became a second mom to me, just like my dad did for Bret."

"Was Bret close to his mom too?"

"That's a long story," he told her, brushing a stray curl from her cheek. She looked about ready to nod off.

"What happened?"

"Oh, Angel..." He sighed. "That's not my story to tell and you need to get some sleep."

"Tell me a little more," she said, then yawned again and snuggled under her blankets. "I won't ask any more questions. Just talk so I can fall asleep."

Jake tilted his head.

Angel was a strong woman, and even now, when she was most vulnerable, a couple of her character traits shone through. First, she always made sure no one else on the ranch ever witnessed how deeply she suffered—even he and Michelle didn't know the depths of what caused her pain. And second, she never showed interest in any other man, yet she asked about Bret regularly.

Jake mentally shrugged. If it helped her to listen to him talk about his friend and their lives together, it was a small price to pay for all she'd done for him.

Still, he resolved to ask Monica once more about Angel's past and discuss his concerns for her future once the time came for him to leave.

40

August, one year later

THE REINS HELD SECURELY in his left hand, Jake brandished a coiled lariat with his right to encourage the cattle to keep moving into the open pen. In the next instant, a yearling bull burst from the group, attempting to head back into the hills. Jake flicked the reins and used his hips and legs to direct his horse into the bovine's path. Back and forth the horse and rider danced until the bull reversed his direction and ran into the pen with the rest of the herd.

"Nice to see you haven't lost your touch, Nichols."

Jake glanced behind him and saw Shawn riding up with a broad smile on his face. Jake scoffed and replied, "I can still teach you a thing or two, Brohm."

Jake and several other people from Angel's ranch, and nearly everyone from Monica's, had been out combing the hills the last few days for

Monica's cattle. This was the last of the herd they needed to drive down into the winter pastures.

Shawn laughed at Jake's retort and slapped him on the back. "Glad to have you here, buddy," Shawn called over his shoulder as he trotted off on his horse, heading for Trevor, who was riding his own chestnut mare not far ahead. "You too, Angel!" Shawn shouted across the open field, using his gloved hand to blow her a kiss.

Angel rolled her eyes and waved off Shawn's antics as one of the ranch hands closed the gate after the last of the cattle passed through.

Shawn grinned and winked at Trevor as he slowed to a walk beside the boy's horse. Trevor chuckled and started chatting Shawn's ear off as they headed back to the house for dinner.

Jake smiled, happy to be back again, and relieved to discover that Trevor and Shawn had grown close in his absence. This was Trevor's first time on a roundup, and he'd done very well. He'd improved a lot just in the last few days. More than once, Jake had observed him and Shawn with their heads together, the boy listening intently and nodding his understanding of the man's instructions. Trevor had made a few mistakes, but after every one he'd consult with Shawn and was careful not to repeat them.

On the first night of their visit, Jake had walked into the dining hall of Monica's home and had nearly been bowled over by a little blonde tornado.

"Jake! Jake!" Kara had shouted as she ran up to him and threw her arms around his legs. Though more reserved, Trevor came up a few steps behind her.

Jake laughed. "Hey, Squirt," he said and scooped Kara up in his arms. "Did you miss me?"

"Yes," the little girl said, her arms wrapped around his neck.

Jake gave her a hug and grinned down at her brother. "How about you, Trevor? You been keeping busy?"

His denim-blue eyes lit up, and he stuck his chest out. "Yep. Shawn taught me how to ride."

"Yeah, I saw that," Jake said and ruffled the boy's hair. "I'm glad we'll have your help this year."

Trevor's smile widened with the praise.

Excited to tell Jake everything they'd done since the last time he'd seen them, the kids had chattered on all through dinner. He didn't get to speak with the adults until everyone was finished eating. He'd slanted Monica a couple of apologetic looks, but each time she only smiled, with promise in her eyes.

The kids' interest in him had waned a bit by the second evening, and they chose to sit with their new parents and then ran off with their friends after dinner.

The scene warmed his heart, and Jake had smiled at the sight of their little family. Shawn saw his glance and nodded. Jake returned the gesture, grateful they had finally merged into a happy family.

The thought also brought back memories of his old friend Bret, and a little pang of melancholy struck him.

At dinner that first night, and during mealtimes for the rest of their stay, he had caught glimpses of Kristine Collins eyeing him darkly, but she avoided him as if he were diseased.

Now, with the final day of the roundup complete, Jake rode toward the barn and sighed, immensely thankful for the disagreeable woman's distance and the good fortune of his friends.

"It *is* good to see you again, Mr. Nichols," Rosa said from the back of her gelding a few feet away, shaking her head at Shawn's silly clowning.

Jake grinned. "Are you ever going to stop being so formal with me, Rosa?"

Rosa laughed, riding along beside him. "I'm glad you were able to come, Jake. We needed the help this year."

"I'm happy to be here."

"I'm sorry we haven't had much chance to catch up since you've been back."

He shrugged. "It's been busy."

Rosa glanced around, leaned toward him from her saddle, and lowered her voice. "Monica misses you."

Jake's grin widened, and he winked at her. "Same here."

Rosa shook her head and chuckled. "You've changed for the better, Jake." She glanced at him. "I'm glad to see it."

Tonight was their last night on Monica's ranch, and Jake expected dinner to be the same as it had been for the last few evenings, though he was looking forward to his time after the meal more.

From the back of her horse, Monica had been giving him heated looks all afternoon as they searched for cattle. She'd even teased him with stolen kisses in the brush. The last time she'd directed her horse to follow him into the undergrowth, she'd surprised him by grabbing his shirt and yanking him toward her. Her soft lips on his sent bolts of desire flashing through his body. One of her hands slipped to the back of his neck as her tongue darted into his mouth, while her other slid slowly up his inner thigh. His muscles tightened and he reached out to pull her to him, but she broke the kiss and sidled her horse away.

"Un-uh," she'd said with a smile. "That was just a teaser. You'll get the rest tonight."

Shoulders sagging, he groaned. "You're killing me right now."

She laughed. "I'll make it up to you later."

* * *

Jake made his way upstairs, looking for his luscious tormentor, but as he neared Monica's bedroom door, he saw Angel exiting.

"Evenin'," he said by way of greeting. He hadn't spoken to her much today, but he'd noted her downtrodden appearance growing more pronounced as each day passed and autumn drew closer.

"Hi," she replied and then waved toward Monica's door. "She's on the deck if you're looking for her."

"Yeah, thanks." He paused at the entry to Monica's room and stared at Angel's back as she strolled down the hallway to the guest room. Head down, shoulders bowed, she looked so beaten down it made his heart clench. "Angel?"

Eyebrows raised, she glanced at him over her shoulder.

"Are you all right?"

Her lips curved up in a weak smile. "I'm fine, Jake. Just tired from all the riding."

"You sure?"

"Yeah, I'm sure. Have a good night." She fluttered her hand in farewell and then disappeared into the guest room.

Jake shook his head and went to find Monica.

He paused just inside the French doors leading out onto the deck to admire the woman who'd stolen his heart. Her blonde hair hung in loose waves around her shoulders as she gazed out at the pink and orange clouds in an indigo-lavender sky. She was dressed in a red bathrobe that made her skin glow in the sunset light, and he spared a few moments to fantasize about what she did or didn't have on underneath.

"Are you going to stand there and stare all night, Cowboy?"

Jake chuckled and crossed the deck to wrap his arms around her. She leaned back into his chest and dropped her head on his shoulder.

"Howdy, handsome," she said glancing over her shoulder at him with a soft smile.

"Howdy, yourself." Seeing her twinkling eyes and soft lips, he wanted to kiss her, and he could tell she wanted the same thing, but he held off—a little payback for all her teasing that afternoon.

"I've been waiting for you."

He raised an eyebrow and gazed down at her. "Have you?"

She slapped his forearm at her waist. "You know I have. Did you forget my kisses already?"

Grasping her hips, he turned her to face him and lowered his head. She gasped softly. Their lips barely brushed as he spoke. "I don't know. I think you need to remind me."

He closed the distance, and her mouth opened immediately. She wrapped her arms around his neck to pull him closer. He bent her backward, slanting his head to deepen the kiss, intent on making the most of his last night with her for a while. His hands gripped her backside, grinding his hips against hers, letting her feel how much he wanted her.

She moaned into this mouth, but then she broke the kiss.

"I think we should take this inside," she said, and the desire in her eyes shot right to his groin.

"Whatever you say," he said. The sooner he could get her clothes off the better.

Inside, she went into the master bathroom, but he paused beside her red-quilted queen-sized bed, which was nestled against the outside wall between the French doors—exactly the position she'd asked him about more than a year ago, when they were first getting to know each other. The memory made him smile.

He heard the water start in the shower and wondered what she would do next. The teasing wasn't new. Many times over the last year, they'd discussed pushing his boundaries, and she never failed to surprise him. And he loved her boldness in pursuing him.

"Get in here, Jake Nichols," she called, and he chuckled to himself at the excited note in her voice.

He walked in with a smile on his lips, but he found her still in her robe.

"Did you think you were going to sleep in my nice clean bed without taking a shower?"

He lifted one shoulder. "Hadn't thought about it," he said, though he had wanted to clean up before dinner. There just hadn't been time.

She narrowed her eyes, and he chuckled again as she started unbuttoning his shirt.

He closed his hands over hers to stop her movements. "I can undress myself."

"Not like I can," she said with a crooked grin that sent a fresh swell of scorching heat through his already surging veins.

He dropped his hands, a smile playing on his lips. "Then by all means.

Do what you like, I'm all yours."

"You better be," she said, her eyes shining up at him intensely.

Not that long ago the possessive note in her voice would've unnerved him. Now, he only grinned as she leaned toward him and her tongue flicked out to taste his flesh beneath the button she'd just undone. The hot, slick sensation of her tongue sent chills of expectation dancing over his skin, heating his blood and speeding up his heart. His loins clenched, and he sucked in a deep breath. He closed his eyes and sighed. Head thrown back, he savored her attentions and the resulting lust that flooded his body. By the time she swirled the tip of her tantalizing tongue around his navel, he was breathing hard, more than ready to take her in his arms and show her how much he loved her.

She pulled back and paused long enough for him to look down at her again. Then she grinned as she slowly pulled his shirttails from his jeans and the sultry look in her eyes had his heart pounding harder than before. His muscles jumped beneath her fingers as they skimmed over his abdomen and chest to his shoulders. Her soft hands grazed down his arms, sending the garment tumbling to the floor. She tugged at the button on his jeans, slowly lowered the zipper, and pushed the denim off his hips, all while her gaze remained locked on his face.

Her eyes fell to his groin, and then her wicked little fingers traced over the rigid bulge of his erection, exploring the ridges of his hot shaft with deliberate strokes. Her gentle touch along his sensitive skin shot waves of pleasure through him. His breath caught, and his legs trembled with the sudden caress. He clenched his teeth and then he moaned. He saw her smile as her hand traveled downward to cup his heavy balls in her palm. Gently, she squeezed, kneading him as her other hand continued to rub his hardened cock in a slow, seductive motion. Heat pulsed through him, electric tingles shot over his nerve endings, and his genitals swelled further, to the point he felt ready to burst. He groaned and his whole body shook. He reached for her, wanting to feel every inch of her soft heat along his hard frame, but she batted his hands away.

"No," she said, slanting an impish grin his way. "I'm the only one who gets to touch right now."

He groaned and clenched his fists at his sides. She'd done this before, and, trying as it was, he was never disappointed in the end.

"I want to touch you," he said, his voice matching the pulsing, fiery passion inside him.

"You will," she said. "Later." Her tone and the blazing look in her gold-flecked hazel eyes told him how much she was enjoying driving him crazy. He couldn't say he didn't love her attentions, but she was definitely testing the limits of his restraint.

Her fingers gripped the elastic of his navy briefs, and she tugged them down to his ankles, freeing his erection. As he kicked them away, she stepped back. She licked her lips as her eyes devoured every inch of him, stoking the intensifying inferno inside him.

"If you keep looking at me like that," Jake rasped, "I'm not going to make it to the shower."

She giggled in response and then slowly stripped off her robe.

Jake's breath halted at the vision before him. He'd seen her naked many times before, but the sight of her long legs, silky skin, and delectable feminine form always left him stunned and panting.

She stepped into the shower stall. "Let's get you cleaned up so I can finish what I started."

Still a little dazed by her display and the rage of carnal hunger gnawing at his vitals, he swallowed, hard, imagining what she planned to do.

"Get in here, Jake. I want to wash your sexy body."

He huffed out an anticipatory breath and grinned at the teasing note in her voice. *Damn, I love this woman.*

By the time Monica had bathed him—and made him watch while she bathed herself—Jake was once again so hard he thought he might explode any minute. And she still wouldn't let him touch her.

"I need you," he said, his voice low, almost a guttural growl. His whole body felt taut as she turned to shut off the water. She angled her frame just right, treating him to a show of her trim backside and long legs, as well as her beautiful, pink-tipped breasts as they jostled with her movements.

His balled-up fingers tightened a little more at his sides.

Glancing over her shoulder, she giggled, relishing her little game of seduction. "I know," she said, and her eyes purposely looked him up and down, twice. She smiled at him suggestively and then quickly exited the shower.

His back stiffened and he did growl then, in frustration. But seeing how much fun she was having, he decided to let her play a little more.

She handed him a towel as he stepped out of the shower. "Dry off and meet me at the bed," she told him. He reached for her, but she danced away into the other room, her sweet bottom swaying enticingly.

He gritted his teeth, but despite the pulsating need pounding between his legs, he was kind of relishing this game too—though he wouldn't let it go on much longer. His hands itched with how much he wanted to touch her, not to mention his urgent, driving need to be inside her as soon as possible.

She was standing beside the bed when he reentered the bedroom. The covers had been turned down to reveal creamy white sheets. She held out her hand, and he crossed the room to take it. The feel of her small hand in his caused sparks to dash up his arm, but she wouldn't let him pull her close.

"Not yet, Jake," she said as she pushed his hands behind him again.

"When?" His voice was so raspy and full of need, he almost didn't recognize it as his own.

"Soon." She drew his head down and kissed him. Her hardened nipples burned twin holes in his chest, the heat of her luscious body stoking his desire to new heights, and it was all he could do to keep from clamping her to him in an iron grip. Instead, his hands clenched together behind his back to keep them immobile, but he almost lost control when her fingers wrapped around his hardened shaft.

"Monica..." he grumbled into her mouth. "I can't take much more of this."

She shoved against his chest and he stumbled back a step. His legs collided with the bed and he plopped down onto the mattress. Before he got his bearings, Monica's hands gripped his thighs and inched them further apart as she knelt between his knees.

"No," he said and grabbed her wrists. "I want to be inside you."

"You will be," she said, and his heart slammed harder in his chest from the heat in her eyes. "I want to taste you first."

He licked his lips, rapidly sucked in air through his nose, debating with himself as to whether or not to agree to more.

He had no doubt the decision was his.

Her eyebrows lowered and concern filled her gaze. "Is it too much?"

He scoffed. "I'm ready to blow, Monica. You had me going all afternoon."

"Are you not enjoying yourself?"

He barked out another short laugh. "Hell, yeah, I'm enjoying myself, but I don't know how much longer I can wait."

"Just a little longer?"

The eager expression on her face did him in. How could he deny her anything, especially when all she wanted was him?

"A few minutes," he warned, "and then if you don't join me on this bed, I'll drag you up here myself. And not for teasing. I'll get you back for that later."

"Such a romantic," she said with a little pout, but then her mouth pulled up in a broad grin. "I can't wait."

Shaking his head, his lips quirked at her giddiness, and he released her wrists. He leaned back and propped himself on his hands as he gazed down at her. "Not too long, Monica. I mean it."

"Whatever you say, Cowboy."

Head back, eyes squeezed shut, body shaking, he moaned as she took him in her hand and her slick tongue licked a slow, erotic trail up the underside of his cock. He fought down his natural impulses one more time and somehow won the battle. The next instant, he moaned again, louder this time, as her fingers curled around his hardness and her hot mouth engulfed him. The pressure of her lips and hand tightened in a perfect, sensual vice as they slid up and down his shaft once, twice, three times. The need in him swelled to overwhelming levels, and he knew he could stand no more.

"Stop. Now," he croaked, reaching for her. He cupped her face in his trembling hands as she pulled back, licking her lips.

"You taste so good, Jake."

His gut clenched, and another jolt shot through his loins. He grimaced and gripped himself to stop the reaction from going too far.

"Get up here," he grit out between his teeth.

She smiled and stood. "Scoot over, so I can crawl up beside you."

He moved into the center of the bed and lay back on the fluffy white pillows. Kneeling near his hips, her gaze ran his whole length once more, pausing on his almost painfully ready erection as it jutted up from the tangle of golden-brown curls between his thighs.

She licked her lips again.

"Monica," he said, need and desire suffusing her name.

She met his gaze. Lips parted, eyes shining down at him intently, she straddled his hips and reached down to position him at her opening. Then, still staring into his eyes, she deliberately sunk down along his shaft.

His back arching and hands fisting in the sheet beneath him, he groaned at the sleek, wet heat that encompassed him. She folded over his body, the hardened tips of her breasts pushing into his chest, brushing lightly through the curling mat as she whispered in his ear.

"I'm close too," she breathed, a little quiver in her voice. "Touching you is such a turn on, Jake, and I love how you feel inside me. Can you hold on a little longer...for me?"

Her warm breath against his ear sent a shiver along his spine.

"Yes," he groaned, and then his hands grasped her hips, guiding her as she began to move.

She hadn't lied. With a little help from his mouth on her breasts and his fingers caressing the hard little bud between her thighs, she screamed out her pleasure a few minutes later. Jake joined her within seconds.

She collapsed onto his chest and he wrapped his arms around her, cradling this daring, tender, sometimes exasperating woman close to his heart.

"I love you, Jake," she murmured against his neck.

"I love you too," he whispered in reply, his fingers caressing the soft skin of her back.

She pushed up to look into his face, and he used a finger to tuck her damp hair behind her ear.

"Thank you," she said, "for letting me play." He heard the unspoken "You've come so far" in her words.

"You know I like it when you touch me."

"Yes, but I tested you a little hard today."

"Yes, you did."

"I'm going to pay for it later though, aren't I?"

He lifted his brows and nodded. "Oh, yes."

She giggled and wiggled her body against him. "Goody."

He laughed and hugged her tightly.

She rolled to the side and cuddled up against him.

"Just think," she said as she settled her head on his shoulder, "a little over a year from now, if I can afford you by then, we can play like this all the time."

"Yeah." Jake sighed.

She tilted her face to his. "What's wrong?"

"Nothing's wrong. How could anything be wrong when I have you in my arms?"

She smiled, but she wasn't deterred. "That's very sweet, but something's bothering you."

He glanced toward the bedroom door briefly, and then his eyes returned to Monica, debating if now was the best time to voice his concerns.

"What is it, Jake? You've had something on your mind all day."

He raised an eyebrow. "You noticed that, did you? I should've known."

"Yes, I did, and I've been waiting for you to tell me. Now, spit it out already."

A rueful grin tugged at his mouth. "All right. I'm worried about Angel."

Monica sighed, and a shadow of sadness veiled her face. "Yeah, me too."

"She doesn't look good."

Monica nodded. "She was crying earlier too."

An uneasy weight settled in Jake's heart. He didn't like hearing that. "Why?"

"I've already told you more than I should."

"Yeah, I know, but..."

"But?"

He glanced at her. "I'm worried about more than right now."

"You're worried about leaving her."

Jake nodded.

Monica traced a finger through his chest hair, making little figure eights and starting goosebumps on his skin.

"I know I asked you to look out for her," Monica said and then lifted glistening eyes to his face, "but I want you back."

"I want that too, and I don't have a problem helping her," he replied. "I just don't want anything to happen to her later."

"Theo could...maybe..."

"Theo has his own issues to deal with," Jake said. "Friends or not, I'm sure Peggy wouldn't appreciate him having to run up to the house in the middle of the night to take care of Angel."

"Probably not," Monica conceded, and she laid her head back on his shoulder. Jake knew she understood the exact situation he was referring to; she'd lived through it with Angel herself.

Hearing the disappointment in Monica's reply, his arm tightened around her as he stared up at the ceiling. He felt the same way, but he also felt an obligation to Angel now too.

"Don't get me wrong," he said after deliberating on his thoughts, "but I don't want just anyone looking out for her."

"Me either," Monica replied, but something odd entered her tone.

With a finger curled under her chin, he lifted her face to his. "You're not worried about me and...her...?"

Monica frowned and lightly slapped his chest. "Of course not. It's just that I know it might take me more than one year to save enough to pay her back, and we've already waited so long. As selfish as it might sound to say it out loud, as soon as I can make it all official, I want you here with me."

He squeezed her a little tighter. "Me too."

"We'll just have to look for the right person to take your place when the time comes," Monica said, cuddling against him and draping her arm across his ribs. Her fingers drew small circles on his skin. "If we get lucky, maybe we'll find a man she'll fall in love with too."

"Who's the romantic now?" Jake said, kissing her forehead.

"She needs someone to break through to her. Someone she can't push away or hide from behind the walls she's erected to keep everyone out. I know she loves me"—she glanced at him—"loves us, that our friendship is important to her, but she needs...more."

The sad note in her voice made his stomach tighten.

It was time to lighten the mood.

She squeaked as Jake rolled her onto her back and kissed her. When he finally pulled back, they were both breathing hard.

"I need *you* again right now," he rasped. Then he gently tugged her wrists above her head and held them there in one hand. He kissed his way down her neck and over the swell of her breast. The smell and taste of her skin heated his blood and numbed his brain, until no one and nothing else existed but her. He licked her taut nipple and she inhaled sharply. He sucked the sensitive tip into his mouth and teased it with his tongue and teeth, then let it go with a loud pop.

"Jake," Monica moaned in disappointment and frowned as he looked up into her face.

He winked and gave her a wicked grin. "It's my turn to play."

Monica's face lit up, and she giggled with glee. "Oh, goody!"

41

December 31st of the next year

JAKE NICHOLS STAMPED HIS FEET on the snow-covered ground and dug his fists deeper into the pockets of his thick wool pea coat. A slight breeze knifed through the air, but the knit cap covering his close-cropped hair kept the cold from stealing too much of his body heat. He shifted his feet while he glanced around the Auction Hall compound and shivered as he remembered his own time here.

He'd spent several weeks in this awful place after his capture, and two years of his life in the cesspool of suffering that was Darla's home, about a mile to the north of where he now stood. His stomach twisted up being this close to her center of power, and nausea caused by outright disgust churned deep inside his belly like a pit of angry vipers. Unfortunately, need brought them back here today.

"I'll take care of his duties," Angel had said almost two years ago now, after Dr. Beck had passed away. Over the nearly four years he spent with them, Dr. Beck had trained Angel in medicinal care, which made her decision to carry on his work unsurprising.

"Are you sure?" Jake had asked, concerned the responsibilities might be too taxing for her at times. The look she gave him said otherwise.

"You need to stop worrying so much, Jake. I'm not that fragile."

Jake wasn't so sure. He'd only been at Angel's for a year at the time, and though he no longer lived in fear of women, he hadn't known her well enough to argue.

Now, speaking his mind with Angel didn't faze him.

"You don't have to come along," Angel had told him a few months ago when she finally decided to find a replacement doctor.

"Do you really need to go?"

She frowned. "Yes, I do. I told you, if Peggy gets pregnant again, she needs a real doctor. I don't think she could take another miscarriage, and she and Theo want a baby so much. I can't let them down."

He nodded. "Then I'll go with you."

"I know how much you hate that place, Jake. And Darla and her cronies will probably be there. You don't need to go."

"Didn't you say there's been recent rebel activity in the area again?"

Her eyes narrowed, and her lips thinned as she pressed them together. They'd argued about the risks of her traveling alone before, but he wouldn't back down when it came to her safety.

"Yes," she answered in a clipped tone.

"Then I'm going with you."

Jake now stood with the other male slaves who had escorted their Mistresses to today's auction. They milled around by the barns, some gossiping, some glaring at everyone, and some hunched in the rear, trying not to draw attention to themselves. Others avidly monitored their Mistresses, while the women mingled and checked out the new "merchandise"—what most of the women there called the men who were put on display before they were sold. Jake avoided looking at the poor souls chained up across the yard. His recollections, though five years old, were still too sharp, too raw to take in what he would see.

He shouldered his way through the crowd of men to reach the periphery. His eyes skimmed the large group of women several yards away, hoping to catch a glimpse of one particular blonde. Monica had told him she would be here today, and he didn't want to miss the opportunity to see her, if only briefly.

As much as he anticipated spending a little time with Monica, Jake couldn't wait to get back home. In the last three years, Angel's Lazy A Ranch had become a home for him. Although the conditions of his sale had come to an end and he longed to be with Monica full-time again, he felt torn about leaving.

Each autumn, Angel pretended she was fine, but the mood swings and last year's leanings toward suicide had frightened both him and Monica. After that—and Jake swearing to keep the details to himself—Monica had explained what she knew of the deeply painful losses Angel blamed herself for. Knowing the story helped him understand Angel better, but it made him feel worse about leaving her alone when Monica could finally afford to purchase his papers and he could return to her.

"I won't have enough to by your papers from Angel," Monica had said with tears in her eyes during his visit for Christmas last week. Both ranches had grown in the last two years and trips to each other's homes had diminished due to their work responsibilities, but holidays were still special occasions.

"We'll figure it out," he had said, brushing a loose tendril of her golden hair behind her ear as they lay together, once again sharing her bed.

"I know, but I hate not having you here."

"I miss you too." He brushed a tear from her cheek. "But there's still the Angel problem."

She nodded. "Isn't there any man on her ranch that you'd trust with her?"

"I trust Theo, but..." He shrugged. "I can't think of anyone else I'd want knowing about her past. Can you?"

She shook her head, and he tightened his arms around her.

Jake knew he couldn't leave until Angel sold him. None of them wanted to raise red flags with Darla or her friends by having Jake leave Angel's ranch before Monica reimbursed her—which meant, for the time being, he was stuck with Angel, not that it broke his heart too much. He might miss Monica like a drowning man longs for air, but he liked working Angel's ranch. He liked Angel too. Their friendship was important to him; *she* was important to him.

Sometimes he thought he might be being overprotective by not wanting to leave Angel without someone else to look out for her. Then he would see the pain in Angel's eyes when she woke screaming in the middle of the night or when he found her crying under the huge willow tree, and his resolve to make sure she was kept safe returned.

An angry but subdued rumble among the men behind him brought Jake back to the present and the cold, dreary prison yard of the Auction Hall. When he turned, he saw two men pushing each other and exchanging heated words. He couldn't hear what they were saying, but the body language was clear enough. Several of the others, knowing the punishment for fighting, separated the two individuals before punches could be exchanged, and the commotion quickly died down.

Jake glanced at the guards, stationed nearby to keep an eye on the slaves and punish them if necessary, but they appeared not to have noticed the hubbub. He breathed a little sigh of relief. The expressions of the men around him mirrored his feelings, but some also showed a mixture of fear and anger, clearly not as tame as their Mistresses believed them to be. He shook his head, about to return to his search for Monica, when someone else caught his eye.

Animosity bubbled up and burned in his belly as his gaze locked on a familiar face: Toby Lonset. He hadn't seen the hated man since Angel sold him to Carrie Simpson just over two years ago.

An image of Toby, bound hand and foot as they hauled him from the barn to the wagon that would take him away, popped into Jake's mind. Toby had struggled against their hold, screaming that Angel would regret her actions and vowing revenge against her.

How he planned to do that, Jake had no idea.

A nasty grin tugged at Jake's lips as he glared at Toby. He wondered if Toby had fared any better with Carrie Simpson than Jake had when the crazy woman purchased his breeder services years ago. Just thinking about how she'd hurt him while thoroughly enjoying his pain sent icy prickles down Jake's back and set his teeth on edge

I wonder if Toby regrets hurting Angel now?

He shook his head again. After what Toby had tried to do to Angel, Jake didn't pity him one bit.

Right now, Toby fixated on something beyond the crowd of men that surrounded them. Jake turned his head, and when he realized Toby was ogling Angel as she watched her stallion prancing in the horse corrals, fury raged through him like wildfire devouring a parched forest.

That bastard, Jake railed as his protective instincts kicked in. *Still lusting after what he can't have.*

Feeling the need to shield Angel from Toby's leering gaze, Jake purposely stepped into his line of sight. Toby's pale blue eyes focused on Jake's face and narrowed when he recognized his one-time adversary. Jake straightened his shoulders and pulled his fists from his coat pockets, prepared for anything. He gave Toby a meaningful look, happily noting the slight curve of the man's now-healed broken nose. Toby glowered right back. Jake took several steps toward Angel, blocking Toby's view completely. Toby sneered his contempt as he began to move through the crowd. Jake turned and headed toward Angel. He needed to get away from Toby before he did something stupid.

Yeah, he thought sardonically, *like breaking his damned face again.*

As Jake strolled across the compound, he glanced toward the slaves being auctioned off. His eyes slid over the rows of chained, naked men, trying not to focus on them. A pang of empathy twisted his heart seeing their plight; he remembered all too well what it was like to be in their place. So cold and alone, desperate and terrified. He remembered...

He stopped cold.

What the—?

His brain stumbled to a halt, and his feet refused to continue along his path to Angel's side.

He stared at the men on display across the compound. Even with the women thronging around him, one stood out like a brilliantly colored banner waving in the chilly wind. Jake could not believe his eyes.

It can't be...

42

That cannot be him. Jake's mouth went dry as his stunned mind struggled with what his eyes told him. His breath halted. His heart drubbed a rapid rhythm against his ribs as he squinted at the heavily chained man across the yard. Women ebbed and flowed around the new slave, and while Jake stared, waiting for another break in the crowd, a few stopped to run their hands over the man's quaking body. Jake rubbed his eyes and focused on the man once more as the women dispersed.

He might be crazy, but...

I think it is *him!* A wild, stupid hope surged to life inside his chest.

Just like every other slave in the display yard, the man's blindfold made clearly identifying his face impossible. What Jake perceived of the other man's features, however, made him believe his eyes told the truth. The man appeared to be the same size and height. He had the same bearing, and, knowing his friend, the overabundance of chains made sense too.

"Bret?" he whispered, and his heart stuttered. Five years was a long time, and despite the similarity of his appearance, from across the yard Jake couldn't be sure it was him.

The blood-red tag on the man's metal collar flashed in the sunlight and branded him as a high-quality breeder, the same category Jake himself had been labeled, which meant his price would be high—too high for nearly every woman there. Only a handful could afford a breeder of that caliber, and whether it was Bret or not, Jake was not surprised to find this man categorized as such.

Even from a distance he could see the man had already been sorely abused; red welts and bruises covered him. Too far away to tell how serious his injuries were, Jake wished he could approach the slaves on display. But doing so would earn him an inescapable flogging.

How to...?

Maybe Angel...

And then Monica could...

A smile bloomed on his lips, and he felt a little breathless.

Bret's presence could be the catalyst that changed things for all of them.

Jake's family—his father, Jim, in particular—suddenly popped into his mind. Jake had always been grateful for his parents, but his father had played a big role in Jake's relationship with Bret. Jim's acceptance of Bret as part of their family had made a difference for the lost young man Bret was back then.

"Why don't you come camping with us, Bret?" Jim had said not long after Bret and Jake started hanging out together. "Bring your guitar and you can entertain us by the campfire."

Bret's eyes had brightened, and the corners of his mouth had ticked up at the invitation, but it quickly slipped away and he dropped his chin. Hands in his pockets, his shoulders hunched forward, Bret stared at his feet.

"Come on, Bret. It'll be fun," Jake had said to encourage his friend, suspecting how much Bret needed to get away from home for a while. "You can show off some of those outdoorsman skills you keep bragging about."

Bret's eyes flicked between them and then he shrugged. "I'll ask my mom."

That trip led to dozens of others. Bret seemed to become a different person in the woods—not so angry or withdrawn—and their time outdoors together strengthened their friendship in the process. Jake often wondered if his dad knew about Bret's home situation and whether the knowledge incited Jim to see Bret as a second son.

Another scene from years later flooded Jake's mind—one where they'd been hungry for days, unable to stop or hunt for food because of the numerous raiding parties scouring the mountains. Jake's shoulder had been injured, which made him next to useless.

One morning, after days of running, Jake had woken up alone. Weak as he was, anger at Bret's suspected departure and fear for what that might mean gave Jake the strength to leap to his feet and frantically survey the surrounding area.

At first, he hadn't believed Bret would leave him, but after an hour of futile searching and another filled with expectant waiting, doubt began pecking at his faith.

"Mornin', Jake," Bret's voice had sounded from behind him, and Jake nearly jumped out of his skin. The sudden movement aggravated his shoulder, and he groaned. Then he stood tall and released the irritation that had been brewing since he'd woken up alone hours earlier.

"Where the hell have you been?" Jake didn't have any reason to doubt Bret, but after two days without anything to eat, the constant threat of capture by the Raiders, and the pain in his arm, waking up to find his friend gone had been too much.

Bret's eyes narrowed. "I thought you might like some breakfast," he said as he dropped the load of sticks he'd carried under one arm and then dangled two plump grouse from his other hand for Jake to see.

Jake's stomach fluttered at the sight of the birds, and then shame for mistrusting his friend tightened his throat. "Oh," he said, feeling like the biggest jerk on the planet. Heat pulsed up his neck as Bret set their breakfast aside and began building a fire.

Then Bret paused and glanced up at him. "You thought I left you." He sounded disappointed and hurt.

Jake shrugged. "I thought..." He shook his head. "I don't know what I thought."

Bret sat back on his heels, his green eyes intent as he looked up at his friend. "I'd never leave you, Jake."

It had been a simple statement and one that Jake never doubted again.

Until Bret *did* leave him.

Yet aside from that one incident, he'd never let Jake down.

You were wrong that day, Nichols, Jake thought. Maybe... *Maybe you're wrong about what happened with Amy too.*

Either way, Bret had been family for over twenty years, and despite everything that had happened because of Bret's bad judgement, Jake would do anything to help or protect his family—blood or not.

Angel was as much a member of his family now as Bret had once been, and her struggles this last fall troubled him. And just as disconcerting was the fact that he would never be able to live with Monica if he couldn't leave Angel or find some way to help her heal.

Unless someone else took his place.

I wonder...

Now, standing in the yard at the Auction Hall, staring at a man he thought to be his long-lost friend and ruminating over the last three years, a spark of hope sprung to life inside Jake. Regardless of what happened, if he could trust anyone to take care of Angel in his absence, it would be Bret. The man would never hurt her, and if he gave his word to take care of her, the Bret that Jake knew would do whatever was necessary to keep his vow.

The question now was: Is Bret the same man he used to be?

No, that's not the first question, Jake thought. The first question was whether the man chained up in the breeder's section of the display yard was actually Bret Masters. There was only one way that remained to find out:

Someone must ask. He couldn't do it, and he needed to discuss the other ramifications with Monica, which left only one person: Angel.

Jake surveyed the mob of women to the south as he resumed his search for Monica. He saw her bright, flowing locks and waited for her to look his way. When she did, he held up one hand, all five fingers splayed out. Monica nodded, understanding his message to meet in their usual place in five minutes.

Jake turned away to locate the second most important woman in his life.

Angel still stood by the horse corrals, and he made his way to her. He wasn't sure he could talk her into saving Bret by purchasing him, and he thought of and dismissed a dozen or more ways to broach the topic. Knowing the tenderness of her heart, Jake finally settled on straightforward. Well, mostly straight anyway. Despite her unusual wealth, Angel couldn't afford the doctor she needed and an expensive breeder too; he must convince her that Bret had a lot more to offer her than sexual services she didn't want. Considering her atypical interest in his stories, Jake thought he might have a good chance of persuading her.

When her gaze settled on him, Angel's face lit up with a friendly smile. He forced himself to return her grin, but his dropped away almost immediately. Still, as he watched the mischievous twinkle bloom in her eyes—the one that said she plotted to tease him about something—Jake realized what he could say to sway her to his cause.

43

JAKE LEANED AGAINST THE BACK WALL, wrinkling the gray curtains hanging floor to ceiling over the uneven surface as guards led man after man onto the elaborate platform at the front of the room, like stallions up for sale. The tightness in his chest made breathing difficult, but the cause was purely psychological. Being in this glamorous room with its black-and-white tiled floor and silver-gray accents always made him justifiably nervous, and his anxiety then affected everything else.

He had been right to think Angel wouldn't like the favor he asked, but he'd still persuaded her to check on the man he thought to be Bret Masters.

"I'm not promising anything, but I'll find out if it's him or not," she had said right before she crossed the yard to investigate.

As soon as she stepped away, Jake made his way to the barn to meet Monica. He saw no sign of Toby Lonset as he passed the group of men waiting nearby, and he breathed a sigh of relief. Having another problem with Toby was the last thing Jake needed.

"Where are you going?" one of the guards demanded as Jake reached out to open the barn door.

He turned at the question, with an answer on his lips. "I was told to meet Miss Avery inside," he explained, enduring the woman's stern gaze. He dropped his arm to his side and remained silent while she looked him up and down, clearly attempting to uncover any deception on his part.

Apparently not finding any, she nodded her head, and he went into the barn.

Monica met him in the last stall. Always so happy to see him, she pulled him into a quick kiss that set his pulse racing. They were both breathing hard when she pulled away again. He rested his forehead against hers, unwilling to step away just yet.

"So what's the big emergency?" she asked, her soft breaths teasing the skin on his neck.

"Bret's here."

"Your friend?" She pulled back and her voice rose in pitch, delighted for his good fortune. Even more than Angel, Monica understood what Bret meant to him.

"Yeah, Angel's talking to him now to make sure, but I'm sure enough. It's Bret."

"You must be excited."

"He's a breeder," Jake said in a flat tone.

Monica's happy expression fell away so fast he almost laughed, but they both knew what Bret's classification meant.

"Oh, honey," she crooned, placing a consoling hand on his arm. "Is Angel going to help him?" The question was tentative.

"She wouldn't make any promises," Jake said, "but I'm going to ask her to buy him."

"She's here for the doctor."

"I know, but I can't take the chance of Bret ending up with Darla or Carrie. I just can't let that happen."

"I'm so sorry, Jake."

"You could help," he said, his eyes pleading with her. "And maybe make things better for us too."

"How so?" Her expression perked up.

"If you buy the doctor, Angel would be able to save Bret," Jake said.

"How's that going to help us?"

"Bret can run her ranch far better than I can," he explained. "If you have the doctor, you could trade him for me. The amount you'd need to acquire to buy my papers wouldn't be nearly so high; her need would offset much of the cost."

"But what about Angel? I thought you didn't want to leave her in the care of just anyone."

"Bret's not just anyone."

Monica's enthusiastic squeak was his only warning before she jumped up and down and wrapped her arms around his neck to kiss him again. This one lasted a bit longer than the last, not that he minded.

"If you're sure we can rely on him, I think your plan might work," Monica breathed when she broke the kiss.

"The exchange won't happen right away. He'll need to recover from whatever they've done to him first, and taking over for me might take a little convincing too," Jake said. "I haven't seen him in five years. We'll have to get reacquainted, but I don't think it'll be too hard. What about you?"

"What do you mean?"

"Can you do it? Will you?"

"Of course I'll do it," Monica said in a tone that questioned his sanity. "The women have been talking about a new breeder they all intend to bid on. I'm guessing Bret's who they're talking about."

"Probably," Jake groaned.

"That's actually a good thing," Monica informed him. "It means fewer of them will be interested in the doctor. Less competition means I can more easily afford him, and, if Angel and I play it right, we should be able to distract the others enough that they won't think twice about me making such an expensive purchase. Though, I'm sure Bret will cost a lot more."

"Probably," Jake grumbled again. He worried Bret's cost might be so high that Darla Cain would be one of the few women there who could afford him. He could envision her interest in Bret; he was precisely the kind of man she liked to break: proud and strong—a challenge.

Jake rubbed the back of his neck. He must convince Angel to put out the funds. A heartbeat later, a smile pulled at his lips. Considering her unusual interest in the stories about Bret, his current condition—and Angel's abhorrence of the abuses heaped on the men here—could mean that swaying her to his cause might take less effort than Jake first thought.

That had been several hours ago, nearly the entire duration of the auction.

Once Angel had confirmed it was Bret chained up in the yard and Jake had convinced her to help, they proceed with his plan.

Monica's purchase of the doctor had gone much better than expected, and now the last of the breeders was being led on stage. Jake didn't have to guess if Bret was coming next—only one remained.

Even with the unpleasantness of his plight, Bret seemed overly distraught as the guard yanked him forward and secured his lead chain to a steel ring embedded in the floor. When they removed the blindfold, the man looked sick, terrified, and furious all at once. He bared his teeth and inched backward, away from the buzzing crowd, plainly afraid as he jerked at the chains, hoping to escape what was coming.

"Hold on, Bret," Jake mumbled to himself. He remembered the terror of standing naked before a mob of hungry, uncaring eyes, and he could see, even from this distance, the effect the situation had on his friend. *Not much longer now, brother, just hold on.*

Jake couldn't believe his luck. Bret was here! Right here, only a couple dozen yards away. And Angel had agreed to help. He knew Angel thought she owed him and Monica something, but he didn't see it that way. Aside from benefiting him and Monica, this whole scheme was about helping the rest of his family: Bret and Angel.

"She's a wonderful woman," Monica had said during their meeting in the barn, "and from what you've told me, he's a decent man. If he agrees to take over for you, maybe something more will grow between them."

Jake didn't know about that.

"One issue at a time," he had said with a smile, and then swiftly dropped a kiss on her mouth before they left the barn. "Let's save him first and worry about the rest later."

The opening bid for Bret was outlandish, and the rest of the bidding went much the way Jake expected. The numbers women rabidly shouted out, sometimes one over another, increased in price quickly, and soon less than a handful of women were still making offers. Angel wouldn't join in until only the serious bidders remained, but the questions she unexpectedly shouted out to the auctioneer about Bret's health brought everything to a screeching halt.

That's my little sis, Jake thought with a fond chuckle. She had detailed Bret's injuries to him, and the fury he read in her blue eyes as she did so told him she was angry about his friend's condition. Still, he had not expected her to scold the Auction Hall's owner and employees in front of everyone. But that's exactly what she did.

When the auctioneer attempted to cut her off and asked her to make a bid or sit down, Angel shocked the entire room with her scorn-filled response.

"Yes, I wish to make a bid: Ten thousand, gold."

Her words jerked Jake away from the cloth-covered wall, and he straightened up in attention. The whole room went deathly quiet, stunned by the enormity of her bid. After a few seconds of disbelief, a loud drone of whispered astonishment buzzed around the room.

Damn! Can she afford that much? Can the ranch? He wanted his friend back and safe from the horrors Jake had faced when he first became a slave, but... *Ten thousand in gold?* Most slaves, even the well-educated ones and the breeders, went for a lot less. Jake didn't expect Angel to spend so much, even to fulfill a favor to him, and the bidding wasn't over yet.

Jake's anxious fists clenched so tight all of his knuckles turned white.

He took a deep breath and glanced around him. No one noticed his behavior.

Good, he thought. The last thing they needed was for news of Jake's interest in this sale to get back to Darla. She'd make sure Angel never acquired Bret if she thought Jake was vested in the outcome. In that scenario, if Angel won the bid, Jake wouldn't put it past Darla to find a way for Bret to be "mysteriously" killed or suffer some mishap that wouldn't endanger Darla or the empire she'd built for herself.

Jake searched the crowd for Monica's blonde head, hoping she could curb Angel's ire if it got out of hand. Angel seemed to be on a vendetta, which shouldn't have surprised him. As Jake had predicted, their treatment of Bret had angered her.

"She cares too much about people to let Bret go to someone cruel like Darla," Monica had responded inside the barn earlier, when he'd questioned whether Angel would take on the trouble and expense that helping Bret would cause her. "And she always finds a way to survive the costs."

"I know," Jake answered, "but if she gets mad, she won't stop until she wins. She's done it before. It's dangerous..."

"It's a possibility, but she's not stupid, Jake. She knows she must be prepared for future challenges with the ranch or anything else that comes up. Give her a little credit."

Jake had nodded, understanding, but now, with so much on the line, his uncertainty started an acid fire burning in his belly. He wondered silently if Bret managing Angel's ranch could ever fully recoup the cost of his purchase today. With Bret's skill and knowledge, the ranch's crop and cattle sales over the next year should double, if the other variables worked in their favor. Still, Angel's bid was a huge risk.

Jake's other fear was Darla. If she wanted Bret for herself, or if she thought winning the bid would harm Angel, she would cause problems. If that was the case and Angel outbid her, he didn't want to consider the possible ramifications for them or for Bret.

A few minutes passed, and half a dozen more bids were exchanged between Darla's proxy and Angel. The tension in the room settled in Jake's muscles, every single one taut to the point of snapping as he waited with the rest of the audience for the final outcome.

Somehow, Jake sensed a change in Angel. He heard something in her voice when she placed her last offer to best Darla's most recent one. She sounded weary and irate, and Jake felt Angel's determination to end this battle of wills and gold like a physical weight on his chest.

Jake stared at Darla's profile. She appeared calm, but he knew her expressions better than most. She was raging beneath her mask of tranquility. When Angel made her final, astoundingly-high bid, Darla's face, for only a split second, showed all the hatred and rage she harbored for Angel. He blinked, surprised Darla would allow so much to show, especially here, but when his lids lifted, the look was gone. Darla shook her head, and the battle was over.

Chattering broke out among the crowd as Jake breathed a sigh of relief, but his eyes stayed locked on Darla Cain and the tension refused to leave his shoulders. She grinned, and a shiver ran through him like a wide, icy river. Darla's smiles never boded well.

As Angel made her way through the crowd, Jake's gaze went to Bret, still standing on the stage. Mortification painted his features, and then his chin dropped to his chest.

"I know the feeling, brother," Jake muttered, understanding Bret's distress. The fear drug they undoubtedly gave him must be wreaking havoc with his pride too. Jake commiserated, though he didn't dwell on it long. He never intended to end up in that position again. He'd die first.

Angel made her way up the aisle toward Jake, an expression of determination on her face. He met her gaze and frowned, perplexed by her behavior with the bid, but he didn't say a word as he followed her out the rear doors.

Jake took a deep breath, and the anxiety that had him wound tighter than a guitar string all day dwindled. He exhaled, turning his face up to the afternoon sun, and thanked the fates or whatever had brought Bret to him today.

He had no idea how this all would play out, whether Bret would agree to his request or not, but those were all worries for another day. For now, he had his friend back, a safe, warm home to return to, and a loving woman waiting for him.

44

JAKE PROPPED HIS SHOULDER against the windowsill, his arms crossed over his bare chest, as he stared out Angel's guest room window. He and Monica had spent an hour before dinner rearranging Jake's apartment to accommodate Bret as his new roommate. They still had a few things to do, and since they both were tired after the long day—and wanting to spend as much of their remaining time together alone—they'd decided to sleep here and finish the rest in the morning.

He gazed over the beautiful landscape lit starkly by the moon. The huge weeping willow on the hill held his attention as the long, thin limbs stirred in the breeze and moonlight streamed through them, casting moving shadows on the snow-covered ground, like snakes writhing through the white-dappled darkness. The tree was a beautiful sight in the spring and summer, with its array of light-green leaves whispering in the wind. In the fall, when the foliage turned to shades of red and brilliant yellow, the willow was just as lovely. But in the barren silence of winter, the tree's nude appearance made the willow and the hill look dead and desolate.

The hour was late, and the house was as still as a crypt, but he couldn't sleep. Restlessness rolled him out of bed and drew him to the window to think. Now, the forlorn scene outside caused painful images from his past to flood his tired mind.

Anna...

He sighed. He had not thought about her for a while now, but going to the Auction Hall earlier that day and watching his best friend be sold like an animal brought everything back.

He couldn't change what had happened to Anna or forgive himself for his part in her demise, but at least he had finally found some peace and safety of his own.

A soft rustling on the bed behind him disturbed his morbid train of thought. He turned from the bleakness outside to stare at the beautiful woman bathed in moonglow as she stretched in her sleep, one arm reaching out, searching for him. The pale, ambient light turned her hair the color of silvered honey, and her smooth skin appeared opalescent against the light-blue sheets. Her loveliness swelled his heart with love and pride, while the memory of their lovemaking warmed his chest and stirred his desires once more.

A smile pulled at the corners of his mouth.

When they had returned to Angel's ranch after the auction, they'd all gone about their daily chores. At dinner, they ate together, as always and celebrated the coming New Year with their friends. Afterward, he asked another ranch hand to check on the cattle before bed, and he had followed Monica up to the room they would share for the night, to engage in a private celebration of their own.

They made love for most of the evening until they were both sated, and Monica had curled up beside him to drift into dreams. Jake had lain there for some while, not wanting to disturb her slumber, but the excitement and stress of the day were still with him, and despite his exhaustion, he couldn't relax enough for sleep to take him.

Bret was scheduled to arrive sometime tomorrow, and Jake's anxiety would not let him unwind. Only a few more hours and he would be reunited with his old friend once again—and the countdown of his departure from Angel's ranch to Monica's would begin.

He was troubled by Bret and Angel and his own leaving, but, as he kept reminding himself, he couldn't change what was already done.

While he stared at Monica still lying on the bed, her pretty eyes fluttered open and took in his nakedness with a lengthy perusal. She grinned at him like a woman with a big secret, making his lips curl anew.

"Howdy, handsome," she greeted sleepily. "What are you doing over there?"

"Just thinking," he responded.

"Everything all right?" she asked as she sat up. The sheet tucked beneath her arms, she rested her back against the headboard and studied him more closely.

"Everything's fine." He dropped his arms as he went to sit on the edge of the mattress, hands flat on the bed beside him. She stayed where she was, sensing his mood and giving him space.

"Are you nervous about tomorrow?" she probed lightly.

"Yes," he said without hesitation.

"About Bret? About your friendship?"

"Yeah, that and what may be happening to him now. Darla doesn't take losing well."

"She wouldn't risk her wealth and position over losing one man to Angel."

"She would if she got angry enough. Or if she thought she could get away with it."

"True, but I'm sure he'll be fine."

"Yeah, I hope so."

They fell silent for several seconds before Monica spoke again.

"So, what else is bothering you?"

He glanced at her, his hands curling around the mattress edge as he leaned forward, bracing his arms against the bed. He averted his gaze and stayed quiet for a long minute before Monica said, "You're worried, aren't you?"

He glanced at her, then back at the floor. "Yes, a little," he admitted.

"Why? Bret's safe, and you'll soon be able to come home with me. What's to worry about?"

He dropped his head, took a deep breath, and then looked out the window at the winter darkness.

"I'm not sure about him...about Bret...about...this..." He waved one hand as if to encompass everything around them.

"What do you mean?" Monica asked, cocking her head and frowning in confusion. "You said he would take over for you, now you don't think he will?"

"I know what I said. I've just had a little more time to think about it, and I'm realizing precisely how long it's been since I've talked to Bret. He may be a different man now."

"I suppose that's possible, but do you think he would've changed that much? The man you told me about seemed very..." She faltered, searching for the right word. "Loyal," she finished.

"He is with those he's closest to, and when he gives his word he keeps it, but, like I said, it's been a long time."

"He's your family and you're his," Monica said. "I doubt he's forgotten that. Plus, from what I know about him, I'd say he's been carrying a lot of guilt for what happened to you."

Jake nodded. "I blamed him for that for a long time too." He spoke so softly she had to lean forward to catch his words; he felt the movement through the bed.

"And now?"

He glanced at her, and then his eyes slid away again. Unable to remain seated, he stood up and went back to the window. He braced his hands on the ledge and stared out at the cold barrenness, remembering the nearly two years of hell he had suffered at Darla's and the dark hole in which he'd been chained up and left to die. Three years had passed since he'd been rescued from his misery, a long time to consider how he felt. He dropped his forehead against the cold glass.

"Now," he said and sighed, his breath fogging the window as he spoke, "it no longer matters."

"How you feel matters, Jake," Monica said, coming to his defense as always. The corners of his mouth tipped up slightly at the thought but slid downward again.

"That's not what I meant," he said, turning to face her. He leaned back against the ledge and crossed his arms over his chest again. "I don't hate him; I never could, even when I was furious with him. But I know where he's been, what he's been through, and I understand why he did what he did with Amy. At least, mostly. Now that I'm with you, I can imagine how hard it was for him, needing someone to care about him, wanting happiness. I could've handled the situation with Amy better myself. I'm not pleased with what happened, but you're right. Bret would've blamed himself, and what happened would've eaten at him all these years.

"By accident, I found happiness, and if it weren't for him and his bad decisions, I would've never met you." He paused, thinking again. "I forgave him a long time ago, but realizing it took a little while."

"Then why are you worried?"

"Trust is hard for him."

"Yeah, so you've said...and?"

"He finds trust hard with women in particular. I'm concerned how he'll react to Angel and being made a slave."

"He won't have the same experience with Angel that you did with Darla."

"No, but he won't be pleased with the situation either."

"No one would," Monica said, "but how does that change your mind now?"

"It doesn't, not exactly." Jake shook his head. "The problem is I'm not sure what he's like now, what else may have happened. Maybe he won't help, won't give her a chance."

"You think he won't like her?"

"He won't like that she paid money to own him," Jake clarified.

"But she'll win him over. She always does. He won't have a choice. He'll like her."

Jake scoffed. "Oh, he'll *like* her alright, what man wouldn't? She's adorable, but she needs a friend more than she does a lover. Hell, she's never even shown interest in wanting one. And Bret..." He shook his head again. "He was difficult to get through to before, who knows what he'll be like now."

"Jake," Monica said, drawing his eyes to hers with the sternness of her voice, "you can't do anything about it now."

He nodded but remained silent.

"Besides, the man you told me about would never let his friends down, would never purposely hurt anyone, and would, in fact, fiercely defend those he cares about. He hasn't forgotten you, I don't think he could. Even not knowing him myself, I know this much: he'll be happy to see you. The rest will come in time."

"But we don't have a lot of time to—" Jake said sadly and cut himself short. He glanced at her guiltily. There was so much he still must tell her, but not tonight.

"We have plenty of time," Monica assured, misinterpreting his pause as additional worry for his friend.

Jake nodded. "I want Bret to be happy and safe. I want the same thing for Angel, but I want to be with you too. I love you, Monica. I'd do anything for you, but you deserve better than this." He gestured again to indicate the enormity of their circumstances. "I can't do right by you, especially while I'm stuck here."

"I told you before, Jake," she said in an annoyed tone that grew more spirited as she spoke. "I deserve the man I love, and that man is you. Right now, to me, our living situation doesn't matter if everything between us is good. We can work out all the rest. If Bret wants to be stubborn, fine, let him. He won't be able to stand up to both of us. We're a team, Jake. Together, we can do anything."

He grinned at her, loving the ferocity of her affection for him, and humbled by it too.

"You know, you're really cute when you're feisty," he kidded, and he chuckled at the glare she gave him. "And you're right, we'll figure it out. All of it. Together."

"That's all you have to say?" she queried, raising an eyebrow, but there was fondness in her gaze.

"I love you too," he said with the soft smile he knew would melt her like ice in the summer sun.

She held her frown for a moment longer and then relented.

"Good," she said and grinned at him playfully. "Who knows, maybe one day we can have our own happy little family like Shawn and Kim and the kids."

The idea choked him up. "I'd like that," he said hoarsely. "A little girl as sweet and beautiful as her mother would be perfect."

"I'd like a little boy as brave and handsome as his father."

Warmth swelled in his chest at the love in her eyes. "We'll have to practice...a lot."

Her eyes twinkled with desire again. "Well, get over here then," she said. "I'm not done with you yet tonight."

He chuckled.

"I thought you were tired," he teased as he crawled under the covers and pulled her into his arms.

"I had a nice nap," she said brazenly while sliding her hand down his torso. "I'm rested and ready to take you again."

"Take me?"

She propped herself on an elbow and kissed him, a quick peck on the lips.

"Take you, have you, love you. However you want to say it," she said still grinning. Then she leaned forward and whispered, so close to his ear her lips brushed the sensitive edge seductively. "Make love to me, Jake."

Gooseflesh pebbled his skin, and a shiver of desire shot down his spine.

"Yes, ma'am," he answered and rolled her onto her back, pinning her to the mattress with the weight of his much-larger frame. He kissed her thoroughly, demanding her response. She clung to him and gave him all he needed: her.

His lips nibbled on her cheek, her jaw, down her neck, along her collarbone, relishing the hot little pants emanating from her parted lips. Her fingers raked through his hair as his downward progression continued. He moved slowly, wanting to hear her moan and cry out his name.

Lust pounded through his veins, screamed in his mind, throbbed between his legs, but he kept his deliberate pace, stroking her, caressing every inch of her delectable skin. Sucking, licking, touching, nibbling, he savored every inch of her.

Kissing her lips once more, his hand slid between her thighs, marking the heated wetness of her opening. His balls cramped, his cock jumped, yearning to slide into the slick, soft warmth of her core, but still, he postponed his needs to stoke her fires into an inferno. Teasing her with his fingers, he let her feel his readiness, but held back, waiting for her to tell him what she wanted.

She shifted her hips, widened her thighs so his shaft fell into position. She bucked as her body surged downward to seat him inside her. He didn't allow it. Instead, he pressed himself against the moist heat, only the head of his erection touching, rubbing, teasing, but without penetration. He lifted himself as he pressed forward, skimming his whole length along her swollen folds, and she quivered as a shaky groan burst from her mouth.

"Oh, Jake, please!"

"Not yet," he growled as he took her mouth with his, tongues lashing, clashing, insistent in their need for one another. It would be awhile before they could be together like this again; he wanted to make the most of their time.

He positioned himself at her opening, barely broaching the folds of her sex. Everything in him demanded he thrust home, but he held back. He sucked on her nipples one after the other, drawing them into his mouth and teasing the tender buds, as his fingers snaked between their bodies to massage the hot, pulsing nub waiting, wanting, and needing his touch.

At his first soft caress, she jumped, moaned, and clutched his shoulders. He repeated the movement, over and over, tantalizing her moist flesh, while he rained kisses from her mouth to her collarbone. She tensed beneath him, her hips lifted, body arched, her nails dug into his back as she screamed into his mouth, once again covering hers.

As her waves of passion diminished, her fingers eased, skimming over his shoulders and arms, her nails trailing lightly over his skin. Goosebumps rose in their wake. He kept kissing her. His fingers kept kneading, rubbing between her thighs. She shivered and wiggled beneath him. Her fingers traced the groove of his spine. He drove forward and slid inside her an inch, only enough to entice her desired response.

Her internal muscles tightened around the head of his shaft, her body trembled, and she moaned again.

"Oh, God," he muttered, but held firm to his task of leisurely seduction.

Still, she made his mission very hard indeed.

Her hands clamped onto his ass and attempted to use her hold to plunge him inside her. When that didn't work, she tried to shimmy downward. She writhed, pushed, pulled, anything to propel him farther into her yearning depths. Gently, he clamped his teeth around her nipple and tugged, flicking the sensitive peak with his tongue while using his fingers to taunt the other. She arched her back and groaned louder, her body thrashing against him, her fingers digging into his ass, everything in her straining for him.

"Jake! Jake, now. Please now. Jake..."

In the same instant, he pulled his hand out from between them, braced his arms beneath his shoulders, and lunged forward, driving himself deep. Her hands on his rear tightened and her hips rushed up to meet his. He had wanted to keep his rhythm slow, but the moist heat and the tightness of her channel, coupled with her wild response, spurred him to speed. Her legs wrapped around him, encouraging him, and she matched every thrust with earnestness and a lust to rival his own. He dropped onto her, chest to chest, her hardened nipples drilling through him. His arms wound around her back and he ravaged her mouth with the need of a desperately lonely man. Still moving inside her, the strength of his release building to an epic crescendo, his heart ached with the love he felt for this woman.

"I love you," he whispered against her lips. "God, I love you. I love you..."

"Same here, Cowboy," she answered, mocking him a little with the nickname that didn't quite fit.

"Jake," he said holding on just a little longer. "Call me Jake."

"Jake," she breathed. "Oh, Jake. My Jake..."

His name on her lips was the final impetus that ripped his restraint from his tenuous grip. He thrust inside one last time, plunged deep, and held there as his orgasm slammed through him. Back arched, head thrown back, eyes closed, teeth clenched, every muscle tightened as his body rocked against her, and he trembled from the power of his release. He felt her quivering with spent passion as she lay under him. Her final cry still echoed in his mind as he buried his face in her glorious hair and inhaled her soft, feminine scent. His arms wrapped around her and her legs encircled his lean waist, neither of them ready to let go.

"That was...fantastic," Monica gushed and kissed his neck. "As always," she added quietly, closer to his ear.

He chuckled. "I have always loved your enthusiasm." He was only half kidding.

"That isn't all, I hope," she pouted impishly as her fingers playfully traced the curve of his spine and the flex of his muscles.

He pulled back to gaze into her beautiful, smiling hazel eyes.

"Of course not," he grinned back. "You're a snappy dresser too."

He laughed at the frisky glare she threw at him and winced when her nails dug warningly into his ass. He rolled onto his back, dragging her against him, his arm curled around her. She placed her hand flat on his chest and propped her chin on it, still frowning. He met her dark gaze then reached over with his free hand and poked her nose. "Don't look at me like that," he said lightheartedly. "You know I love you. Nothing will change that."

"Good!" Her instantaneous grin told him she hadn't taken him seriously and that her feigned annoyance had been a ruse to tease him.

He chuckled again.

She shifted so her head was on his shoulder and her arm draped over his chest. She sighed with satisfaction, and Jake smiled as the thought of her contentment warmed his heart.

"Are you still worried?" she inquired a little later.

He opened his eyes and forced his sleepy brain to focus. "Hmm?" he hummed to give himself a little more time, and to actually hear the question this time.

"Are you still worried? About Bret and Angel and everything else?"

"I suppose I am," he said, "but I'm also happy being here with you. And like you said, we'll figure it out. Together."

"That's my Jake," she said as she snuggled closer to his side. He didn't miss the possessive note in her voice, telling him again, without so many words, they belonged together.

"Yep, all yours, baby."

She sighed, her breath swirling through his chest hair, and, to him, she seemed to purr like a contented kitten. Her body relaxed against his, warming him as she drifted to sleep.

Once again, hope burned in his heart, but not just for himself this time. In a few hours, his best friend would be safely under the same roof. Monica was right—they were family, and Bret wouldn't forget that. Accepting that as truth warmed Jake more. What happened in the past was done and gone. All that mattered now was the future...for all of them.

He still had much to tell Monica about that future and his part in it, but he had already convinced himself to wait until after he moved back to her ranch. She might be upset, but he doubted it. Nothing he did now, or would do in the future, would hurt anyone they cared about. In fact, his actions might help them all in the end.

He sighed, settling into the comfy pillow, holding Monica's hand against his chest while the fingers of his other traced intricate patterns over the silky curve of her hip and waist.

Our time apart is finally coming to an end, he thought languidly. He could, at long last, lower the hard shell he'd erected around his heart for protection against disappointment and pain, and allow a glimmer of hope to burst into life inside him.

Wrapped in the blanket, and with Monica draped over his side, Jake began to relax in the warmth they created together. Drowsily, he glanced at the woman sleeping on his shoulder. Seeing her lying so soft and content in his arms amplified the love in his heart for her. The power of the overwhelming emotion startled him every time, just as the knowledge that she was his still amazed him.

I am a lucky man, he thought. His lips tugged up at the thought as sleep dragged his eyes closed, enticing him into dreams of a bright future, where he, Monica, and their friends were alive and free, happy and healthy...and together.

* * *

Monica and Jake's story continues and Angel and Bret's story begins in the first book of *The Angel Eyes Series: Masters' Mistress*, scheduled to be release in early 2020.

If you enjoyed this story, please leave a review. Reviews help other readers in their decision to purchase or download a book and help authors be seen by more readers. This is especially true with new, independent authors like me. So, again, please go to Amazon, or Apple, or Barnes & Noble, or wherever you purchased your copy, and leave an honest review so you can help me reach others who would enjoy this series. Your support is very much appreciated!

I would like to, once again, express my deepest "Thank You" to all my readers—that would be you!—for taking the time to read my first novel. I truly hope you enjoyed the story and are looking forward to finding out what happens next!

* * *

About the Author

Jamie was born and raised in the wonderful Pacific Northwest and she has always wanted to be a storyteller. As a child and young adult, she spent countless hours dreaming up stories to entertain herself and her friends. She kept long-running, developing stories in her head for years, knowing someday she would write them all down.

She still has many stories still floating around the back of her cluttered mind (and haunting her hard drive as well).She hopes they all will make their way out into the world for your enjoyment someday (soon)!

She still lives in Pacific Northwest with her husband, her family, and her fur-babies.

You can learn more about Jamie and her books on her website: www.jamieschulzauthor.com.

And connect with her on:

- www.facebook.com/jamieschulzauthor (@jamieschulzauthor)
- www.amazon.com/Jamie-Schulz/e/B07K7X6JV5/
- www.goodreads.com/author/show/18580547.Jamie_Schulz
- www.bookbub.com/authors/jamie-schulz
- www.twitter.com/TheJamieSchulz (@TheJamieSchulz)

Made in the USA
Lexington, KY
22 June 2019